LAST BATTLE OF THE ICEMARK

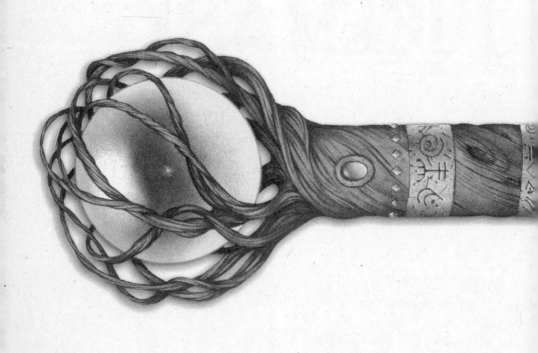

LAST BATTLE OF THE ICEMARK

STUART HILL

Chicken House

SCHOLASTIC INC. / NEW YORK

All rights reserved. Published by Chicken House, an imprint of Scholastic Inc.,
Publishers since 1920. CHICKEN HOUSE, SCHOLASTIC, and associated logos
are trademarks and/or registered trademarks of Scholastic Inc.
www.scholastic.com

Published in the United Kingdom in 2008 by Chicken House,
2 Palmer Street, Frome, Somerset BA11 1DS.
www.doublecluck.com

Library of Congress Cataloging-in-Publication Data

Hill, Stuart.
Last battle of the Icemark / Stuart Hill. — 1st American ed.
p. cm. — (Icemark chronicles ; bk. 3)
Summary: Queen Thirrin's tiny kingdom of Icemark has enjoyed peace
since the banishment of her murderous daughter Medea, but when Medea
allies herself with the King of Darkness and his terrifying Ice Demons,
the queen must respond to the threat of war.

ISBN-13: 978-0-545-09329-3
ISBN-10: 0-545-09329-5

[1. Fantasy.] I. Title. II. Series.

PZ7.H55738Las 2009
[Fic]—dc22

2008023005

10 9 8 7 6 5 4 3 2 1   09 10 11 12 13

Printed in the U.S.A.   23
First American edition, April 2009

The text type was set in M Horley Old Style.
Book design by Elizabeth B. Parisi

To Clare

1

The gentle crackle of burning logs was the only physical sound that disturbed the peace. Outside the window the cold autumn night sparkled and glittered with stars, and the moon ladled a silver puddle of light across the floor of the darkened room. It was the night before Samhein, or "Halloween" as some of the older country folk still called it, and the veils between the physical and spirit worlds were so thin that Oskan Witchfather could clearly hear the whisper and echo of voices beyond.

None of this held any fears for him. As a warlock and wielder of magic, he knew he was simply listening to part of the natural—and supernatural—order of the Cosmos. His ear automatically sifted through the various calls and voices of the ether, identifying and categorizing each and every phenomenon it encountered: ghost, banshee, undead, demon, angel.

He rested his mind for a moment in the peace of the Spirit Realms; its sounds of birdsong, the perfume of flower-scented breezes, and the gentle sibilance of falling silver rains marked it as the residence of the Goddess and the place of heavens such as Valhalla and the Summer Lands.

He slowly drifted toward sleep, most of his powers veiled in that protective state that kept them safe from the clamor and noise of the living and unliving worlds. But then a sudden gust of wind breathed around the stonework of the window, the rush of air finding a voice in the cracks and crevices and softly wailing with a note of such despair and omen that it shook the Witchfather from his rest. Oskan fully opened his mind again, searching for signs of danger. Immediately his head was filled with the entire tumbling, tangling cacophony of the spiritual and natural worlds, and he listened carefully.

He soon found what he was looking for. An unmistakable "voice" calling in the Darkness and growing stronger day by day. A tone that was deeply evil . . . and familiar. Medea!

A time was fast approaching when he'd need to face this new threat and either destroy it or be destroyed. He sighed and settled back into his seat, trying to recapture the peace that had fled. There was always time enough for confrontation, and he wasn't ready yet for the struggle that would come. He needed to gather his strength and prepare his powers before he would be ready for battle. And, if he was completely honest with himself, he had to admit that he was more than a little afraid of what he'd found.

For the time being, he wanted to rest from the dangers of the world and the Cosmos, and for the next two days or so he was determined to enjoy the celebrations of Samhein. He closed his psychic ear and listened instead to the physical activities of the palace around him.

The kitchens had been busy all day, preparing food for the great feast that would take place the following night, and the faint clatter of pots and pans reached him as the chefs and scullions hurried around in a desperate attempt to spread the heavy workload over two days. Of course, most of the cooking would need to be done on the day of Samhein itself, but some of the cakes and pastries would actually improve if left to mature for a few hours in a cool pantry. And many of the cold meats and pickles would take no harm if stored away carefully.

Dozens of guests had already settled into the citadel, and, most important, Tharaman-Thar and Krisafitsa-Tharina, the giant Snow Leopard monarchs of the Icesheets far to the north, and their daughter Princess Kirimin, were due to arrive in a matter of a few hours or so. But there was still time for peace in all of the joyous chaos and the threat of new Powers arising in the Darkness. He decided to steal a few minutes' sleep before the demands of the festival became too great.

He'd just wriggled his shoulders deeper into the cushions and composed himself for rest when a familiar sound floated into his consciousness. Outside the firmly closed door, the huge expanse of the empty Great Hall echoed like a bell. The servants had finished decorating it for the Samhein feast and were wisely keeping all the housecarls and werewolves out until the actual day of the celebration, so the crunch and tread of a pair of chain-mailed boots as they paced across the flagstones sounded almost as loud as an entire advancing army. With great determination Oskan ignored it, but the noise was getting closer and closer until, with a rattle and bang, the door was wrenched open and his wife and warrior-queen, Thirrin Freer Strong-in-the-Arm Lindenshield, burst into the room.

"Arse, arse, and arse again!" she shouted.

The Witchfather was used to this sort of drama, so it was only reluctantly that he opened his eyes and watched as his wife, dressed in full armor, busily handed her shield and weapons to one of the housecarl door guards.

"Good evening, dearest," he said, deciding to use quiet irony as his shield against her noise and bluster.

"And arse yet again," she answered. "And a mucky one at that!"

3

"Yes, I'm very well, thank you. And yourself?"

"I'm thinking of banning all messages and news over the Samhein period. At least that way I'll be able to relax and enjoy it."

"Yes, it is a lovely evening, isn't it? The stars and moon-light are truly splendid."

"I can't imagine why we thought the werewolf relay was a good idea. All it does is tell us of war and death and chaos."

"Yes, I love the night before Samhein, too. It's so peace-ful. The lull before the chaos, I suppose—but still, it is pleasant."

Thirrin paused and looked at him. "What are you witter-ing on about, Oskan? Here I am worrying about the latest reports from the Polypontian Empire, and all you can do is whine on about moonlight like some love-struck teenager!"

He sighed, his attempts to hang on to at least a semblance of domestic peace completely defeated. "I know all about what's happening in the Empire. I heard the reports."

"Fine!" said Thirrin, taking off her mail-shirt and draping it over the back of a chair. "So what are we going to do?"

"Watch events carefully, and see what happens," he answered wearily. "It's all we've ever been able to do."

She drew breath to reply irritably, then paused before finally saying, "You're right, of course. When has the Icemark ever dictated events?" She crossed to a chair that stood facing Oskan's on the opposite side of the hearth and sat down heavily. "But wouldn't it be nice to be in control of events, just once? I mean, here we are, the defeaters of the Bellorum dynasty, the breakers of the Imperial host, and all we can do is watch while the Polypontian Empire destroys itself fighting dozens of internal wars, and wait to see who comes out on top!"

Oskan nodded. "And by the looks of things, whoever does finally get to be top dog will be a threat to us . . . again."

Thirrin leaned back in her chair and closed her eyes. "But we already know who it'll be, don't we? Erinor of Artemesion and her unstoppable Hordes."

For a while he didn't reply and just sat gazing deeply into the flames of the fire.

"I somehow get the impression I don't have your undivided attention!" Thirrin snapped. "I mean, is there any real point continuing this conversation?"

He looked up and smiled apologetically. "I'm sorry, Thirrin. I'm a bit distracted."

She threw up her hands in despair. "Ye gods! What can be more distracting than the breakup of the Polypontian Empire and the possibility of a war with Erinor and her invincible army? Come on, man, spit it out!"

Oskan shuddered as all of his instincts suddenly screamed at him that the moment had come. He would have to tell his wife the secret he'd been harboring, the very subject he'd been trying to avoid for months. He looked at her quietly as he gathered the strength he'd need to tell her the terrible truth.

"Medea," he finally replied, and the name seemed to fall like a lead weight into the middle of the room.

"Medea?" said Thirrin quietly. "But . . . but she's dead."

A silence developed, deepening as Oskan turned back to the flames. "The Icemark and the allies banished her . . . no, no. Let's be honest, now that we've come to it; *I* banished her to the Darkness after the last war. And by all the laws and rules of normality, she should have died." Oskan looked up and held his wife's gaze. "She *should* have died, Thirrin. But our daughter is beyond the laws and rules of normality."

"She's alive?" came the reply in a horrified whisper. "Medea's alive in that dreadful, hideous place?"

He nodded. "But if it's any comfort to you, please don't think she's in any sort of torment or pain. Oh no, not our dearest daughter! If anything, she's the tormentor; she's the inflictor of pain!"

Thirrin heard almost none of this. Her mind was in turmoil. Medea was alive: their child, the daughter they'd raised and loved. Medea, the traitor who'd disrupted her own country's war effort and who'd tried to kill her own brother! Medea, the Adept who could have helped to defeat the Empire, but who instead had plotted against her family and helped the enemy!

Thirrin was racked by a tumult of conflicting emotions: undeniable joy that her child had cheated death and still lived; seething anger for the crimes that child had committed. But at the base of it all was something else: a terrible, crushing guilt that she'd never been able to relate to the child who'd had no interest in the military and warfare. Could her neglect, her inability to reach out to her strange, aloof daughter, have somehow pushed her toward the Dark? Could she, Thirrin, be responsible for her embracing evil?

"Are you listening to me?" Oskan asked, breaking into her thoughts and dragging her attention back to the present.

"Yes . . . yes. Medea, she's alive."

"More than that, I'm afraid —"

"Why didn't you tell me?" she interrupted quietly. "Why didn't you tell me my daughter's still alive?" Then, with sudden suspicion and a rising tone, "How long have you known?"

He turned away again to look into the fire. This was another question he'd been dreading. "I've known for certain only a short while. But I've suspected for some time."

Thirrin slammed her hands down hard on the arms of her chair. "Why didn't you say? I'm her mother; I have a right to know!"

"You know now."

"Not good enough . . . not nearly good enough! You should have told me when you had the first inklings of a suspicion! Not wait until you knew for sure and needed to talk about . . . about . . . Well, about what, exactly? How glad you are, perhaps? How relieved you are that she's alive; how sorry you are that you were driven to send her into the Darkness in the first place?!"

"No. None of that. I'm not relieved she's alive or sorry I exiled her," he said quietly. "Exactly the opposite, in fact. I regret she survived, and I'm only sorry the Darkness didn't finish her once and for all. But sometimes that . . . *place* reacts in ways that even I can't fathom."

Thirrin leaped to her feet, a raging outburst rising in her throat. But then she stopped and stood quietly instead, fully aware that her anger stemmed from her own terrible sense of guilt. "What can we do?"

"I'm not sure. We need to make a decision, but to do that you need to know all the facts."

Thirrin sat down again and rested her head against the high back of the chair. "Go on."

He paused, uncertain how his wife would take what he was about to say. But then, taking a deep breath, he plunged in. "She's evil, more evil than you can ever imagine. And her power has grown enormously. I've been watching her ever since I first detected her unmasked mind and recognized it. I'm not entirely sure what she's planning, but we must be on our guard. She still hates the Icemark, in fact even more so since her exile, and I think she's after revenge." He poured it all out in one breath and waited for her response.

"Is there no hope of rescuing her and perhaps . . . well, I don't know, making her see sense?"

Oskan laughed despite the terrible nature of the situation. "She doesn't want to be rescued, Thirrin. Don't you see? In the Darkness she has status and power. She's almost a queen. And she has only one more test to pass and she'll have proved herself the most powerful Adept in the domain. The most powerful of all, save for one . . ."

"Save for one? And who might that be, exactly?" Thirrin asked, catching the significance of the phrase, and then she watched as he drew into himself, unable to go on. It was almost as though a huge weight had been levered onto his shoulders and his skeleton were being crushed under the burden.

"My father," he finally answered quietly. Suddenly his head was filled with a raging fire of sensations, as light and sound, rich scents and terrible stenches, flooded his senses.

Thirrin screamed as he slumped forward in his seat, but then stood back when she recognized the symptoms of the Sight. All she could do was wait and hope that he came out of the trance quickly.

But deep within his head, Oskan was feeling completely in control. After the initial explosion of sensations, he was now standing on what looked like a hillside under a sky that was gray but bright with a soft light that spilled over the world in a gentle wash of brilliance. He watched as a figure walked toward him through a glowing mist that was slowly gathering in rolling banks. As far as he could tell, the figure was female, dressed in flowing robes and with long golden hair that waved and rolled in a wind that Oskan couldn't feel at all. Obviously whoever or whatever the figure was, she had some significance in his vision, so he waited quietly until she was near enough for him to call out politely. But before he could say a word, the figure was suddenly standing before him.

"Oskan Witchfather," she said in a beautiful, musical voice. "I am a Messenger sent by the Goddess herself. Listen well to what I have to tell and show you, because the decisions and actions you must take afterward could change everything you have ever known and ever will know."

Oskan opened his mouth to ask exactly what she meant, but before he could speak, his head was filled once again with a raging fire of sensations. He seemed to be falling from an incredible height, tumbling over and over as he desperately tried to regain some sort of control. His vision was nothing but a blur of speeding colors as he fell, and his ears were stuffed with a roaring wind. Then he hit the ground with a jarring, bone-breaking thud that drove through his spirit form and left him almost senseless.

He lay unmoving for what seemed like hours, but gradually sensation returned and he looked around him at a gray, lowering sky and a stark landscape of twisted, tortured rocks. Immediately he knew he was being granted a vision of the past, of the *deeply ancient* past. He somehow knew he was looking at a place from before the world was made; before the universe had been shaped and molded from the chaos; before even time itself had been originated and calibrated and set on its infinite way. This was the domain of the Goddess, from a time when Creation had hardly begun.

Then suddenly the mysterious Messenger was with him again, a gentle and sad smile playing around her lips as she looked at him. "Come with me, Oskan Witchfather," she said.

Silently he took her hand and allowed himself to be led to a rock that rose out of the plain. In the distance he could see a gathering of figures, and closing his eyes, he felt himself being taken closer. When he opened them again, he gasped aloud in awe and fear. He was looking on the Goddess herself.

Thirrin looked on in mental agony as Oskan squirmed in his chair, but there was nothing she could do other than watch and wait. Dragging her chair closer, she sat and gently took her husband's hand, taking care not to disturb the trance.

Meanwhile, deep within his vision, Oskan noticed movement. A group of fifty or so figures was being brought to stand before the Mother of All, and realizing the huge importance of the vision, he steeled himself to watch.

"Who are these who stand before me?" a voice of polished clarity asked.

"You know well who we are, and you know even better who *I* am," a voice answered. "We are the spirits and angels who were brave enough to stand against the tyranny of the Goddess. We are they who challenged your power and right to rule; we are they who made the very foundations of heaven itself tremble.

"I stand not in judgment over you, but offer instead forgiveness," the gentle tone continued. "Come back to me, accept my love, return to the perfection of unity, and all dissent will be forgotten."

The mild good reason of the voice flowed like cool wine slaking a raging thirst, and Oskan waited, confident that its offer would be accepted. Then, as he watched, almost all the rebel angels and spirits moved forward to be welcomed and embraced by the light and benevolence of the Goddess.

But seven figures still stood, in defiance, outfacing the Goddess. Then at last the leader of the rebels spoke.

"You have destroyed my army and reduced my allies to broken-spirited cravens. But I will not give you the pleasure of seeing me beg for mercy. I defy you still! I will defy you forever! Victory may be yours today, but tomorrows will dawn when you will know the bitter savor of defeat. Look to your walls and ramparts, and arm your angels and sanctified dead, for one day you will see the banners of Cronus riding against you again!"

The Goddess remained silent for a long time after that, and when she replied, it was with actions rather than words.

With a deep cracking sound, the ground beneath the feet of the seven figures gaped open and they fell.

Wails of despair and rage rose up to fill the ether, and suddenly the scene disappeared as Oskan, too, began to fall. Once more his senses were overwhelmed as the wind of his speed filled his ears with a roaring sound, and he seemed to be tumbling and rolling through endless miles of air.

He was filled with a deep, unending agony of despair as he felt the emotions of the defiant spirits. The Goddess had rejected them! Despite her promise to forgive, she'd withdrawn her love and compassion, and now the rebels were falling through eons into a black and empty exile. Oskan could feel their rage and sense of betrayal as it burned their souls with a livid fire. But then, out of the pain, a towering hatred grew, and a ravening need for revenge.

Thirrin watched as her husband writhed and struggled in his chair, and, unable to help herself, she gathered him up in a restraining hug as she tried to calm him.

But Oskan was aware of nothing other than the Fall he'd just witnessed. The spirit who had openly defied the Goddess in his vision had been Cronus himself. The mighty one whose power was only just a little less than that of the Mother of All; he was the Evil One, the maker of wars and hatreds, the enemy of heaven.

Oskan opened his eyes and found that he was lying on the hillside again beneath the glowing sky, and nearby the Messenger stood watching him with concern. "So, Oskan Witchfather, now you, too, have experienced the Fall and know of the rebellion against the love and judgment of the Goddess. What have you to say?"

For a moment he could say nothing and simply shook his head. But then he looked up. "They were fools," he answered simply. "The greatest of all fools. Who else could have rejected such unconditional forgiveness?"

The Messenger smiled as though relieved. Stepping closer, she sank down to sit beside him. "Yes, they were fools, but even so, they were powerful and a threat to all Creation, and they remain so to this day." She fell silent and Oskan waited, knowing more was to come.

"And now I must give you a warning, Oskan Witchfather: You must know that a time of terrible danger is approaching, a time when the very fabric of all Creation itself could be ripped apart and made again into something hideous and corrupt. And you must also know that only you can stop it."

The terrible burden of her words settled over him with a crushing dread. "Why me?" he asked at last. "Why can't the Goddess destroy them?"

"Because the Goddess is the Mother and Creator of All; she doesn't destroy her own children! But she recognizes that unless the Evil Ones are stopped, all of the Cosmos is endangered. Therefore she has appointed you, Oskan Witchfather, to stand against this threat, and to stop it before all that is good and beautiful is ended."

Panic engulfed him as a sense of such hideous, boundless responsibility ripped aside all semblance of self-control. "But . . . but how can I stop them?" he asked in despair.

The Messenger took his hand and gripped it firmly. "I am to tell you that the Goddess will give you a weapon: a means of breaking the power of this enemy and defeating it once and for all. But you must also know that this weapon has no physical form; it is neither blade nor gun, fire nor explosion. It is a weapon of knowledge alone, and you will find it within yourself. But before I give you this knowledge, you must also know that it can cut both ways. The biter can be bitten, and a terrible sacrifice will be asked of the one who uses it."

Oskan shuddered, but after a time of silence he looked up and said, "Tell me."

The Messenger said not a word, but placed the knowledge within his mind, and immediately he collapsed as all the terrible implications hit him.

"But how can I use such a thing?" he whispered, appalled.

"To stop the Evil Ones and their allies, you must. But the Goddess, even now, does not command you to use it. When the time comes, you must make your choice."

Oskan nodded, accepting that he could never truly understand the reasons behind the decisions of the Goddess. She had chosen him and he must make of it what he could. But when the battle began, he would have to choose what to do.

"There is one thing more you need to know," the Messenger said, interrupting his thoughts. "All knowledge of this weapon must be kept secret. No one must know, not even your closest and most beloved, not even Queen Thirrin. Its power lies in the fact that no Adept, whether evil or not, has ever known of it. In this way the wicked have been kept under some control down the millennia. But if ever its secret is revealed, then all of its power will be lost; it will be rendered useless. Know, too, Oskan Witchfather, that only you, of all Adepts who have ever lived, have been given this knowledge; such are the times that we live in. The final confrontation is almost upon us, and the Warrior of Light must stand forth."

Oskan was rendered speechless; the responsibility was too great. If he could have, he would have run away, far from the Goddess and her Messenger, and far from what was being asked of him. But before he could think or act further, the world suddenly shifted and swirled around him and he felt himself falling again. On and on he fell, until at last he shuddered to a halt as his spirit entered his body again, and he drew a deep breath. His head whirled as he opened his eyes and saw Thirrin anxiously watching him.

"Oskan, are you back; are you with us again?"

He nodded, and immediately regretted it as a deep pain drove through his forehead.

"Here, drink this," Thirrin commanded and held a flask of some burning spirit to his lips. He coughed and spluttered, but then everything seemed to swing back into place and he was able to look around without feeling dizzy.

"Well, was it the Sight? What did you see?"

Oskan nodded weakly. "Yes, it was the Sight."

"And . . . ?"

"And? And I witnessed my father being banished from heaven," he said almost lightly, hiding the thoughts that clamored in his head.

Thirrin looked at him sharply, but knew she'd get nothing more from him until he was ready. "Well, sit still until your head clears properly, and I'll see if I can get one of your witches to make up a draft to help."

He watched silently as she left the room, and breathed a sigh of relief as he was finally left alone with his thoughts.

In many ways he'd learned very little that was new, but often the quality of information was more important than the quantity.

2

Medea, sorceress and Adept, had spent more than two years in the Darkness, so she was used to the endless night of glittering stars and frozen skies. The constellations were completely different from those of the Physical Realms; here, monsters and devilish faces could be seen in the patterns of countless stars glimmering in the perpetual night.

The moon was different, too. It was larger and always full. And the shadowy "seas" and craters on its surface made it look like a grinning skull that leered over the frozen land of snowfields and sheets of ice. But unlike the natural tundra that lay far to the north of the Icemark in the Physical Realms, here in the Darkness each flake of snow and tiny crystal of ice was all that remained of the soul of one of those stupid enough to travel to this most evil of domains. Only the very strongest could withstand the malevolence that haunted its wastes, and of those who couldn't, their spirits were drained and reduced to glittering shards of ice that would fall in a blizzard, together with countless other lost souls, to become part of the frozen wilderness of the Darkness.

"They've come to witness my victory, Orla," Medea said, nodding at the constellations of stars and smiling coldly at the hunched figure dressed in black rags that stood in attendance on her.

"Yes, Mistress," the figure replied in a voice of rusty creaks and groans. "And then you can take your rightful place among the greatest Adepts of the Darkness."

"Yes! Just think, Orla, I only have to fight one small battle and I'll have proved my right to be accepted as a citizen at last."

"Just one small battle, Mistress," the figure answered, but Medea's sharp ears detected a tiny note of uncertainty and she whirled on her companion.

"Do you dare doubt me, you piece of black rag? Only one other Adept in the entirety of the Darkness is greater than me! Who else can revive frozen souls and restore them to sentient life, as I did with you, and who else can then create a body for the vulnerable spirit to live in?"

"Only you, Mistress," Orla replied. "Only you and one other."

Medea nodded. "Don't ever forget that I rescued you from the torment of the tundra, you ingrate. It's thanks only to me that you have life and a body again. Always remember, Orla, that unlike you and millions of others, I was strong enough to survive my arrival in the Darkness, even though I was badly injured and exhausted after fighting a battle with my beloved father!"

"I do not forget it, Mistress. You're good enough to remind me every day," Orla, Witch of the Dark Power, answered.

But Medea didn't seem to hear. "Even in my weakened state I was still powerful enough to blast the hideous Ice Demons to smoking skeletons when they tried to kill me! And then I managed to fight my way to the shelter of a cave, from which I fought off everything sent against me!"

She fell into silent thought. For months she'd been forced to fight for her life, but eventually she was left in peace, and she'd begun to realize that the evil realm had become a home to her; its malevolence suited her perfectly, and as the weeks had passed, she'd eventually understood that this was where she belonged—truly belonged.

In all the hatred and fury, in all the evil and the hideous death, she'd at last found a sort of family, one that loathed as she loathed, thought and acted as she did, and which expected nothing from her in return but violence and rage. Here nobody would be disappointed in her. Here her ability as an Adept could bring her power without limit. So what need did she have of the Lindenshields? What need did she have of parental love and acceptance?

All she wanted now was to sever all links with her hated family, and to mark the occasion she would kill her hated brother, Charlemagne. What black joy such an act would bring. The final snuffing out of the life that had filled her parents' very existence with love. Perhaps then they'd find it in their hearts to share out their care a little more evenly!

But why should she worry about such things? She had her power. Nothing else mattered. All she needed was to be accepted by the Darkness, and now before her lay the test that would finally allow her to become part of the realm. She faced battle with her fellow Adepts; she faced possible death and degradation, but she was willing to sacrifice all to secure her place within the power that she felt sure would one day challenge the Goddess herself.

She drew a deep breath and looked out over the land. From her position standing high on a peak of rock and ice that towered into the frigid sky, she had an unimpeded view of the frozen plain that lay before her. Far off in the distance, she could see the range of broken peaks and pinnacles where the enemy stood, and she nodded calmly.

Opposing her were the six Adepts who for countless thousands of years had helped to rule the realm. It was their task to prove she wasn't worthy of her position as Sorceress of the Darkness, and this they would try to do by destroying her and reducing her soul to one more frozen crystal of ice among the endless millions that formed the tundra.

And standing in judgment over them all, making sure that strict protocol was observed in the ritual of battle, was her grandfather himself: the Arc-Adept and king of all that lay beneath the grinning skull of the moon.

She turned to the east and bowed toward the single towering pinnacle of rock where she knew he stood watching. She applied her Farseeing Ability, unable to resist focusing her psychic eye and looking at the mysterious figure of pure evil that stood in unmoving silence. His form was wrapped in a swirling mist of ice crystals, but every now and then a random breeze would tear a hole in the enveloping vapor and she would catch a glimpse of a figure, pale as moonlit mist, white as time-bleached bone.

Aware of Medea's scrutiny, Cronus turned his head, and the black, endless depths of his eyes held her for a moment. She flinched as the malevolent power of his gaze seized her.

"He's watching us, Orla!" she said to her servant, her voice edged with fear.

Immediately the Witch of the Dark Power collapsed into a heap of black rags and groveled in the ice crystals at their feet. But Medea grabbed her and hauled her upright.

"Stand up, you spineless wretch! I won't have Cronus judging me by my handmaid! Show a proper respect, but hide your fear. Remember you serve the greatest sorceress in the Darkness, an Adept whose power is second only to his!"

Orla managed to control her terror enough to stay on her feet, but she continued to cringe, feeling the malevolence of his gaze. "Perhaps, Mistress, I'd need to be as powerful as you to stand in the presence of the Arc-Adept. But my Abilities are weak. There's nothing to protect me and little to give me the right to be here in the Darkness. Perhaps all I have is a long memory, which might be interesting to those who'd otherwise blast my soul to the tundra again."

Medea regarded her handmaid quietly. Sometimes it was easy to forget that Orla was one of the oldest souls in the Darkness. She'd been one of the first mortals to be drawn to its evil power, and she'd also been one of the first to be destroyed by it and have her spirit reduced to a tiny crystal of ice. Only Medea's need for a companion in the vastness of the domain had caused her to use her powers to bring the witch back from oblivion. And even Orla didn't know exactly how old she was.

There were other elements to be considered, too. Medea might have accepted the Dark as a substitute family, but the links between Cronus and herself were even stronger. She trembled as she remembered the day she'd discovered exactly who the Arc-Adept was.

It had been the end of her first year in the Darkness, and she'd just fought off yet another attack by the hideous Ice Demons, when she'd become aware of a mind probing her. The force and evil of it had made her gasp aloud, and she'd fallen to her knees in horror as it ripped open her soul and gazed at leisure within. But then, as quickly as it had arrived, it withdrew, and she was left sprawled in the ice of the tundra.

Trembling and shocked, she'd retreated to her cave, but her journey back to safety was made easier by the knowledge she carried with her. A probing mind, no matter how well shielded, reveals something of itself when it enters a soul, and Medea had noted a familiar "tone" as Cronus had examined her. It was a tone that had sounded like that of another, one she had once loved and now hated. It sounded like the tone of the one who had guided her magical development and had then opposed her in a battle that had almost killed her. It sounded very like Oskan Witchfather! As alike, in fact, as a father's face can be to his son's!

Looking into the mind of Cronus was almost like looking at a mirror image of Oskan. It was reversed, of course, like all reflections, and it was dark and deeply corrupted, but otherwise their minds were almost identical.

She'd slept for two days as the awful, wonderful knowledge she'd acquired had overwhelmed her and sent her into a protective state of dormancy. At last! At last she'd discovered who Oskan's mysterious father was! The venerated and revered Oskan Witchfather, savior of the Icemark and champion against evil, was the son of Cronus the Mighty, the fallen Immortal who'd made war on the Goddess herself!

"I *will* stay here, Orla," Medea said, emerging from her memories. "The Darkness is my home, and the Arc-Adept himself is my grandfather."

But she was under no illusions. She might have been related to Cronus, but here in his domain, the concept of family had little influence; only strength and ruthlessness could guarantee safety and acceptance. Hastily she bowed to the mysterious figure on its pinnacle of ice, and her thoughts returned to the urgency of the moment.

If she was to defeat her opponents and win her right to remain in the Darkness, she would need to concentrate.

3

For Kirimin, this was the best part of Samhein. All of the rituals were finished, all of the ceremonies performed, and now the ghost stories and games could begin. As she walked toward the eaves of the Great Forest, she could clearly see the jack-o'-lanterns hanging in the trees, the candles inside the hollowed-out pumpkins making the faces grin and flicker weirdly in the gathering shadows. In the sky the first stars were only just beginning to appear, whisper-thin and pale like polished silver through mist, but under the trees, night had already gathered like black drapes drawn across the window of the world. Kirimin shivered, enjoying the gentle stroke of fear that ran all the way down her spine to the tip of her spotted tail. This was the very spirit of Samhein: dark shadows, the fluttering of cool winds that somehow sounded like whispering voices calling your name, and tales of the dead visiting the lands of life again. But best of all, on this special night of magic, there was a new moon. It rode in the slowly darkening blue above her, cold and brilliant like a strongly drawn bow of ice just before its arrows of light are released.

Looking around her, she could see others from the city of Frostmarris scuttling through the gathering darkness, some already trying to hide from their friends, others still in laughing, whispering groups, and some completely alone, on some private business of their own on this Samhein night. Hugging the ground close, she slid over the terrain like a breath of fog blown by a wind. There was no sign of Sharley or Mekhmet, but she knew they were following nearby. This time she was determined to give them a scare. All night they'd been making her yowl with sudden fright as they leaped out of the shadows at her or told her hideous stories of corpses coming back from the dead for revenge.

A light sprinkling of snow had already fallen, the first of the season, and the dusting of white over the shadows and contours of the land blended perfectly with the spots and rosettes of Kirimin's coat. Every now and then she paused and became invisible as fur, snow, and shadow blended into one. Her brilliant amber eyes scanned all around her as she searched for the boys. They wouldn't startle her this time; she was ready.

She moved swiftly on, reaching the first trees of the forest and sliding beneath their shadows to hide and watch. Soon her hunter's eyes narrowed as she spotted them. They were dressed all in white and moving cautiously through the dusk, hoping to spot her before she saw them.

"Too late," she whispered to herself. "I have you already."

One of the other human revelers from the city trod heavily on her tail, but she didn't make a sound or move a muscle. In the deepening gloom of twilight she looked exactly like a snow-sprinkled bank of earth, and with a bit of luck, the boys wouldn't notice her until it was too late.

She narrowed her glowing eyes until only the merest glimmer could be seen, like embers gleaming beneath white ash. "This way," she urged as Sharley and Mekhmet drew closer. "I'm waiting for you."

Soon they were near enough for her to catch their scent, and she held her breath. Any moment now!

"I saw her come this way, I'm sure," said Sharley.

"You must be mistaken," Mekhmet replied. "There's no sign of any paw prints."

"Oh, that means nothing with a Snow Leopard; they can move as lightly as mist if they need to. I've seen an entire squadron of them walk over a muddy field and leave no trace at all."

"And yet they must be as heavy as warhorses," said Mekhmet, moving toward the trees.

"Heavier," said Sharley, joining him. "Anyway, she's given us the slip. Let's go back to the city and hide there. She's bound to show up before too long."

Suddenly the ground beneath his feet rose up roaring into the sky, and his gimpy leg, which had been badly weakened by polio when he was little, gave way, dumping him hard on his backside. Mekhmet leaped forward to his defense and ran into a solid wall of fur and muscle. Again the huge monster roared, and then began to giggle.

"Yes! Yes! I got you! I scared you witless! Admit it, you were pooing your pants!"

"Not at all!" said Sharley, struggling to his feet. "We knew you were there all along."

Kirimin giggled again, knowing full well that he was lying. "Yeah! I got you good! Sweet, sweet revenge!"

Both boys leaped on her, and soon they were all rolling around in the dirt and snow of the forest floor, laughing and screeching and throwing handfuls of dead leaves at one another until they were all completely filthy.

Eventually they sat down together and surveyed the damage. "We'd better try and sneak in by a back way. Cressida's bound to notice and get snotty," said Sharley. He was sixteen years old now and spent most of his time in the Desert Kingdom with Mekhmet. But even though he was now recognized as a great warrior, and had fame and standing throughout all the known lands after his role in the last war with the Polypontian Empire, he still didn't like to get on the wrong side of his sister Cressida. Neither did the other two, and Kirimin also had to remember her mother, who would think her behavior "unladylike." After a quick discussion, they decided to go back to Frostmarris and try to get in through one of the small postern gates that were set into the perimeter walls.

For ease and speed, the two boys climbed on Kirimin's back, and soon she was running swiftly and silently through the gathering night. The effects of their wrestling match in the leaves could soon be wiped clean from her coat by the use of her tongue and paws. But if the boys got into trouble, both her mother and father would naturally assume that she was partly to blame, and that could mean she'd be sent to her quarters early so she'd miss the ghost stories and huge supper.

Her mother, in particular, was always telling her that she must be more ladylike, especially as she was now almost fully grown at more than two years old. But she found it so difficult to behave in the way Krisafitsa wanted; she wished that Snow Leopard ages and human ages were the same, and she'd once tried to argue that a two-year-old human child could behave more or less as it liked without anyone complaining. But her mother had pointed out that there was a difference, as she well knew; humans grew up much more slowly than Snow Leopards, and in real terms she was almost the same age as Sharley and Mekhmet.

The walls of Frostmarris stood in black silhouette against the polished brilliance of the moonlit sky, and as they approached, they could clearly see the tiny figures of house-carl and werewolf guards patrolling along the battlements.

"Go to the eastern wall, Kirimin," said Sharley. "There's a postern gate about halfway between the gateway and the corner tower." The small entrance would be guarded, of course, but Sharley knew almost all the housecarls and were-wolves who were likely to be on duty, and it would be easy to slip inside without anyone being told.

An icy wind had followed from the Great Forest, whipping around them as Kirimin galloped through the darkening night, bringing with it a scent of leaf litter and approaching winter. Mekhmet shivered and drew his cloak tighter around himself. As much as he loved the Icemark, there were times when he thought the weather must have been created by the One as an exercise in extremes. It never occurred to him that the climate of the Desert Kingdom could be described in exactly the same terms, being equal and opposite to the conditions of the northern country—fire to its ice, dry to its wet. To Mekhmet almost permanent drought seemed perfectly normal, whereas the lightest shower was a thing of endless wonder.

"We'll have to hurry if we're going to be ready for the banquet," he suddenly said. "The other guests on the top table will be expected to be seated long before the Queen and the Thar arrive."

"I know," Sharley answered. "But as long as there are no holdups, we should make it in time."

"There's the postern," Kirimin interrupted, her keen night vision easily spotting the small gate among the shadows. "I'll have us there in a moment."

The curtain walls of the city stood on a huge rocky outcrop that rose out of the Plain of Frostmarris like an island out of a sea, and each gateway was served by a path that zigzagged up the steep incline at an angle that made it possible for carts to climb up with ease. But ignoring this, Kirimin leaped up the almost sheer wall of granite, her claws finding holds among the rocks, and her powerful legs driving them up to the small gateway in a matter of seconds.

The boys scrambled down from her back, and Sharley limped over to the gate, where he knocked with the hilt of his dagger. The gate suddenly burst open and the ferocious face of a werewolf guard thrust itself out at them.

"It's us, Sergeant Moon-runner. Let us in, quick."

"You'd better hurry; Crown Princess Cressida's been wondering where you are. And your mother's been asking for you, Princess Kirimin. It'd be wiser to take the back way into the citadel."

They nodded their thanks and hurried across the court-yard to the service entrance of the Great Hall. After that it was easy to lose themselves in the winding passageways of the citadel, and soon they arrived at the boys' room. "Wait for us, Kiri. We won't be long," said Mekhmet.

"All right. But hurry."

Within seconds the sound of splashing water and the slamming open of clothes chests could be heard beyond their closed door, and Kirimin started her own cleaning-up process while she waited in the corridor. After only a few minutes of careful washing and grooming, her coat gleamed in the torchlight and she relaxed. No one would have anything to complain about now. Not even her mother . . . perhaps. She just hoped the boys were as successful in their sprucing-up.

On cue, their door was wrenched open and they stepped out into the corridor. Kirimin gasped. They were both dressed in the robes of the Desert Kingdom, Mekhmet in a beautiful blue embroidered with gold, and Sharley in his usual black, but so expertly picked out with silver stars that he seemed to be wearing a fragment of midnight that had somehow been captured in fine cloth and beautifully tai-lored. She purred deeply in appreciation, but she'd have sooner died than actually tell them they looked wonderful. "Not bad," she said after a moment. "Come on, I think I can hear people on their way to the Great Hall."

4

Medea turned her gaze outward over the tundra, watching for the enemies' advance. She needed to concentrate if she was to finally win her right to stay in the Darkness.

Orla stood a few paces away from her mistress, her twisted and misshapen body trembling with a combination of cold and fear. The enemy was formidable, and with countless eons of magical experience to call upon, they would surely sweep Medea aside and destroy her. Orla's soul would once again be frozen to a shard of ice and drift forever in the winds of the Darkness.

But Medea showed no such fears. Throwing wide her arms, she exploited the Power of the Dark and drew on the surrounding materials to transform her body.

Power! Huge bolts of power were needed to transform her slight frame into the hideous fighting creature she was making. She grafted the crystalline structures of stone and ice to her bones, and stretched and molded their shapes so that her arms and legs, her spine and skull and all of her skeleton, grew and strengthened; she enmeshed the cosmic dust of stars and meteors, comets and suns, to her skin, weaving it in and kneading it to form diamond-hard scales that covered her growing form.

Now her teeth grew as the molecular structures of iron and steel were added to them, and they sharpened and expanded until they burst from her mouth like swords. Then finally she molded wings on her back, their span reaching wide over the tundra below her and beating the air with a rumble of thunder. Medea had become a huge glittering dragon, ferocious and powerful. Her massive body quivered with pent-up strength, and heat pulsated from her scales as the fires within were stoked to greater and greater temperatures.

At last Medea was ready, and throwing back her head, she let out a blast of fire that illuminated the wastes of the Darkness with a bitter golden light. A huge sense of strength and power flowed through her magical form. She was invincible. Medea the dragon stepped into flight and swept across the sky. She was calling them out, laying down a challenge of personal combat.

The world of the Darkness fell silent as the entire domain waited for Medea's opponents to appear. Only the low moaning of the wind gave voice to the tension that filled the air. Then at last a deep rumble, like distant thunder, rolled over the plain, and six gigantic figures loomed on the horizon, their bodies hulking and enormous, each one a threat to Medea's dragon form. She watched as they approached, and counted each monstrous body as its details came into focus. Giant wolf and bear, eagle and bat, troll and boar. These were the shape-shifted companions of Cronus himself, who, many ages ago, had stood before the Mother Goddess and rejected her offer of forgiveness. The reward for their loyalty was to fall with the Arc-Adept, and they had helped to rule the Darkness ever since.

But in the heat and excitement of battle, Medea had chosen to forget their loyalty to her grandfather and what they might mean to him. All she allowed herself to remember was the fact that it was the Adepts who wanted to stop her from taking her rightful place alongside Cronus. With a great roar she swept over the tundra to meet her enemies, landing a few yards ahead of them. But now she shocked all who watched as she returned to her natural form, sloughing away the magical additions of metal and mineral, cosmic dust and ice, to stand before the Adepts unarmed and undefended.

Medea's enemies raged aloud in triumph, assuming she had surrendered in despair. Then, just as her senses were overwhelmed with the stench and power of the enemies' gigantic forms, she shifted her shape again. Medea was risking a clever strategy, and the enemy quailed and fell back before her as she paced gently over the frozen souls of the tundra. She'd taken on the form of Cronus, the Arc-Adept himself. And such was her power that not even the enemies' most incisive probing of her mind could reveal her true identity.

Immediately the companions of Cronus's original exile returned to their natural unprotected forms. Medea gazed at them in fascination. The endless years of their time in the Darkness had twisted their already foul minds still further until it showed in their outward appearances. All six were hideously ugly with white, bloodless skin stretched thinly over a deformed skeleton. Their heads were huge and nodded and lolled on their bony necks, and their mouths were lipless gashes that could barely contain the tangle of broken and jagged teeth. They gazed on Medea's shape-shifted form and bowed.

"Dear companions in power," said the cold and cruel voice emerging from Medea's shape-shifted throat, "this confrontation has continued for long enough; hear now my pronouncement, and prepare yourselves to obey my orders."

The six enemy Adepts bowed obsequiously before what they believed to be their lord and commander.

Medea was jubilant; she'd tricked them. Completely fooled by her deception, they'd laid aside all of their shields and defenses, proving that she really was the most powerful Adept but one.

She drew a deep breath and smiled. "Die," she said quietly. "Die in agony." And she released the pent-up energy she'd so carefully gathered in a raging fire of destructive power. Flames and white-hot plasma spewed into the atmosphere, blasting a crater into the ice and engulfing the unprotected Adepts in an explosion of searing destruction.

Their bodies began to rip apart; blistered skin was flayed from the flesh and muscles beneath, which then began to scorch and burn until their blood started to boil. Then, at last, with Medea's final cries of rage echoing on the frozen air, the Adepts' bodies were blasted apart with a sound like sheets of saturated leather being split open.

But even though their bodies had been destroyed, the Adepts still hadn't been defeated. Slowly they began to link mind to mind, and their power and confidence grew. As one they called on the energy of the surrounding ether, conjuring a cascade of liquid ice that flowed and undulated high in the blackness of the sky, like a curtain stirring in a breeze. All who saw it knew its touch would mean death, every last drop of warmth and life drawn away by its deadly cold.

Medea watched as the scintillating sheet slowly descended and draped itself over her slender form. The liquid ice then flowed over the surface of the tundra, dragging Medea down to the ground and oozing over her slight form so that soon there was no sign that she'd ever stood in defiance before her enemies. The six Adepts let out a shriek of triumph, their voices echoing over the frozen wastes.

But if Medea truly was dead, then her corpse was not lying quietly, and soon the surface of the pool of liquid ice began to shiver and creep like the pelt of a huge animal. Gradually, stealthily, the movement gathered pace until the liquid began to roll and flow; then, incredibly, it started to give off steam, and bubbles began to burst and pop all over its surface. The Adepts' freezing curtain of ice was beginning to boil.

The Adepts tried to probe the mass of liquid below them, searching for Medea. But there was no need; Medea exploded from the boiling mass in a crescendo of flame and steam. She had become a Fire Wraith, a creature of pure flame that incinerated anything it touched, and her brilliant light blazed out over the frozen tundra like a sun. She screeched a challenge in a voice that roared and crackled like a forest fire, and shot across the sky like a comet. She smashed into the conjoined minds of her enemies with a mighty explosion that drove all who heard it to their knees, and the shattered spirits of the Adepts were flung across the sky like windblown leaves.

Medea now slowly resumed her true form as a teenage girl. Then she watched with quiet satisfaction as the broken remains of the Adepts' souls floated gently down like a scatter of snow to join the countless millions of ice crystals that made up the tundra of the Darkness.

She smoothed her skirts, smiled quietly, and, turning to the distant peak where the watching figure of Cronus stood, she bowed her head.

Then the black joy of her victory seized her and she couldn't resist laughing loud and long, her voice echoing over the frozen wastes and settling like snow among the corpses of the fallen Ice Demons.

"I did it, Orla! I did it!" she shouted joyously to her servant. "I defeated the six most powerful Adepts that the Darkness has ever known! Only one other is more powerful than me, and that's Cronus himself!"

5

Sharley, Mekhmet, and Kirimin set off for the Samhein feast hoping to get to the dais before the Queen and Thar arrived. But in the event they didn't have to worry; they were the first ones to arrive at the top table, and they sat down and looked out over the hall, where the lower tables were quickly beginning to fill up.

Kirimin happily absorbed the atmosphere and shuddered with delicious dread. Some of the older country folk who called the holiday "Halloween" kept up the folk traditions of ghost stories and carved pumpkin lamps. In fact, all of the tables were glittering and grinning with jack-o'-lanterns and white papier-mâché skulls, and the huge hammer-beam roof was festooned with orange and black streamers as well as ghosts and black cats cut out of thin cardboard. The scent of candle wax and slightly toasted pumpkin flesh was the absolute epitome of Samhein for Kirimin. No matter what time of year it was, she only had to sniff the rich scent of cooking pumpkin and she was immediately transported back to cool twilights and the happy dread of ghostly tales.

Some of the off-duty housecarls down in the hall had also dressed up as Zombies and ghouls and sat now chatting away happily with their comrades as though they always looked like they'd been dead for several weeks. The werewolves, of course, didn't have to bother to wear costumes; they already looked monstrous, but they seemed to enjoy helping their human friends look as hideous as possible. One huge member of the Queen's Ukpik bodyguard was patiently helping a housecarl friend make himself up as a Zombie, delicately dabbing a green dye onto his cheeks and then stepping back to properly gauge the effect.

"It's going to be a good one this year," said Sharley, happily gazing out over the hall. "I wonder if the Wolf-folk will start dancing again like they did last time. That was great; I've never seen anything so ridiculous."

"Yeah, I particularly liked it when King Grishmak decided to partner that little woman from the Southern Riding. She just about came up to his knees, or at least she would have if she'd stood on a stool," said Mekhmet.

"Baroness Gunhilda, you mean?" asked Sharley. "She might be small, but she's the best shot I know with a throwing ax. Still, she did look like a complete pillock dancing with Grishmak!"

"What about the pie-eating competition?" said Kirimin. "I didn't think Dad would ever stop being sick. But I suppose that's the price you pay for taking on Olememnon."

"He won, though, that's the point," said Sharley. "Only a Snow Leopard could've done it. Uncle Ollie's a legend among the Hypolitan."

"Is he here this year?" asked Kirimin. "He tells great ghost stories and even better dirty jokes."

"No. The Hypolitan have their own ceremonies and rituals for Samhein. But the big meeting about the Empire, and all the wars that have happened since Bellorum's death, is scheduled for the day after tomorrow, and Uncle Ollie and the Basilea will be here for that."

A sudden commotion down at the main doors drew their attention, and they watched as two werewolves maneuvered a sedan chair into the hall. Once through the doors, they raised the carrying chair to shoulder height and paraded between the tables as they headed for the dais. Maggiore Totus surveyed the decorations and activities all around as he was carried along, and he waved enthusiastically as the housecarls and werewolves began to thump the tables in greeting.

"It's Maggie!" said Sharley excitedly. "I didn't expect him until much later — the roads from his home in the south are already beginning to freeze over." He stood up and waved as the ancient scholar approached the top table.

For a moment there was no response from the sedan chair, but then a pair of enormously thick spectoculums turned toward the dais and Maggie's face lit up. "Sharley and Mekhmet! And I do believe I spy Princess Kirimin!" he called down the hall. "My, my, you're all so grown-up!"

Why do adults always say that? all three of them thought as they watched the little old man approach. But he was so obviously happy to see them, they forgave him immediately.

The werewolves reached the top table, removed the carrying poles from the sedan chair, lifted the seat onto the dais, and then positioned Maggie next to the boys.

"Thank you, Sergeants Sky-howler and Moon-watcher. I trust I can call on your services again at the end of the night?"

"Yes, Sir," said the larger of the werewolves. "Though the ride might be a bit bumpy after a few beers, like."

"Well, I intend to have a few myself, so I probably won't notice," Maggie replied with a grin. The soldiers saluted and trotted down to the lower tables to join their comrades.

The old scholar turned to the three friends and laughed. "It's so good to see you all!" Sharley and Mekhmet hugged him, and Kirimin purred thunderously and rubbed her enormous cheek against his wrinkled face. "I hope you've lots of news to tell me; I'm a bit out of the way down in the South Farthing, so I miss out on things."

"Lots and lots, Maggie. Where shall we begin?" said Mekhmet.

"Well, I'm glad you said that because I need to clarify a few points on your father's campaigns in the southern provinces of the old Empire."

"Glad to, but later tomorrow would be best, when things are quieter."

"Oh, absolutely. In fact, I intend to be less than quiet myself tonight. Bring on the wine servers!" A chamberlain immediately appeared at his elbow, taking him completely by surprise. "Eh? Not yet, not yet, my man. Far too early to start drinking."

The boys grinned and sipped their goblets of sherbet, the alcohol-free drink produced in the Desert Kingdom. "Perhaps you'd like to try some of our refreshments, Maggie?" said Sharley.

"That's enormously kind of you, but I'm afraid I'm just an old reprobate who expects his drink to make his head spin when he's had too much. Sometimes the infidel is beyond help, eh, Mekhmet?"

"I would have you no other way, Senor Totus," the Desert Prince replied formally and salaamed.

Medea breathed a sigh of pure joy as she arrived back in her cave. The old witch scuttled like a twisted crab to her mistress, ready to take her heavy furs.

"I defeated them, Orla; I defeated all of my enemies!"

"You did indeed, Mistress. But now come in out of the cold and warm yourself by the fire."

Medea stopped and looked around, as though seeing the cave she lived in for the first time. "What's this? The second greatest Adept in all the Darkness doesn't live in a cave!

Stand clear, Orla; your mistress will now create the architecture that truly reflects her status!"

Medea closed her eyes, concentrating as she drew on the Power of the Dark, and ghostly white structures of arches and flying buttresses slowly began to evolve from the warp and weft of starlight and ice. Not surprisingly, they were cold and white, being made up of countless glittering shards of ice, and they soared through the air in huge leaping arches, slender bridges, and buttresses designed to look like the most delicate of skeletons: ribs and elegantly curved fingers, spinal columns, and the most graceful of thighbones. All around her a palace evolved from the void, like a cathedral built in homage to refined death.

She then made a high-backed chair that was almost a throne—almost, but not quite. *He* would've been angry if she'd allowed herself that. Then she placed white cobblestones over the ice of the tundra. Everything in the Darkness was monochrome: dead white, or the void of black. But these cobbles were different: They were the rounded domes of thousands of skulls, stretching away into the distance until she raised a wall on which blazed torches with pure white flames.

Orla stood transfixed as the palace grew around her. As a spirit who'd been resurrected by Medea from the ice of the tundra, and who'd then watched as her mistress had fashioned a new body for her, she was well aware of the sorceress's power, but this massive display of Magical Abilities was almost overpowering.

Medea smiled as she looked on her new home; at last she had earned her status and the right to remain in the Darkness. But even now, in the moment of her success, a tiny shiver of fear slowly trickled down her spine as she remembered the victory over her enemies.

"Orla, how do you think Cronus will . . . react to the deaths of the enemy Adepts?"

"I'm not sure, Mistress," the witch replied fearfully. "But it's said that he likes to control every aspect of the Darkness, including exactly who lives . . . and who dies."

Her voice trailed away to silence, and she flinched as Medea suddenly smashed her hands down onto the arms of the chair-that-was-almost-a-throne. "Why didn't you remind me of this? I can't be expected to remember everything when I'm preparing for battle and then fighting for my life!"

Orla trembled before this outburst, but she knew there was more that Medea needed reminding of. "Mistress, I didn't know that you planned to kill your enemies, otherwise I would have warned you against such an act. But . . . but I'm afraid there are other facts that have slipped your mind in the elation of your victory."

Medea turned a cold eye on her handmaid. "Remind me."

Orla drew a deep, steadying breath. "After the war against heaven, almost all of the rebel army betrayed Cronus and accepted the mercy of the Goddess. Only six remained loyal and were exiled with him into the Darkness, where together they healed their psychic wounds and then helped him to create the realm as we know it today. . . ." Orla's voice trailed away to silence again, but then she went on: "Those six Adepts now lie dead on the field of battle, their souls blasted to ice by your powers; they're lost among the countless thousands in the tundra that they helped to create."

Medea gasped as the truth of Orla's words hit her. Her grandfather could easily decide to avenge the deaths of his most loyal allies by destroying her! For a moment blind panic threatened to seize her, but then she spied a glimmer of hope.

"Orla! We must return to the battlefield and I can revive their frozen souls, just as I did yours! I'll put a check on their powers and house their souls in small, easily controlled bodies. Then I can present them to Cronus to do with as he wishes!"

But Medea's excitement was interrupted by a small, careful cough. "Mistress, I'm afraid the situation's more complicated than that."

"What are you talking about, woman?"

"Your powers, Mistress. They're different; they combine the Abilities of a fallen Immortal with elements that are purely human. Feelings, for instance; your hatred ripped apart the Adepts' souls and scattered them over the tundra. There are fragments and shards spread over the entire width of the Darkness. It'd take a lifetime of searching to find all the parts."

Medea let out a great howl of rage, and siftings of cosmic dust trickled down from the ceilings of her palace. What had she done? How could she hope to survive the wrath of Cronus?

Orla quietly withdrew into the shadows. Centuries of life, before she'd become one of the first to fall in the Darkness, had taught her precisely when to make herself scarce, and this was definitely one of those times. Orla had no intention of returning to the oblivion of the tundra if she could help it. Within a few seconds she'd quietly withdrawn to the doors of the Bone Fortress and disappeared into the frozen night. She'd either return when her mistress had found a solution to her difficulties, or simply fade permanently into the background if she did not. After all, if Medea was destroyed by Cronus, she could hardly punish Orla for absconding, could she?

Medea didn't even notice that Orla had gone as she desperately tried to think of a way to convince Cronus that the deaths of the six Adepts were somehow good for the Darkness. But as she wrestled with the impossibility of the situation her thoughts were suddenly interrupted, as the tall ivory doors of the palace creaked open and a breath of deadly cold slipped over the floor like an invisible glacier.

Her mind scanned the ether and she leaped to her feet. It was him! Quickly she smoothed her dress, and as her every nerve and fiber screamed under the strain of the unbearable tension, she peered into the gloom.

The ripple of faint footsteps echoed through the towering halls of the palace, and as they drew closer, she began to sweat in spite of the deep, penetrating cold. At last a long shadow slowly encroached on the skull-cobbled pattern of the palace floor, and with it came a dense mist of ice crystals.

Closer and closer the shadow came, and as its grave-scented clamminess touched the hem of her dress and slowly rose up her legs to her waist and finally over her whole body, she shuddered and almost cried out.

She forced herself to wait quietly until the swirling mist of Cronus's presence coalesced under the icy archway that led into the hall where she stood. In a state of controlled terror she curtsied. "Welcome, Grandfather."

She watched as the mist of ice crystals swirled as though driven by internal winds, and then were torn aside to reveal Cronus himself. He was ugly, horribly ugly, though outwardly he looked almost normal. His tall figure glided over the floor. His skin was as creamy white and as dry as parchment; his face seemed little more than a skull, though the bone structure was fine and beautiful. His eyes were as wide and as black as moonless midnights and had no pupils or irises. They reflected neither light nor emotion and were blank and flat.

He looked neither young nor old, he seemed neither living nor dead, and as he walked, there was only a small, distant echo of footsteps, receding like ripples in a pond.

"Granddaughter," he said in greeting, drawing his white lips away from his sharply pointed teeth. His voice held the senses in a grip of iron and ice; it was deep and toneless, as though spoken into a wide, lightless cave where blind creatures scuttled in the shadows.

The smile of greeting was then carefully packed away and he looked at Medea with expressionless eyes. "You have destroyed my allies. Exactly why did you do this?"

Near panic, Medea couldn't think of anything to say. Her legs began to shake, and she sank into her great chair, where she tried to look as though she were so at ease in Cronus's presence that she could sit without his permission.

The dead black eyes held her gaze in a grip of ice, and she felt her control slipping. She mustn't show fear, even though he knew full well she was terrified. "I killed them because I wanted to!" she blurted, like a child caught with its hand in the cookie jar. Then suddenly defiance swelled up within her, and with a growing anger she went on: "They were my enemies. If I'd been defeated, *they* would've killed *me!*"

"Undoubtedly," the deep, toneless voice agreed.

"So, then, my actions were justified!"

"No. The battle had been won and you were victorious. There was no need for you to destroy them. Your actions were premeditated and murderous."

"Yes, I won, but could you guarantee that they wouldn't have been a threat to me in the future?"

"No."

"Then surely you must agree that destroying them was the only thing I could do."

"They deserved better. We fought together against the Goddess herself, and even in defeat we were glorious."

She found herself snorting. She'd no idea where this courage came from; perhaps there was more of the Lindenshield in her than she cared to admit. "Should I have let them live just because they were once great enough to make war on the Goddess?"

Cronus answered with a silence that stretched into long, endless seconds and seemed to echo on the frozen air. She looked up and met the empty black gaze for as long as she dared, before dropping her eyes.

"Truly you are now a citizen of the Darkness," he said at last. "Your attitude reminds me of the admirable Bellorums."

"No. They failed!" she spat in reply.

"They did. A disappointment, after so many years of manipulation. But now that the Polypontian Empire's destroying itself in a welter of vicious wars, I've a huge cast of characters to choose from. Warlords and generals and homicidal maniacs."

"But you've chosen already, haven't you?" she asked with certainty.

Once again the black, endless pits of the Arc-Adept's eyes held her for a few agonizing seconds. "Yes," he said at last. "Erinor of Artemesion is a fitting successor to the Bellorums. I've already manipulated events so that she could break out of her mountain kingdom, and now no one can stop her."

"And the point of all this is what, exactly?" she asked.

"That will stay a secret, for now. But I'm prepared to say that all of your family will be heavily involved."

"Really?" she asked with excited glee. "Then my hateful little brother could die, at last! How delightful!"

The mist of ice crystals swirled around Cronus like clouds around a mountain peak as he ordered his thoughts. Medea, as a powerful Adept, would be a useful addition to his arsenal of weapons; all he needed to do was to shape her to his needs. The simplest of tasks.

"You have an endless capacity to kill those who should hold your loyalty, Medea, whether the greatest Adepts of the Darkness or your own blood kin. This hatred of rivals, and even of your family, shows a preoccupation with revenge that reveals a dangerous flaw in your character. As an Adept, you should be above such petty concerns."

"You hate," she dared to snap. "You kill for pleasure. Why is it different for me?"

"I hate in the abstract, not the particular. I hate all things with equal malevolence, and so rise above dangerous private obsessions. But you hate with a personal passion that can distract an Adept from the purity of magic. It's a flaw and a weakness that could be exploited by a clever enemy, and one that could yet see you destroyed." His black, empty eyes held her for a brief, terrible moment.

He truly believed that his evil was pure and unsullied by the taint of emotion, but in fact his every act was a considered manipulation of the world and all around him as he searched for the means of attacking the Spirit Realms once again. Cronus had spent eons scheming and planning revenge on the Goddess for defeating him and driving him into exile. Medea was just one more piece in the giant and complex plan that he hoped would one day see him defeat the hated Mother of All and secure him the throne of the Cosmos. But he believed that all of his strategies were formulated in cold, emotionless calculation, and so he felt nothing but contempt for his granddaughter's intense feelings of jealousy and rejection.

He regarded her for a moment longer, and then, without another word, he turned and walked away across the wide floor of the palace. Medea watched him go, sinking back into her chair and breathing a long sigh of relief. She'd done it! Cronus had forgiven her for murdering the six Adepts and had accepted her right to stay in the Darkness. But even now there were still dangers: The hatred and rage against her family that she believed to be her true strength, Cronus saw as a weakness. Obviously she'd need to be careful as she plotted against the Lindenshields and Sharley in particular.

Whatever happened, the Arc-Adept mustn't know what she was doing. And in truth he didn't. But neither did Medea know that her grandfather had begun to mold her thoughts and actions in ways that would make her useful to his plans.

It had been more than a day since Oskan had told Thirrin that Medea was still alive, and he could see she was still trying to come to terms with the devastating and unexpected news. Her eyes filled with tears, she shifted in the chair that stood opposite Oskan's in their private rooms, and waited for him to look up.

"Did I fail her?" she suddenly asked, unable to wait for his attention any longer.

"No," he answered, understanding her question immediately. "Medea is her own creation; nobody else is responsible."

"But if I'd given her more of my time . . ."

"It would have made no difference. Don't forget that I spent endless hours teaching her, showing her how to use her Gifts. If anyone failed her, it was me."

"But I'm her *mother*. A girl needs female guidance; perhaps I should have spent less time running the country and more time with my family."

"In which case we'd all be dead," Oskan answered sharply, recognizing her words as a cry for help and reassurance. "The threat of Bellorum and the Imperial armies took every moment you had to spare. We all know that; Cressida and the boys know it; the entire country knows it. Of all our children only Medea has become . . . has turned to the Dark."

"But only she could. She's the only Adept among them!"

"The only *Adept*, yes. But Cressida . . ."

"I should have spent more time with her and less training with Cressida and the boys in the lists. Perhaps . . . perhaps she felt left out somehow; I should have let her know that it didn't matter she wasn't a warrior. . . ."

Oskan slammed his hands down on the arms of his chair in frustration. "Thirrin! You're not responsible for Medea becoming evil! You didn't neglect her! It has nothing to do with the fact she wasn't a warrior; neither was Sharley at first, and he never once thought of turning to evil!" His voice rang out into the room, shocking her to silence. He drew a steadying breath, and then went on more quietly. "If anything's responsible for our youngest daughter becoming the foul creature she now undoubtedly is, it's her heritage. Her grandfather's blood . . . my blood."

He stood up and walked slowly over to the window, where he stared out at the moonlit night. "Like all children and descendants of Cronus and his allies, she was given a choice, and quite simply, she chose to be evil."

A small whisper of doubt nagged at the edge of his consciousness. He'd once believed that the choice only had to be made once in an Adept's life, but now he was slowly becoming aware of a . . . temptation within himself, of a need to explore other possibilities. He was beginning to allow himself to think the unthinkable. He was, after all, the son of the second-most powerful being in the entire Cosmos; what would happen if he allowed himself to accept his heritage and opened his mind at least partially to the Dark? Perhaps he'd be able to control it and use the massive increase there'd be in his powers to serve good!

Thirrin joined him at the window, interrupting his thoughts and bringing him back to the immediate problem of Medea. The Queen leaned her head on his shoulder. "Then was her . . . fall inevitable?"

"No!" he said sharply. "*I'm* a child of Cronus's and I was strong enough to reject the Dark, and all the power it could have given me. Nothing's inevitable. . . . It's just that for some it's more likely."

Thirrin nodded. "You've never really told me about your father. Can there never be any hope for him or his followers? Is he completely evil?"

"Oh yes! Completely and utterly! I once searched the Darkness itself for more information about his mind, about the way he thinks. And I found his history imprinted on the very atoms of the atmosphere."

"Tell me!" said Thirrin eagerly. "Tell me everything. I need to know this creature that's corrupted my daughter."

"There's too much to tell in one short lifetime. But perhaps everything can be summed up by the beginning of his evil. You know he fought a war against the Goddess, of course, and that one of his many titles is 'He who refused the mercy of the Goddess.' Even in defeat his hatred and iniquity raged on. Cronus and six others proudly rejected forgiveness. . . ." Oskan fell silent and shuddered as the memory surfaced. "His voice had once been as beautiful as deep-toned bells, but as he faced the Goddess, pride and hatred cracked its beauty, and it rasped and rattled as he defied his enemies.

"She knew then that he would never change, and he and his six allies were cast down into the void between the Physical Realms and the Spirit Realms that was known as the Darkness. But even in this desolate place their pride wasn't quenched, and over time they created a world that was to become a corrupt mirror of the purity they'd lost."

The wind moaned around the walls of the citadel, filling the silence as Oskan fell quiet.

"And our daughter willingly chose to follow this creature," Thirrin said, her voice rendered completely flat and emotionless by the sheer weight of her feelings.

"I'm not sure that 'follow' is quite the term to use. Essentially evil is selfish, and even the greatest allies it gathers are there purely for their own ends." He sighed. "I'm afraid, my dear, that we have to accept that Medea chose to be evil for her own reasons. Nothing actually corrupted her. She's a creature of her own making."

Thirrin nodded, accepting his words. Then, remembering her role as Queen of the Icemark, she forced herself to consider practicalities. "And you think she could be a danger to us?"

"Yes. But I'm not entirely sure how or in what way. It could be that she'll be content just to cause mischief, but if she does move against us, I somehow think it'll be on a larger scale than mere troublemaking."

"Will . . . will you kill her?" Thirrin asked, her voice barely more than a whisper.

Oskan was deeply shocked. "Kill her? No, no, I can't kill her," he answered. *Not without truly terrible consequences.* Although he could not tell Thirrin, this was the knowledge the Goddess herself had given him to use as a weapon against Cronus in the struggle he knew was coming.

But once again the voice of doubt nagged at the edge of his mind. Surely there had to be another way; perhaps even Dark Power could be used for good, if wielded by a good man? He struggled to clear his mind of doubt and concentrate. "All I can do is try to destroy Medea's power . . . render her impotent in some way."

"And in the meantime, we have the possibility of a war to consider," said Thirrin wearily. "Our lives are never less than complicated, are they?"

"No, my love," Oskan replied with a grim smile that masked his relief at the change of subject. "What do the latest reports say about the Polypontus?"

"That the Empire's crumbling and Erinor marches on, sweeping all before her."

"She's a problem that definitely needs addressing," said Oskan thoughtfully.

"As she will be, just as soon as the allies are gathered and we can discuss our response," said Thirrin with vigor.

The Witchfather nodded, happy to see his wife distracted.

The sound of marching feet and growled orders then percolated into the room as the Queen's Ukpik bodyguard arrived at the door, ready to escort her to the feast of Samhein in the Great Hall.

Thirrin stood, smoothed her gown, and straightened her shoulders as she donned her public persona as the warrior-queen of the Icemark. But just before the bodyguard entered the room, she quickly turned to her husband and took his hand. "Promise me . . . promise me that I didn't fail her, Oskan. Tell me that I didn't condemn her to evil."

He raised her hand to his lips and kissed it. "I truly believe that it is impossible for Thirrin Freer Strong-in-the-Arm Lindenshield to either commit or cause evil of any sort anywhere in Creation. And any who have fallen into the Darkness have done so by their own choice."

A small sad smile touched her lips, and she blinked rapidly to clear her eyes of tears before the escort of werewolves came in.

Once again she assumed the role of monarch, and raising her head proudly, she said, "Then let us join in the feast of the Goddess. Our people await."

6

Suddenly a fanfare sounded, and all of the guests turned to look out over the hall. In the past few minutes the tables had been filled to capacity, musicians had started to play in the minstrels' gallery over the main doors, and acrobats had begun their glittering displays of tumbling and diving all along the walkways between the benches. But now everything froze and fell silent, as though one of the amazing painters from the Southern Continent had captured the entire scene on an impossibly broad canvas.

All eyes were turned to the massive double doors, and a murmur rose up as the Queen's Ukpik bodyguard appeared, marching in step, their ferocious faces glaring rigidly ahead. Then Queen Thirrin herself arrived, walking with Tharaman-Thar and Grishmak, King of the Wolf-folk. Behind them came Krisafitsa-Tharina and Oskan Witchfather, and at the rear walked Crown Princess Cressida. All the guests in the Great Hall stood and bowed as they swept past.

Kirimin couldn't help noticing that her father had on his "regal face," as her mother put it, and he inclined his head haughtily to right and left as the royal party processed to the dais. But catching sight of his daughter, he winked and let his whiskers droop comically, before resuming his royal dignity and surveying all from the huge height of his regality.

Krisafitsa soon spied her daughter already seated at the top table and critically scanned her appearance. She approved enormously; Kirimin was almost fully grown and was very beautiful indeed. If only she could iron out the more *exuberant* parts of her personality, then perhaps she would make a fitting princess. Of course, the enthusiasm and playfulness came from her father, and there was very little that could be done about that, but a true member of the royal family of the Icesheets should learn to control her nature and present a restrained and dignified face to the world.

They arrived at the top table, and all sense of decorum was lost as Tharaman started to fuss over everybody, making sure everyone had enough cushions and was comfortable, rearranging the chairs and knocking over jugs and bowls.

"Darling, might it be a good idea to leave the arrangements to the chamberlains?" asked Krisafitsa gently.

"Eh? What? I'm just making sure everyone's comfortable. . . . Ah, Sharley! Mekhmet!" he boomed, immediately distracted from his reordering of the seating arrangements as he caught sight of the boys. "Well, you look smart in your . . . in your desert robe thingies! Yes, very smart!"

Both boys stood and bowed correctly. "Oh yes! Very . . . Don't they, Krisafitsa, my love?" he went on.

"Yes, darling, they do. Now, sit down. Thirrin wants to formally announce the start of the feast."

"Oh, right! Yes . . . well, why didn't you say so?"

Thirrin had been waiting patiently during Tharaman's chaos, and now stood forward and looked out over the hall. "The great ceremony of Samhein is upon us once again, my people. And, as has been decreed by the Mother Goddess herself, and her consort, the God, we have acknowledged the day with rite, ritual, and holy procedure. Let us stand now and receive the blessing of Oskan Witchfather, the senior priest in the service of the Lady."

A great scuffling and scraping of benches then sounded throughout the hall as everyone stood and turned to face the dais. Oskan stepped forward, dressed entirely in black but for a thin circlet of silver, etched with the phases of the moon, around his brow. His stern face was beginning to show the lines and furrows of the many harrowing experiences he'd lived through, and his once-jet-black hair was now touched with gray at the temples. As he stood rigid and unmoving before the gathering of human, werewolf, and Snow Leopard, he looked like a statue of some wise and mighty king from the far heroic past. None guessed of the struggle and uncertainty that were tormenting him. They saw only the great Adept and Witchfather who had helped to guide them through the troubles and chaos of two wars. Everyone believed they could rely upon him and his powers to keep them safe, no matter what the strength of the enemy. Everyone believed he would always be unswervingly loyal to the cause of the Icemark.

"Children of the Goddess, be reminded at this feast of Samhein that all of us here are mortal and destined to die. Such is our lot in life. If accident or war, disease or unlawful death, does not take us, then the creeping enfeeblement of old age certainly will. The mightiest warrior cannot defeat the Reaper of Souls, nor can the greatest athlete outrun him. He will always be victor in the long run of life."

His somber words echoed over the silent hall, and everyone felt the truth of them sinking into their very souls. But then Oskan's face broke into a wide and warmly loving smile. "But at the moment we're alive! The fire is warm, the food is good, and the wine and beer are just begging to be drunk. Let us celebrate these gifts of the Goddess! She is the greatest of all mothers, and loves to see her children enjoying their lives. But also remember that the spirits of the beloved dead move among us, so let us do them proper honor by singing and dancing and also by drinking and eating more than we should!"

A great cheer rose up, the musicians started to play, and the acrobats cascaded into the air in a dazzle of sequins and skill. Chamberlains and servants now poured into the Great Hall, carrying huge trays and platters of food that steamed and bubbled, hissed and sizzled, as delicious aromas filled the enormous space.

Soon the top table was mountainous with food of every imaginable type. Grishmak heaped his plate hugely, demolishing half of it in one mouthful. "Great grub as usual, Thirrin," he bellowed, then turned his huge bloodshot eyes on the Snow Leopard King. "Are you ready for a small duel, Tharaman? I choose beef and gravy as the weapons, the winner being the one who eats the most and can still walk out of the hall at the end of the evening!"

"Right!" said the Thar, the light of battle in his eye. "You're on!"

"Oh, please!" said Krisafitsa in despair. "Does every meal have to be a competition? Can't we just enjoy the food for its own sake, for once?"

Kirimin laughed. "I think Dad's determined to defend his crown as Chief Glutton of the Alliance."

"Indeed I am, especially as it was so hard-won from Olememnon last year. It's a pity he's not here tonight."

"He'll be with us soon," said Thirrin.

"But when he does arrive, I don't think there'll be much time for party games, Tharaman," said Crown Princess Cressida sternly. "The Polypontian Empire may be dying as we speak, but its passing is far from quiet and easy. Wars are raging throughout its lands, and there are rumors of a movement of people far to the south that could become a threat to us all."

Thirrin suddenly looked tired. Unlike her husband, she seemed untouched by the passing of time; her complexion was still flawless, and her red hair was as fiery and as lustrous as ever, but at the mention of war she physically sagged. It felt as if she'd spent most of her reign on horseback, fighting to save her tiny land from invasion and defeat. And even now, after the Empire had finally started to break up following the deaths of Scipio Bellorum and his sons, there were still threats to the Icemark's liberty in the form of Erinor and her undefeated Hordes. And added even to that was the devastating news about Medea and her fall to the Darkness. There were times when a quiet life lived in obscurity seemed far more attractive than mere power and rule. She thought she'd quite like to have been a baker, with a little shop in a quiet town somewhere. But her pleasant daydream was interrupted by Oskan nudging her.

"Can't you do something with your daughter?" he murmured. "It's so typical that she should spoil the party atmosphere with talk of war."

For a moment Thirrin thought he was talking of Medea, but then realized that it was Cressida who was the cause of his annoyance. "She's your daughter, too, you know!" she murmured back. "But yes, you're right. I'll distract her and then you can zap her with a happy spell!"

He smiled. "It wouldn't work. She's immune to magic."

"She's probably even more immune to happiness!" said Thirrin. "Try and get Sharley and Mekhmet going; they'll soon liven things up."

He nodded in agreement and turned to the boys. "How are your horses recovering after the sea crossing?"

"Great, thanks, Dad," Sharley replied. "Suleiman's almost back to normal, and so's Jaspat, isn't he, Mekhmet?"

"Yes, we're hoping to go for a trek through the Great Forest for a few days, to blow away the last of the cobwebs and get the horses back up to strength. Kiri's coming, too."

"Oh, *is* she?" said Krisafitsa, looking up. "That's news to me."

Kirimin removed her muzzle from the bowl of apple custard she'd been eating and gazed at her mother entreatingly as cream dripped from her long whiskers. She loved human food, particularly the puddings, but in the sudden crisis she forgot all about eating as she desperately tried to think what to say. She knew she should have spoken earlier about going with the boys to the Great Forest, but she'd just kept putting it off. Sometimes talking to her own mother was more daunting than meeting a room full of strangers.

"Oh, *please* let me go, Mama! I meant to ask you earlier, but the time never seemed quite right. It's perfectly safe in the forest, ask the boys, and there'll be three of us, anyway, and they'll have their scimitars and armor and I can fight well, ask Eodred and Howler, I helped break their shield-wall only this lunchtime, and there're no enemies in the forest, anyway, but if there were, we'd be able to beat them easily, wouldn't we, boys? Yes, see, no problem, and we'll be sensible, especially me, and we won't take any risks and we're only going for three days, if you let me go, that is, so we won't be able to go that far, and even if we did, we still wouldn't be in any danger, would we, boys? No, see . . ." Her voice trailed away as she remembered that she had to breathe, and she looked imploringly at her mother, who was licking her paw.

"I'm not sure that the Great Forest is the right sort of environment for a young princess, even if there aren't any dangers," said Krisafitsa doubtfully.

"Why not?" asked Kirimin, trying to ignore the sense of despair that was growing inside her. "There's . . . there's nothing *vulgar* or *improper* about the forest. It just *is*! It's nature, and . . . and natural things, and you said yourself that a proper interest in the natural world was a good thing for a young lady."

"Indeed I did," Krisafitsa agreed quietly. "But I meant that the subject could be studied in a classroom, with a tutor and with a proper sense of *decorum.*"

Kirimin lowered her head sadly as she sensed defeat. For her mother, decorum and correct behavior were the most important things in the life of a young princess, and anything that threatened these things must be avoided at all costs. Sometimes she hated being a member of the Snow Leopard royal family; everything she wanted to do had to be analyzed and studied before she dared even move.

"I wonder . . . I wonder if I might make a contribution to this discussion?" said a voice. All eyes turned to look at Maggiore Totus, who'd been watching the small but desperate battle of wills between Krisafitsa and her daughter.

"Please do, Maggie," said the Tharina graciously. "I'm sure your undoubted wisdom will make my daughter see sense."

"Well, first I'd like to volunteer my services as a tutor to the princess. I've found retirement to be endlessly boring, and I feel Kirimin would add a much-needed sense of *energy* to my life."

"Ha, accepted, Maggie!" boomed Tharaman, who'd been watching the struggle between his mate and daughter with the usual sense of despair. "She'd benefit massively from your input, wouldn't she, dear?"

"Indeed she would," Krisafitsa agreed.

"Oh, I'm so pleased," said Maggie, beaming through his thick spectoculums. "Then may I assume that I can begin my duties immediately and set the princess an assignment to be prepared before our first lesson . . . say, in four days' time?"

"Indeed, I'd like nothing better, Maggiore," said Krisafitsa, purring deeply.

"In that case, Ma'am, I'd like your permission to send Kirimin on a field trip to the Great Forest."

"Oh! Well, I'm not sure . . .."

"I would, of course, insist that the study had a proper scientific basis, Ma'am," said the old scholar, and turning to Kirimin, he continued: "I want you to observe the preparations for winter on the part of the wildlife of the forest, my dear. I will expect a detailed report on such activity categorized as either flora or fauna and subcategorized by species. Do you understand?" he asked in a stern teacherly voice, but when no one else was looking, he winked and smiled.

Kirimin purred happily. "Of course, Maggie!"

"That's Senor Totus, to you," said Krisafitsa. "I think it's important to establish discipline from the very beginning."

"Yes, Mama," said Kirimin diffidently, but discreetly looking at Sharley and Mekhmet, she raised her lips over her enormous teeth in her best imitation of a human grin.

"That's settled, then!" said Tharaman with a sense of relief. "Grishmak! Did you say beef and gravy for the duel?"

The noise and bustle of the celebrations enveloped the top table, and Kirimin sighed happily. She was going on the trip to the Great Forest, thanks to Maggie, and there was still a whole evening of partying ahead. The Samhein celebrations would go on until well past midnight and would only really finish when the last guest had sunk drunkenly to sleep.

A slow, soulful moaning reached Kirimin's sensitive ears as a rising wind blew around the walls of the citadel, and once more she shivered with delicious dread. The atmosphere almost crackled with excitement and also that slight undercurrent of fear enjoyed in safety that made Samhein so special. Happily she looked out over the hall and picked out the housecarls who'd dressed up as ghosts and Zombies. There was even a Snow Leopard in a white sheet and a huge skull mask, but he only managed to look silly rather than frightening.

Kirimin purred and turned to the boys, who were chatting quietly together. "Come on, it's Halloween! Tell us a ghost story from the Desert Kingdom, Mekhmet."

"Ghosts are rare in my country," he answered. "Apart from the Blessed Women, of course, but they're not quite the same thing, and djinns have never really had a physical life."

"Look, if you're going to get technical and quibble about everything, I'll go and talk to the housecarls on the lower tables. They seem to be having a great time, and I bet they've got lots of stories to tell."

"All right, all right, don't go all moody on us," he finally said. "I do know one, about a young boy who lived alone in an old house in an isolated desert town." He then told a story that was so hideous, Kirimin found herself looking over her shoulder, half expecting a cold and clammy hand to settle on her back at any moment.

As Mekhmet finished the tale, the noise and activity of the Great Hall began to percolate back into the listeners' minds, and Kirimin shook her head. "That was horrible," she said. "Sad and nasty at the same time."

Mekhmet shrugged. "It's a traditional tale of the desert; fearsome places make fearsome stories. Would you have preferred it if I'd changed the ending to make it happier?"

"Well, no," she answered. "But don't you know any *nicer* ones?"

"The dead who stay on the earth to make ghosts of their souls are often not happy to be here. Remember that if you see something tonight."

Kirimin shuddered but didn't comment.

"Cheer up, Kiri," said Sharley. "Here's some more puddings. That'll keep you occupied for a while."

"I don't know what you mean. Anyone would think I ate like a pig or something!"

"Not at all," said Sharley. "You just eat like a Tharaman."

As the evening wore on, the celebrations, unlike all other parties and gatherings in the Great Hall, became quieter. The tables were drawn aside, and revelers gathered together in small knots to tell one another stories or read fortunes on the night when the veil between the natural and supernatural worlds was at its thinnest. The musicians in their gallery seemed to be affected by the atmosphere, too, and they began to play tunes in the minor keys that had a strangely brittle and disjointed quality.

"They sound just like I imagine skeletons walking in moonlight would look," said Sharley, confusing nobody with his odd sentence.

"Yes, exactly," said Kirimin, raising her muzzle from another bowl of suet pudding. "Especially if it was frosty."

Most of the torches around the hall had been allowed to burn out, and the huge space was lit by the central fire and by a few candles that burned in holders on some of the tables. Shadows leaped and danced up the walls or were deformed by perspective into hideously twisted shapes, so that the hall seemed to be populated by a convocation of monsters.

Even the guests on the top table were touched by the creepy atmosphere, and the conversation had dropped to a low buzz on the edge of hearing. Thirrin and Oskan sat quietly, holding each other's hands under the table, while Cressida glared around as if daring anything even vaguely supernatural to show itself, but eventually even the Crown Princess's vigilance began to wane and her eyes slowly closed. Krisafitsa shuddered gently as the wind moaned around the citadel and Maggiore snored, his hand still firmly grasping his half-full goblet of wine as he dreamed of spirits that stood over his bed, their mouths wide and silently screaming while the cold air of the grave billowed out of their jaws and pooled over his face.

Only Tharaman-Thar and Grishmak seemed active, and they were reaching that stage of their eating duel when the very smell of food was nauseating.

"Would you be prepared to negotiate a draw?" asked the Werewolf King, as the mouthful of meat he'd been chewing slipped greasily down his throat.

"Not at all!" Tharaman replied, resolutely seizing a rack of ribs in his jaws. But then the gravy oozed over his tongue and he dropped the meat with a gentle shudder. "Oh, very well. I declare honors even."

"Agreed," said Grishmak, and both contestants leaned forward slowly until their heads rested on the table and they slipped into a deep, ghost-haunted sleep.

The night was at last coming to a close; even Sharley and Mekhmet were blinking owlishly at each other, and after a few moments they, too, had closed their eyes. In the main body of the hall the whisper and mutter of ghost stories still flowed over the shadows, but eventually these, too, ebbed away into near silence.

Kirimin looked out over the dark space, unwilling to let the celebrations end. She watched with her excellent night vision as the shades and thick textured blacks of the dimly lit hall seemed to weave themselves into distinct shapes, then slowly dance around the walls like dirty cloth undulating and billowing in underwater currents. The ghosts of the citadel had at last come out to celebrate Halloween, but only those who cared to look closely would see them. Kirimin blinked and shook her mighty head; she must be getting tired, she thought. But she wasn't ready to surrender to sleep yet; she still wanted to savor the delicious fear of the haunted darkness. And where better to find it than in the Great Forest?

If she crept out now, she could be walking under the dark trees within a few minutes.

On her silent Snow Leopard paws she padded down from the dais, across the hall, and out into the night. Only two figures in the dark cavernous space saw her go, and nudging each other, they climbed to their feet and hurried to the stables. They knew exactly where she was going, and if they were going to keep up, they'd need horses.

Down in the city, in the small houses made cozy against the dark with candles and lamps and warm log fires, people were telling one another tales of hauntings and spectral visitors who knock on doors late at night, but few were prepared to seek out the real ghosts of Frostmarris, who watched the living from cellars and attics and lost secret rooms. Their tales were too true, and often too terrible, to be comfortable on Samhein night.

Kirimin's whispered tread passed their doors unnoticed as she made her way down to the gates, and soon she was flowing like a silent bank of mist through the entrance tunnel and out into the night of stars and the breathless beauty of a new moon.

7

The horses clipped and clopped through the silent streets, the sound echoing and clattering from the densely packed houses, seeming to make a cavalry of the two animals. Both riders wore black hooded cloaks, skeleton masks, and a full panoply of strangely exotic armor, making them look like long-dead warriors who'd returned to earth in search of revenge. Anyone who dared to peep out of their windows on this Samhein night and saw them riding by would have hurriedly closed their shutters and called on the Goddess for protection.

They reached the long entrance tunnel of the main gate and trotted briskly to the outside world. A freezing wind, with the clean scent of winter on its breath, eddied around them as they looked out over the Plain of Frostmarris.

"There she goes!" said Mekhmet as he caught a slight movement in the Dark.

"Where?" asked Sharley, scanning the dense tumble of shadows and blackness, but as he spoke, Kirimin's huge form crossed a cart track that glowed dimly in the starlight, and she stood out in solid black relief. "Ah, yes. I see her."

They urged their mounts forward and were soon trotting across the plain, relying mainly on instinct to take them in the same direction as the Snow Leopard princess.

As far as possible they avoided riding along the road, not only because it reflected what little light there was and would make them stand out to any watching eye, but also because Suleiman's and Jaspat's hoofbeats rattled over the hard surface like hammer strokes in a busy forge. If they were going to get their revenge for the fright Kirimin had given them earlier, they needed to catch her unawares.

After half an hour the eaves of the Great Forest loomed before them, and Sharley raised the pace slightly. Several jack-o'-lanterns still hung in the branches, their glowing eyes gazing eerily over the night as the two boys approached.

"Surely any candles would have burned out hours ago," said Mekhmet, voicing the worry that Sharley had been trying to ignore. "It's been ages since anyone came from Frostmarris."

"Perhaps someone came along later," said Sharley nervously. "Or perhaps people who live nearby lit them."

Mekhmet scanned the land around in search of any cottages or farmhouses, but the wind moaned over nothing but empty farmland and heath. He shivered and nestled down inside his cloak. He wasn't so sure that trying to scare Kirimin was a good idea anymore.

After a few more minutes of steady riding, the boys dismounted and inspected the ground to look for paw prints, but it was a futile search. Although huge, Snow Leopards were amazingly light on their feet, and the already frozen land revealed nothing.

"She must have come this way," said Sharley, with more conviction than he felt. "Come on, we're bound to catch up with her soon."

Mekhmet drew breath, and his friend braced himself for what he knew was coming. "Have you noticed that the jack-o'-lanterns have moved?"

"I think it just looks that way," Sharley answered quickly. "Remember, we're closer to the forest now. I'm sure Maggie would explain it as *perspective* or something like that."

Mekhmet, looking at the weirdly glowing eyes and teeth that seemed to laugh at him from the nearby trees, was unconvinced by the explanation. "Well, if we're going to catch up with Kirimin, we'd better go now." He didn't like to add that unless they moved soon, he might not dare go on.

Both boys climbed back into their saddles and headed off again. Suleiman shook his head and snorted nervously, the chink and rattle of his harness echoing on the cold night air like tiny discordant bells. After a few minutes Mekhmet pointed to the trees. "There! There's something big moving in the shadows."

Sharley peered ahead. "Well, I commend your eyesight; all I can see is darkness. But I'll take your word for it. Come on."

They urged their horses forward and headed for the forest at a brisk trot.

Kirimin had been moving through the trees for almost half an hour, her superb night vision revealing nothing but a tangle of shadows and blackness that constantly shifted as the night breeze blew through the branches. Her other senses were ras sharp as a boxful of knives, her ears flicking and turning to hear every creak, every whisper, every tiny smothered snicker. Her nerves, too, sent constant ripples of movement cascading over her pelt like waves on the surface of a restless sea, every individual hair of her gloriously thick coat vibrating with the air currents as she moved through the night, and her nostrils twitched and snuffled at each new scent and drew it in to be almost unconsciously analyzed. Even her sense of taste examined the world around her as she drew the night air over the roof of her mouth and on to that special feline organ that made each smell a flavor.

Kirimin knew exactly what lay around and about her, but it was her cat's intuition rather than any of her superrefined physical senses that told her she wasn't alone. She shuddered with a mixture of fear and delight. This was precisely what she wanted of Samhein: mystery and laughter, darkness and that shivery feeling that something was secretly watching from the shadows.

She didn't actually know what to do next. Should she just continue walking through the shadows, or should she sit down and simply watch in the hope of . . . well, *what*, exactly? She had no answers to give herself, so she continued on her way, sliding through the trees like a gentle movement of air that had somehow acquired a physical body.

Above her in the branches, a jack-o'-lantern glowed weirdly, appearing as though from nowhere, and seeming to follow her route as she passed beneath it. A sound like whispering laughter echoed in her head. She decided she'd imagined it; after all, the grinning mouths of the lanterns suggested that they were cackling wickedly, and she supposed her mind had just provided the sound. There were more of the faces appearing now; obviously the people of Frostmarris had come this way earlier. They seemed to have taken the trouble to place their pumpkin lamps on some quite high branches. Then, as suddenly as they had appeared, the fiery, grinning faces were left behind and she walked on through the shadows.

After a few minutes, a soft green-blue glow started to bloom in the blackness. It was faint at first, but then it began to etch the outlines of twigs and branches and eventually the trunks of entire trees. It wasn't very bright, but in the deeply shadowed forest it seemed to fill her eyes and paint the dips and hollows of the woodland with even deeper shadows as the contrast between light and dark became gradually stronger. What could it be?

She moved toward its source, her brilliant amber eyes narrowing as she drew closer to what looked like a faintly pulsating ball of light. After a few minutes the area of light grew larger, and Kirimin realized she was approaching what looked like the mouth of a cave, sitting at the base of an outcrop of rocks. She'd never seen it before but quickly decided that that wasn't unusual; she hardly knew the forest at all really. A few days earlier Sharley had taken her and Mekhmet to the cavern where Sharley's father had grown up, but that had been in an entirely different direction, and anyway, these rocks looked completely unlike those. These were oddly smooth, almost as though they had been polished, and in the pale light she could clearly see that they had lines of various colors meandering through them, like veins and arteries through flesh.

There were more jack-o'-lanterns around the mouth of the cave. These had somehow been attached to the rock so that they swung and nodded in the breeze almost as though they were laughing and talking to one another as they watched her approach. She paused, and the lanterns grew still, their fiery eyes watching her closely. What should she do? She was fascinated and at the same time scared. Deciding that this was exactly how she should feel on Samhein, she walked on. Just at that moment a breeze caught the lanterns and they nodded and bobbed, filling the air with imagined snickering and whispering.

Sharley and Mekhmet picked their way cautiously through the dark forest. Both Suleiman and Jaspat had excellent eyesight, but even they found the deep shadows and darkness difficult, and eventually the boys reined to a halt, dismounted, and led the horses on into the night.

"You know, we're probably being completely stupid here," Sharley whispered. "Finding something even as big as a Snow Leopard in a pitch-black forest without the help of a torch or tinderbox is nigh on impossible."

"You're probably right," Mekhmet agreed. "Perhaps we should . . ." He stopped suddenly and grabbed Sharley's arm. "There—something white, moving off through the trees!"

"Are you sure?"

"Yes, absolutely. I could even see the spots on her coat."

"In this light?"

Mekhmet nodded emphatically, and Sharley shrugged. It seemed unlikely, but his friend never lied. "All right, let's see if we can creep up on her."

But even moving with as much stealth as they could, their horses' hooves still thudded and thumped on the thick forest litter, and neither boy was surprised when they didn't see anything else.

"She's gone," said Sharley finally.

"Yes, but we know what direction she's going in now. Come on."

Sharley followed his friend with a growing sense of futility. They'd lost Kirimin and she'd be forever one up in their game of scaring each other witless. They might get a chance of revenge the next day, but it wouldn't be the same as doing it on Halloween. Somehow, frightening someone to a gibbering wreck didn't have quite the same sense of satisfaction as it did on the day of the great celebration of ghosts and monsters.

After several minutes of stumbling along in pitch-darkness, the grinning faces of more pumpkin lamps relieved the gloom and their flickering eyes watched the boys as they continued on their way. Mekhmet was convinced they were closing on Kirimin and urged Sharley on.

Soon he had evidence to support his confidence: They found a tuft of white fur caught on a thornbush. It seemed to glow in the dark of the forest almost as though it were trying to draw attention to itself, but neither boy said anything about that, even though both thought it a little odd. Perhaps a break in the thick canopy of the trees had somehow funneled starlight to shine on the fur.

They continued on through the shadows until a strange blue-green light started to percolate through the densely interwoven undergrowth. Both boys drew their scimitars; there was an unhealthy quality to the light that neither of them liked, and there was something comforting about carrying a razor-sharp sword, even if you did suspect that you were dealing with the supernatural.

They emerged into a clearing that Sharley didn't recognize at all. The odd light pooled and pulsated before them, illuminating a cave that he knew for a fact shouldn't be there. But before he could say a word, he saw Kirimin disappearing into the mouth of the cave under an archway of jack-o'-lanterns.

"What *is* she doing? That cave's obviously not natural! Who knows where it'll lead?"

"What do you mean, not natural?" asked Mekhmet nervously. "It looks real enough to me."

"Well, of course it's *real*! I never said it wasn't *real*! It's just not natural. Look, we haven't got time to discuss it. Come on!" He charged across the clearing.

Kirimin stepped into the cave and immediately felt herself enfolded in an atmosphere that was cold and clammy. The walls glowed unhealthily with some odd fungal phosphorescence, and ferns grew in every nook and cranny, dripping with moisture that condensed on them from the misty, moisty air.

She sniffed experimentally and sneezed. The atmosphere was rank with a thick scent of decaying wood, leaves, and even flesh. She didn't like it; she didn't like it at all. But something stopped her from turning around and walking out. The cave might be creepy and smell like the worst sort of garbage dump, but it was also beautiful. Stalactites hung from the roof far, far above her head, glowing luminous greens and brilliant blues, and at her feet stalagmites grew from the floor, each one strangely twisted and contorted as it reached toward the roof. The crystalline structures seemed to pulsate as the phosphorescent colors washed over them, and sometimes she could have sworn they'd actually moved as they loomed up at her from the shadows.

A strange wispy mist, like wet silk, began to writhe around the shadows, folding and weaving itself into fantastic shapes that were sometimes beautiful and delicate, like elegant dancers draped in the sheerest gauze, and sometimes grotesque and twisted, like the most hideous humpbacked beasts. And once again the phosphorescent light tinted the mist with blues and greens, sometimes refracting through the tiny droplets of water to create a flowing bank of rainbow color.

"It's like a fairy grotto," she said to herself, and almost leaped out of her skin as an echo threw her words back, twisted and transformed into a hideous, threatening whisper: ". . . *fairy grotto . . . otto . . . otto . . .*"

"Oh, stop it!" she snapped.

And after a second the echo answered: "*Stop it . . . op it . . . op it . . .*"

She considered roaring just to see what sort of effect it would have, but quickly changed her mind. She had a feeling it would be truly awful, and she wasn't sure she'd be brave enough to stand her ground. After taking a few seconds to consider her next move, she stepped out again, heading toward what she supposed was the back of the cave. There actually seemed to be a path of some sort, and she was curious about how it might have gotten there. Perhaps she might meet a wood sprite. Sharley had said they were very rare but sometimes came out on Halloween. It would be great to be able to tell him she'd seen one. He'd be green with envy.

With this happy thought she plunged deeper into the cave, not noticing that the roof was getting higher and higher, and soon it disappeared from view completely. The sound of dripping water gave way to a chuckling gurgle as a small stream began to rush across the floor, and when a breath of fresh night air washed over her fur, Kirimin suddenly realized that there was a thin strip of starry sky slicing the shadows above her head like a razor cut through black velvet.

She breathed the night air deeply, savoring the scents of the rich damp earth and forest greenery. Obviously the cave had actually been a tunnel, and she'd emerged on the other side. An evil chuckling issued forth from the shadows of the steep-sided chasm, reminding her that it was still Samhein, and her keen amber eyes raked the darkness around her. Thick-textured shadows scuttled away to merge and blend with the darkness, and she silently raised her lips to reveal her massive teeth. If it was real enough to make a noise, it was real enough to bleed, she reasoned to herself, and it might as well know exactly who and what it was laughing at. She was Princess Kirimin of the Icesheets, and she'd already killed enough Ice Trolls to make an entire regiment of the dead.

"Look on me and tremble!" she suddenly called into the blackness.

And the echo quickly answered: "*tremble . . . emble . . . emble . . .*"

"Yes, '*emble* indeed," she said, too quietly for the echo to reply.

* * *

Sharley and Mekhmet entered the cave leading Suleiman and Jaspat, who blew and whickered nervously as the atmosphere of pungent scents, oddly glowing light, and sly, slithering movements enveloped them.

"So, what you're saying is that this cave is magical in some way?" Mekhmet asked, his voice taut with nerves.

"In a nutshell," agreed Sharley.

"Then why are we going in?"

"Because Kiri's in here and unless someone catches up with her who understands the dangers, she's bound to end up in trouble . . . serious trouble."

"Yes . . . yeah, of course," Mekhmet agreed reluctantly. "The only problem is, this is *northern* magic; this is ghosts and wood sprites and goblins, not djinns and Blessed Women and demons. I've no idea how it all works, so I'm just as helpless as Kirimin, really. What use am I going to be?"

Sharley didn't like to admit that he was just as inexperienced as his friend about all things magical. After all, he was the son of the most powerful warlock in the known world, and somehow he felt this should have qualified him to sort out any magical or mystical problems in an instant. But the truth was that he was as baffled, confused, and—he had to admit it—as scared as everyone else. Samhein had always been a time of fun and excitement to him; ghosts and monsters, and dark, forbidding places that people stupidly decided to investigate, had always been safely contained in stories told by candlelight. But now here he was walking into a cave that he just knew was haunted and would lead to places and situations that were almost certain to be hideous.

If he allowed himself to think too much about it, he was sure he'd just turn around and go home. But he couldn't do that; Kirimin was in here somewhere, and the longer she stayed, the more likely she was to get into trouble . . . bad trouble. *Thank goodness, Mekhmet's here,* he thought to himself; just his friend's presence made him feel better.

They moved slowly forward into the luminous dimness of the cave, their ears and eyes constantly baffled by faint sounds and sights that flitted on the very edges of their senses. Voices seemed to whisper their names, but whenever they turned toward the source of a particular sound, another whispered voice would call from a different direction.

"Someone, or some*thing,* is playing games with us," Sharley said, his firm, confident tones deserting him as his voice cracked. "In fact, I'm beginning to think all of this could be a trap and not just Samhein mischief."

At that moment something large and repulsive slithered by their feet and disappeared into the shadows. Both boys grabbed each other, their nerves finally at breaking point, and the horses squealed in terror. The echo immediately seized the sound and filled the cave with a hideous, tangled explosion of screaming that was added to by Sharley and Mekhmet. All rational thought and common sense fled before the terror of the cave, and suddenly, without any time for thought or discussion, both boys leaped onto their horses and galloped away from the horrible, nerve-breaking sound. Unfortunately this took them deeper into the shadows, and soon Sharley and Mekhmet needed all their concentration just to stay in the saddle and avoid hitting the rocks and stalagmites that loomed without warning out of the darkness.

After a frantic few minutes that seemed to last forever, the horses burst out into a narrow ravine. On they galloped, splashing through the stream that ran along the rocky base of the chasm, their nostrils flared wide in panic and their flanks foamed with sweat. But eventually the insistent pulling on the reins and the familiar voices of command began to percolate through to their brains, and after a few more minutes of barely controlled galloping they started to slow down and gradually succumbed to human control again.

The boys allowed them to trot on for a few minutes, keen to put more of a distance between themselves and the horrible, haunted cave. In fact, their own nerves were less than steady and they rode on in silence, taking deep calming breaths and trying to order their thoughts. Neither of them liked the thought that to get back home they'd probably have to retrace their steps and go back through that horrible glowing darkness. Perhaps they'd be able to ride around it in some way, but Sharley was well aware that this wasn't the nature of magic and the Magical Realms. You either went on until you found some other route back to your own time and place, or you retraced your steps exactly.

As they gradually regained control of both themselves and their horses, Sharley and Mekhmet began to take stock of their surroundings, and what they saw was less than comforting. The chasm had slowly opened up, and the boys found themselves riding through a wild and desolate landscape that seemed to be composed entirely of the color gray, with a few variations on a theme of charcoal and black. The air was filled with banks and billows of thick mist and steam, as geysers erupted huge plumes of vapor into the air, and hot springs bubbled around them.

"I know this place," said Sharley, rubbing his lame leg, which was throbbing as painfully as it always did in times of stress. "Dad told me about it once. I think we're on the Plain of Desolation."

"The where?" asked Mekhmet fearfully.

"The Plain of Desolation. It's a sort of halfway house between the peace and beauty of the Spirit Realms and the evil of the Darkness. I think it's supposed to be a mixture of the two . . . you know, both good and bad."

"Well, it looks like the bad bits are definitely in control at the moment," said Mekhmet as a huge geyser suddenly erupted nearby with a sound like an exploding kettle.

"Yeah," Sharley agreed. "I must admit that the little Dad told me about it didn't sound very . . . *balanced* between good and bad. There are supposed to be ghosts and lots of other nasties around the place, and he said there was some sort of close link between here and The-Land-of-the-Ghosts. You know, a sort of *seepage* that allows some pretty horrible spooks through to the Physical Realms."

"Oh, that's just great!" said Mekhmet with feeling. "As if things weren't bad enough, now we can look forward to meeting something horrible in the very near future!"

"Well, about time, too," a voice suddenly boomed from the shadows. Both boys screamed in embarrassingly high voices and grabbed each other.

Kirimin was so pleased. She'd managed to scare them again. She was two up on them now.

8

There was something really satisfying about carefully laid traps going exactly to plan. Medea had baited her snare with deadly skill and lured her brother and his friends to just where she wanted them to be. Of course, trapping Kirimin and Mekhmet was just a by-product of her real plan, but when she finally got her prey into proper position, she'd be able to kill them in front of Sharley, and so increase the horror of what was an already horrendous situation.

But she had to be careful; she couldn't risk bringing them to the Darkness, where Cronus would immediately know who they were and what she was doing. He still believed that acts of revenge were a sign of weakness. Even if the emotions driving them were hate, jealousy, and vengefulness.

Medea sat back in her chair-that-was-almost-a-throne and thought things through. She'd need to lure her brother and his friends across the Plain of Desolation and wait until she was completely certain that Cronus had no idea what she was doing. Then, when the time was exactly right . . . she'd strike, and finally wipe Charlemagne Athelstan Redrought Weak-in-the-Leg Lindenshield, Shadow of the Storm, from the face of the worlds.

*   *   *

Thirrin walked along the corridor trying to concentrate on the business in hand. She was on her way to a meeting of the Allied High Command, which had been scheduled to discuss the collapse of the Polypontian Empire and the threat of Erinor and her Hordes. But the thought of Medea and her willing acceptance of the Dark kept interrupting. It was almost as though Thirrin's subconscious was trying to tell her something, trying to warn her that she'd somehow overlooked something important. But no matter how often she analyzed the situation, nothing became apparent.

There seemed little point in wasting any more mental energy on the problem, and she tried to discipline herself to concentrate fully on the definite physical threat of Erinor. In fact, if all of the reports coming in from the old Polypontian Empire were true, then the future could be grim, and everybody would be looking to her for answers. For a moment she felt almost angry with the way things had turned out in her life; here she was, the queen of a land that had been invaded twice by one of the greatest military powers the world had ever seen; a mother of five children; wife to the most powerful warlock in existence; and *still* she felt like a young girl who was almost certain to mess it all up. Just when would she finally feel like an adult? When would she feel mature and responsible and, best of all, capable? Cressida looked and acted more grown-up than she did! Cressida frightened everyone. As Oskan said, she was the world's headmistress and she was more than ready to put everyone in detention!

She found herself grinning inanely as she walked along the corridor and only realized she was doing it when a werewolf guard stamped to attention and she was forced to frown in her best martial manner as she returned the salute. Everyone would think she was going mad! She must concentrate. She cleared her throat and stomped along like a warrior-queen should, arriving at the meeting chamber before she was ready.

All eyes turned to her as she blinked in the bright sunshine that streamed from the windows. But then she caught sight of Maggie snoozing happily in his chair, and felt a little better. She wasn't the only one unprepared for the importance of life.

The guards on the door announced her arrival as she entered, and everyone in the room stood, apart from Maggie, who slept on regardless. Grishmak, Tharaman, and Krisafitsa greeted her happily, and Oskan smiled as she took her place next to him.

"Wake up," he muttered, so that only she could hear. "Everyone expects you to be a queen."

She looked at her husband darkly. As usual he could read her perfectly and was always ready to be mischievous at her expense if it would distract her from thinking about Medea. "Thank you, oh my beloved one," she answered ironically. "I wasn't aware my regality had slipped."

"No matter. Only those who know you well would be aware of anything amiss."

"What a relief," she said and looked around the table. The Hypolitan contingent had arrived early that morning, having celebrated Samhein in the ancient manner beneath the trees of the Great Forest. Thirrin noted that Olememnon's hair was now almost white, but he looked as hale and hearty as an old oak tree. Beside him sat the Basilea Olympia, her bright eyes and stern warrior's face making her look like an eagle as she stared around the room as though looking for prey.

Much of the discussion would be important to the Hypolitan, so Thirrin was glad she looked alert. Their input would be valuable.

* * *

"Right, I call the meeting to order, as we all seem to be here," said Cressida in her usual bossy manner, and she started shuffling an alarmingly thick pile of papers.

"Actually we're not," said Krisafitsa. "All here, I mean. Kirimin's missing and so are the boys."

"Missing?" asked Thirrin, suddenly alarmed. "What do you mean?"

"Exactly that, I'm afraid," Krisafitsa replied. "Kirimin's quarters and the boys' room show no signs of being slept in last night. But I'm sure it's nothing to be alarmed about. They probably went off to the Great Forest for a last Samhein experience and just forgot the time. I expect they'll be back sometime today, all contrite and hoping to get away with any punishment they're certainly due."

"But when did you find out they were missing, and why wasn't I told?" asked Thirrin agitatedly.

"Only a few minutes ago," said the Tharina calmly. "Kirimin usually calls on her father and me before attending any official functions, and when she didn't arrive, I sent a werewolf guard to find her. He came back and reported her room empty and unslept-in. I immediately thought of the boys, and when their room was checked, my suspicions were confirmed."

Thirrin turned to Oskan and raised her eyebrows questioningly. He shrugged in reply. "If anything had happened to them, I'd have known. Perhaps Krisafitsa's right and they just went off to the forest for a laugh. I'm sure they'll be back when they're ready."

"But they all knew there was an important meeting this morning. Surely they wouldn't miss that?"

"They're teenagers; call something 'important' and they'll immediately ignore it. It's what they do; they're strange beasts," Oskan said reassuringly. "Come on, we've got a lot to discuss. We can give them a summary of proceedings when they finally get back."

Cressida nodded, cleared her throat, and prepared to take control again. Nobody had actually appointed her as chair of the meeting, but she'd assumed the role, anyway. Somebody had to do it, she reasoned, and she was probably the best qualified, being confident, competent, and efficient.

"Right, now that everyone seems ready to begin, I'll start by calling this meeting to order." She raised a small wooden hammer and smacked it smartly on the table.

Maggiore awoke with a snort. "Yes, Grishmak. Good idea, I'll have a pint of ale," he said loudly and blinked at everyone in confusion.

"I agree with you, mate," said Grishmak happily. "But unfortunately we've got the very dry business of a meeting to get through first."

Cressida coughed meaningfully and silence fell. "All right, it's Woden's Day. The first of November, the Year of the Boar, and present are Queen Thirrin, Oskan Witchfather, King Grishmak, Tharaman-Thar, Krisafitsa-Tharina, Basilea Olympia of the Hypolitan and her consort, Olememnon Stagapoulos, Maggiore Totus, and myself, Crown Princess Cressida. Absent are Prince Charlemagne, Crown Prince Mekhmet of the Desert Kingdom, and Princess Kirimin of the Icesheets. We've gathered to discuss the growing crisis in the lands of the disintegrating Polypontian Empire and will attempt to agree on a united response to it." She fell silent and turned to the gray-haired clerk who was busily scribbling notes. "Have you got all of that?" she asked, and when the clerk nodded, she drew breath to continue.

"Aren't there going to be any refreshments?" Tharaman interrupted. "I always think better with a little snack to keep me going."

"I'm with you there," said Grishmak. "Bring on the nibbles!"

"There aren't any!" Cressida snapped. "This is all far too important, and besides, once you lot start eating, it'll only turn into a party."

"Can't say I have a problem with that myself," said Tharaman. "What about you, Grishy?"

"None at all. Bit of food and fun helps the boring bits along, in my opinion. Let's call a chamberlain and order some grub."

"No!" Cressida insisted. "We all need to concentrate, and I for one find it difficult to think once you and Tharaman start cracking bones and spitting out gristle."

"I never spit out gristle!" said Tharaman in miffed tones. "A terrible waste of protein. It just needs a little extra chewing, that's all."

Thirrin had watched the exchange in silence, but now she sat forward in her chair. "Actually I wouldn't mind a sandwich myself."

Cressida looked at her thunderously. How dare her own mother not support her stance? The chaos that was the Icemark's government needed to be controlled and subjected to a little discipline, and her decision to ban food from important meetings was the first of many reforms she had planned. "Madam, I really feel that eating and drinking—"

"Ah, drinking, good idea!" said Tharaman. "Beer would go down nicely at the moment. There's a particularly good brew just in from the Southern Riding. I sampled a few bowls last night and—"

"We can't have alcohol in a meeting!" Cressida almost wailed.

Thirrin sighed. Her daughter was an excellent Crown Princess, but she dreaded to think what sort of puritanical state she'd introduce once she ascended the throne. She really had to learn that you cannot suppress people's natural exuberance. Even trying could be disastrous; she'd probably make herself the most unpopular monarch since Theobold the Thin, who had tried to introduce a tax on food and was finally sent into exile when he decided to ban all alcoholic drinks.

"Cressida, every meeting I've ever attended in the Icemark has been liberally supplied with food and drink," she said gently. "And, do you know, for all the debauchery and lack of etiquette, we really didn't do too badly, did we? Every coastal raid pushed back into the sea, every invasion defeated, and the dreaded House of Bellorum wiped out. All of that planned in meetings and forged in alliances that were steeped in alcohol and buried under an avalanche of food. If you think *we're* bad, you should have experienced your grandfather's gatherings. King Redrought firmly believed that he'd failed as a host if most of the delegates to his meetings weren't carried out at the end of the day."

"But . . . but that was in the olden days!" Cressida spluttered. "It's the modern world now. The Empire's dying, and a new order is emerging, where efficiency and discipline will reign supreme—"

"And where people will still be people, no matter how many times you tell them they're simply cogs in a beautiful machine," Thirrin interrupted. She really would have to have a quiet talk with Cressida once the meeting was finished. Crown Princess or not, she really had to accept that populations only ever really *consented* to be ruled. Any monarchs that made themselves unpopular could expect to lose their throne in double-quick time.

"Grishmak, see if you can find a chamberlain. I'd like a beer myself and a cheese sandwich," Thirrin said firmly as Cressida subsided into an affronted silence.

"And don't forget the pickle," Oskan suddenly added.

"Absolutely," she agreed. "Now, where had we got to?"

"'And don't forget the pickle,'" the clerk, who had been busily scribbling notes, informed her helpfully as he read back through his papers.

"Fine. Grishmak, you have some news for us, I believe."

The Werewolf King finished muttering to the chamberlain who'd answered his call and sent him on his way before turning back to the room. "Ah, yes! You mean the information we've gathered about the south?"

"Information from the south? Very exciting! But how exactly did you come by this intelligence?" Maggie asked, his interest revived by the promise of food.

"From the werewolf relay. The southernmost links have been talking to the migrating birds and animals that have been coming north over the last few months, and we've built up a fascinating picture."

"About the Empire, you mean?"

"Yes, and basically everything points to it being finished. The Desert Kingdom in its southernmost regions has been completely victorious; the Venezzians and Hellenes have taken control of the Central Ocean and all coastal areas; in the north the Imperial legions got a good kicking from us; and in the east and west . . . well, that's what we're here to discuss, isn't it?"

"It is indeed," Thirrin agreed. "And I believe it's the news from the east that's the most . . . disturbing."

"Very," Grishmak said.

"Is it still as bad?"

"The last reports from the relay suggested that it's getting worse. Unless we act soon, we could all be in danger."

"I suppose it all depends on how we react to the information we have."

"Well, if you shared it with us all, there might be a chance that something could be done!" Maggie said exasperatedly. "I'm too old for dark hints and riddles; I might be dead before they're answered!"

"Nonsense, Maggie," said Krisafitsa warmly. "You'll outlive us all."

"Ha, only if you all die tomorrow! Now, will somebody please explain what's happening?"

"Yes. I will, Maggie," said Oskan, sitting forward in his chair. "There's a movement of people in the east of the old Imperial lands. Now that the legions have been defeated, there's a greater freedom in the world than has been seen for many generations, and entire populations seem to be migrating."

The Witchfather stood and paced backward and forward as he tried to order his thoughts. "But something else has happened. Something . . . odd. We're being forced to realize that perhaps not all freedom is good after all."

Maggie's spectoculums almost fell off his face. "What on earth can you possibly mean? How can a fundamentally beautiful principle such as freedom ever be anything other than good?"

"When one group of people has the freedom to make war on their neighbors simply because they happen to want their land. When blood feuds, long ago suppressed by the laws of the Polypontian Empire, now have the freedom to blossom again, and children are left as orphans and entire towns and villages are laid waste; and when warlords can rise to power and divide once-prosperous lands into private domains that fight continually among themselves." Oskan laughed bitterly. "Ironic, don't you think, that we should have fought long and hard to see the end of Bellorum's Imperial strength, and then live long enough to see chaos and death rise in its place? The fact is that the Polypontian Empire may well have been an oppressive, despotic, and basically cruel power bloc that suppressed the rights and individuality of the people it ruled. But it also crushed local vendettas, smashed warlords, and made people accept that what they had was enough for their needs."

Maggie stared at him in silence for a while. "I see," he finally said. "And all this is happening now?"

"At this very moment, apparently. But there's something more we need to consider. Something that brings the danger very close to home." He suddenly turned and looked sharply at the Basilea and Olememnon. "And it directly concerns the Hypolitan."

The Basilea raised her head and held his gaze in the iron grip of her icy blue eyes. "Exactly how?"

"I'll tell you, if you'll just allow me a moment to set the scene for those who have only a working knowledge of ancient history," said Oskan and sat down again while he composed himself. "First of all, I ought to explain that our information comes from several sources and isn't just reliant on the gossip of migratory beasts. Human beings have crossed our borders, too, and some of them have trekked over many countries and land boundaries before they arrived here. All of them tell the same tale: People are moving and fighting on a huge scale as the Polypontian Empire dies."

"Then we should look to our borders and secure them now, before we're swamped!" said Tharaman-Thar.

"I agree," said Cressida, coming out of her sulk at last. "We can't just sit back and watch as Hordes swarm through the mountain passes."

"The *Hordes*, as you put it, haven't reached this far north yet, and probably never will. The few that have crossed our borders have fled before the rumor rather than the fact of invasion. And I think we have to accept that the Icemark isn't a very attractive prospect to most people."

"What do you mean?" asked Grishmak, offended for his adopted land.

"It's quite simple really," said Oskan gently. "Most of the refugees, invaders—whatever you want to call them—come from southern lands where the weather is warmer and dryer. The idea of coming to a land that's covered in snow for almost six months of the year, and seems to be lashed by heavy rain for the rest of the time, would probably seem like madness to them. Let's face it, we're the wild and woolly north: a place of mists and mystery, witchcraft and mon-sters. It was here that even Scipio Bellorum and his mad sons were defeated. In fact, we're famous throughout the known world as the bane of the Empire; almost everyone knows our names, and they tell tales about us that make us living legends. In short, the biggest and fiercest of Hordes would probably be too afraid to set foot in the Icemark."

"Then we're safe," said Tharaman happily.

"Not quite," Oskan replied. "There are always exceptions to any rule."

"And the exceptions are?" Cressida asked.

"The Hypolitan."

"What?!!" came the collective shout, and then the voices broke up into a storm of questions that filled the room with an indecipherable babble. The arrival of the food and drink then added further to the pandemonium, and Oskan waited quietly for order to return.

Even the puzzlement and outrage caused by the Witchfather wasn't enough to distract Grishmak and Tharaman from the foodstuff, and they postponed their inquisition until they'd filled their plates. In the relative quiet that followed, the Basilea was at last able to make herself heard.

"Please explain yourself, Witchfather. How are the Hypolitan a threat to the Icemark?"

"I think it would be best if Thirrin explained from this point on. Her mother was a member of the Hypolitan aristocracy and so she's better qualified in this matter." He turned to his wife with a smile and then sat down.

Thirrin suddenly felt very light-headed. The room was getting warm and the smell of roast beef, pork, and mutton was overpowering. For a moment she thought she was going to black out, but she shook her head; obviously the importance and danger of the news from the disintegrating Empire was getting to her. She realized that even a warrior-queen with years of battle experience could get stage fright. *The only way forward is to advance,* she thought, and plowed on.

"We've been told that the middle lands of the Empire are mountainous. They're difficult to control, and even the best Imperial generals — even Bellorum — found it impossible to impose undisputed rule. As a result they were left more or less autonomous — self-ruling — as long as they acknowledged the Emperor and paid some tribute occasionally.

"Well, now even that restriction has gone, and the fierce tribes who live in the clouds began a fight for supremacy among themselves. It didn't last long — just a couple of months, according to our sources — and now they're united under one leadership, banner, and Basilea."

Olympia's fierce eagle face became fiercer as realization set in. "What is the name of this mountainous region?"

"We're told it's called Artemesion."

"The original homeland of the Hypolitan, from which we migrated as a people over twenty lifetimes ago."

"Precisely so," Thirrin agreed. "The werewolf relay has gathered huge amounts of information from migrating beasts, but it was only when a Polypontian refugee was taken and questioned that the fullest details began to emerge. And the fact that this refugee was General Berengetia of the Imperial

Eastern Army might give you some idea of the depth of detail he gave."

"A general of the Empire, you say?" said Olympia in shocked amazement. "Has his army been completely defeated, then?"

"No," Thirrin replied simply. "Let's just say that he thought it wise to make good his escape before the enemy was 'inevitably victorious,' as he put it." She paused and looked at the faces of her allies and friends, who were all looking at her so trustingly. With a sudden sense of guilt she drew breath to speak. "Forgive me, Grishmak, and you, Tharaman, my fellow monarchs, for not revealing the full import of what we found. But I must ask your forgiveness especially, Olympia. My only excuse is that we didn't want to cause unnecessary panic unless we could confirm that our sources were correct."

"And obviously you've now done that," said Olympia quietly.

"Yes. Last month a squadron of Vampires flew south to find out what they could. They returned three days ago. They made contact with the people of Artemesion and found them to be fierce, independent, and powerful. They're ruled by Basilea Erinor and they call themselves the Hypolitan."

"Fascinating! Quite fascinating!" said Maggiore, taking a large gulp of beer. "And are they definitely of the same ethnic stock as our own northern allies?"

"If you mean are they related to Olympia and Olememnon's people, then yes, they are. In fact the fame of the Icemark's war against Bellorum brought our Hypolitan to their attention over twenty years ago, but it wasn't until the Polypontians were defeated for a second time that they were able to break out of their mountain stronghold and begin their crusade."

"Crusade? What crusade?" asked Olememnon calmly.

"To seize control of the old Imperial capital, to reestablish the Empire under their rule, and ultimately to wipe out the northern Hypolitan, whom they consider traitors."

A silence followed as the importance of the information sank in. But then Olememnon spoke up. "And could they do this?"

Thirrin shrugged. "They head an alliance of mountain people. They're fierce, warlike, and ruthless. On top of that, I strongly suspect that Basilea Erinor is more than competent as a war leader. The remnants of the Polypontian army have clashed with her in five major battles and countless skirmishes. They lost every time. She now threatens the southern borders of the Polypontian heartland. It'll take her several months to prepare for invasion, but nonetheless she certainly will invade."

"Then what do we do?" asked Olememnon.

"Couldn't we send an envoy or embassy of some sort?" asked Krisafitsa. "Unpleasantness can often be avoided by the use of simple diplomacy and good faith."

"In effect, that's exactly what the Vampire party was. Her Vampiric Majesty chose the most intelligent and personable of her subjects; they were under strict instructions not to reveal their true natures and to transform to their flying forms only when there were no witnesses around. Even so, Basilea Erinor arrested them, and five of the ten were destroyed before they escaped."

"Then there's no hope of a peaceful solution?" asked Krisafitsa, her voice tinged with despair.

"I think it remote. Before she started murdering the envoys, Erinor let it be known that not only does she consider our Hypolitan to be traitors for deserting the homeland so long ago, but that the Icemark itself is a target because, as the daughter of a Hypolitan woman, I, too, am a traitor and my lands forfeit."

"Complicated sort, by the sound of things," said Grishmak as he crunched a rack of beef ribs. "It's amazing how some of the most violent types have to find an excuse for their actions. Bit annoying, though. I don't know about you, but I could do with a bit of a rest from fighting."

A general rumble of agreement greeted this, and then a silence followed that was broken only by the sound of chewing and the cracking of marrowbones.

"What tactics do they employ?" Cressida asked, her obsessive military brain hungry for details.

"Much the same as our Hypolitan, I'd have thought," said Tharaman, chewing a huge beef knucklebone.

"Similar, it has to be said," Thirrin agreed. "But there are factors that make them . . . dangerous."

"Well, whatever it is, it can't be worse than the Sky Navy," said Grishmak. "And if it's just the usual problem of us being outnumbered by something stupid to one, then we've all been there before. In fact, to be honest, after taking on the worst that Bellorum could throw at us, I find Erinor and her Hordes less than worrying. After all, don't let's forget that the Empire did keep them trapped in their mountains for centuries, and if they couldn't defeat the people that we have beaten twice in a row, I'd say there's little to worry about."

"Ordinarily I'd agree with you," said Thirrin, sipping her beer. "But there are factors that need to be considered. First, the Empire built a wall around the entire region of Artemesion; it was over thirty feet high at its lowest point and had lookout towers more than fifty feet high at one-mile intervals. On top of that, there were fortresses with half a legion every two miles *and* a full-sized castle garrisoned by two full legions every six miles. Breaking out of that particular stranglehold would have taken something that was the equal of the Imperial army at the very least."

"By the Goddess, just what were they afraid of?" asked the Basilea in an awed voice.

"Good question," said Thirrin, looking out over the room. "Let's just say that you don't build a cage of stone and steel to house a pussycat."

"What are the other factors?" asked Cressida.

"Our sources have recently given us more information about Erinor's battle tactics," Thirrin continued. "Apparently Artemesion is a land not only of high mountains but also of wide and flat plateaus that stretch for miles between the towering peaks. Most of these lie thousands of feet above the level of the sea, and it was here that the feuding tribes fought their wars. The land was ideal for chariots, swift and strong ones, with razor-sharp scythes on their wheels, drawn by powerful armored horses and crewed by two warriors: the driver and the fighter. The fighter is equipped with a bow. Not the usual compound bow of our own Hypolitan's mounted archers—Erinor's army has those, too, in abundance—but a longbow, huge and powerful and with a range that is at least the equal of our own archers' weapons. These chariots are devastating, and as soon as the wall around Artemesion was abandoned by the Imperial legions, Erinor made her people dismantle their chariots and carry them through the mountains and out into the lands of the disintegrating Polypontian Empire. Here they smashed aside all opposition. They shoot murderous waves of arrows that rain down on the enemy long before they come into range themselves, and then the armored horses smash through what remains, the scythed wheels carving a bloody path through anyone who dares stand against them."

"I'd have thought our ballistas would easily be the equal of the biggest longbow," said Grishmak as he licked gravy from his fingers. "Especially those that Archimedes designed to use against the Sky Navy. Their range is enormous."

"Yes, but they're not mobile, Grishy," said Cressida quietly.

"Precisely," Thirrin agreed. "Any weapon brought against them is usually heavy and cumbersome and can easily be outrun. Even archers with bows equal to the range of those of Erinor's Hordes are usually on foot and fighting from fixed positions. These chariots sweep down on a region in devastating squadrons that so far have been unstoppable."

"But they can only be used if the land is suitably flat and rock free," Grishmak objected.

"True, but the lands they've conquered so far have been just that. The central steppes of the Polypontian hinterland. And in the few places where it's been unsuitable for chariot warfare, they've fallen back on yet another weapon."

"Go on," said Grishmak resignedly. "I dread to think what's coming next."

"You'd be wise to do so, I'm afraid," said Thirrin darkly. "The Hordes have an unusual . . . cavalry, of sorts. Huge beasts, reportedly bigger than a house, ferocious and unstoppable."

"Elephants, you mean?" asked Maggiore excitedly. "As are supposedly used in the far, far east of the world?"

"No. If I understand the description of those particular mythical beasts, they have tails at each end, and are said to be noble in nature and loyal to their riders, even to the point of death. But these beasts are different: They're savage, controlled only by steel and threat; they're huge and have heads that are naturally armored with three horns, and necks that are protected by circling plates of bone and tough hide. In battle they carry wide platforms on their backs, from which archers and slingers can rain death down on the enemy. And they fight in their own right, too, trampling the opposition under their massive feet and skewering anyone who gets in the way with their horns. But they can also be used in siege warfare, smashing down gates and breaching walls like massive living battering rams. In fact, three Polypontian cities have fallen to them already."

"But I've never heard of any beast that sounds even vaguely like that," said Maggie in puzzlement. "And yet every creature that walks under the sun is part of a *genus*, or group with recognizably similar physical attributes that confirm their status as a species member."

Thirrin shrugged. "I've no answer to that, Maggie. You're the scholar, but if I remember my lessons from so many years ago, did you not say that there are isolated areas of the world where animals can develop in astonishing and unique ways? Where certain characteristics can become exaggerated according to the needs of their surroundings?"

"Very true, my dear Thirrin," the old scholar agreed. "And I must say I'm most gratified that at last I have evidence that you did indeed listen to me occasionally. But to return to your point, I might also add that there are locations where species survive after all others of their type have become extinct. Perhaps, then, this could be said of the mountainous regions of Artemesion, and we may hypothesize that this beast is of some antediluvian species that has died out everywhere else."

A hugely cavernous burp echoed around the room, and Tharaman held his paw delicately to his mouth. "I do beg your pardon. The gravy was exceedingly rich. Most remiss of me. But now that I have everyone's attention, might I ask if these thingies you're discussing are edible, and how big are their steaks?"

Thirrin looked at her Snow Leopard ally incredulously; she sometimes wondered why she bothered. Here she was warning them all of impending doom and disaster, and all Tharaman could contribute to their emergency meeting was a question about the culinary possibilities of the enemy's war beasts.

Grishmak let out a bark of laughter. "Ha! You'd better hope they're not too big for the palace ovens, Tharaman. I think you've become a bit too refined to eat your meat uncooked anymore."

"You know, I never thought of that. Perhaps I'd better have a word with Archimedo Archimedes. I'm sure he could find a solution."

9

Proper daylight didn't happen in the normal way of things in the world Sharley, Mekhmet, and Kirimin had entered. When it did occur, it was usually a deep, dreary gray, or sometimes a sort of glowing white as the perpetual mists and fogs reflected the light around. But in the day or so that the three friends had been lost in the strange Plain of Desolation, light had dawned four times and lasted for about half an hour at the most, and then night had taken control again. Actually they found themselves preferring the night, because then most of the fogs disappeared and it was possible to see the sky. But even then things were still not normal. The moon was either full, new, or nowhere to be seen at all, with none of the usual in-between stages of quarters and halves. The stars encrusted the sky as densely as scales on a silver celestial fish, and none of them recognized any of the constellations.

After the boys had gotten over the shock of Kirimin leaping out at them again, they'd tried to become businesslike and give the impression that they knew exactly what they were doing. But Kiri soon saw through this and ignored them when they tried to tell her what to do.

"Apart from the name, you've no more idea than I have about where we are," she'd said to Sharley as he was telling her with great authority about the Plain of Desolation. "If you had, we'd have found the cave again by now and simply walked back through it to the Great Forest. We're lost, it's as simple as that, and none of us has any idea how to get back home."

Sharley sighed. "All right, I admit it. I've no idea where we are, but I do know one thing: There's no point hanging around here in the hope that we'll find the grotto again. Dad told me lots of stories when I was little about things like this, and if mortal people in the stories got lost in magical places, they were in trouble. The only thing to do is to travel on and hope that another doorway between the worlds will appear."

"But how will we recognize it?" asked Mekhmet in worried tones.

"Well, usually they're in caves or tunnels, but not always. All you can do is keep your eyes peeled and investigate anything that seems unusual."

"*Unusual?* In this place? Everything's unusual," said Kiri irritably. "There are bats the size of eagles, deer as small as mice, and snakes that could swallow a mountain! How are we supposed to notice anything unusual when nothing is ordinary?"

"I don't know," Sharley admitted, his weak leg beginning to ache as it always did in tense situations. "We'll just have to trust to instinct, that's all. I suppose the longer we're here, the more likely it is that we'll recognize something that doesn't fit in with what passes for normal."

"Then let's hope we stumble on a doorway by pure chance," said Mekhmet. "I'd hate to be so used to this insanity that I see an escape route to the natural world as something odd."

"And another thing," said Kirimin tersely. "What about food?"

"Well, perhaps we can hunt," Sharley replied.

A sudden beating of wings announced the arrival of something, and they all automatically ducked as an odd-looking creature suddenly loomed out of the mists.

"What's a flying monkey doing here?" Mekhmet asked, drawing his scimitar warily.

The creature swept in for a closer look, and then powered back into the sky as Mekhmet's scimitar whistled through the air.

"What did you call it?" Kiri asked.

"A monkey. It's a sort of small human being, but not as intelligent, and they're also very hairy. People keep them as pets in the Desert Kingdom."

"Well, I don't think this one'd make a good pet," said Sharley, drawing his scimitar, too. "It looks like it'd bite off your hand if you offered it a banana."

The creature flew in a little closer, giving the three of them a much clearer view of its small, red, scaly body, black-feathered wings, and long, forked tail. It had a sneering expression of amusement on its face, and it easily veered out of range whenever the boys swung their scimitars at it.

"Ah, mortals!" it suddenly said, as though all of its worst fears about stupidity had been confirmed.

"You can speak, then," said Kiri.

"No. You must be having a nervous breakdown. I can't speak at all," the creature answered sarcastically.

"*And* you have a nasty tongue," the Snow Leopard added evenly.

"So, what do you want with us?" Sharley asked.

"Nothing. I'm just curious," it answered, sweeping in low again and grinning contemptuously.

"About what?"

"About whether mortals really are as stupid and pathetic as I've heard." It paused, its head on one side as though assessing them. "And, yes, I think you are."

"Fine. Well, now that you've reached that conclusion, you can leave us alone and get lost," said Sharley, raising his scimitar again threateningly.

"Or you'll do what?" the creature asked in mock terror as it swept up out of range of their weapons. "Come on, tell me! I'd be shaking in my boots, if I were wearing any. What could you possibly do to me?"

"This!" Kirimin shouted, and gathering her powerful body to a crouch, she suddenly leaped skyward like a massive spring. Her huge paws stretched out and swatted the creature to the ground, where she pinned it in a cage of glittering claws.

The creature screeched and raged, but it was trapped, and the friends gathered around to inspect it.

"Ugly," Sharley concluded. "Colorful, but ugly."

"It has an ugly attitude, too," said Mekhmet.

"I'll show you even more of my ugly attitude once I'm out of here!" the creature spat.

"Who says you're getting out?" asked Kirimin quietly. "We might decide to crush you, or perhaps I could impale you on my claws."

"You wouldn't dare!"

"Why not?"

"Because . . . because . . . well, you just wouldn't, that's all!"

"I'm afraid your confidence is badly misplaced," Kirimin answered, her voice low and threatening.

"Look, just tell us who and what you are and we might consider letting you go," said Sharley firmly.

"I'm telling you nothing," the creature answered angrily. "Let me go now, and I might consider not taking this any further!"

"And just what would *taking it further* entail?" asked Sharley. "Do you have Powers of some sort?"

"I think we can safely say that if it had, it'd have used them by now," Mekhmet pointed out.

"Exactly!" said Kirimin in triumph. "It's just bluffing."

"Oh, am I?" the creature snarled. "Even those that don't have Powers may know those that do; and some of us just might have some very *Power*ful friends indeed."

"What do you mean?" asked Sharley in sudden suspicion. "Did someone send you to spy on us?"

"They might have," the creature answered airily, and then started to screech as Kirimin's paw began to squash it into the ground.

"That's decided it! Spies and traitors are always executed!" Kirimin roared.

"Wait!" Sharley ordered. "Let's find out who it's spying for. . . . Then you can destroy it."

"No! No! I'm not spying for anyone! I was just curious to see mortals, that's all."

"Well, you've done just that. And now that you've achieved that ambition, we can't risk you passing on the information to anyone else — so, Kirimin . . ." Sharley gestured to the giant Snow Leopard, who prepared to squish the creature.

"No, wait!" it screeched. "I'm not spying for anyone; I'm just an innocent citizen of the Plain of Desolation trying to fill his dreary day with a bit of free entertainment! Is that any reason to kill me? Where's the justice in that? I heard that the society of mortals was free and fair, and that no one was punished without just reason!"

Sharley raised his hand again, and Kirimin waited. "It's certainly true that *some* mortal societies are free and fair, but how do you know that we're from one of those? We could be from the Eastlands, where khans and potentates put people to death just because they're bored, or perhaps we're from the Westernholds, where it's said people die every year in the name of what they call 'justice.'"

"Well, you're not! You're from the Icemark, and the other human's from the Desert Kingdom, where Suleiman the Great once ruled and gave all his people the protection of just laws!"

The three friends looked at one another, their suspicions now thoroughly aroused. "You know a great deal about us for one who just happens to be casually curious. Why is that, exactly? You wouldn't have been briefed by someone with an interest in us, perhaps?" asked Sharley suspiciously.

The creature managed to sneer even though half of its face was squashed into the mud underfoot. "*Everyone* knows about the Icemark and its allies; ask the next creature of any species you meet. You're all famous for beating Scipio Bellorum and his empire despite all the help he got from . . . other quarters." Then, suddenly becoming even more agitated, it exploded: "Look, we're not talking about the mysteries of Creation here! No mortal's that enigmatic; everything you do is watched every day! Even the most stupid among you is sometimes aware of it; haven't you ever felt that you're being watched, or that someone's standing behind you when there seems to be no one there? Well, that's when we're watching you; believe me, you mortals have no secrets from us!"

Sharley looked at the others and shrugged. "What do you think?"

"I don't trust it," said Mekhmet decisively. "I think it's lying."

"Well, if it is, that means someone's spying on us, in which case we may not have stumbled into the Plain of Desolation by accident." He paused to allow the importance of his words to sink in. "We may have been lured here!"

"I don't believe that," said Kirimin confidently. "We got lost during Samhein; everyone knows that the Physical and Spirit Realms are close to each other at that time and that people sometimes slip between worlds. We were just unlucky enough to find a cave that led us here, that's all."

"You mean *you* were unlucky enough to find a cave," Mekhmet pointed out. "Sharley and me had nothing to do with it."

"Well, you didn't have to follow me," Kirimin replied hotly. "I don't think I can be held responsible for the fact that you're a pair of sheep without the brains to think for yourselves!"

"Bickering among ourselves doesn't really help matters," said Sharley. "We still have to decide what we're going to do with this . . . thing."

"Good point," Kirimin agreed. "Anyway, what is it exactly? We haven't even decided that yet."

"You could always try asking me," the creature said snottily from under Kirimin's paw.

"Yes, I suppose we could," she said with a light laugh. "All right, then, what are you?"

"Isn't it obvious?"

"Quite frankly, no, it's not," said Kirimin crisply. "I mean, just look at you! You've got wings like a giant bird of some sort, but arms, legs, and a head like a little human being, apart from the horns, that is. And as for your body . . . well, have you ever seen anything like it?" she asked, turning to the boys.

"No," Sharley answered decisively. "It looks like it's been stitched together from spare parts. In fact, I don't know of any creature that has bird's wings *and* a scaly body. And as for the tail with that strange arrowhead point . . ."

"I think I've seen it before," Mekhmet interrupted quietly. "In fact, it seemed familiar from the moment we first met it, but it's taken me until now to remember exactly where."

"Well, spit it out. Where?" Kirimin asked.

"In a book I read once about creatures of the night. It's a demon, a little devil, sometimes called an *imp*."

"That's correct," the creature agreed. "I *am* an imp. My name is Imp-Pious Blasphemosa."

"Pleased to meet you . . ." Kirimin began to reply politely, but she was interrupted by the sound of a scimitar being drawn.

"Stand away, Kiri! Imps are evil, children of the devil, who bring pain, havoc, and death to the world."

"Children of the devil?" said Kirimin confusedly. "Now, just give me a moment. . . . He's part of some obscure human mythology, isn't he? Something to do with evil . . ."

"Perhaps I can help you," said the imp and smiled coldly. "According to some beliefs, the devil is the Supreme Negativity; the antithesis of divinity and lord of all darkness and chaos. He rules a domain that according to many religions occupies an area vaguely postulated as being somewhere beneath our feet. A place of torment and evil; a place often of fire, and I believe the term is *brimstone*. But of course these myths have a habit of appearing and reappearing in many different beliefs. And I believe I'm right in saying that the devil is known by many names: Beelzebub, Lucifer, Cronus . . ."

Sharley drew his scimitar and joined Mekhmet, who was watching the creature warily. "You seem to have signed your own death warrant, Mr. Imp. I must admit that normally I prefer the idea that everyone is innocent until proven guilty. But here in the Plain of Desolation I don't think we can afford such a luxury."

"Now just a moment!" said Kirimin. "Let's not be too hasty. Impervious here could be a useful guide and adviser."

"That's Imp-Pious!"

"Yes, all right," the Snow Leopard said dismissively. "But the fact remains that he knows the Plain of Desolation, and as we don't, he could be valuable."

"But we can't trust him," said Mekhmet.

"I think I've adequately explained my position," said Imp-Pious, suddenly becoming aware of his mistake in admitting to a knowledge of the devil. "I was simply curious and wanted to see mortals at firsthand, as it were. And as for the claim that imps are 'children of the devil,' well, that's a wild exaggeration." He paused as he realized he was beginning to babble, and then went on. "The Snow Leopard's right. I *do* know the area very well and could be very useful to you as an adviser and guide."

"Why, so that you can lead us into trouble?" asked Mekhmet darkly.

"And why should I do that? What would I gain from it?"

"We've no idea," Sharley said. "That's the problem. We know nothing about you — why you're here or who you're working for . . . if anyone. But maybe Kirimin's right; you could be our best hope of getting back home."

"Indeed I am. If you'd just let me go, I could show you the way out," said the imp eagerly. "Now, do you have any ideas about how to return to the Physical Realms?"

"Some, I suppose. We know we need to look for a doorway between the worlds, and that these usually take the form of a tunnel of some sort. But where they're likely to be, we've no idea. You wouldn't know, would you?"

"Yes, absolutely. Though they may take a while to find."

Sharley paused as he thought things through; then, taking a deep breath, he looked up. "I know I could be making a terrible mistake here, but I don't think we really have any choice. . . . Kirimin, let him go, and Mekhmet, tie his wings together so that he can't fly off. Important, you are now our official guide."

"Imp-Pious!" the creature corrected him, but he was too relieved to sound really indignant.

* * *

Howler was annoyed. He was sitting in the armory of the Regiment of the Red Eye, with Eodred, his friend and fellow commander of the fighting unit that was made up of equal parts human and werewolf soldiers. Howler felt it was deeply insulting that, as princes of the human and werewolf worlds, they hadn't been invited to the meeting discussing the collapse of the Polypontian Empire. For his part, Eodred had long ago accepted that he wasn't bright enough to make much difference to any discussion or debate. He was quite content to wait until the decisions had been made and then be told where to go and whom to fight.

But Howler was different; he understood the subtleties of diplomacy and the complicated tangle of government and its workings. But nobody expected him—being nearly seven feet tall and as solid as a fortress wall—to understand even the simplest of intellectual tasks. King Grishmak, his father, attended all such debates, but Howler suspected that much of what was said went over the king's head. His philosophy of governance could generally be summed up in the phrase "Agree with me or I'll rip your filthy head off."

"Sharley and Mekhmet were expected to go," said Howler grumpily. "I bet even Kirimin was. Why're they different from us?"

"Yeah, but they *didn't* go, did they?" Eodred replied, placidly polishing the blade of his battle-ax. "Nobody knows where they are. Everybody thinks they're in the Great Forest, but I bet they're not there now. It was Samhein when they disappeared, so I think they're probably lost in the Magical Realms. But nobody listens to me; they'll come to their own conclusions soon, and then there'll be panic."

"But they *were* invited, weren't they?" said Howler, ignoring most of what Eodred said. "Why them and not us?"

"Because Mekhmet represents the Desert Kingdom, as does Sharley, and Kirimin needs the experience of how these things work."

"And we don't?"

"Well, I don't. Nobody listens to me, anyway, so it'd be a waste of time inviting me along to any discussion. Though I suppose I could keep Maggie awake."

"And that's another thing! Maggie was invited! Why him?"

Eodred looked at his friend witheringly. "Look, I'm the stupid one and even I know Maggie's the cleverest politician this side of Doge Machiavelli. You're just letting the fact that you're in a bad mood get in the way of your brains. Pass me that sword; it's getting a bit dull."

The werewolf prince handed the weapon to his friend automatically while he continued to mull over his resentments. "I mean, I only found out that it'd been agreed we'd invade the Polypontus from one of the housecarls!"

"No, you didn't!" said Eodred, beginning to get annoyed with his friend's unconscious distortion of events. "You might have found out that it'd been agreed we'd look into the *possibility* of an invasion, but that's all. Nothing's been finalized."

"Just a matter of time, I'm sure," Howler muttered sullenly.

"Yeah, well, when that happens, you can relax, because they won't be going anywhere without us. Our regiment's too good to leave at home, and if everything I hear about the southern Hypolitan and their Basilea is true, anyone who tries to stop her is going to need everyone they can get."

"She certainly sounds formidable, it has to be said," Howler agreed quietly. "It's ironic, really: You get rid of one homicidal maniac and his sons, only to find that once Bellorum's dead, his place is happily taken by another nutter who might actually be worse than him. I mean, did you hear the relay report on the fall of that city in the southern-most province of the Polypontus heartland?"

"I *do* understand werewolf speech, you know," said Eodred, defending his scant intellectual abilities with a nicely judged sense of outrage.

"Yes, I know. But you sleep a lot, and when you're not doing that, you're fighting, or eating, or drinking. . . . I thought you might have missed it, what with being busy in so many other areas."

Eodred finished polishing the sword and put it back in the rack. "Well, there's just a chance I might have been doing something else, I suppose. . . . Just remind me again, what was the town called?"

"Right, so you didn't hear the report, then. I thought not," said Howler. "The place was called Tri-polis, which literally means 'three cities,' and it had three complete sets of defensive walls, each one protecting a huge sweep of the city that was built as a set of rings, one inside the other; like a big onion. Anyway, Basilea Erinor took the place in three days, one for each set of walls. Not only that, but she killed *all* the inhabitants, not just the soldiers, but *everyone*. And then she burned the place to the ground and demolished whatever was left standing."

"Thorough," said Eodred, climbing to his feet and stretching hugely.

"Mad, you mean."

"That, too. But what's happened to the Imperial army? One of its generals is killed and it falls to pieces. Why?"

Howler sat in thought for a few moments, his sensitive nostrils unconsciously twitching as the distinctive scent of cleaning oil rose up from the old rag Eodred had been using. Eventually he said, "I suppose . . . I suppose there must have been a combination of factors at work. Not only the death of Bellorum *and* his tactically brilliant sons, but also the war with the Desert Kingdom in the south, and the Venezzians and Hellenes on the high seas. It probably would have survived one or even two of these pressures, but all three was just too much for it."

"Perhaps," Eodred conceded. "But just because your army's stretched to the limit doesn't make it less brilliant than it was before. The Imperial legions were feared and respected throughout the known world, and now they lose every battle."

"Pressure may not make your army less 'brilliant,' as you put it, but it will make it less efficient," said Howler. "And couple that with the fact that the loss of the coastal ports has interrupted vital lines of supply, *and* with the breakdown of the Empire's manufacturing industry because of that disruption of supply, and you have a perfect recipe for military failure."

Eodred gazed at his friend admiringly. "They just didn't know what they were missing when they forgot to invite you to the emergency meeting, did they? Come on, I'm hungry; let's see what the mess has cooking."

"How can you even consider eating at a time like this?" asked Howler incredulously.

"Why not? We've got to keep up our strength for the trials ahead. It's no use meeting Erinor and her Hordes all thin and wasted, is it? I see it as one of my duties to eat like a Tharaman."

"Not possible," said Howler. "But perhaps you're right, I could do with a sandwich myself."

"A sandwich! That won't even touch the sides! You'll have a side of beef or I'll want to know why not!"

10

They'd been traveling through an area of boiling mud pots and erupting geysers for over two hours, and it was getting hotter by the minute. The daytime probably wouldn't last for more than another hour or so, but in that time the clammy, swirling mists would absorb more and more of the geysers' heat, making it feel like they were swimming through a sauna. Everywhere insects flew and darted through the dappled shadows. Most of them were recognizable, but truly enormous, from dragonflies that had wingspans wider than Sharley could stretch his arms, to maggots that were as big as slimy loaves of bread. Once, a bluebottle rumbled across their path with wings as big as the sheets of glass Maggie claimed could be found in the cathedrals of the Southern Continent.

At one point they'd had to ride by a hornet's nest and the creatures had attacked, forcing Sharley and Mekhmet to draw their scimitars and, along with Kiri, fight their way clear of an angry swarm. The insects were the size of large dogs, and their stings dripped venom as they swooped into the attack. Fortunately no one was stung, and they managed to kill over a dozen before the monster hornets gave up and flew back to their nest.

Food was becoming an acute problem. Kirimin in particular was beginning to feel the effects of the lack of sustenance; her huge, muscular body demanded a massive daily input of energy in the form of fresh meat. But the boys were small and wiry, with the sort of hard stamina that could keep them going all day, and that, added to the fact that they were battle-trained and war-hardened, meant that they were coping with the privations of life on the Plain of Desolation far more easily than the giant Snow Leopard.

"The large cat needs sustenance," said Imp-Pious to Mekhmet, as though Kirimin were some sort of pet.

"Yes, I know," he agreed. "But there doesn't seem to be anything big enough for us to hunt that would satisfy her appetite."

"An interesting problem," the imp replied. "In fact, I might hazard a prediction and say that all three of you are soon likely to meet a creature that would feed an entire regiment of Snow Leopards."

"What do you mean?" Mekhmet asked suspiciously.

"I feel something getting close. In fact, it's almost upon us! UNTIE ME, UNTIE ME! I'LL BE LOOKOUT!" Imp-Pious suddenly screeched. "THERE'S AN ELEPHANTA COMING THIS WAY!"

"A what?" asked Mekhmet in mild surprise, loosening the rope.

"AN ELEPHANTA! RUN! FOR GOD'S SAKE RUN!"

The imp then flew off, rising high into the air, where he hovered, calmly watching events as they unfolded.

"All right, anyone want to make a guess about exactly what an elephanta looks like?" asked Sharley, unsheathing his scimitar and settling his shield on his arm.

Kirimin raised her head, taking an interest in her surroundings for the first time in several hours and narrowed her eyes as she gazed across a wide clearing in the mists. "Well, that's easy. . . . We've all heard of the mythical elephant, haven't we? You know, big as a house and a tail at both ends. In fact, I should imagine it looks something amazingly like that," she said quietly. "Except this one's as big as two houses."

The boys followed her gaze and watched as the biggest creature any of them had ever seen crashed into the clear space before them. Sharley knew full well that elephants did exist; he and Mekhmet had seen them in Arifica, but they hadn't been bright green like this one, and neither had they stood as high as four warhorses at the shoulder, nor been as long as half a squadron of cavalry.

"Lances, I think," said Mekhmet calmly, and sheathing his sword, he drew one of the three long spears he carried in a scabbard on his saddle. Sharley did the same, and they quietly urged their horses forward into the clearing that was still continuing to widen. Kirimin stood her ground, raising her head and scenting the strange beast. The smell was so strange that she sneezed, the enormous eruption of sound echoing through what was beginning to look suspiciously like an arena. The creature swung its hideous tailed head ponderously toward her, the pupils of its red eyes suddenly dilating as it focused on her. It raised its thick face-tail, opened its mouth, and let out a huge trumpeting sound. Kirimin gave a huge roar in return, but she kept her eyes on the long, sharp teeth that grew out of the creature's head on either side of its tail.

Then, with the speed of a loosed arrow, the creature charged, crashing over the rocky ground with a clumsy, lumbering power that took all three friends by surprise. Both boys screamed in alarm and leaped into the attack. But Kirimin was its target, and it ignored them even when they drove their lances deep into its flanks.

Kirimin rose up on her hind legs, roaring, and was smashed backward into an outcrop of rocks as the creature's momentum drove it forward. She hit the ground with a jarring force, curled into a tight ball, and rolled into a boulder. Immediately she uncurled and leaped through the air in a ferocious explosion of tooth and claw. She landed on the creature's enormous head and seemed to freeze in position, sinking her fangs deep into its flesh.

The elephanta staggered in a half circle, roaring and trying to dislodge her by shaking its head and smashing it on the ground. Mekhmet and Sharley had now drawn their second lances, and, crying out the war cries of the Desert Kingdom and the Icemark, they charged. Suleiman dodged the thrashing tusks and Sharley drove his lance deep into the thing's chest, while Mekhmet rammed his into its neck just behind the wide sail of its ear.

The elephanta trumpeted and reared up on its thick hind legs, still shaking its head as Kirimin continued to maul its face. Then at last, with a mighty convulsion, she was dislodged and flew through the air, to land with a crash on a wide area of broken scree.

The horses now moved in shoulder to shoulder, and, drawing their last remaining lances, the boys charged. The creature crashed forward from its mighty height, and the boys stood in their saddles as the wide belly rushed down on them. The lances were driven deep by the elephanta's own massive weight, and it roared in agony, its headlong earthward crash stalling for a moment and allowing the horses to gallop clear.

They circled and drew their scimitars. "Mekhmet, check on Kiri and get her away to safety. I'll try and hold the thing off for as long as possible!"

"Don't be stupid! You can't hold it *and* get away. You'll be killed!"

As the boys spoke urgently, the huge creature suddenly let out another roar of agony and began to stagger almost blindly around the clearing. "I don't think it's as dangerous as it was. We've weakened it," said Sharley.

But before they could say anything else, a spitting, raging lightning bolt of fury slammed into the creature. Kirimin's huge paws boxed the monster's head with mighty swinging blows that sent it staggering backward, huge bloody gouges opening up in its thick hide as her razor claws bit deep.

The horses now charged, driving close as the boys whirled and struck at the creature with their swords. Then once again Kirimin jumped at the thing's head, swarming around to cling beneath its face-tail while her powerful hind legs drove again and again into its throat, her long deadly claws slicing deep into the flesh. With a roar of rage and agony the thing reared up again. Sharley and Mekhmet drove their scimitars to the hilt into its exposed belly. But then a cascading deluge of steaming blood drenched them, and they looked up to see its throat gaping wide.

Kirimin moved nimbly away, and the boys turned their horses and withdrew to watch as the giant monster swayed, probing at the cavernous wound in its throat with its strange face-tail. Its eyes rolled, and huge gouts of blood erupted skyward until at last it pitched forward slowly, like a falling column, and crashed to the ground. A deep silence settled over the clearing, broken only by the gasps of the three friends.

"Dinner, I think, is served," said Sharley, his voice shaking with exhaustion.

"Do you really think it's edible?" asked Kirimin.

"Yes, I should think so. Hack off some of that rump, or a steak from the ribs, and I bet it'll roast up nicely."

But before any of them could move, the creature began to shimmer like a mirage conjured by the heat of the desert, and as they all watched, its huge, solid bulk slowly faded away to nothing.

"Well, that more than suggests it was magically conjured. It's as if you can meet your worst nightmares here," said Sharley quietly.

"Yes, but who conjured it?" Mekhmet replied.

A rustle of wings announced the return of Pious. "You killed it! You killed an elephanta!" said the imp in agitated amazement. "No one's ever done that before!"

"Well, no *one* did this time, either," said Kirimin. "There were three of us."

"Five, counting the horses," said Sharley.

"True," the Snow Leopard agreed.

"Yes, but you killed *an elephanta!*" Pious squeaked again in awe.

"Did you expect us to die?" Sharley asked interestedly.

"Quite frankly, yes, I did," Pious replied.

"You seem almost disappointed."

"No, no, I can assure you not," the imp said, nervously eyeing Sharley's drawn scimitar. "My tone is affected only by awe at your fighting prowess."

"It's strange that the monster appeared almost immediately after you gave the warning," said Sharley conversationally. "Nothing to do with you luring it to where you knew we were resting, I suppose?"

"Nothing whatsoever. Indeed, it could even be argued that I saved your lives by giving you warning. On the Plain of Desolation the difference between life and death can be a matter of the merest seconds."

"Really?" Sharley asked with interest and swung his scimitar in a glittering arc in the vicinity of the imp's head.

"If you'll excuse me, I think I'll take a nap," said Pious nervously. "The atmosphere has become a little *charged* around here." He flew off to hide in the dense swirl of mist that was once again rapidly closing over the scene of the battle.

Orla stood back in the shadows and watched as her mistress quietly seethed. Fear of being found by Medea and punished had driven her back to the Bone Fortress before she'd even been missed. And now she watched in quiet trepidation as the Adept ranted.

"If I didn't know better, I could believe my little brother had the Goddess on his side. But the very fact that I've managed to trap them on the Plain of Desolation proves that the forces of so-called good have no interest in what happens to their creation, as usual." She paused and drummed her fingers on the arm of her great chair. "Even so, something must be helping them. How else could they have done it? How else could they kill a giant elephanta, of all things? I mean, it should've been able to wipe out an entire squadron of cavalry and at least ten Snow Leopards!"

The Witch of the Dark Power waited quietly, and then when Medea sat wearily back into the chair-that-was-almost-a-throne, she shuffled forward and coughed politely. "Perhaps I can suggest an answer, Mistress."

Medea looked up moodily. "You? What do you know? I'm the second-greatest Adept in all Creation and even I don't know how they did it!"

"Friendship, Mistress . . . and love," the witch said simply.

"*Friendship?* What do you mean?"

"Willing self-sacrifice. It's a powerful weapon against evil magic such as yours, Mistress," Orla explained patiently. "Anyone who risks his or her own life to save others weakens Dark Power."

Medea thought about this for a moment, a deep frown on her face, then her features cleared. "Of course, you're right! So that's how they did it! My revolting little brother told his pathetic friends to save themselves while he fended off the creature. Ha! And what should have been embarrassing bravado saved their skins!"

"Exactly, Mistress," said Orla.

As far as Medea was concerned, this act of bravery was just one skinny runt on a horse the size of an underfed deer holding off an *elephanta*! Stupid! Ridiculous!

She seethed quietly for a few more minutes, but eventually she began to calm down and think rationally. There was still hope of death and mayhem; after all, for altruism to save them from magic, the kids would have to know about it and use it as a weapon. But they obviously had no idea that they'd killed the huge monster because Sharley had decided to play the hero and let his friends escape. In fact, they probably thought their victory had everything to do with their prowess as warriors and nothing else.

Medea laughed happily. All she had to do was conjure some sort of trap that wouldn't allow the stupid idiots to even consider sacrificing themselves. She could hit them with a huge bolt of plasma that would incinerate them where they stood—but on second thought, that might warn the ever-alert Cronus as to what she was planning, and she didn't dare do that. No, all she had to do was keep them in so much danger, they wouldn't have time to do anything stupidly noble.

Simple, really. Now all she had to do was think of a scenario. . . .

Cronus drew on the Power of the Dark, giving his mind the strength it needed to cross the border between his domain and the Physical Realms. For a moment the interstices resisted his probing, but soon they began to yield, and finally he was able to tear through the membrane and emerge into the sky of a bright autumnal day in the Polypontus.

Below him lay the battle formation of the Hordes, like a huge schematic plan of Erinor's tactics. They were advancing on a walled city that was defended by a garrison under the command of what appeared to be an experienced officer. But Cronus could clearly see that he was hampered by poor supplies and a demoralized fighting force. It should be a fairly simple matter to capture the city; all he had to do was manipulate Erinor's simple warrior mind, and victory would be theirs . . . and his.

Quickly he found the Basilea. At first, flesh, blood, and bone resisted him, but gradually Cronus gained control of her mind and body, and soon he was looking at the world through Erinor's eyes. It was now just a matter of time before the city fell, giving the Icemark even more reason to intervene. And then, once the land was empty of its army of humans, Snow Leopards, and werewolves, it would be simplicity itself to invade. Providing, of course, Oskan and his hideous White Witches were distracted elsewhere.

The wide front of the Tri-Horns' phalanx advanced ponderously across the plain. There were over five hundred of the huge beasts, many of them roaring like gigantic lions and rumbling like distant storms as they stepped heavily forward. Each one was as high and as broad as a house, and their immense heads, with the three horns that gave them their name, hung low from their massive shoulders and jutted forward like formidable battering rams. Tri-Horns were definitely not built for speed, but they were enormously strong and virtually unstoppable once they'd begun their advance, and any target could expect to be annihilated.

Basilea Erinor and Cronus watched the slow approach of the city impatiently from her position high on the lead Tri-Horn's back, where she sat in the traditional fighting platform or "howdah," avidly studying the defenses as they drew nearer. The whitewashed battlements, curtain walls, and towers gleamed like quartz against the pristine blue of the sky, dazzling the attackers and giving the impression of impregnability. They'd all been built in the heyday of the Empire's powers and were truly awesome, but in these times of Imperial decline the garrison was at less than a third of the strength needed to defend the city, and their supplies of weaponry and munitions were almost exhausted.

Erinor's eye was made to follow the ebb and flow of the battle for the walls, and something told her it was exactly the right time to send in reinforcements. Ever since she'd first had the idea to break out of Artemesion and attack the Polypontian Empire, it was almost as though there was something in her head, guiding her actions and telling her what to do. But being the great and arrogant warrior she was, she simply attributed this to a highly developed tactical instinct.

The Shock Troops of the male regiments were almost exhausted, having completed their task of "softening up" the defenders. Probably less than a quarter of their numbers would have survived to this point, but like all men, they were expendable. Her conscience wasn't troubled by this: They were well trained and equipped and had been given the signal honor of opening the battle. And there would always be others to take their places; the male animal was really quite superfluous to civilization's needs, and by fighting and dying for their Basilea, they at least partly justified their existence. True Hypolitan society had always been organized in this way: Men were useful tools that could be discarded once their usefulness was over, and for the Shock

Troops, that point had just about been reached. Soon the elite female regiments would go in and continue the battle for the walls. A useful diversion while she, Erinor, led the Tri-Horn assault on the main gates. She laughed aloud in pure excitement and elation as they closed in on the latest victim of her lightning campaign.

Her animal groaned, rumbled deeply, and began to sidle, threatening to collide with its neighbor in the phalanx and disrupt the line. Quickly Erinor snatched up her goad and dug its spike deep into the thick hide of her mount until it redressed its position and plodded on. They were evil-tempered beasts with no sense of loyalty, and they'd kill their riders as happily as the enemy. They only served the Hypolitan at all because of strict training and iron control that involved using hot, razor-sharp goads and a constant threat of death.

Some might argue that the beasts reflected the society they served perfectly, but Erinor didn't care about any of that; like the men of the Shock Troops, the animals were useful tools, and now, as the walls of the city approached, she gave the command and the phalanx of Tri-Horns formed itself into a fighting arrow with the Basilea at its point.

From the walls, the defenders watched the approach of the war beasts with dread. They'd been used against three cities in the province just south of the Hypolitan heartland already, and all of them had fallen. What chance had they with an under-strength garrison that was desperately trying to defend the walls against the almost suicidal ferocity of the Shock Troops, and which would soon be called upon to protect the main gates from the Tri-Horn attack? Surrender wasn't an option: The Basilea wiped out the citizens of every settlement she took, and then repopulated it with her own people. Fighting for every inch of land kept her army in tip-top battle condition.

The garrison commander had had the foresight to evac-
uate the noncombatants, so he only had himself and his
soldiers to worry about, but this was cold comfort as he
watched the Tri-Horns approach the gates. He snapped
an order, and the few cannon he had left were loaded with
chain and grapeshot. He only had enough powder for precisely three salvos, so every one had to count. He couldn't
risk solid shot, even though a seven-pound cannonball was
about the only thing that would bring down a Tri-Horn; he
just didn't have enough cannon, powder, or ammunition to
make any impression on the hideous beasts that were bearing down on him. At least with grapeshot he could take out
as many Hypolitan as possible, and maybe he'd injure some
of the Tri-Horn enough to render them hors de combat.

The cannon all roared at once, and Erinor watched as
the fighting howdah of one of the Tri-Horns erupted into
splinters. All of the six Hypolitan soldiers it was carrying
were killed, and she screamed in rage and hurled abuse at
the defenders, but there were no other casualties and the
advance continued.

The beasts began to bellow, as they always did when they
neared their target, and immediately the cannon answered,
sending an explosion of broken metal and chains smashing into the phalanx. Once again the Basilea looked around
her; several of her soldiers were dead or wounded, but not
enough to have a significant effect on the advance. Some
of the Tri-Horns were also bloodied, but the injuries were
superficial, protected as they were by their massively thick
hides and also by leather and canvas surcoats that draped
over their backs and almost reached the ground on either
side of them. Their heads needed no such protection, being
naturally armored with the three horns and with a wide
"ruff" of bone and hide that protected their skulls and
their necks.

They were almost close enough now to begin their charge, and Erinor stood in the howdah and yelled the order. The Tri-Horns bellowed and surged forward at a fast walking pace, which powered the phalanx along like a living avalanche. The cannon roared again and one of the beasts fell, a chance shard of metal piercing its eye and brain. Two others stumbled over the fallen animal, dislodging their howdahs, but they scrambled to their heavy feet again and continued with the charge.

The Basilea now fitted an arrow to the string of a longbow, and on her word a dense flight of arrows rained down on the city's walls. Many of the defenders fell, but now Erinor and her Hordes squatted down in their howdahs and braced themselves for impact. The Tri-Horns were thundering down toward the hugely thick and tall gates. Erinor screamed in elation and hatred; another city of the Empire was about to die!

With a splintering, groaning crash her animal smashed into the portal, which was made of the trunks of entire trees, all roughly dressed and pinned together with long steel bolts. For a moment the gates resisted, while the defenders rained arrows, musket fire, and rocks down on the phalanx. Erinor and her soldiers replied with their deadly longbows and javelins, but then, with a massive heave, her Tri-Horn was through. The gates fell with a booming crash, crushing dozens of soldiers who'd braced them with great spars of wood.

Nearby, a section of the wall next to the gatehouse began to crumble, then fell with a booming rumble as three Tri-Horns, working in unison, forced their way through. Another breach was made as four of the huge beasts burst through the stonework. Then walls crumbled and fell seemingly everywhere as more and more of the Tri-Horns, working in teams, rammed the masonry.

The defenders retreated before them, the superb Polypontian discipline holding in the face of unstoppable power as ranks of musketeers fought skirmishing retreats, and shield-bearers risked all to scale the mighty legs of the beasts and fight hand to hand with the soldiers in the howdahs.

Erinor's face was a fire of glowing red flesh and ragingly mad eyes and mouth. "DIE! DIE!" she screamed repeatedly as her Tri-Horn waded through the houses and buildings that barred its way, like a child walking through long grass. To either side of her the army fanned out and rolled forward over the city, flattening all before it.

The commander of the defenders died futilely casting a spear into the face of a Tri-Horn. He was trodden beneath one of its massive feet, wondering in his last thoughts if the ants he had crushed as a child had felt like this.

The elite female regiments of the Hordes now poured through the breaches and fallen gates killing everyone and everything in their path, while the Tri-Horns rolled on flattening and crushing buildings, stomping defenders underfoot, and carving paths of destruction for the following Hordes to use.

The city fell in less than an hour, the last act of violence perpetrated against it being Erinor's javelin pinning a ten-year-old child, who had missed the evacuation, to the tree he had been hiding behind.

Cronus nodded in satisfaction as he withdrew from the Basilea's mind. One more city had been added to the growing tally of Erinor's victories. It could only be a matter of time now before the Icemark and its allies rode gallantly to the rescue. Everything was going wonderfully according to plan.

He returned to the Darkness, where other preparations awaited his attention. His granddaughter really was an admirable Adept, whose powers would be very useful; all he needed to do was to influence her way of thinking a little more. In particular, he must crush her feelings, her capacity to hate in a way that threatened her ability to wield her magic efficiently. But also he must manipulate the need to love that still contaminated her psyche and then convert its strength into an ability to act with cold calculation.

11

"Then they're definitely missing?" said Thirrin quietly.

"No sign of them anywhere," Oskan answered. "Werewolf and housecarl scouts have searched throughout the city and surrounding plain with no result, and so far nothing's been found in the Great Forest, either. And yes, before you ask, I've alerted the Holly and Oak kings and they're sending out search parties, too."

"What about the . . . magical plain?" she asked, not yet daring to refer to the Darkness by name.

Oskan sighed; this was the question he'd been expecting. "Not a sign," he said, and paused before adding, "at least, I don't *think* there's a sign."

Thirrin immediately swung back from the window in their private apartments, where she'd been staring out over the frosty garden. "You don't *think* there's a sign? What do you mean?"

Oskan scratched his head contemplatively. "Well, it's odd. Sometimes I get the faintest echo of something . . . but I'm not sure. It could just be wishful thinking."

Thirrin felt a thrill of fear shoot down her spine. "Oskan! Don't you see what this could mean? They could be trapped there; perhaps even lured away, and then their presence in some way masked because . . . whoever has them knew you'd be looking for them!"

Oskan was very well aware of this possibility; he just didn't want to acknowledge it. Sometimes, when dealing with the Dark, just accepting that a thing might happen could actually bring it about. He'd considered lying to Thirrin and telling her that he'd sensed nothing, but she was his wife, and if anyone deserved honesty from him, it was her. The fact that she was the Queen had no bearing on his decision at all; Oskan would happily lie to a roomful of emperors and a houseful of monarchs if he thought it would make his life easier. But Thirrin was different; she could somehow always guess when he wasn't being completely truthful.

"Look, I don't think we should panic just yet. It could be that they stumbled across a gateway—it *was* Samhein, after all—and they're just taking their time finding a way out."

"But what about the possibility they've been abducted or lured there?"

"We don't actually know that's the case," said Oskan in what he hoped were encouraging tones.

"Then where are they? Two young men, complete with horses, and a giant Snow Leopard don't just vanish! They've got to be somewhere!"

"Well, yes. Obviously. But finding out exactly where is a different matter."

"Just what is the point of you being the most powerful warlock in the land, and possibly the world, if you can't use your Gifts to find your own son and his friends?" Thirrin asked in frustration. "I mean, *why* can't you find them?"

This time Oskan decided to at least withhold the truth, even if he didn't directly lie. He was actually more worried than he was admitting. In one regard Thirrin was absolutely right: As a warlock, he should have been able to find the kids with ease, and the fact that he couldn't suggested that someone was masking their whereabouts. Someone, or something, that was very powerful indeed.

Had the time now come to use the Power of the Dark himself? If he opened his mind to it now, he would have all the Ability he'd need to rescue Sharley and the others. Perhaps he'd even have enough strength to destroy Cronus without the need to sacrifice anything! Surely it wasn't inevitable he'd be corrupted?

He shook his head as though to clear such thoughts and temptations from his mind. He must concentrate on the problem at hand. Deep down in the recesses of his brain he felt that opening his mind to that wickedness was not the answer. He must be strong.

Thirrin was watching him now, waiting for an explanation as to why he couldn't find Sharley. She reached up and placed a hand on his arm. Suddenly Oskan found her very presence blindingly irritating. Even her simple gesture of touching his arm incensed him.

"In the name of all that's holy, woman, must you be forever pawing at me?" he exploded. "I'm doing everything I can, and if you think it's not good enough, then try finding your precious son yourself! Now leave me be!"

Thirrin gasped and stepped back. She hardly recognized her own husband as his face darkened and his eyes glittered with a vicious rage. "Oskan, I . . . ."

"You what? You just want me to sift through the entire Cosmos for your son, is that it? Or perhaps you want me to sift through every grain of sand on the seabed, eh?"

Thirrin watched in horrified fascination as he seemed to actually grow before her eyes: His shoulders became heavier and rounded, and his face grew broader. "Well, let me tell you, there's just not enough of me to go around! There are too many demands on my time; I mean, just how do you think your precious little kingdom has survived for so long against all the muck and maniacs of the world? Can you guess? No? Well, I'll tell you: because my witches and I have been there to protect it, that's why. And now I'm getting a little bit tired, so I'm sorry if I can't find your son at the precise moment you demand; it just might take me a little bit longer, all right?"

"He's your son, too," Thirrin whispered.

Oskan looked up and was just drawing breath to renew the attack when he saw his wife's face. Her eyes were brimming with tears and she looked almost afraid, if such a thing were possible for the undefeated Queen of the Icemark.

Immediately Oskan felt the anger drain away, almost as though some evil energy had been withdrawn, and he slumped against the window frame. "Thirrin, I . . . I'm sorry. I wasn't thinking. . . . The words just came into my head. . . . It wasn't me. . . ."

She watched as her husband seemed to shrink back to his normal size, and sighed in relief. She'd seen these fits before; once, in the first war against the Polypontus, when they'd both been little more than children, Oskan had exploded in just such a way, and it was only by keeping her head and talking normally to him that he'd come back to her.

With all the resolution of the warrior she was, she suddenly gathered him into a hug. "That's all right, my love. You're just tired; we all are. We've had nothing but war for years and now it looks like it's all happening again. I'm sorry, too."

Oskan buried his head in her shoulder and waited for the last dregs of anger to finally drain away. But what had it been? Where had it come from? Thirrin was bound to ask, and he wasn't sure he had any answers . . . or, at least, no answers that anyone would want to hear. He was just composing an excuse that would explain it all when he was saved by the arrival of Tharaman and Krisafitsa. Getting two very large Snow Leopards into even a good-sized room took some maneuvering and effort, so Thirrin was sufficiently distracted to allow diversionary tactics.

"Any news?" asked Krisafitsa immediately.

"None, I'm afraid," Oskan replied, regaining his composure completely. "But I know for a fact that they're all still alive and well. If anything had happened to them, I'd have known."

"Well, that's one small mercy, at least," said Tharaman. "Now all we need to do is find them. They can't just have disappeared."

"We've been over that ground, Tharaman," said Thirrin hastily. "Let Oskan rest for a while."

"What if Oskan took us into the Spirit Realms?" asked Krisafitsa, ignoring Thirrin as fears for her child put her usual consideration aside. "We could search properly then, and with the Witchfather to guide us we'd be perfectly safe."

"Perfectly safe?" cried Oskan, shuddering at the very thought of what an enormous responsibility two Snow Leopards and a Thirrin would be. "I'd never describe even myself as *safe* when I go into the Magical Realms; no one's *safe* in there, not even if they're armed and armored with every protective charm on the planet. The place has this habit of changing the rules and pulling the rug from under your feet. . . ."

"Is it carpeted, then?" asked Tharaman.

"What?"

"The Magical Realms, are they carpeted? It's just that you mentioned pulling a rug from somewhere and I just wondered if perhaps . . ."

"I think it's a figure of speech, my dear," said Krisafitsa. "I do believe it means to be taken by surprise when you least expect it."

"Oh, I see. . . . Odd expression . . ."

"Look, never mind that," said Oskan, beginning to feel the strange anger rising again. "The fact is, I couldn't guarantee anyone's safety, and the idea of two of the most powerful monarchs in the northern hemisphere *and* their consorts mucking about in a dangerous place like—"

His outraged flow was interrupted by King Grishmak bursting through the door in his usual brisk manner. "What's up, hairy arses! How's things?"

"Not good, Grishy," said Thirrin. "Oskan was just about to have a stroke at the thought of guiding us through the Magical Realms, and there's still no sign of the youngsters."

"Ah, you won't enjoy the bit of news I've just heard from the relay, then."

"What news? It's not about Sharley, is it?" asked Thirrin in a panic.

"No, no!" Grishmak replied hurriedly. "I just meant it's even more pressure at a stressful time, that's all."

"You'd better let us have it, then," said Oskan wearily.

"Erinor and her Hordes are closing in on the southern border of the Polypontian heartlands, and if they continue at the same rate of advance, they could be at the capital within weeks."

"Oh, great!" said Thirrin angrily. "Where'd the information come from?"

"Another military refugee. Staff officer of the High Command, no less. I suppose his tactical eye has shown up all the flaws in the Polypontian response to the emergency, and he's getting out while the going's good."

"Where is he now, Grishy?" asked Thirrin. "None of the Wolf-folk got . . . peckish, did they?"

"What do you mean?" asked the Werewolf King in outraged tones. "We only eat the occasional prisoner of war if the moment merits such an act. And at the moment there's officially no hostilities between ourselves and what's left of the Empire."

"Right, so he's safe, then?"

"Yes, of course. He's being held at the southern border."

"Good. I want him transported here as quickly as possible. And make it quick; I think the weather's closing in."

"I don't think there'll be any blizzards for a day or two yet," said Grishmak, eyeing the lowering sky through the window.

"Three days and five hours, to be precise," said Oskan.

"They should just about make it, then, if a werewolf patrol brings him north immediately," said Thirrin briskly. "Well, my friends, I think we're just going to have to put our plans into action. I never thought I'd see the day when an Alliance army would invade the Polypontus and certainly not to defend the capital from an attack."

The room fell silent as everyone pondered such an idea, but none of them could concentrate on the emergency exclusively. Sharley, Mekhmet, and Kirimin filled a good part of their thoughts. The boys might have been battle-hardened warriors, but to Thirrin, Sharley was still her little boy, and she physically ached with the need to find him and bring him home safely. But at the same time a nagging fear and . . . *doubt*, for and about Oskan, worried at the edge of her mind.

Basilea Erinor sat quietly while the sounds of the camp flowed over her. She'd been pleased to revive the ancient tradition of the *yurt*, which the ancestors had used during their migrations between the grazing pastures high on the mountain plateaus of their homelands. They made ideal campaign tents, being much more robust and weatherproof than the average tent, and their domed "beehive" shape, covered in hides and carpets, gave a greater sense of solidity and permanence than the usual canvas. This in itself was useful, as any enemy spy who observed an encampment gained the impression that Erinor and her Hordes had arrived to stay and had built a town already.

Erinor smiled; the war of minds was sometimes more important than the fighting. When an invaded people saw their camps, they feared the Hordes had come to stay, and when they heard the tales of the Basilea's ferocity, they often surrendered without a fight. She wasn't entirely sure why; after all, she never showed mercy. Everyone was always slaughtered. In a fast-moving campaign there was no room or time for prisoners. Perhaps the conquered people were like rabbits that would crouch and scream in terror when a stoat was on their trail, waiting for the hunter to come and kill them.

But she had no more time for such theorizing. Her designated time of an hour's quiet was at an end, and her most important strategic and tactical decisions had been made.

As often happened at such times, her mind seemed to clear suddenly and she regained the ability to think about things in a less rigid and unbending way. It was almost as though something had been controlling her mind and had released its hold now that the important business of tactics and warfare had been dealt with. Erinor smiled again; she believed it was at such times that the Goddess herself guided her thoughts and actions, proving that the Hordes truly were the instruments of the Great Mother Goddess in a flawed and evil world.

Sighing contentedly, Erinor now called for her second in command, and within a matter of seconds Ariadne Artimesou arrived, still dressed in full armor. She'd been training with the Sacred Regiment of mounted archers, but had almost literally dropped everything when Erinor's order for her presence arrived. She bowed low, expertly gauging the Basilea's mood as she did so.

"Sit," said Erinor curtly. "The archers were on target?"

"Two missed more than the allowed percentage. They'll be whipped tonight."

"Then don't lay on with too much vigor."

Ariadne was amazed. The Basilea had never shown concern about punishments before, but everything was explained when she added, "They'll be needed in the battle the day after tomorrow. The Polypontian army's the biggest we've faced. And Andronicus is a good general. We'll need every soldier we can get."

Ariadne decided to risk pushing harder than she usually dared for information. "Do you expect the Imperial troops to be more effective than of late?"

"More effective, better led, and more desperate than any we've fought so far." Erinor stared at Ariadne with her bleak gray eyes until she was squirming. She may have had more than fifteen years' experience as a field commander in the endless tribal wars high in the mountains of Artemesion, but the Basilea could still reduce her to a quivering wreck with just a twitch of her head. "Make no mistake, Ariadne; desperation's their greatest weapon. Since the death of the Bellorums they've never won a battle, they've lost most of their Empire, and now we're about to invade the heartland of the Polypontus. They have to stop us, or die trying. And I intend to see that their trying isn't good enough, and that they do die, preferably screeching in agony."

Ariadne bowed her head. "The Hordes will be prepared."

"'Will be'? 'Will be'?" Erinor suddenly exploded. "They'd better be prepared *now*, at this very minute!" She leaped from her low divan and drew her sword. "We'll inspect every regiment now, and if I find one that is less than ready, your head will be my battle standard!"

The Basilea stormed out of her yurt, with Ariadne scurrying behind. There then began a detailed inspection of each and every regiment, during which weaponry, equipment, and knowledge of all tactical moves were checked and rechecked. It wasn't until the small hours of the morning that the last division was dismissed and the Basilea nodded to herself.

"Adequate. Barely, but your head's safe for now. Make this a learning experience, Ariadne, and be sure that every soldier is ready at all times of the day." The second in command bowed deeply, her face an expressionless mask. "You may stand down for now," Erinor continued. "Training at first light."

Returning to her yurt, she laughed out loud. "That'll keep you on your toes," she said happily. But then a tiny movement in the darkened shelter made her draw her sword and leap forward with a bark of challenge. "Who's there? Come out and die!"

A tall man stepped into the small pool of light from the night-lamp.

"Alexandros!" She sheathed her sword. "Must you sit in darkness? I might have killed you!"

He bowed deeply. "As a man of the Hypolitan, I realize that this may happen at any time."

Erinor glanced at him sharply, but his face was completely impassive. In truth, she wasn't sure what she'd do if she thought her consort was showing a "rebellious insubordination to the Rule of Law," as the statute books put it. She'd been with Alexandros now for twenty years and she truly wondered if she could bring herself to kill him, even if he were to openly preach revolution against the rule of women.

"You've eaten?" she asked.

"In the male mess tent, earlier," he confirmed.

"In that case we'll turn in. It's going to be a full day tomorrow."

Her consort remained standing, his eyes on the ground.

"All right, what is it?" she asked, immediately recognizing the mute request for discussion.

"The Shock Troops of the Dragon Regiment are under-equipped. They're short of ammunition for crossbows. If they're to perform adequately in the coming battle, they'll need supplying."

Erinor removed her quilted winter coat and let it drop, knowing that Alexandros would pick it up and store it in its proper chest. "Very well. Anything else?"

"Some in the same regiment lack body armor. I realize they're only men and therefore expendable. But the longer they survive, the greater their effectiveness."

"True," Erinor agreed. "Talk to the quartermistress."

Alexandros bowed, at the same time neatly gathering the Basilea's coat and packing it away. He then helped his wife remove her felt boots.

"Ah, that's better," she said with relief. "My feet haven't seen daylight in twelve hours."

"You'll be in the saddle for longer than that when we fight the Imperial army."

"Will I, now?" the Basilea replied, interested to see just how much of the coming battle's tactics and strategies he was aware of.

"Well, I presume you'll be leading the Sacred Regiment rather than the phalanx of Tri-Horns. They're too slow — fine for siege warfare or as the anvil of a battlefield assault, but you prefer to be the hammer."

She laughed affectionately. "I do at that, and you're right, I'll probably be in the saddle from dawn till well after dusk. Oh well, that's the joy of conquest and command."

Alexandros watched her for a moment, assessing her mood. She seemed happy to talk, so he decided to try and gather some more information. "And after the victory, I suppose we must prepare for the assault on the Polypontian capital?"

"Of course," she answered, quirking her eyebrow to show him that she knew perfectly well he was milking her for facts and figures. "But I won't be leading it."

Her consort dropped the tray of drinking vessels he'd been tidying to give his hands something to do in the Basilea's presence. Fortunately they were bronze and simply bounced over the thick carpets, and he quickly gathered them together. "You won't be leading the assault?"

"No," she replied, enjoying his shock. "I've decided to forgo the glory as a sacrifice to the Great Mother Goddess. Ever since breaking out of the homelands of Artemesion I've led the Hordes in victory after victory. Too much success for one commander can lead to overconfidence. The Goddess hates such human arrogance, so Ariadne will lead the assault on the capital."

"Does she have the necessary experience?"

"Are you doubting my judgment?" Erinor suddenly snapped, her voice like a whip-crack in the quiet yurt.

Alexandros, already on the carpet to collect the fallen goblets, bowed his head to the ground. "Such disloyal and misguided thoughts had never entered my head, Your Eminence. And I beg forgiveness that my demeanor should cause you to believe that they had."

Erinor left him prone at her feet for a few moments while he relearned his role and position as her consort. As the premier couple among the Hypolitan, they reflected their society perfectly. Like all men, Alexandros was there to serve his spouse and comfort her as she saw fit. Like all men, his comfort and shelter depended entirely upon his wife, and like all men, he had no rights to property or representation within either law or government. In fact, if Hypolitan edict was followed to the letter, no man owned anything at all, including the clothes he wore or even his own body. Once married, he was entirely the property of his wife, and before marriage he belonged to his mother or his next-nearest female relative.

"I hope your head isn't wearing out my carpet," Erinor finally said lightly, to show that he was forgiven.

"No, Your Eminence," said Alexandros, jumping to his feet. He was aware that the Basilea was now joking, but he'd never smiled in his wife's company before, and would be shocked at the idea of doing so now.

"Good. I'm tired. You may prepare the bed. Oh, and this time, make sure you warm my side properly."

Her consort bowed low and went immediately to prepare the sleeping quarters.

Far off within the depths of the Darkness, the Arc-Adept Cronus analyzed what he had just witnessed. There were times when the Basilea thought for herself, and the results were rarely good. But as he scrutinized Erinor's decision to sacrifice her command of the attack on Romula, he could find little in the way of difficulties. After all, the Polypontian Empire was on the brink of collapse, and even with the help of the Icemark and its allies, it was unlikely to survive.

But at base its survival or destruction was of little real interest to the Arc-Adept; the war for the Empire was purely a diversion, a decoy that was designed only to draw Oskan and his witches away from the Icemark, so that he, Cronus, could begin the invasion of the Physical Realms. Of course, he could simply have begun his invasion at some other point on the physical globe. But the Icemark was a perfect place to establish the first bridgehead of his occupation. Not only was it close to the agreeable Land-of-the-Ghosts, but the presence of Oskan and his witches had saturated the atmosphere with psychic power. Power that could be utilized to evil ends by the most powerful Arc-Adept in all Creation.

His strategies really were flawless, and so far everything was going perfectly as planned.

*   *   *

Olememnon crept into the bedroom as quietly as several pints of beer and a huge steak pie would allow. He'd spent most of the evening with Grishmak and Tharaman, and though the Thar had been quieter than usual, the Werewolf King had been his normal boisterous self, and, as always, had managed to persuade the consort of the Basilea to eat and drink far too much.

Olememnon groped through the darkened room, hiccupping gently and trying to navigate his way to where he thought he remembered the bed had been the night before. The amount of beer he'd drunk suddenly made him supremely confident, and he strode out with determination and walked into a chair, barking his shins painfully.

For the next few seconds he hopped around in slow circles, holding first one leg and then the other as he whispered obscenities to himself. But eventually the pain subsided, and he set out for where he believed the bed to be with undiminished determination.

"Oh, for goodness' sake, it's over here, Ollie!" said a voice from a point directly behind him.

"Eh? Oh! Are you still awake, my love?"

"Well, I wasn't," said Olympia, the Basilea of the northern Hypolitan, "but three hundred pounds of beer-steeped warrior staggering around your bedroom tends to wake you up."

"My most profound apologies, Ma'am," Ollie replied with deep formality. "I was . . . I was discussing tactics with the Thar and King Grishmak."

"Oh yes. I'm sure you were," said Olympia with deep skepticism. "And what gems of military genius did you come up with?"

"Ah well! They were truly brilliant . . . but unfortunately, they seem to have temporarily slipped my mind," he replied, sitting on the edge of the bed and wrestling with his boots.

"But when they return, the world of military tactics will be astounded."

"Undoubtedly," said Olympia, lighting a candle and squinting at her consort as he finally managed to remove his last boot and throw it into the farthest corner. "How was Tharaman?"

"A little quiet, actually," Ollie replied. "There's still no news of Kirimin or the princes."

"No. As if we haven't enough to worry about with the Hypolitan of Artemesion destroying the world, now two of our best commanders are distracted by the fact their children are missing!"

"*Four* of our best commanders are distracted, if you count Krisafitsa and Oskan."

"Yes . . . yes. I suppose so. Have you seen the Witchfather recently?"

"No, he's too busy preparing the medical units for the upcoming campaign or searching the Magical Realms for the kids."

Olympia sighed, her mind suddenly overloaded by the stresses of the pending war. "Ollie, do you . . . do you ever feel guilty?"

"About what?"

"About the fact that it's Hypolitan who are causing this war?"

"No. It might be Hypolitan causing the war, but it's not *our* Hypolitan, is it?"

"I suppose not, but we share a culture."

Ollie, having finally managed to peel off his clothes, leaped into the bed with an ecstatic sigh. "I wouldn't be too sure about the culture thing, either. Some reports coming in from the Polypontus suggest we're dealing with some very backward types here. You know, expendable males used as shock troops, no rights for men in either law or administration, that sort of thing."

"Yes, I know. But let's face it, some of our more . . . old-fashioned citizens might think that a good thing. I've even heard one or two talking about the *purity* of Hypolitan culture being preserved by the Artemesion tribes."

Ollie put his hands behind his head and gazed contemplatively at the ceiling. "You'll always get nutters and fanatics in any society, but most of us realize things are better than they were."

"Yes, I suppose so," Olympia agreed. "But if Thirrin and the rest hear comments about cultural purity too often, they might start doubting our loyalty."

"Surely not; they'll know it's only the rantings of a few fundamentalist loonies."

"You're probably right, but perhaps the time's right for purging the ranks of some of these unsavory types."

Ollie sat up and tried to focus his beer-fuddled eyes. "Olympia, Basilea of the northern Hypolitan, do you really want to be remembered as the first leader of your people in more than half a millennium who ignored their rights as citizens and inflicted punishment without due process of the law?"

She held his gaze for a few moments and then sighed. "No. No, I don't. But even so, there are elements that need watching."

"There are always elements that need watching. But in the meantime I have a steak pie and too much beer to sleep off." With that he fell immediately asleep.

Olympia looked at him for a few seconds, caught between annoyance and amusement. Then she covered him up, snuffed the candle, and snuggled up to what felt and sounded like a hibernating Greyling bear.

12

Cressida helped herself to wine and lay back in her chair. She was tired after spending several hours training in the lists, but at last she had a little time for herself, and she chose to spend it with Eodred and Howler.

Her brother's quarters were always so much more "lived-in" than her own. The floor was littered with pieces of armor, old belts, and discarded lacings, and the place smelled like a housecarl's armpit after a day spent fighting in the hot sunshine. But somehow she felt comfortable here. Her own rooms were gleamingly clean and as tidy as an ironed shirt; in fact, if they'd been anything other than spotless, the chamberlains would have been in serious trouble, and she wouldn't have been able to relax until order had been restored. But Eodred and Howler's room was different. Perhaps it was precisely because it was the complete opposite of her own space that she could relax so completely. She didn't have to worry about keeping up with the expected standards of the Crown Princess and could wind down in the company of two fellow warriors who had no interest whatsoever in etiquette or the correct procedures of court life.

"So you think we'll be ready to march in a month or so?" Eodred said, lying back on his bed and stretching luxuriously as he slowly thought things through.

"Yes," Cressida replied, focusing her mind on the conversation. "About five weeks, in fact."

"How far then to Romula?" asked Howler.

"I'm a bit sketchy on that, I'm afraid. But a week or so of steady marching, I should think."

"Hmm, the latest relay reports say that Erinor and her Hordes are about to invade the Polypontian heartlands," said Howler, scratching his chin thoughtfully. "General Andronicus is trying to stop her with a scratch army cobbled together from remnants and garrison troops, but nobody thinks he's got a chance."

"I shouldn't think he has," Cressida said, sipping her wine. "Though Andronicus is more than competent, according to all the intelligence we have, and if his supplies were better and he'd had time to train his troops, then I think Erinor might have gotten a shock."

"Really," said Eodred, sitting up. "Could he have stopped her?"

"I didn't say that. The Hordes are brilliantly ferocious and, some believe, unstoppable. But I think it would have taken more than one battle to settle the matter. Don't forget that Andronicus was second only to Bellorum in the Imperial military hierarchy. In fact, we're told that his was the loudest voice in the Senate against invading the Icemark, and he led the peace faction that wanted to recall Bellorum when the war dragged on longer than anyone thought."

"Shrewd, then," said Howler.

"Very."

"So what'll happen?" asked Eodred.

"With a bit of luck, Andronicus will slow Erinor down, perhaps even hurt her enough to stop her for a while, and so give us a better chance to establish ourselves before she's ready to march again."

"And what about these Tri-Horns?" Eodred went on. "Are they as unstoppable as everyone claims?"

Cressida shrugged. "Who knows? We can only judge by the reports we receive, and they suggest the animals are virtually indestructible. But no one here's actually witnessed them in action. Even the refugee Polypontian officer the werewolves brought north from the border has no idea. To be honest, I don't think he's actually seen any active service, just admin and supply and that sort of thing; useful for details about logistics, but no good when it comes to the sharp edge of the fighting."

Howler paced the room, suddenly restless. "It's a shame we can't go in and bring someone out!"

"What do you mean?" asked Cressida.

"You know, a small raiding party to seek out and capture a Polypontian officer with experience of fighting Erinor."

"I see your point, but it's too risky. They'd need to go to the front line to get someone with the relevant knowledge, and striking so deep into unknown territory and then getting out again, undetected, would be nigh on impossible," said Cressida briskly. "And not only that, but if they fell into the hands of the Hordes, then all chance of taking them by surprise would be lost. Erinor mustn't know we're coming. By all accounts she's a brilliant tactician and strategist; if she finds out that we're on the way, she'll be ready for us."

"I suppose so," Howler reluctantly agreed. "But without information we're fighting blind."

Cressida shrugged. "We'll just have to be as adaptable as the enemy, then. Until the Empire began to fragment, they were just a scatter of mountain tribes bickering among themselves. It took someone with vision and power to stop them from attacking one another and teach them to fight together. Erinor forced them to adapt to new circumstances, and now *we* have to adapt to *her*."

The sound of marching feet, roaring voices, and galloping hooves percolated faintly through the shutters that were closed against the weather of a late Icemark autumn.

"Someone's busy learning to adapt right now," said Eodred, climbing to his feet and opening the window so that a blast of freezing air howled around the room. "Not many of us are used to campaigning in the winter weather. Still, it'll be warmer in the Polypontus . . . slightly."

Down on the plain that surrounded the city of Frostmarris, Tharaman-Thar and Krisafitsa-Tharina watched as a division of the cavalry put a contingent of infantry through its paces. Already there'd been several light falls of snow and the frozen land was covered in a ragged blanket of white. In the distance the Great Forest roared and howled as an icy wind found a voice in the naked branches of the trees, and an ominously gray sky threatened more snow before the end of the day.

"Does she really need to do this now?" Tharaman asked cantankerously. "We were at it all day yesterday and things got so . . . *vigorous,* almost half the infantry and upward of thirty cavalry ended up in the infirmary!"

"Don't exaggerate, dearest," said Krisafitsa calmly. "It was much less than a quarter of the foot soldiers and only fifteen cavalry."

Tharaman humphed moodily, then added, "Yes, and five of those were Snow Leopards! That just proves how violent it was; it takes pretty energetic war gaming to put our warriors in the hospital."

"You know she's desperate to get the army battle-ready and keep them that way. And besides, she needs to distract herself. Sharley's still missing, and she's afraid."

"And we're not, I suppose."

"Well, of course we are, my dear," she answered quietly. "That fact is made abundantly clear by your complaints about Thirrin. I don't think I've ever heard you say a word against her until now."

Tharaman lowered his head. "I'm tired, Krisa. We've a war to fight—an invasion, no less—and all I can do is wonder where our daughter has gotten to. How can I concentrate when one of our cubs is lost on the Plain of Desolation?"

"No more than I can. But we must, Tharaman. This new threat from the south could destroy the Icemark and the Hypolitan, our friends and allies. We can do nothing to help Kirimin and the boys now. We can only trust that Oskan traces them and brings them home safely."

"But he's already admitted that he can't find them, and that someone, or some*thing*, is masking their whereabouts," said Tharaman desperately. "That in itself is a huge worry; why would anyone hide them from a potential rescuer unless they meant them harm?"

Krisafitsa flattened her ears with fear. "I've no idea, and I must admit it looks bad. But we have no choice, my love, we can only wait while Oskan continues his search and pray that he succeeds."

"And if he doesn't?" the Thar asked quietly.

"If he doesn't . . . if he doesn't, then for a time the stars will stand still in their courses, and the sun will be dimmed to a gray parody of day," said Krisafitsa in a whisper. "But still, Tharaman, still our allies will be threatened, and our friends will be in danger, and I for one will fight in their war, though my heart may mourn for the rest of my days and my life will be changed to a cold and dark shadow of what it once was."

The Thar gazed out over the darkening plain, his amber eyes glowing like the heart of a winter fire and the icy wind stroking patterns in his richly dense fur. Then at last he hung his head low for a moment before turning to his Tharina. "You're right, as ever, my love," he finally said.

"From now on my heart will still be in the Magical Realms, but I will try to use my teeth and claws here in the physical world. Our friends are in need and the struggle is about to begin. Let none say that Tharaman and Krisafitsa ever betrayed those in need of the Snow Leopards' strength!"

And, throwing back his head, he sent out a mighty roar that was answered by all of his people, until the Plain of Frostmarris echoed with the power and might of the Icesheets.

Oskan searched slowly through the Plain of Desolation again. Eventually he turned away and looked beyond the steaming geysers, mud pots, and hot springs to the narrow area of rocky scree that led down to the chasm bordering the land. He knew that beyond the border lay the supreme evil of the Darkness, and he was desperate to find the boys and Kirimin.

But despite his sense of urgency he was distracted; being so close to the evil realm filled his psyche with a frisson of almost unbearable excitement. He was well aware that all he had to do was lower his defenses and the Dark Power would fill his mind to capacity, and then no amount of shielding would be able to hide Sharley from him. But what then? Would he just become as evil and as twisted as every other fool who'd opened himself to the Dark, or would he be strong enough to control it? He was, after all, supposedly the son of the second-most powerful being in the Cosmos. . . .

"And that second-most powerful being was also made evil and twisted by the Dark," said a voice, and Oskan watched as the Messenger of the Goddess approached. He hadn't seen or spoken with the powerful spirit since she'd appeared in his psychic trance. Oskan raised his hand in greeting and wondered what this second visitation heralded.

"I rather thought that Cronus was evil before he created his realm," he said.

"And so he was," the Messenger agreed as she stood before him. "But the creation of the Darkness has compounded his wickedness. He's steeped and bathed in its power every second of his existence; it permeates every part and particle of his being, corrupting and deforming his very soul. Exactly as it would do to you if you chose to open your mind to it."

Oskan nodded. "And she has sent you to warn me of this?"

"Yes, and also to remind you of the weapon of knowledge that the Goddess has placed in your hands. You must choose to use it freely for it to be truly effective."

Oskan remained silent. The sacrifice that its use demanded was appalling, and he still resisted accepting his task.

"The Goddess will expect an answer from you soon, Oskan Witchfather. She knows of your pain, as she knows the minds of all of her children. But the existence of the entire Cosmos depends upon your decision. She must think of the many."

Oskan nodded and looked up, meaning to tell the Messenger to ask the Goddess to allow him a little more time. But she had gone, and he was alone in the ether of the Plain of Desolation. He sighed; when would there ever be time for Oskan Witch's Son again, the boy who'd once met a princess in the forest and given her shelter from a storm?

He scanned the plain around him, and for a while he could see nothing—but then, for a moment, a tiny flicker of identity broke through an obscuring fog.

"Sharley!"

The mask that had been hiding the three friends had slipped, and now he could see why. Whoever it was that had enticed them away to the Plain of Desolation was about to attack, and maintaining the energy levels needed to hide people while preparing to strike was almost impossible.

Quickly Oskan assumed the shape of a giant hawk and sped to the chasm. As he flew, he could sense a building of negative power in the ether. Whoever it was that was trying to kill Sharley and his friends was almost ready to strike! The kids would be defenseless against magical power.

He arrived just as a bank of black thundercloud rose out of the void and moved threateningly toward the two boys and the Snow Leopard. Bolts of lightning flickered around its huge bulk, and deep, rumbling notes of thunder muttered and boomed ominously. Swiftly Oskan projected a bridge that leaped out over the yawning chasm, an ideal place of safety; nothing could harm anyone who stepped onto magical bridges, because the levels of magic needed to make them were so high that all other power in the vicinity was rendered null and void.

Oskan could also see that Sharley and Mekhmet were drawing their scimitars, and Kirimin was crouching, ready to spring at the approaching storm. Desperately he shouted a warning, but it emerged from his hawk throat as a piercing screech. There was a small flying creature nearby, and when it heard the hawk, it flew around the friends' heads and seemed either to be urging them toward the bridge or harrying them in some way.

By this time lightning bolts were striking all around them, and huge hailstones were ricocheting from the ground and thumping deep depressions into the turf. Reluctantly the boys and the Snow Leopard stepped onto the bridge and within the blink of an eye were gone.

Oskan breathed a sigh of relief, and then, with a screech, powered into the storm cloud. Immediately he was caught in the mighty turbulence that raged and tumbled through the thunderhead. He sent out a great burst of power that burned away a large segment of its bulk. A thunderbolt exploded as the storm writhed in agony, then it quickly recovered and struck at him with all its power.

The lightning burned away every feather and he fell. Quickly he negated the burning energy by becoming a fireball himself, and, rising, he turned and smashed into the cloud, drawing energy from the storm itself and growing in strength as he seared a burning path through the vapor of the thunderhead.

The storm boomed and roared, striking at him again and again with lightning, but Oskan merely used the energy to grow in power, crackling and raging at the very heart of the cloud.

In triumph he sensed the enemy fading. He was almost certain he could kill it with just one more burst of power!

But then it was gone. Oskan hung suspended in the air, the constellations glittering and scintillating all around him, and no sign of the storm. He'd won, but it had escaped, and he tried to convince himself that he didn't know who or what it had been. Not only that, but Sharley and his friends had crossed the bridge and he had no idea where they'd gone to. Now he'd have to start the search again, and if the enemy recovered before he found them, they could be in deadly danger.

Medea fell screaming through the ether and smashed into the frozen lands of the Darkness. The tiny shards of ice that made up the endless tundra hissed and spat as they came into contact with her burning wounds, but eventually the heat dissipated and the souls refroze over her ruined skin, soothing the pain and stopping further damage.

She writhed in mental anguish and screamed again into the wide nothingness of the Darkness's sky. Oskan, her own father, had beaten her in battle, and she had been so sure she was now stronger than him! Such was her rage and pain, she almost forgot to direct her magic into its healing mode. But at last her mind turned inward and damage was repaired; charred and blackened skin sloughed away, ruined limbs crumbled to charcoal, and the rebuilding began.

Such was her power that even in her injured and dormant state she was able to keep the ravening packs of Ice Demons at bay, and in less than two hours she was healed, physically at least, and climbing to her newly re-formed feet, she willed herself back to her Bone Fortress. She arrived in the Great Hall and sat in the huge chair-that-was-almost-a-throne while she sought order from the chaos of her defeat, and for a moment she allowed the silence of her home to wash over her, finding in its quiet a calmness and peace that was healing in itself.

But if all was quiet around her, within she was a seething mass of conflicting emotions. The battle she'd just fought and lost was the first contact she'd had with her father since he'd banished her to the Darkness. She felt a need to feel nothing but undiluted hatred for the man she believed had betrayed her, but deep in the darkest corners of her mind the smallest note of longing sounded. She'd seen Oskan again! Her father; the man who'd raised her; the man who'd nurtured her childish Magical Ability . . . the man who'd loved her.

The hiss of her intake of breath echoed around the walls of her palace as the thought arrived unbidden in her mind. In raging anger she forced herself to remember that it was also her father who'd sent her to die in the Darkness.

With a supreme act of will she regained her confidence and she gloried in her power. The Witchfather had merely been lucky, taking her by surprise. Next time she'd be ready, and then they'd see who was the stronger.

Orla emerged from the shadows where she'd been hiding, and she curtsied as deeply as her twisted body allowed.

"Oh, there you are!" Medea snapped. "I was beginning to think I'd need to thaw another soul from the tundra. Where have you been?"

"Close enough to do the mistress's bidding if she had needed me."

"Well, if you were that close, you'll know I was badly injured in a battle with my beloved father." Once again a far-distant echo of regret for what might have been sounded in her mind, but she ruthlessly squashed it. "But you, my dear handmaid, were conspicuous by your absence! Exactly where were you when I needed you?"

The witch managed to look concerned. "I'm sorry to hear the mistress was injured, though surely the wounds can't have been too serious, especially as she is so obviously in good health now."

"My *good health,* as you put it, is due purely to my superb Abilities as an Adept. Now, you can get me—"

But Orla had disappeared. Suddenly Medea became aware of another presence, something much more powerful and evil. Medea then watched as her grandfather paced his measured step across the skull cobbles of her hall. His white frock coat flowed elegantly in the breeze, as did his hair that swept back from his forehead and down to his neat and pristine collar, and his pale face was expressionless.

"Granddaughter!" he called as he approached. "You have clashed with your father."

"We fought, as well you know."

"And what was the outcome, now that you claim to be the stronger?"

"My Powers *are* greater than his, but he has more experience and utilizes what he has with enormous skill."

"Aren't *skill* and *experience* to be considered Powers, too?" he asked tonelessly.

"No . . . yes. But they're not magical in the truest sense of the word."

"And yet they helped to defeat you."

Medea observed him in silence. How far dare she push his supreme evil by arguing back? "My lack of experience will be remedied by time, and therefore my skills will soon be equal to his."

"But, Granddaughter, his experience will also grow with the same passage of time. How can you ever catch up, unless you kill him?"

"There *will* come a time when I will walk away from a meeting with Oskan the Warlock, and he will remain forever silent."

"I admire your confidence; I hope it isn't misplaced."

"I will destroy him," she answered quietly.

Her grandfather turned the empty depths of his eyes upon her and held her in the crushing vise of his regard for several long seconds. "Medea, your right to exist in the Darkness is called into question by your inability to defeat your father. He has never fully embraced his magical potential, denying the power of the evil within him, and yet despite this he can still crush you in a straight contest."

"I have secured my right to the Darkness by virtue of the fact that I destroyed the six Adepts in battle," Medea answered, her voice almost cracking in panic.

Cronus's eyes suddenly glinted in a rare display of open malevolence, and then he granted Medea a view of his unguarded, undiluted mind.

For a moment she was made aware of the appalling depths of his evil. Here was a being, she suddenly knew, who would again try to depose the Goddess if he could. How could she compete with such depths of depravity?

"Something to aspire to, Granddaughter," he said quietly, and then he went on: "Tell me, in all the depths of my mind, did you detect even a hint of emotion?"

"No," Medea replied automatically, though there *had* been the faintest suggestion of something buried beneath the layers of his malevolence. Something that had almost seemed like a sense of betrayal and a deep, unhealed pain. Perhaps here the two Adepts had something more in common than simply their family link, if either would dare to acknowledge it.

"No, there are no emotions," Cronus agreed. "Because I will not allow it. Feelings weaken the strength of the depraved mind, something you still haven't accepted, Granddaughter. But understand and recognize this: You will never defeat your father while you allow emotions to dictate your actions. The passion of your mind threatens both the Darkness and my plans for the Physical Realms. Therefore, you *will* lay aside all human feelings."

The echo that usually haunted the place scampered away in terror, leaving his words to fall flat and stark into the gloom.

Strangely Medea was reminded again of Oskan, who had also tried to make her conform to his ideas on what was acceptable and right. The two hugely powerful Adepts were so alike; only their loyalties differed. She forced herself to concentrate on her grandfather, realizing it was dangerous to do otherwise.

He held her eyes for a few crushing moments, then turned and slowly walked away. Mind-shaping, he thought, needed to be carried out with a little more subtlety. Medea was now all too aware of his presence in her head. He would wait until later, when he'd disguise his molding of her opinions and attitudes as her own thoughts and feelings.

Medea watched him go, her heart pounding. Whatever happened, Cronus must never find out what she was trying to do to Sharley and his friends. Death and terror would be inevitable if he did. Quickly she sent her mind questing out to the Plain of Desolation and, locating her brother and his companions, she quickly increased the levels of psychic masking that hid them from view.

Erinor seethed and boiled with greater levels of rage than she thought possible. Already her Shock Troops had been broken by a simple pincer movement of cavalry into their left and right flanks, and even the chariots and Sacred Regiment of mounted archers had been almost completely wiped out as they'd charged into a series of cunningly hidden ditches around the enemy's position.

General Andronicus was proving himself a very worthy opponent, even without the artillery that usually accompanied an Imperial army. The problems with supply continued to dog the Polypontians and cripple their armies. But even so, under the right leadership they still packed a considerable punch.

Erinor surveyed the wreckage of her opening moves against him, and incredibly a sense of calm suddenly returned. For a moment she found herself wishing that she and Andronicus could have met in battle when the Imperial legions were at their height, with none of the present troubles with supply and morale. But then she dismissed the thought. Circumstance and chance were the makers and levelers of armies, the architects and destroyers of empires. The Polypontians had had their day, and it was her task to literally clear them from the face of the world.

She looked out to the general's position, where she could clearly see him, training his monoculum on the battle before him. Then, incredibly, his viewing instrument came to rest on her, and she watched as he raised his hand in greeting. She smiled, genuinely amused, and bowed her head in acknowledgment.

General Andronicus was indeed a worthy opponent, she thought to herself. But even so, he was fighting from a position of terrible disadvantage; the Polypontians had lost every battle in the war so far, and the Imperial soldiers really believed she was invincible.

"So, General, if you cannot be outflanked, a frontal assault remains the only option," she said quietly. And then her face was transformed into a mask of rage and hatred as she screamed out her orders.

With a bellow Erinor's Tri-Horn moved forward, leading the phalanx of mighty beasts toward the Imperial lines. Their pace quickly increased to a lumbering charge, and the Polypontian legions began to fall back. Now Andronicus sent forward the pike regiments, their eighteen-foot-long spears swinging down into the engage position as they advanced.

This would be the general's greatest test. The Tri-Horns were considered unstoppable, but he'd watched them in action once before and thought them unsteady. If the morale and courage of the pike soldiers could hold, and they advanced in close order, he believed the animals could be turned and made to inflict huge damage on their own army as they fled.

Down on the front line the pike phalanx pushed through the retreating lines of the Imperial legions, while before them the Tri-Horns advanced like a disciplined mountain range, their massive feet sending up clouds of dust and their deep bellows vibrating through the air.

Arrows began to rain down on Polypontian soldiers as the archers in the howdahs came into range. But the pike regiments continued their advance. Soon the overpowering smell of the huge animals washed over them, and their enormous bodies filled the horizon as they rolled forward. The Tri-Horns now raised their heads and roared, and, with a heave, drove forward into the enemy.

The pike lines immediately buckled as the long spears snapped and shattered against the tough hide of the animals, but more and more of the weapons swung down into the engage position from the ranks of soldiers marching behind. Still the Tri-Horns advanced through the densely packed lines of the enemy, and Erinor laughed aloud. What hope had such puny efforts against her mighty war beasts?

But more of the pikes were now engaged, and the soldiers closed ranks into a solid wedge of bristling razor-sharp steel, each individual fighter becoming a part of a single killing machine that stood against the power of the Tri-Horns. The shafts of the immensely long spears were driven deep into the ground, and held at a deadly glittering angle that drove their blades deep into the armored hide of the animals, and though many splintered and fell, more and more were engaged to take their place. Through blood and terror, sweat and hatred, the Imperial fighters held their line—then, slowly, slowly, the seemingly unstoppable advance of the huge animals faltered, and finally, incredibly, stopped.

Erinor raged and howled out orders, and arrows and spears rained down on the Polypontian ranks.

All around her the Tri-Horns bellowed as the impenetrable hedge of steel bristled before them, and then suddenly, with a scream of rage and frustration, several of the beasts turned and lumbered away, trampling the ranks of elite female regiments that were following in support. More and more of the animals now turned and crushed all in their path, the soldiers in the howdahs tumbling like straw as the beasts stampeded away.

All through the ranks of the Hordes a murmur arose. The Basilea heard the rumbling dissent and knew she had minutes to save her position. But before she could act, the roaring war cry of the Shock Troops sounded on the air.

The soldiers erupted through the dust and haze of the battle and charged the pike regiments.

Erinor's consort, Alexandros, had regrouped his forces after they'd been broken in the opening moves of the battle, and now returned with a fury to smash into the unguarded flanks of the enemy. In a seething wedge the soldiers of the Hordes drove deep into the Polypontian ranks, splitting them apart and breaking up their cohesion and order.

For several long minutes the field commanders struggled to counter the attack, ordering sections to lay down their unwieldy pikes and fight back with sword and dagger against the ferocity of the Shock Troops. But the initiative was lost, the invincible Hordes were fighting back, all was lost, all was lost! With a roar of despair the Imperial soldiers folded and then broke, casting down their long spears and turning to run. Erinor seized the moment, and, gathering the remains of her Tri-Horns, she charged.

On a nearby ridge General Andronicus watched it all. He snapped shut his monoculum and shrugged almost humorously. Such was the fickle nature of battle. Turning his horse, he gathered as many of his cavalry as he could and galloped away. His goals were now simplicity itself: first to escape, and then to seek out Queen Thirrin of the Icemark. She was the only one now who could stop Erinor and her Hordes, and he had learned several lessons in his battle that would prove useful to the northern Queen. With luck his valuable experience and knowledge would earn him a position at her side.

13

"That was Dad, Mekhmet! That was Dad!" Sharley shouted as they ran across the bridge.

"Yes, but what was the other thing?"

"I don't know! Something evil. Who cares? The important thing is, it was Dad; he's found us!"

"And lost us again. I don't think there's—" Mekhmet's reply was cut short as he came to the end of the bridge and fell back onto the Plain of Desolation. Sharley fell on top of him, which was no hardship, but then Kirimin's massive frame landed on them, too, and everything was knocked out of them, from air to consciousness.

They came round several minutes later to find Pious fanning them with his wings, and Kirimin staring anxiously into their faces. "Well, thank the One for that!" she said with a sigh of relief. "I thought I'd squished you for good."

"I think you very nearly did," said Sharley, sitting up and wincing as all of his bruises complained.

"Nothing's broken, I checked."

"Oh, good, I'm so glad," said Mekhmet sarcastically as he rubbed his head. "That makes being knocked unconscious completely unimportant."

Kirimin decided to ignore him. "Anyway, hurry up and get your wind back; we've got to explore."

"Yeah, where exactly are we?" asked Sharley, looking around at a dark and gloomy landscape.

"On the Plain of Desolation," said Pious. "Where else?"

"Well, it certainly doesn't look like it—"

"Just a minute, where are the horses?" Mekhmet interrupted in a panic.

"Calm down; we've tethered them over there," Kirimin answered, nodding to the animals that stood a few yards off. "They're fine. You weren't riding, if you remember, and they just jumped over you when you fell."

"I'll take your word for it," said Sharley in relief. "Now, what were we saying?"

"I was telling you that you're still on the Plain of Desolation," said Pious. "And the sooner we start searching for the way out, the better."

"Well, we can't move on from here," said Sharley. "Dad'll come soon to take us home."

"No, he won't, I'm afraid," said Pious. "Magic bridges never end in the same place twice. It'll have disappeared as soon as we crossed, you see, and when your dad calls it back, it'll take him to a completely different part of the plain."

"Oh, great!" said Sharley. "So we're back to square one."

"Precisely," Pious agreed. "You're lost; your father doesn't know where you are; you don't know where the exit from the plain is; and you all have about as much chance of surviving as a snowball in a furnace."

"Thanks," said Sharley, understanding that they were well and truly back in trouble. "But if this really is the Plain of Desolation, why does it look so different?"

They looked around them apprehensively and saw a land of villages and towns under a full moon. They stood on top of a steep rise of pasture that swept down to a river and an intricate pattern of hedgerows and fields. Small woods and copses punctuated the open farmland with dark shadows under the subtle light of the moon, and in the distance stood a neat town with a castle at its center.

"It looks . . . pretty and ordinary," said Sharley at last. "Like parts of the Southern Riding. I would imagine it's almost inviting when the sun comes up."

"That's just it," said Pious quietly. "The sun never comes up. This is a magically conjured landscape; obviously some very powerful Adept has really got it in for you, and whoever it is, they've decided to set a little trap personally tailored for your good selves."

"I'm not sure I like the sound of that," said Kirimin with masterly understatement.

"Nor me," said Mekhmet.

"You're not meant to," said Pious in tired irritation. "I suspect that ghosts 'live' here and it's obviously going to be their job to kill you."

"Look, just a minute!" said Sharley in agitation. "What did you mean about an Adept setting a trap for us? What Adept, and why?"

"I don't know," Pious replied. "But to create a landscape like this, they've got to be hugely powerful."

"Yes, but why would they want to trap us?"

"Well, who knows? But obviously you've annoyed them at some point in the past."

"But we don't know any Adepts, apart from my dad and his witches!"

"Well, at least one knows you, and they seem to have a very low opinion of you," the imp answered forcefully.

"Is this really helping us?" asked Kirimin. "Adept or no Adept, let's just get going and try to find the tunnel or whatever it is that'll get us out of here."

An ice-cold wind sprang up and moaned around them like tormented souls in the lowest pit in hell. "Kiri's right," said

Mekhmet. "There's no point in trying to analyze anything in this place. Let's just get going."

This was greeted with a general murmur of agreement, and after the boys had untethered the horses, they all trotted on under the gibbous moon, while Sharley continued to worry about malevolent Adepts.

Within a few minutes they reached a small river that meandered across a valley floor. Nearby was a stone bridge that seemed to be decorated with carved skulls, but as they drew nearer, they realized they were real.

"Very nice!" said Kirimin shakily. "I don't think much of their taste in decor around here."

"No," Sharley agreed. "This Adept who's got it in for us certainly has a vivid and nasty imagination."

"The troll puts them there," said Pious conversationally. "Every time he kills whoever's stupid enough to try and cross his bridge."

"What troll?" asked Mekhmet. "I thought you said this place has only just been magically conjured."

"And so it has," the imp answered. "But bridges always have trolls when an Adept creates them. It's a sort of tradition."

"Like in 'The Three Billy Goats Gruff,' you mean," said Sharley.

"Well, yes, I do believe the mortal world has acknowledged this ancient fundamental truth of the Cosmos by encapsulating it within a *fairy tale*," Pious agreed disdainfully. "I suppose we can expect no better. However, none of this alters the fact that the troll will contest your passage over the bridge."

"Fine, we'll swim across," said Mekhmet. "It doesn't look very deep."

"You can't do that!" said Pious, squeaking in horror. "The water spirits'll get you, not to mention the flesh-eating frogs, slime fish, and drowned corpses!"

"Another tradition, I suppose?" asked Mekhmet.

"Absolutely."

"So how do we get across?" asked Sharley in a tone that suggested he didn't expect an easy answer.

"Well, *I'll* fly," said Pious. "Don't know what *you're* going to do."

"Oh, come on!" said Kirimin. "I'm getting annoyed now. If any troll thinks it can stop me, it's welcome to try!"

Seeing no option, the boys shrugged and, drawing their horses close in to their bristling companion, they set off across the bridge.

They'd just reached the halfway point when a flurry of churning water and a slithering thump announced the appearance of the troll. It was dripping wet and slimy, smelled of rotting fish, and filled the entire width of the bridge with its bulk. Kirimin stared at it with blazing amber eyes.

"Move!" she snapped angrily.

The troll roared, engulfing them in a smell like rancid farts, and all three retched and coughed. Even the horses blew in disgust. But then Kirimin stepped forward. Raising her paw, she brought it down with crushing force on the troll's head. The monster was driven to its knees, but sprang up almost immediately, only to be met by two flashing scimitars that quickly removed its arms and buried themselves in its chest. Kirimin then tore off its head and lodged it on a spike that had obviously been prepared for the skull of the troll's next victim.

"That's that problem solved," she said lightly. Trotting forward, she heaved the creature's body over the bridge and into the river. "Shall we proceed?"

"You can't do that!" Pious exploded. "There are rules and procedures!"

"Meaning the troll's supposed to kill *us* and put *our* heads on a spike, I suppose," said Mekhmet.

"Well, something like that, yes," said Pious. "I mean, it's nothing personal, it's just that trolls have a role to fulfill! It's the unnatural order of things; it's what happens!"

"Not anymore it isn't," said Kirimin briskly, and all three friends trotted over the bridge and on toward the distant town.

The imp watched them go in an agony of indecision. What should he do? He seemed to have become embroiled in a cell of revolutionaries! Then, quickly deciding that the mortals' actions were both refreshing and exciting, he hurried to follow them.

Thirrin was racked by excruciating fear and exquisite relief at one and the same time. Oskan had found the boys and Kirimin; he'd seen them, alive and well, but then he'd lost them after he'd fought off some evil . . . *thing* that seemed intent on killing them!

"You're sure they're safe now?" she asked for the umpteenth time as she paced their private quarters.

"Yes," Oskan answered patiently. "No magic, or magical being, can harm anyone once they're on a bridge. So at least we know they're safe."

"But now you can't find them because someone or something is masking them again?"

"That's right."

"It's Medea, isn't it?" she suddenly said, giving voice to a fear that had been with her since Sharley had first gone missing.

Oskan almost smiled as Thirrin's warrior-spirit refused to shy away from even that most terrible of situations. "Yes. I said she still hated us, and she hates Sharley more than anyone."

"But why?"

He shrugged. "I'm not sure. But if it wasn't so laughable, I might suggest jealousy."

"Jealousy! Of whom, or what?"

"Of Sharley."

"That's ridiculous!"

Oskan shrugged again and said nothing, knowing that Thirrin was adding the possibility of Medea's jealousy to the long list of guilts she already felt about her lost daughter. If Medea was jealous of Sharley, then there must be good reason for it. Perhaps she and Oskan had neglected her in favor of Sharley in some way. Perhaps they'd lavished too much time and affection on him after his illness when he'd almost died of polio. Well, maybe that was true, but it was a perfectly natural reaction on the part of any parent.

Then, in the deep recesses of her brain, an awful, unforgivable thought stirred. It just might be that Sharley was a much more lovable person than Medea had ever been, and even if he'd never been ill, perhaps she still would have loved him more than his dark, moody sister. For a moment she was shocked to silence by her own wicked thoughts, but then was forced to accept the undeniable and asked again the tired question that had just resurfaced.

"You're absolutely certain that Sharley and the others aren't in the Darkness?"

"Completely," Oskan answered with the air of one who'd answered the same question dozens of times.

Thirrin sighed in frustration and tried to ignore the panic that boiled just below the surface. Sharley might be a proven warrior who'd helped to save the Icemark, and who'd also fought on the southern borders of the disintegrating Polypontian Empire, but he was still her youngest child and, in her subconscious mind, would be forever the little boy who'd almost died of polio.

"Rescue them for me, Oskan," she whispered, suddenly unable to trust her voice.

"Thirrin, it's my most pressing priority," he answered, his anger threatening to spark again. "Don't you think they'd be here now, in this very room, if I could bring it about? Fathers fear for their children, too, you know!"

She nodded, acknowledging the obvious fact, but she remained unaware of another fear, which he had kept hidden deep under the cares and worries of the coming war and his missing child. Medea was much more powerful than she'd been in their last encounter. Obviously she'd passed the final test that had allowed her to stay in the Darkness, and now she was thriving and growing stronger by the day. He couldn't help feeling a sudden and unexpected pride for his hugely talented daughter. Her Gifts might have been dedicated to evil, but their power and potency was undeniable.

He decided not to tell Thirrin about Medea's growing strength. It was a situation she couldn't help with, and she had enough to do in the physical world without worrying about the Magical Realms. This psychic war was his alone, and he had no idea how it would end. Would the defeat of Medea and, ultimately, Cronus see a new Power sitting on the throne of the Darkness: a Power that the people of the Icemark would recognize and know all too well?

He suddenly felt a need for simple human contact. Walking over to where Thirrin stood in the window, he gathered her into a hug. Grishmak found them still locked in the embrace when he burst into the room several minutes later.

"Put him down, woman, you don't know where he's been!" he said, grinning hugely and revealing his enormous teeth.

"What is it, Grishy? Anything important?" she asked, still in Oskan's arms.

"Could be. The southern border guard has just sent a message by the werewolf relay saying that they have a Polypontian officer asking permission to enter the country."

"Oh yes? Who, exactly?"

Grishmak grinned again. "General Andronicus."

"What?" Thirrin barked, leaping out of Oskan's arms.

"I thought that might get your attention," laughed the Werewolf King. "He's got over two thousand cavalry with him, and he says he's just come from fighting Erinor herself."

Thirrin paced excitedly around the room. "He lost, then, as predicted."

"Yes, but he seems to have bloodied her nose, even though he only had a scratch force of garrison troops and veterans. Didn't have any artillery, either, by all accounts."

"He's giving information freely?"

"To whomever will listen. But he says he wants to see you as soon as possible."

"When can he get here?" Thirrin asked eagerly.

Grishmak frowned as he thought things through. "His horses are pretty well foundered, apparently. Seems to have ridden directly from the battlefield with hardly any rest. Even bypassed Romula itself, saying in the circumstances the capital's indefensible."

"Could be a week before he reaches Frostmarris, then."

"Judging by the way he's just thundered across the Polypontus, I'd give it four days. He'll probably rest his nags for twenty-four hours and then set off again."

Thirrin stopped. "Grishy, send a message via the relay. Tell Andronicus we'll meet him in Learton — that's halfway between here and the Dancing Maidens. You, Tharaman, and Krisafitsa can come with me. Oh, and tell Olympia and Ollie they're coming, too." She suddenly laughed in elation.

"At last we'll be able to talk to someone who's actually fought Erinor!"

Oskan watched as the two warriors then went into the minutiae of military planning and felt about as useful as a chocolate teapot. It was amazing the way Thirrin could snap from one mode to another; just seconds earlier she'd been a terrified mother afraid for her child. And now she was the strong leader of armies with no thought for anything but weaponry, troop movements, and supply. Or so it would seem to anyone who didn't know her; Oskan was very well aware that she'd simply learned to compartmentalize her problems; it was the only way she had even the vaguest chance of functioning on so many different levels.

Even so, he couldn't help feeling the smallest spark of contempt for the warrior mind; distract it even for a moment, and all other thoughts were forgotten or "compartmentalized." It was lucky for the Icemark—and even the world in general—that *he* had a brain that could cope with more than one thought at a time. But he supposed he couldn't expect too much from simple mortals. Their lives were so short and insignificant, it was wrong to expect them to be aware of *higher matters*. . . .

He checked himself in horror; where did these thoughts come from? He'd swung from needing the basic human contact of Thirrin's arms to a deep contempt for mortal frailty in a matter of moments. How did these thoughts find their way into his brain?

Not daring to seek an answer, he dragged his thoughts back to the present and coughed politely, hoping to attract Thirrin's attention. After a few minutes of being ignored, he said, "I'll just go and see if dinner's nearly ready, shall I?" He waited for a reply, but, getting none, he added, "Yes, fine. I'll do that, then."

And he walked away from the gathering of warriors, wrestling with a growing sense of anger and disdain.

Maggiore Totus slept peacefully in a shaft of sunlight that pooled over his desk and chair. He'd just finished reading through one of the illuminated manuscripts of his *History of the War Part II*, which had recently arrived from the scriptorium of the Holy Brothers on the Southern Continent. Of course his work had been available for scholarly study a matter of months after Bellorum and his sons had been defeated in their second attempt to add the Icemark to the Empire, but these were special editions, destined to grace the libraries of Thirrin's allies.

He'd been mightily pleased with the superb scrollwork along the borders of each of the volumes' vellum pages, and the illuminated capital letters that began every chapter were works of art in their own right, but it was the individual illustrations of major characters and battles that pleased him the most. The artists in the scriptorium had let their imaginations run wild, and both Grishmak and Tharaman-Thar were truly mountainous and horrifying creatures with enough teeth and claws to furnish an entire army of monsters.

Maggie was happily imagining their reactions to their portraits when he fell asleep with the ease only ever achieved by the very young and the deeply venerable. He snored now in happy oblivion as the world accumulated the new histories he would write in the future. The pool of light in which he slept deepened to a rich honey color as the sun sank toward the horizon, and he might have slumbered right through the night if Cressida hadn't suddenly hammered on his door and almost leaped into his room.

"How can you sleep, Maggie, when the country's heading for war?"

The old scholar snorted into shocked wakefulness and blinked owlishly at the Crown Princess. "One would need to be an insomniac if sleep were only allowed in the Icemark when it wasn't under threat of conflict."

"Ha! Very true, Maggie! Very true!" Cressida said with a grin, and grabbing a nearby chair, she slammed it down facing the old man and sat down heavily.

Of all the royal children, Maggiore thought, it was the Crown Princess who was the most like her mother and also like her grandfather Redrought. She was loud—not to say explosive—aggressive, argumentative, and yet at the same time loving, sensitive to the needs of others, and downright annoying. She also very rarely indulged in social visits, so, settling his spectoculums squarely on his nose, Maggie gazed at her inquiringly. "To what do I owe the pleasure of your presence?"

"Nothing!" she answered in breezy surprise. "Does there have to be a reason to visit my old tutor and friend?"

"Yes."

"You old cynic."

"Yes."

She looked sharply at him for a moment or two, then finally gave up. "Oh, all right! I'm just annoyed not to be going with everyone else to meet General Andronicus!"

"Hmmm?" Maggie said noncommittally.

"Well, I wanted to be there when we finally meet someone who's actually fought Erinor. I mean, I could be useful."

"Uh-huh."

"Yes. I've got one of the most militarily analytical brains in the High Command. All right, I know Mother and Ollie will be more than adequate in their debriefing techniques, but for a sharply incisive insight, you can't really do better than me."

"Umm."

"I know that Mother thinks it would do me good to hone my administrative skills and master the day-to-day running of the country's internal affairs, and the only real way to do that is in her absence, learning by my mistakes and all that. But even so, the arrival of Andronicus is a hugely important event, and I ought to be present."

"Ah."

"Oh yes, you might argue that I'll be able to read detailed reports, and that the man himself will be here in the capital in a week or so, anyway. But none of that will give me the sort of insight that a firsthand interview would reveal."

"Uh-huh."

"And it's no use saying that I'll probably be able to spend weeks talking with the man while we prepare our response to the threat posed by Erinor. The fact remains that I'll have lost the initial unsullied *freshness* of the first interview and debriefing."

"Aha."

"I mean, I suppose a really incisive and analytical mind might argue that I'm simply behaving like a spoiled brat who's disappointed because everyone else is going off on a treat while I have to stay in my room and do my homework. But I'd counter that argument by stating that such an opinion could only be expressed by a truly cynical and judgmental outlook."

"Hmmm."

"Look! I really believe in the validity of my arguments, and your attitude doesn't make me change my opinion one iota!"

"Umm."

"Oh, all right. Have it your own way!" she shouted. "But I still say I'm better suited than anyone else to debrief military personnel."

Maggie winced as the door slammed behind her. He sighed gently and reflected on the pitfalls of the overly analytical

165

mind, before pouring himself a sherry and leafing through the illuminated manuscripts again.

Cressida erupted into Eodred and Howler's room, making them both leap to their feet in shock.

"Hey, sis, have a little thought for my heart!" her brother said feelingly as he slumped back into a chair. "I thought it was Erinor and her Hordes."

"That insufferable man!"

"Who?" asked Howler. "Eodred?"

"No. Maggiore Totus! I've just spent a fraught few minutes explaining exactly why I should have gone with the party to meet Andronicus, and . . . and he . . ."

"And he what?" asked Eodred.

"Well, he . . . he disagreed with everything I said."

"That's unusual. He's normally politeness itself."

"Oh, he was *polite*," said Cressida, removing a mail-shirt and six pairs of dirty socks from one of the chairs and sitting down. "He just stonewalled everything I said."

"Are you sure?" asked Howler, who'd seen Cressida in what she believed to be conversation before.

"Of course I'm sure! He just sat there and . . . and looked *disbelieving*, no matter what I said."

"Right," said Howler, returning to the bone he'd been gnawing and putting his feet back up on the table.

"*You're* doing it now!" she almost wailed. "And take your feet down!"

"Sis," said Eodred calmly. "This is mine and Howler's room, and if we want to dance on the tables in hobnailed boots, we'll do so. Now calm down, sit down, and pipe down. And when you've done all that, have a drink of this sherbet. Mekhmet gave it to me before he disappeared. That's a point; I wonder what's happened to him and the snotling."

"Don't forget Kirimin," said Howler, crossing his feet comfortably on the table and wriggling his hugely clawed toes.

Cressida seethed silently for a few moments, her eyes almost bulging from their sockets. Then she let out a frustrated scream, leaped to her feet, and stormed through the door, slamming it behind her.

"I believe that's what's called a 'dramatic exit,'" said Howler, still gnawing the bone. "Have we got any salt?"

14

Cronus's dead black eyes regarded his granddaughter appraisingly. "I think the time has come, Medea, to test your Abilities."

"Test my Abilities? Don't you think they've been tested enough?" she asked as irritably as she dared.

"Frankly, no. Not if you are to retain your present lofty position within the Darkness," he replied as he sat back comfortably in Medea's great chair. Of course, his real reasons for wanting to push her powers to their absolute limit was one of simple appraisal. He needed to know where her strengths lay, and whether she was strong enough to be of use in the upcoming invasion of the Icemark.

"Then test away, Grandfather. Do your worst!" she said as she paced the skull-cobbled floor of the Great Hall. "I think you'll be pleasantly surprised."

"I do so hope you're right, Medea," he said as he secretly gathered the strength he needed. "How, for example, would you react to this?"

Suddenly the hall was filled with three giant Ice Demons, their wings clattering and battering at the air as they rolled and hopped along the floor toward her. Tusks burst from their mouths like splinters of rock, and a stench of blood and worse billowed around them in a thick and choking smog.

Medea stood her ground, and with a wave of her hand three Ice Demons of her own leaped into the world.

Immediately she seized control of their minds, and with a roar they charged the demons of Cronus. They met in a tangle of limbs and wings; a great bellowing filled the hall, and black blood splattered the ice-white ceilings in a fine tracery of gore.

Cronus applied his power, and his creatures surged forward in an explosion of unstoppable ferocity, tearing wings to tatters and wrenching limbs from sockets. Medea's demons were borne slowly back, their sharply clawed feet slipping in the welter of slimy blood as they scrabbled for grip.

Rejecting all idea of surrender, Medea sent a burst of homicidal hatred into her creatures. Now they fought back with insane power, ripping and gouging, smashing and tearing, until Ice Demon met Ice Demon in an immovable wall of fighting intensity. On and on they fought, their simple minds controlled by two of the most powerful Adepts in all Creation. Medea trembled and quaked with the effort of fighting her grandfather through the proxy of her demons, but Cronus, too, was feeling the strain. This was the first time he'd personally experienced her strength, and he was almost impressed.

With a final effort he sent a surge of power into his demons, which was translated into the tearing-off of heads and the disemboweling of all that remained. With a great roar of triumph, they trampled their enemies and swallowed huge slobbering mouthfuls of skin and bone, and then they turned on Medea.

Howling and snarling, they stalked slowly toward her, their eyes glittering with insane glee, saliva pouring unchecked from their mouths. But then, with an almost contemptuous wave of her hand, she set them alight and watched impassively as they shrieked in agony. When they were incinerated to ash, Medea restored the pristine brilliance of the Bone Fortress, removing blood and oily smoke damage from ceiling, floor, and walls, and restoring the shattered skulls of the cobbles to their former perfect domes.

Cronus sat in quiet contemplation for a moment, and then, standing, he set off toward the main doors, a nimbus of ice crystals eddying around him.

Medea watched him go and smiled triumphantly as his parting words reached her across the freezing air.

"Well done, my dear. I think we might be ready."

General Valerian Honorius Andronicus gazed ahead to the city of Learton. He could clearly see the reception committee of Queen Thirrin and her High Command waiting before the gates, and quite frankly he was fascinated. It was this woman and her alliance with talking beasts and monsters that had finally defeated and destroyed the Bellorum clan, arguably the greatest monsters the known world had ever produced. But the fact that he, Andronicus, had been an enemy of the late general and his sons, and that he'd bitterly opposed the war with the Icemark in the Senate, gave little comfort now as he approached this almost legendary woman and her hideous allies.

Behind him the two-thousand-strong regiment of cavalry clattered along in smart and disciplined lines, their fierce young faces glaring rigidly ahead, their thoughts and fears masked by their martial frowns. Andronicus's own misgivings were hidden behind his habitual half smile and ironically quirked eyebrow. Bellorum had favored an icy expression when dealing with friend and foe alike, and he'd thought his rival's open friendliness both weak and ineffectual. In fact, the two generals had differed on many points; unlike Bellorum, Andronicus firmly believed that exercise should be restricted to the young. As a result, he had what he termed a "comfortable" figure, but which his wife had fondly described as "fearsomely fat." However, as most of his belly was now encased and restrained in his smartly polished breastplate, he simply looked large and imposing.

The Polypontian cavalry drew closer to the city, and Andronicus could see the citizens milling around the road behind cordons hastily thrown up by the housecarls of the garrison. They were mainly silent as they watched the Imperial troopers draw closer, their emotions definitely mixed. The last time such uniforms had been seen in the Icemark they'd wrought havoc and mayhem and murder. And yet now here they were approaching their Queen as potential allies against a new threat from the south. In all reality, to the ordinary people of the Icemark, rumors of Erinor and her Hordes were so far in the distance that they hardly seemed a threat at all. Most of them were far more worried to see Imperial cavalry on their home soil again.

Andronicus was close enough now to make out details, and the Queen's red hair shone out like a beacon. But it was the stupendous sight of the Snow Leopard Thar and Tharina that held his gaze, as well as that of Grishmak the Werewolf King. As an opponent of the war against the Icemark, he'd never actually seen such creatures before, and even from a distance their presence was overpowering. But Andronicus wasn't the second-most famous Polypontian general for nothing, and he unconsciously straightened his spine as he approached. This challenge would be met with the same fortitude with which he'd fought his wars, both military and political.

Judging himself close enough, he held up his hand and the cavalry reined to a halt. A silence of an almost tangible quality now settled over the day. The people watched proceedings with suspicion, and the Imperial troopers frowned on all around them. Only Andronicus smiled gently, and after a few minutes of silently regarding the surprisingly slight figure of the Queen, he urged his horse forward.

Thirrin and her companions didn't stir, and the sharp clip-clop of Andronicus's horse's hooves on the flagstoned road jabbed small knives of sound deep into his ears. But then at last common sense prevailed; they were not enemies, they were not at war, and they shared a need to control a growing military disaster in the south. Why should he be nervous? Why should any of them be anything other than happy to be in each other's company? With this thought Andronicus relaxed, and his smile broadened into a genuine and warm greeting.

By this point his horse had reached a comfortable distance from the Queen and her party, and he drew to a halt. Andronicus then saluted and bowed in his saddle. He straightened up and gazed in wonder on the group before him.

"Your collective Majesties: Queen Thirrin, King Grishmak, Tharaman-Thar, Krisafitsa-Tharina, and Basilea Olympia, may I say it humbles a man to be in the presence of such living legends. It is truly my honor and pleasure to greet you."

"General Andronicus," Thirrin replied quietly. "I suppose I should say, 'Welcome to the Icemark.'"

Understanding her reluctance and reticence entirely, he smiled again and was just drawing breath to reply when his stomach rumbled as enormously as only an enormous stomach could, and housed as it was in the steel sounding chamber of a breastplate, the noise of it floated over the air and even reached the ears of the watching masses.

"There sits a hungry man," said Tharaman and chuckled.

Andronicus's eyes widened as he heard the refined voice emerging, incredibly, from the cavernous mouth of a wild beast, but he quickly recovered. "My apologies to one and all, but I've been on uncommonly short rations over the last few weeks, and I must say that I miss my tuck!"

"Nothing worse," Tharaman said sympathetically. "The only real drawback to campaigning, in my opinion."

"Precisely so," said the general, warming to the huge animal. "Do you know, I only had time for half a dozen eggs for breakfast and less than half a loaf."

"Nowhere near enough for active service!" said the Thar in outraged tones.

"We must get you fed, General," said Krisafitsa. "There's a feast of welcome prepared. There are just the formalities of greeting to complete and we can go in."

Andronicus bowed again. "Madam, I am forever in your debt."

"What about drink?" Grishmak asked. "If you like beer, we do a particularly fine brew from the Southern Riding."

"Nothing better than beer after a hard ride, in my opinion, and if rounded off with a bottle or two of a warming red wine, then all the miseries of this mortal life are relegated to their proper positions as mere irritations."

"Ha! A man after my own heart!" said Grishmak. "If you'll allow, I'll appoint myself as your guide through the many fine brews of the Icemark. You'll be surprised at the variety!"

"I will be the most willing of travelers," Andronicus replied and smiled again.

Thirrin watched her friends' tentative moves to establish a relationship with the Polypontian general, but found herself totally unable to do the same. How could she possibly even communicate with a man who represented the very nation that had tried to destroy her land twice, the very nation that had killed her father and son and countless thousands of citizens of the Icemark? Let none have any illusions here; the only reason Andronicus was sitting before them on his horse at all was that the Polypontus was in dire and desperate straits. If the circumstances had been different, he might even have been leading yet another invasion against them! She looked now at his laughing face and saw only an enemy.

But then, deep in the recesses of her mind, a small voice started to speak: *The only reason* you *ever made an alliance with the Wolf-folk and the Snow Leopards was because the Icemark was in dire and desperate straits! And yet look at what friendships have grown from an alliance of need. Could the Icemark even function now without the Wolf-folk? Would your life be complete without Tharaman, Krisafitsa, and Grishmak? An alliance of mutual convenience can grow into something far more powerful . . . given the chance.*

Thirrin nodded to herself, then shrugged. There were times when bravery and daring were needed in the field of diplomacy even more than on the battlefield. Taking a deep, steadying breath, she made a decision, cleared her throat, and said, "General Andronicus, the cooks of the Icemark produce a pie that meets with the approval even of Tharaman-Thar and his staunch eating companion, Olememnon, consort of the Hypolitan Basilea. The opinion of a man of your gastronomic standing would be greatly appreciated by the kitchen staff."

Andronicus was immediately aware that Thirrin had fought and won a monumental battle with her understandable prejudices, and he smiled warmly. "Ma'am, nothing would give me greater honor than to judge a pie that has such credentials of recommendation."

Thirrin tried a small smile in return. "Then let us go in and sample the feast that has been prepared."

The Great Hall of Learton's citadel had been scrubbed and polished for this first meeting between Thirrin and the most

important Polypontian soldier to enter the Icemark since
Bellorum himself. The city had been rebuilt by Archimedo
Archimedes after it was flattened by the bombs of the Sky
Navy, and it was now a marvel of design and detail, or so
Archimedes insisted.

The hall was crammed with tables, at which sat the
Polypontian cavalry and the werewolf and housecarl garrison of the city. But instead of the boisterous roaring and
gaggle of laughing, shouting voices that usually accompanied a feast, there was only a low-key buzz, like a hive of
depressed bees.

At the top table Thirrin looked out over the hall and
watched nervously for trouble. None of the garrison had
wanted to share a table with the Polypontian troopers, but
in the interests of trying to integrate the factions she'd
insisted that the seating plan placed every Imperial soldier
between a housecarl and werewolf. This meant that at each
table there were about thirty Polypontians to sixty garrison
soldiers. She admitted to herself that it couldn't have been
comfortable for the "guests," but thought it might be a useful lesson for them to find out what it felt like to be heavily
outnumbered.

Andronicus faced a similar ratio on the top table, but he
didn't seem to mind at all, and spent most of his time telling Tharaman, Ollie, and Grishmak dirty jokes while they
waited for the food to be brought in. Occasionally he would
remember the presence of what he termed "the ladies" in the
form of Thirrin, Krisafitsa, and Olympia, and then he'd chat
charmingly and interestingly about the Polypontus while he
tried to ignore the cavernous roars and thundering rumbles
of his huge belly.

At last the procession of the food began, with chamberlains
and servants being escorted through the hall by a marching party of musicians. But the usual uproarious greeting

for the roast boar, sides of beef, and shield-sized pies was missing, and on one of the further tables a housecarl, an Imperial trooper, and a werewolf began a furtive fight that was quickly quashed by Grinelda Blood-tooth and her fellow Royal Bodyguards of Ukpik Wolf-folk. She was kept busy throughout the entire time of the feast, and the silent and swiftly descending phalanx of white-pelted Ukpiks became a common sight as they broke up fight after fight throughout the hall.

Thirrin sighed tiredly. She'd known the first so-called peaceful contact between Polypontian and allied troops would be difficult, but she'd hoped it would be easier than this. Andronicus caught her mood and immediately leaned across to talk to her. "I wouldn't let it worry you too much. See it as the dynamic resolution of old scores. I'd be far more worried if nothing had happened. If a soldier goes quiet when in the presence of a former enemy, then there's cold murder in his heart. Here there's just hot anger. They'll settle down."

"If we're ever to stop Erinor, they'll need to," she answered. "An alliance of enemies will never work." Her own words seemed to surprise her, and she fell silent as she thought things through. "That's right, Andronicus. An alliance of enemies will never work. We've got to use the hatred or we're lost."

The general nodded. "Undoubtedly. The Hordes, I believe, can be defeated, but their power and ferocity is such that it would take a completely united front to do it. Erinor's strength stems entirely from her ability to unite the different tribal factions of her mountain people, something that had never been done and which, before her, had seemed impossible. To fight her effectively, we, too, have got to achieve the impossible."

Thirrin nodded, and then, with a sigh, she suddenly stood up. Down in the main body of the hall, Grinelda Blood-tooth immediately noticed her mistress and commander waiting quietly, and she raised her mighty voice over the murmur and hissing of the discontented soldiery. "Give silence for Queen Thirrin Freer Strong-in-the-Arm Lindenshield, Wildcat of the North. Shut your feckless noise and listen!"

Thirrin waited until the last mumble had dwindled to silence, and then she drew breath. "I have decided to be honest with you all. I have decided to cast aside the usual restrictions of diplomacy and high politics and talk to you in the language of the everyday and say exactly what I mean. Some of what I say will probably make you angry, but I think in your hearts you'll agree with me, and so together we'll be able to confront our true feelings and use them to make something . . . new. Possibly something great."

She paused and took a sip of wine before looking up and continuing. "We hate each other. We hate each other for good reason. Thousands have died on both sides in the wars between our peoples. You Imperial soldiers probably hate me more than anything else you've ever encountered, and I can assure all here present that I cordially hate you with every fiber of this body that has killed countless numbers of your comrades." Her voice dropped into the cavernous well of silence that yawned over the Great Hall. "So what do we do about that? Anything? Nothing? Do we continue to loathe each other, and every now and then draw blood again to satisfy the detestation that fills us to the very brim? Perhaps. I must admit it doesn't seem a bad proposition to me; I'd quite enjoy killing a few more Polypontian soldiers every couple of years or so." A laugh rose up from the housecarls and werewolves, but she raised her hand and the charged silence returned.

"What a glorious feud that would be; it would keep our respective armies occupied for years. I suspect we'd both secretly enjoy it. But I'm afraid we can't allow ourselves that luxury. As much as it horrifies both of us, we're just going to have to give all that up and at least try to reach an agreement. The Polypontus is on its knees; it's dying, and Basilea Erinor and her Hordes are the ones who are doing the killing, not the Icemark and her allies." She folded her arms and gazed out at the faces that were all turned to watch her.

"So, why should I care about that? Why should I give a moldy fig if what remains of the Empire collapsed tomorrow? Well, I'll tell you: I *don't* care; I *don't* give a moldy fig. I'd happily sit back and watch you all drown in your own blood if I could. But the fact remains that Erinor wouldn't stop at your borders; she'd cross into mine, and she's let it be known that she believes the Hypolitan, who have been part of our country for hundreds of years, are what she calls traitors. She's determined to destroy them and along with them the Royal House of Lindenshield and anyone else who has even the tiniest drop of Hypolitan blood in their veins. Well, I can tell you that over the years there are precious few in our land who can't count the Hypolitan somewhere in their ancestry. So what choice do we have? What choice do *you* have?"

She paused and listened to the beat of her own pulse booming into the silence of her ears. "Well, the answer's obvious, isn't it? We don't have any choice at all. As much as we hate to admit it, we need each other. I and my soldiers know from personal experience, and you Polypontians know it, too, that alliances with even those who've been the bitterest enemies can stand against the most overwhelming odds and win. Scipio Bellorum and his appalling sons found this to be true and countless thousands of your comrades. No one can stand alone against Erinor, but neither can anyone forget the sort of hatred that we have for each other. So don't let's even *try* to forget it. Let's use it as a power and energy against the Hordes, let's convert it to a rivalry where we both try to outdo each other in the fighting against Erinor, let's agree to wait for a more . . . convenient time when we'll be able to smash the hell out of each other again and be happy to do it.

"Soldiers of the Alliance and the Polypontus, all of us have a fine and proud tradition of glorious warfare; let us bring these two traditions together and make one unstoppable power that will sweep Erinor and her Hordes back to their mountain hovels! From detestation let positive rivalry evolve; from hatred let there come energy; from loathing let there grow strength! And—who knows—perhaps somewhere in this coming war, we may find an ability to respect each other. We may even find that there's something to like!"

Her voice rang out into the silent hall long after she'd finished speaking, like the resonance of a struck bell. No one said a word, not one voice was raised in agreement or disagreement, nobody even moved. Then the thunderous sound of a drinking flagon being dragged across a table as a werewolf soldier raised his beer to his lips echoed around the hall, and a babble of voices broke out as Thirrin's words, and all they implied, were discussed.

Andronicus leaned forward and said quietly, "I've never heard a braver speech, not even in the Senate. You've made them all think, and at least it's stopped them fighting . . . for now."

Thirrin nodded unsmilingly. She was completely aware of the bravery of her words; she just wished she could believe them. In all reality, how could she possibly make an alliance with an empire that'd killed her father, her son, and countless thousands of her people?

Erinor sat in her yurt waiting quietly. She'd already arranged herself on the largest chair she possessed so that she looked formidable, and she drew her sword and laid it across her knees. After a few moments the sound of approaching footsteps was followed by the challenge of the guard. The entrance flap to the yurt was then respectfully drawn aside, and Alexandros, her consort, was escorted into the Presence. He sank to his knees and waited, head bowed.

"Leave us," Erinor said, and the guards withdrew. She then allowed the silence to extend into deep discomfort before she finally said, "Your Shock Troops were broken in the battle."

Alexandros bowed until his forehead touched the carpet before his wife's feet. "Your Highness, I can offer no excuse save the brilliance of Andronicus's tactics."

"His soldiers are better than yours?"

"His luck on the day was better."

Erinor nodded slowly. "Two in every ten of your men will be executed as an example."

Alexandros sat back on his heels and looked at her. "Madam, as you are fully aware, we reformed despite great pressure from the enemy and charged the Polypontian pike regiments that were doing so much damage to your phalanx of Tri-Horns. Without us, all could have been lost."

Erinor's pupils contracted to pinpricks of rage. "Do you dare to suggest that mere *men* turned the tide of battle?"

"The fortune of battle lies purely with the Goddess, and it was her hand that guided us to outflank the enemy and break their formation. We were as pawns in her divine game of chance. But had we not been to hand your—"

"Blasphemy!" his wife exploded. "How dare you claim to know the mind of the Goddess?"

"Madam, no blasphemy is intended and none can be seen in the undeniable fact that the Shock Troops broke the enemy line when the struggle hung in the balance. To reward such bravery and fighting prowess with death seems harsh," Alexandros answered quietly.

Erinor glowered over him for fully five minutes before she seemed to relax, focusing on the middle distance while she thought. "Because of their bravery only one in ten of the Shock Troops will be executed," she finally said. "And the rest will receive double rations of wine and beer."

Alexandros recognized that he could hope for nothing better, and bowing to the floor, he said, "Your Majesty is both just and generous."

Erinor nodded in agreement. "I'm ready to eat. You will join me."

Kirimin looked up at the castle that rose above the streets of the town on a low hill. Its walls and most of the houses that surrounded it were ruined, with gaping roofs and black windows like the empty eye sockets of staring skulls.

"Well, I suppose it might be worth searching it for a tunnel," she said to the boys, nodding toward the castle. "But it really is like looking for a shadow in a dark room."

Sharley nodded. "Even so, we have to try somewhere, as hopeless as it seems. We can't just rely on Dad finding us again."

"We could split up and search different areas of the town," said Mekhmet. "That way we'll cover three times as much ground."

A Zombie suddenly appeared from a dark alleyway and lurched by, leaving behind it a trail of oozing flesh. Kirimin flattened her ears in disgust. "I for one refuse to search anywhere on my own. If one of those things came anywhere near me, I'd have to wash for a week. At least the ghosts are clean."

"Kiri's right," Sharley agreed. "If we go off separately, we're bound to get into trouble. It's best to stay together."

They found the path that wound up to the main gate and climbed it; it was quite steep and obviously not designed with horses in mind, but both Suleiman and Jaspat managed it after a bit of a scramble. The gates, when they reached them, were hanging at crazy angles on their rusted hinges, and it was simplicity itself to squeeze through and into the courtyard. The moon, as usual, was full, and the cobbles stretched before them drenched with silver light, like the bed of a wide pool awash with crystal water.

"Everything looks so beautiful in moonlight," said Kirimin in a wistful voice.

"That's the time to be wary," said Pious, flapping around her head. "Landscapes that have been created by Adepts are never beautiful, not unless they're trying to lure you in and trap you!"

"Oh, shut up, you pessimistic little windbag!" Kirimin snapped. "Let me enjoy something in this awful place for once!"

"All right, be my guest, but don't say I didn't warn you."

Almost on cue, an icy wind whipped across the courtyard, bringing with it a tumble of mad and menacing laughter.

"Now what?" said Mekhmet wearily. "Do you think we'll ever have a day when nothing out of the ordinary happens?"

By this time the wind had whipped up a whirling maelstrom of debris from the courtyard, and strange wispy white shadows, like ragged banks of mist, began to form.

"Ghosts, then," said Sharley in matter-of-fact tones. "That's a pity; scimitars and claws don't really have an effect on spirits."

"Well, hopefully they won't be able to have any physical effect on us," said Mekhmet. "Their only weapon is fear, after all."

"That's enough, isn't it?" said Kiri, shuddering as she watched the wraiths slowly gathering form from the air around them.

"Who informed you that specters are solely reliant upon fear as a means of inflicting harm?" asked Pious incredulously, settling to hang like a large leathery jewel from one of Kirimin's ears. "If they make their bodies from the debris around them when they materialize, they can do a lot of damage. I once watched a ghost manifest in a room full of broken glass, and nobody got out of there without losing a few pints of blood, at the very least."

"You're such an enormous comfort in times of stress," said Kirimin as she shook her head and sent the imp flying through the air. "Have you ever considered counseling the distressed and suicidal? You'd soon reduce their numbers."

"Stop moaning, you overgrown kitty," said Pious. "Without me you'd have been dead long ago!"

Kirimin didn't bother to answer; she was too busy watching the wraiths as they gathered their bodies from the world around them. Unfortunately for the three friends, they'd decided to manifest in what looked like an old blacksmith's workshop, and soon seven gigantic forms appeared, made up of jagged shards of broken metal, pieces of chain, and glitteringly sharp tools. One seemed to be made almost entirely of different-sized files, ranging from truly gigantic rasps, used to smooth horseshoes onto hooves, to delicate, bladelike instruments that wouldn't have looked amiss in a jeweler's shop.

"Oh, great!" said Mekhmet. "Terrifying *and* more dangerous than an entire squadron of Imperial cavalry. Just what we need."

"Well, it's no good sitting here and talking about it. They've got physical bodies now. Let's do something!" said Sharley. Drawing his scimitar, he charged.

Mekhmet watched openmouthed as Suleiman leaped forward, then, gathering his wits, he, too, drew his sword and galloped into the attack.

Kirimin flattened her ears in fear and anger. "Oh, for the love of the Great Creator," she snarled. "How stupid! How typically male!" And roaring out a challenge, she joined in the assault.

Sparks flew as the boys struck at the wraiths with their scimitars. But encased in iron and steel as they were, the ghosts were impregnable. Kirimin beat at them with her huge, clawed paws, but only succeeded in gashing her flesh on their shells of broken metal. Quickly the friends drew back and turned for the gate. Strategic withdrawal was no disgrace, and at the present time they had no answer for the ghosts' armor. But it was too late. Their retreat was cut off by two of the phantoms standing directly in the gateway.

"Things are definitely not looking bright," said Mekhmet as they retreated to the middle of the courtyard.

"No," Sharley agreed, trying to sound far braver than he felt. "In fact I think this could very well be it. There's nothing we can do against armored ghosts."

Kirimin licked her cut paw and squinted at the wraiths that were howling and screaming in the shadows. "Why don't they just attack and get it over with?"

"I don't know. Perhaps they're just taunting us," said Mekhmet. "You know, like cat and mouse, with us definitely in the role of the rodents."

The ghostly screeching rose to a higher pitch, and the friends turned to one another and hugged. This was it. This was the end. They'd never get back to see friends and family, they'd never get back to their own world where everything was so ordinary and . . . and *real*. They closed their eyes and waited in silence.

But then the screeching took on a different quality; it sounded less murderous and more uncertain, as though the ghosts weren't so sure they could kill them anymore.

After a few minutes Sharley risked opening his eyes, and there before them stood the figure of a man. He was elegantly dressed, and his posture seemed to suggest he was almost bored.

"Oh, *please*! I mean, how clichéd. It's a wonder you're not wearing white sheets and going 'wooo'!"

The ghosts raged back at him in what was obviously a language of some sort, because the man finally stopped inspecting his nails and looked up to answer. "Do you know, as surprising as it may seem, I really don't care if it's your job to kill mortals. You're not killing these."

The wraiths advanced menacingly on him, and the change in the elegant figure was startling and instantaneous. He snapped upright, bristling with fury, and his lips drew back in a ferocious hiss that revealed long white fangs. "One step nearer and I'll rip your ectoplasmic bodies to shreds and freeze your pathetic souls!" His voice barely rose above a vicious whisper, but it echoed around the courtyard and the ghosts retreated.

Again the screeching rose and fell in the semblance of a language, and eventually the man said, "Well, exactly who has sent you on this 'mission'?" A pause, and then: "As you wish. It's of no importance, anyway. If the devil himself had ordered their deaths, I still wouldn't let you kill them!"

This seemed to decide something for the ghosts, and they suddenly rushed the man, their ironclad bodies clanking and clashing like an earthquake in a saucepan factory. As one they converged on the lonely figure, and he disappeared under a tangle of ironmongery. But then, with a sudden eruption of rusting metal, the seven ghosts flew through the air and landed in a clanging, banging heap on the far side of the courtyard. The man now advanced with a slow, stalking stealth like a hunting cat, his lips drawn back over glittering fangs and his eyes aflame with rage.

With a gesture both elegant and powerful, he pointed at the heap and a great howl rose up until a bright point of light hung shimmering in the air above it. For a moment it scintillated, and then fell with a brittle chink onto the stones of the courtyard.

"Your choice has been made; you attacked and I have punished. Now, who else will surrender their soul to my wrath?"

Six ragged skeins of mist rose up from the broken metal and fled screaming, their voices diminishing to a distant echo and then finally silence. The man stooped, picked up the tiny shred of light, and placed it in his pocket, as though he'd found a coin. Then he turned and regarded the boys and Kirimin, who'd witnessed it all.

Sharley and Mekhmet still held their scimitars, but something told them to remain still and offer no challenge. "Who are you?" asked Sharley curtly.

"Someone who has just saved your life, young man," came the reply, and the man walked over to stand before them with indolent ease. "A little gratitude might not go amiss."

"Then have our thanks, and willingly given," Sharley answered. "Please excuse us if we seem overly suspicious, but I'm sure you'll appreciate our caution while traveling in this particular place. You, er . . . you appear to be a Vampire."

The man smiled, revealing his glittering fangs. "Not anymore, technically speaking. You see, I'm the *ghost* of a Vampire."

"But Vampires don't have ghosts," said Kirimin. "Everybody knows that."

"Well, I am the exception to that general rule," the man answered.

"But how? And why?" asked Sharley in confusion.

"It's quite simple really," the man said, folding his arms and shifting his weight to one hip so that he looked exactly like some of the statues Sharley had seen in Venezzia. "At the end of my long physical . . . *existence*, I learned to feel compassion, and friendship—and also, most important, I developed the capacity to love. And as these qualities are

186

the very things that are the building blocks of the spirit, I found that I had developed a soul."

"Who did you love?" asked Kirimin, her romantic nature moved by the idea.

"Ah, that answer is simply given, but would take an age to explain. Suffice it to say that she made the aching burden of Vampiric existence as light as the touch of moonlight; she filled the darkness with the radiance of her beauty, and she gave the formless eons a shape and purpose."

Kirimin sighed. "Does she have a name?"

The man frowned. "I'm afraid we both lost our names down the long ages of the epochs we spent together. But she does have a title." He paused, consciously raising the dramatic effect, then finally said, "She is known as Her Vampiric Majesty, and she is now the sole ruler of The-Land-of-the-Ghosts."

"Then you must be the Vampire King!" said Sharley.

His Vampiric Majesty smiled and bowed. "The very same."

"But you were destroyed in the war against the Empire," said Sharley, trying not to let his jaw drop in amazement.

"Indeed I was," the king conceded.

"Didn't Bellorum destroy you?" asked Mekhmet.

"Definitely not!" snapped the king. "The weapon that ended my long rule was nothing other than treachery, wielded by that loathsome dog. I'd defeated him in fair contest, using only rapier and dagger, and never once resorting to my supernatural powers. He lay at my feet bleeding from the many wounds I'd inflicted. And then, when he raised his hand, I gave quarter, as a gentleman must, and prepared to grant him his final wish before performing the coup de grâce. It was then that the treacherous worm ordered in over a hundred musketeers."

"But lead shot wouldn't have killed you," said Sharley.

"Indeed not," the king agreed. "But each musket was loaded with wooden bullets, and my physical existence was ended there and then."

"I see," said Sharley as he absorbed the information. Then, remembering the needs of the moment, he went on: "But to get back to our present situation, what I don't understand is why you decided to help us against the ghosts just now."

"Quite simple, young Lindenshield," said the king with a small bow. "I rescued you in deference to your mother. Queen Thirrin became a friend despite many long years of enmity between the Icemark and The-Land-of-the-Ghosts. For a mortal, she was, and is, truly great, and had the greatness of spirit to offer friendship even above the demands of treaty and alliance. When you meet again, remember me to her."

"You don't know how we can get back to the physical world, do you?" Kirimin suddenly blurted. "I just thought that as you're a ghost, you might know where the tunnels are."

"Alas, no, Princess Kirimin," said His Vampiric Majesty. "The location of the gateways between the worlds never remains constant. A tunnel to the mortal realms this week may become a simple network of caves the next."

"Oh well, I just thought I'd ask," she said quietly.

The Vampire King smiled sadly, then turned back to Sharley. "And now I would ask a favor of you."

"Of me?"

"Yes, when you return to the Physical Realms, I would deem it the greatest of favors if you would go to the Blood Palace and seek audience with Her Vampiric Majesty. Tell her . . ." He paused as sadness gathered in his features. "Tell her that I exist still, and that if she, too, learns compassion and love, then we will meet again, once she has laid down the terrible burden of her physical continuance."

"I will," said Sharley simply.

"I have been watching her almost nightly, but of course she can't see me, and even when I kiss her, she merely feels a gentle draft across her lips." The Vampire King shook his head sadly, then, seeming to recollect where he was, he bowed with an elegant flourish, and after blowing them all a kiss with his exquisitely gloved hand, he slowly faded away. "Remember," his voice echoed on the air. "Remember."

Kirimin sighed again. "How beautiful."

"What is?" asked Mekhmet.

"That their love should have survived for so many centuries and still live on even after death."

"Oh, that . . . Yes, I suppose it is beautiful. Perhaps the sages are right; nothing is ever completely evil. Even the worst of us have a spark of good somewhere within us."

"I could think of a few exceptions," said Sharley.

A sudden flapping of wings interrupted their thoughts. "It seems that mortals enjoy a surfeit of good luck!" said Pious as he circled above them. "You were in deep trouble before that Vampire arrived. Those ghosts would've reduced you to gooey jam!"

"Oh, shut up," snapped Mekhmet. "Why don't you just flap off somewhere and leave us in peace?"

Kirimin and Sharley both agreed loudly with this, and the imp spiraled away. "I know when I'm not wanted!" he called as he flew off.

"Some power's obviously working against me, and this time I don't think it's the Witchfather," Medea said to Orla as she swept off to her great chair to think.

The old witch said nothing and waited in silence for her mistress to go on.

"It could, of course, be something higher; in fact, it could be something far higher. But if she's getting involved, why doesn't she just perform a minor miracle and transport them back home?"

"The actions of the Goddess are always a mystery," Orla said quietly.

Medea nodded in weary agreement. "Though there's always the possibility that we're all being put through some sort of tedious 'learning process.'" She slammed her hands down on the arms of her chair-that-was-almost-a-throne. "She's so pathetic! Grandfather's completely right to reject her. When he finally begins his war against her, he can count on my support!"

Orla nodded, then, hoping to distract Medea from her worries, she asked, "Would the mistress perhaps like a little wine?"

"No, the mistress would not!" Medea snapped in reply. "The only vintage that would satisfy my thirst would be about eight pints tapped from the veins of Charlemagne Weak-in-the-Leg Lindenshield!"

15

Cressida climbed the tightly winding corkscrew of the spiral staircase and finally emerged on the wind-blasted pinnacle of the highest lookout tower in the citadel. Being in strict battle-training, she wasn't breathless at all despite the hard climb, and she quickly looked around her and smiled when she saw her father.

"Couldn't we have met over a mug of mulled wine in a quiet parlor somewhere?" she asked ironically as an icy gust of wind howled through the tower's battlements.

"This is more private," Oskan answered. "There are things I want to discuss, and I don't want them generally known."

Cressida secretly wondered who'd be foolish enough to spy on the Witchfather but said nothing. Instead she climbed onto the viewing platform and looked out over the Plain of Frostmarris toward the Great Forest, a distant haze of autumnal golds and reds.

"Fine. What do you want to talk about?" she asked in a characteristically direct manner that made Oskan smile despite the grimness of the situation.

"I need your help in the Magical Plains," her father went on, deciding to adopt his daughter's directness.

She swung around in amazement. "You need my help in matters supernatural? But why?"

Oskan sat down on the edge of the viewing platform and patted the cold stone next to him, as though inviting his daughter to sit on a comfortable cushion. Cressida joined him and waited patiently for an explanation.

Her father rested his elbows on his knees and gazed sightlessly ahead. "You've never actually been told this before, Cressida, but you have a powerful magical talent."

"*Me*, magical?" she said incredulously.

"Yes; in fact, in your own way, you're almost as powerful as Medea is."

She wasn't surprised to hear Oskan refer to her sister in the present tense. Somehow she'd known she wasn't dead, and keeping her ears open over the last few weeks had confirmed it. Her mother and father were constantly having hurried and hushed conversations that stopped abruptly whenever anyone walked into the room, but the name Medea had hung in the air like a storm cloud.

"Exactly how am I as powerful as that vixen?" Cressida finally asked.

"You know she's alive, then?"

"Of course," she answered. "You don't get rid of a nasty stain on the family's fabric like Medea that easily. But you still haven't told me; how am I as powerful as her?"

"*Almost* as powerful," Oskan corrected. "But still, your Gift could withstand anything she sent against you."

"Look, are you going to tell me or not?"

He smiled at her impatience. "You're immune to magic."

"Oh, so I can't blast the witch to death, then?"

"No, I'm afraid not. Your Gift is completely passive; you can't actually 'use' it as such; it just is."

"Well, what's the use of that? If I'm going to be magical, I'd sooner have something I can actively use, like . . . like . . .

oh, I don't know . . . the ability to incinerate enemies, or call a storm . . . something like that."

"I know you would," Oskan replied, feeling a huge upwelling of pride for his warrior-daughter. "But the Gift you have is enormously useful and powerful. Nobody can harm you magically; not even Cronus himself could blast you. If an Adept conjured a weapon into existence, it couldn't be used against you; they couldn't even lay a magical trap for you or lead you astray. Don't you see? The ramifications are enormous!"

"Yeah, but they could still kill me with a real weapon; I could still be ambushed using conventional methods, couldn't I?"

"Well, yes," Oskan agreed. "But you could walk through any part of the Magical Realms and not be harmed by anything other than physical means. In fact, you could even walk through the Darkness itself and come out completely unscathed by evil magic, and that's what I want to talk to you about. . . ."

"The Darkness?"

"Yes. I need you to lead a unit of handpicked werewolves and housecarls to hold off the Ice Demons while I . . . confront Medea."

"Ha, now *they* could do me damage," she said, referring to the Ice Demons, which all mortals knew about, especially as they'd peopled ghost stories and nightmares since their earliest childhoods. "They're as physical as a lump of granite smashed on the back of your head."

"Exactly," Oskan agreed. "And I need your fighting expertise to keep them at bay while I attack your beloved sister."

"Is this so that you can rescue Sharley and the others?"

"Yes. If I can injure her enough to break her hold over them, it'll be a simple matter of transporting them back home."

"I see," said Cressida with quiet relish. "When do we go?"

Her father smiled and squeezed her hand. "One thing. Your mother mustn't know about this. She has no magical

Gifts, and she's got enough to worry about with Erinor. I want to go in, rescue Sharley, and get out again without her knowing a thing."

"Agreed," said Cressida.

Over the next few minutes they discussed the logistics of their upcoming raid and finalized the details. Then, with her characteristic energy, the Crown Princess suddenly stood, kissed him on the cheek, and rushed off to begin putting her plans into action.

Oskan watched her go and sighed gently; her fire and tough tenderness reminded him so much of her mother. In fact, there were many strong warriors in his family and all of them were an odd combination of disciplined violence and deeply loving gentleness; Sharley and Eodred, too. How could he ever leave such a fascinating, adorable, contradictory rabble? How could he bring himself to risk losing them forever?

"Because if you don't, you will lose them, anyway, and everything else you've ever known and loved."

Oskan looked up and wasn't particularly surprised to see that he'd been joined once again by the Goddess's Messenger.

"That hardly represents a choice," the Witchfather said quietly. "Use the weapon against Cronus and destroy yourself in the process, or don't use it and risk seeing the world and all you've ever loved falling into ruin."

The Messenger smiled gently. "Even obvious decisions are sometimes difficult to make."

"Why is it so obvious?" Oskan asked with sudden steel. "The only real certainty is that I will definitely die if I use this weapon—but if I don't, there's still hope that Cronus will ultimately be defeated, and all of the destruction and chaos he inflicts on the world can be somehow . . . cleared away and repaired."

The Messenger shook her head sadly. "There is no physi-cal or psychic power that can stand against him. He is the channel and conduit of all the corrupt energy that exists in the entire realm of the Darkness. What chance would any have against him?"

"None," Oskan agreed. "Unless they, too, used the Power of the Dark."

The next day Olememnon and Basilea Olympia reviewed the army. Drawn up in their regiments and squadrons across the Plain of Frostmarris, the warriors looked truly formidable. Werewolves, Snow Leopards, and human beings stretched into the distance, and the variously colored banners fluttered and snapped bravely in the freezing breeze.

The dual heads of Hypolitan society stood on a specially constructed podium, and with an imperious nod from the Basilea the army began to march past. This was in fact only a dress rehearsal for the parade that would take place in a few days' time, when the army would march off to the inva-sion of the Polypontus. Haste was needed if they were going to be ready before the heavy snows of the winter fell and blocked the passes into the lands of the Empire. Once south of the Dancing Maidens they should be safe from the more extreme weather, and even though there'd undoubtedly be snow, it wouldn't fall in the blinding, blood-freezing bliz-zards of the Icemark. It would even be possible to fight and march in the depths of the Polypontian winter, and the far-ther south they got, the snows would probably change to rain. This in itself would bring its own problems with mud and impassable roads, but at least there'd be no danger of freezing to death.

As a result, training and preparations for the war had been accelerated to a greater level than was normal, but Thirrin had demanded that no corners be cut, and she'd even insisted that the traditional parade of the army should take place so that the citizens of the Icemark could have a sense of participation in the coming offensive. So it was that the dress rehearsal for the parade had also been scheduled, even if the Queen did show a reluctance to take part in it herself. In fact, both the Basilea and her consort were only "taking the salute" as stand-ins for Thirrin and Cressida, who were the real commanders in chief of the allied force.

Olympia couldn't help but marvel at the ironic turn events had taken. If anyone had told her only a year ago that an army of humans, werewolves, and Snow Leopards would be preparing to march into Imperial lands in an attempt to defend what remained of the Empire from marauding Hordes, she'd have laughed. And yet here she was, nodding at the salutes of generals and commanders as section after section of the army marched by. And strangest of all was the fact that Polypontian units were included in that relieving force. In the last few weeks, the Imperial sections of the allied army had swelled significantly, as more and more of the Polypontian armed forces had fled into exile to regroup and prepare to strike back at Erinor.

General Andronicus had become something of an icon to the "Free Imperial Army," as they called themselves, and he rode by now at the head of over twenty thousand cavalry, thirty thousand pikemen, and fifteen thousand shield-bearers. There were also ten thousand musketeers, but as they only had enough powder and ammunition among them to fire three rounds each, their weapons had become largely symbolic. Nonetheless, the Polypontian soldiers fiercely defended their right to carry their muskets and had only reluctantly agreed to train as swordsmen to back up their meager firepower.

Olympia watched the fat general fondly as he rode by on his big-boned horse and smiled broadly at her. In the few weeks she had known him, he'd become a dear friend. He was witty, charming, and just plain good fun; Ollie said he had an appetite that almost equaled a Snow Leopard's, and what greater compliment could there be than that? And Grishmak and the general had become almost inseparable as they explored the deepest cellars in search of rare wines and beers. Oskan, it had to be said, rarely spoke to the Polypontian soldier, but then, they had so little in common, and they were more than polite to each other.

Yes, thought Olympia, *there have been very few problems with either the general or his soldiers. Every one of them has settled in nicely, and after a few initial skirmishes even the housecarls and werewolves seem to have accepted them . . . in a qualified sort of way.*

But the Basilea knew full well that Thirrin still had a problem with both the Imperial soldiers and their general. Despite her best efforts and intentions, the idea of forgiving the people who'd killed her father and son, and who'd destroyed the lives of so many of the citizens of the Icemark, was alien to her. As a tactician and strategist, she was fully aware of the value of the Polypontian sections of the army, and she had no doubt they'd fight well. Few others had such firsthand knowledge of their martial abilities, but she couldn't bring herself to happily accept their presence in a force that she commanded.

Olympia had watched the Queen struggle with her understandable prejudices and searched fruitlessly for ways of helping. In the end she had just had to accept that this was a battle that Thirrin would have to fight alone.

"They look very handy, don't you think?" said Ollie, interrupting her thoughts.

"Umm?"

"The army, handy."

"Oh yes, very," Olympia answered distractedly. She continued to mull things over for a while, then asked, "Where did you say Thirrin and Cressida were?"

Ollie turned from avidly watching the march-past and regarded his wife. "Going over the arrangements for supply and general logistics; you know what a stickler Cressida is for detail. Why?"

"Oh, nothing really; I was just wondering if she was . . . well, if she was trying to avoid watching the Polypontian sections marching past."

"Why on earth should she?" asked Ollie in surprise.

"Simple really. Painful memories."

"Oh, I see. Well, we all have those, don't we? Everyone in the High Command's a veteran of at least one war against the Empire, and most of us have fought two!"

"Yes, very true. But none of us has lost a father *and* a son in the fighting."

"No," Ollie conceded. "But . . . but times have changed, and everyone knows that yesterday's enemy is often tomorrow's ally. If we're going to stop Erinor and the southern Hypolitan, by all accounts we're going to need everyone we can get, and Andronicus is a good general with actual experience of fighting her."

"Yes, I know. But emotions are funny things, and especially female emotions."

Ollie was about to say he knew that only too well but wisely thought better of it. No one in his experience could hold a grudge like a female, of *any* species, but somehow, if she was human *and* Hypolitan, there was an unrivaled artistry in her wrath.

The War Room of the High Command was situated deep in the caves beneath the citadel of Frostmarris. It had been moved there during the last war against Bellorum, when the

Polypontian general had sent the Sky Navy and its bombs against the city. Here the gunpowder and blazing pitch that had poured out of the bomber-galleons had had no effect, and Thirrin and her allies had planned their counterattacks in safety. But now the Queen and her daughter were preparing for a very different war; they were no longer fighting a defensive strategy but preparing to invade what remained of the Polypontian Empire.

Cressida glanced through the lists of supplies almost sightlessly. The walls of the cave were lined with cressets where torches blazed and brightly illuminated the planning tables. She and her mother had been going over figures all morning, and she was deeply and profoundly bored. But what made it particularly excruciating was the fact that she knew full well the Queen was simply using the checking of supplies as an excuse to avoid the dress rehearsal of the parade.

"Can the supply route through the pass be easily defended?" Thirrin asked.

Cressida sat back in her chair and stretched. "Well, as the pass isn't in enemy hands and we hold all three forts that defend both entrances, I'd say it was pretty safe."

Thirrin heard the note of quiet sarcasm and decided to ignore it. "Good. Even so, I think I'll leave a regiment of werewolves as extra defense."

"And deny the army their strength? Besides, which regiment do you have in mind? Every one of them is designated a frontline role."

"Perhaps Eodred and Howler's . . ."

Cressida laughed aloud. "You'd have to tie them up first, and even then you wouldn't stop them following as soon as we'd marched over the horizon."

"They're all soldiers of the Icemark. They'll follow their orders to the letter."

This was too much; Cressida wasn't going to sit by and watch the army being denied the power and experience of the Regiment of the Red Eye. Besides, her brother and his werewolf friend would never forgive her if she let such a thing happen. "Mother! There'd just be no point in leaving them to defend the pass. It's safe! The supply route's safe! And we'll need them when the campaign really gets going."

Thirrin looked at her daughter sharply. Cressida never called her "Mother" unless she was really angry or determined about something. For a few moments she held Cressida's eye in a contest of power, but at last she sighed and sat down heavily. "All right," she conceded. "I suppose they'll be useful against the Hordes."

Cressida snorted. "Invaluable, more like."

"Fine. I thought we'd just check through fodder supplies for the cavalry, after which there's the ration packs for the human infantry. . . ."

"You're about to go to war, Mother, and part of your army's made up of Polypontian soldiers. In fact, one of your most experienced generals was second only to Scipio Bellorum in the Imperial military hierarchy. . . . You're just going to have to get used to it, and stop putting off the moment when you have to acknowledge these facts," Cressida pointed out in a reasonable, if forceful, voice.

"I'm not sure I—"

"Understand what I mean?" the Crown Princess interrupted.

"I was about to say, 'I'm not sure I like your tone,' young lady. You *are* talking to the Queen, you know!"

"Then, for goodness' sake, act like it! I'd expect such obvious and immature diversionary tactics from a junior officer who'd messed up a duty roster, not from the greatest monarch the Icemark's had in more than a thousand years of history." Cressida thumped the table with her mailed fist for emphasis. "Now, I don't know about you, but I'm thoroughly sick of supply routes, quartermasters' reports, and the problems of logistical support. So if you don't mind, I'm going to see how the cavalry's shaping up in the dress rehearsal."

"Well, yes, I do mind, actually," snapped Thirrin, deeply resenting being put in her place by her daughter . . . yet again. "I happen to believe that supplies and logistical support are important to an army."

"And so do I," Cressida snapped back. "Which is exactly why I've already checked, double-checked, and *triple*-checked every item and all procedures on every single one of these inane lists!"

"Oh! Oh . . . have you? Fine. That's . . . all right, then, isn't it? Well, in which case I suppose you'd better run along, then."

"And you?"

"No . . . no. I'll just check over these—"

"MOTHER! IT'S ALL DONE! For the love of all that's sane, leave it alone!"

A long silence stretched out between them, and then at last Thirrin drew breath and said quietly, "I can't."

"Why not?"

"You know why not. If I stop doing this, I'll have to review the army, and then I'll finally have to admit to myself that I've . . . I've made an alliance with the very people who killed your brother and your granddad."

Cressida looked at her mother, both appalled and embarrassed to see her in such a vulnerable state. Calling on all her reserves as a great warrior, she forced herself to look up and say, "I know, but things have changed. We need them, and they need us."

Thirrin shrugged helplessly. "But that's just the point: Things haven't changed; your brother and granddad are still dead, and some of those soldiers marching in the parade might have been there when they died. They might even have been responsible!"

Cressida sat down heavily. "Well, as to that, King Redrought died nearly twenty years ago, and it's historical fact that he wiped out the entire Polypontian army that was sent against him. And according to eye-witness reports, Cerdic was shot by Octavius Bellorum, and then Sharley killed *him* in the final battle of the last war. So who's left of the guilty ones?"

Thirrin gazed at the table, unable to accept the logic of what she heard. "But . . . but they're all the same! Every Polypontian soldier is a fanatical killing machine who could invade us again if we save their Empire now. They're evil, Cressida, as a race they're evil."

"There's no such thing as an evil race, just evil circumstances that make people do evil things. You know that as well as I do. I shouldn't imagine there's one nation in this entire death-riddled, war-torn, disease-riven world that hasn't carried out one atrocity or another at some point in its history. So let's have no more of this talk about evil races! The Polypontians are just people who have done some truly terrible things, and who's to say that we wouldn't have done exactly the same if we'd been in their position?"

"Never! Never in an age and an age of warfare would I have done what Bellorum did to us!"

Cressida looked at her mother, admiring her certainty. "Never? Not if by invading his lands and wiping out his cities you could have prevented Cerdic's death? Not if by some sort of preemptive strike you could have stopped the wars with Bellorum before they'd begun? Even if it meant killing thousands of noncombatants to do so? Just imagine if you'd *known* exactly what his plans were, and you'd been in a position to stop him. How many civilian lives would you have snuffed out to kill him? How many children would you have been prepared to see wiped out to save your own child?"

Thirrin shook with rage, incensed that her own daughter was forcing her to confront her vulnerabilities. "That's not fair. I was never in a position to invade the Empire."

"But you know as well as I that you would have done it if you could," Cressida answered quietly.

"I am *not* Bellorum!"

"No. But you *are* human, and just like the rest of us you have the potential to be both a devil and an angel. There's no such thing as an evil race, just a *human* race."

"Trite!" Thirrin spat.

"But true," Cressida replied.

"This is ridiculous! No amount of playing with words is going to make me feel any different about the Polypontians. I can't bring myself to even talk to them, let alone lead them in battle."

"And yet you must if we're to successfully confront Erinor and her Hordes."

"I can't. I just can't!"

Cressida began to feel desperate. In a day or so she'd be crossing into the Darkness with Oskan to confront Medea, and she was determined to have this particular problem solved before she left. The country must have the strongest of leaders, without any distractions.

"What need does a country have for a leader who will not lead? You are without purpose or point," she said with quiet ice. "Give up your throne."

It took Thirrin a few seconds to realize what had been said, and then she gasped aloud. "To even think such a thing is treasonable; to *say* it is a matter for the executioner!"

"Or for the Wittanagast," said Cressida, naming the Council of Wise Ones who, in an emergency, could remove a reigning monarch from power and select a replacement.

"You threaten *me* with an outmoded tradition that hasn't been used in fifty years?"

"Forty-three years, actually," Cressida said calmly. "And you know full well the Wittanagast still exists."

"And on what grounds would you call them?"

"As I've already said, dereliction of duty. If you refuse to lead the army because there are Polypontian troops in the ranks, then you'll be failing in your role as Monarch."

Thirrin breathed deeply to calm her raging nerves. To be threatened by her own daughter was so unbearable she could have screamed aloud in fury and frustration. "Many of the Wittanagast will be veterans of the wars against Bellorum. They'll understand me; they'll support me. Don't forget I'm a tried and trusted war leader with more than twenty years of successful rule to my credit. Do you really think they'll depose me in favor of you?"

"No, not a chance," said Cressida easily. "Even though I, too, am a tried and tested war leader, my experience is negligible compared to yours. But the very act of being called to explain your actions and attitudes before a council of elders *and* the people of the Icemark will sully your . . . mystique. You'll no longer be Thirrin Freer Strong-in-the-Arm Lindenshield, irreproachable leader of the nation, but an ordinary woman who's facing enough opposition to force her to defend her actions. In short, Mother, you'll be exposed in all your ordinary lack of glory."

"And do you really think that will bother me?"

"Yes. Your pride is equaled by mine alone in all of the Icemark."

Thirrin looked at her daughter appraisingly. How had she produced such a ruthless, calculating monster? But then the answer came to her in shocking clarity. Cressida was her mother's daughter; she was a flawless reflection of herself.

"Why are you doing this?" she finally asked.

"Because the Icemark needs this alliance with the Empire. Unless we throw our combined weight against Erinor and her Hordes, we'll be defeated. It's as simple as that. Survival, Mother, pure survival."

Thirrin bowed her head and shuddered involuntarily. "But how can I lead soldiers of an empire that have committed genocide in my country?"

"None of the soldiers marching today have taken one allied life; they're all too young, and the general that leads them actively opposed the war against us in the Senate. Your conscience will be clear, Mother. And if that doesn't make it any easier, then simply see them as another weapon in your armory to use against Erinor; they're like a sword or a bow, and when you've finished fighting, you can put them away."

"Put them away?"

"Cast them aside, end the Alliance, however you want to put it. We haven't signed any treaties of undying mutual support and friendship. All of us know this is a marriage of convenience. General Andronicus knows it, as do all of his soldiers. We just need each other at the moment, and when the moment's passed, we can start hating each other again. This is diplomacy, Mother. You know better than I that today's trusted friend is tomorrow's bitter enemy. You even said something very like it in your speech at the feast of welcome for Andronicus. Why else is politics the perfect refuge for every liar, cheat, and self-serving toad that was ever born? All you need is a good set of teeth and the ability to smile convincingly with them!"

"Well, you certainly have a refreshingly clear view of the diplomatic service," said Thirrin, amused despite herself.

"I'd sooner face the entire Bellorum clan armed only with a feather duster than spend longer than is absolutely necessary with a diplomat or politician."

"You know, you could have a point there," said Thirrin and laughed, immediately breaking at least some of the tension.

"I *know* I have a point. But at least the Polypontians we're working with now are just soldiers. There's something honest about the armed forces. It's pretty obvious what they mean when they attack you with a sword. No metaphors, no hidden messages, just the clarity of 'kill or be killed.' We all *know* where we stand; it's just that Erinor is a bigger threat to us both at the moment. There's plenty of time for us to fight again later."

Thirrin sighed. "You're right. . . . Of course you're right. But I can't help myself, Cressida. All I can promise is that I'll do my level best to work with them. Who knows, perhaps I'll get good enough at lying to convince even myself."

"Perfect, that's all we really need! And if your prejudices start to show, I'll be there to remind you."

"Oh yes, I know you will, my darling daughter," said Thirrin with an ironic smile. "I know you will."

Cronus and Medea watched as, far off in the distance, a large area of shadow slowly encroached on the pristine brilliance of the tundra. It was almost like watching dirty water soak into a beautifully crisp and ironed linen sheet, but both knew it was a gathering of thousands and thousands of Ice Demons, which they'd summoned by the power of their minds.

These hideous creatures would become the invading army that would crush the Icemark, but before they were ready, they'd need to be trained in the fine art of killing human beings and werewolves.

"I think now would be a good time," Cronus said quietly, and together he and Medea applied their minds and began to create bodies and forms from the ice and rock of the Darkness. Such was their power that soon rank upon rank of housecarls and Wolf-folk warriors stood waiting silently in the freezing gloom of the Darkness. Their rigid lines receded into the distance, where they stood like the trees of an oddly disciplined forest.

"Shall we install the souls now?" Medea asked eagerly, and when her grandfather nodded in silent assent, she sent out her mind to thaw some of the spirits that made up the individual ice crystals of the tundra. Gradually the atmosphere became murky, with a dense rolling fog, as more and more souls that had been cursed and exiled were freed from their icy prisons.

Cronus applied his power, and each of the newly created bodies gave a start and then shook itself as a soul entered it and began to move its limbs and head. A great murmur of excitement rose up as the spirits realized what had happened. They were alive again!

"Silence!" Medea roared into the gloom. "Cronus the Great has decided to have mercy upon you and give you a new life. All he asks is that you prove yourselves worthy of his generosity and defend yourselves against the army of Ice Demons that even now advances upon you. Take up your weapons and fight for your right to live!"

For a moment all was confusion as the liberated souls stared around them, and then they saw the Ice Demons bearing down upon them. Some screamed and tried to run, others collapsed to the ground in pure terror, while others simply wept. But here and there could be seen housecarls and werewolves who'd been warriors in their previous lives, and they drew their weapons or flexed their claws and waited grimly for the enemy to reach them. Gradually even those who'd wailed in despair took heart from their examples and, drawing their own swords and axes, prepared to defend themselves.

The Ice Demons were drawing ever closer, and now the dark sky was filled with their bellowing and roaring as they swayed and rolled over the tundra toward the newly created soldiers who waited for them.

"Smell their sweet scent!" Cronus shouted over the din, as great billowing waves of stench enveloped them. "It's the aroma of martial fervor; it's the smell of victory!"

Medea rather thought it was just the sickening stink of blood and dung, but she smiled, anyway, and nodded in agreement.

A huge roar rose up into the frozen sky as the two armies met. Immediately the white brilliance of the ice was drenched in a wide splatter of gore and blood as the huge demons ripped into the opposition. Limbs and heads flew through the air as the newly made soldiers were torn apart, and their smoking entrails were greedily sucked into the tusked jaws of their enemies.

Medea smiled. She was really rather proud of the attention to detail that both she and Cronus had shown when they had created the bodies for the revived souls. They really were anatomically perfect and accurate, and she spent a happy few minutes trying to identify body parts as they flew through the air.

The battle had become a rout, and even those spirits who'd been soldiers in their former lives fell back before the dreadful ferocity of the Ice Demons. It seemed that nothing could stop them. As each body was torn apart, its soul fled with a wail of despair and loss for the new life that had been so short.

Soon much of the fighting was hidden from view by a blizzard of falling ice, as each spirit was then frozen by the malevolent Magic of the Dark and fell as a small crystal shard to join the countless millions of the tundra.

In less than an hour, the Ice Demons had destroyed all opposition and now stood steaming in the gloom as their stupid, hating eyes cast about for more victims.

"I think you could call that a complete success," Cronus said happily. "Our army has proved its abilities, and each and every one of them is now imprinted with an image of the enemy."

Medea nodded and smiled. "May I invite you to the Bone Fortress for a victory feast?"

"You may, indeed," her grandfather replied. And they stepped elegantly over the blood-soaked ground while the ferocity of the Ice Demons was quashed by the power of the two Adepts and they marched away to wait in designated holding areas in readiness for the coming war.

Two days later, Oskan and Cressida, along with a unit of more than forty werewolves and housecarls, prepared to enter the Darkness. All of the warriors had received special training from the Witchfather on how to survive in the Magical Realms, and all had been handpicked for their bravery and toughness. But the fact remained that Oskan didn't actually know if he could transport such a large body of living people through the interstice that divided the physical and magical plains. He could only hope and trust to his Abilities.

For several days now he'd been preparing for a battle he knew would be crucial to the survival of his son and his friends and perhaps even to the Icemark itself. But he was also very aware that his battle would be against his own daughter, the child he'd raised and nurtured. The child whom, in the very depths of his soul, he knew he still loved.

But the times and circumstances demanded that he put aside all such emotions. He'd already been on a number of reconnaissance flights into the Magical Realms and knew exactly where his enemy was. And he also knew that there were several contingents of Ice Demons nearby who acted as a sort of unofficial bodyguard to Medea. It was these that

Cressida and her soldiers would be keeping busy while he dealt with his other, far less pleasant daughter.

Medea might have been able to mask the whereabouts of Sharley and the others with consummate skill, but she'd been surprisingly lax in covering her own tracks. Perhaps she thought no one would dare attack her in the Darkness and so had built her Bone Fortress in the nothingness of the magical plain without bothering to disguise it in any way at all.

Oskan smiled coldly; how shocked she'd be when he attacked her in her own lair. He took a deep breath, crossed into the Darkness, and immediately assumed the form of a speck of cosmic dust. He didn't want the hideous Ice Demons seeing him and giving away his presence; surprise was crucial. But before he began his assault, he paused as he allowed the barriers in his mind to slowly fall and gazed into the abyss of evil that he kept hidden securely away.

Once again he felt the almost irresistible call of the power that dwelled in the unexplored recesses of his mind and allowed himself to answer it. Immediately he was filled with a sense of indomitable strength and unstoppable purpose, and his mind expanded to fill the universe of evil he'd entered.

He turned in the emptiness of the Darkness, focused on the Bone Fortress, and arrived in the ether above the pinnacles and turrets of its roof. Then, assuming his human form, he wove an intricate pattern of magic symbols and signs in the air, and successfully brought Cressida and her command through the interstices between the worlds. Striding across the tundra, the Crown Princess immediately raised her sword and, drawing breath, gave the war cry of the House of Lindenshield: "The enemy is upon us! They kill our children; they burn our houses! *Blood! Blast! And Fire! Blood! Blast! And Fire!*"

Her living voice raged like a flame over the frozen wastes of dead. Ice Demon guards at the gates of the Bone Fortress turned their blazing eyes on the mortal intruders, and battle began.

Oskan watched the onset of the fighting from his vantage point high above the roof of Medea's stronghold, and, once satisfied all was going well, crashed through the tiles and slates of the fortress as he descended from floor to floor. Finally, with an explosion of ornate plasterwork and gilded chandeliers, he landed before Medea's great chair and looked on the startled face of his daughter.

"Medea," he said simply. "I am here."

For a split second she gazed at him in amazement, but then, with a scream of terrified rage, she lifted her hand and struck at him with a bolt of plasma. Immediately he was engulfed in the crackling power of the white-hot light, but with a wave he threw it back, and her great chair exploded into ash.

Medea paused; this was the first time she'd been in the same room as her father since he'd exiled her so long ago. For a moment she felt a rush of longing, but quickly crushed it. Her mind began to race. How had he found her? Before she could think further, she was suddenly seized in a field of energy that crushed her breath from her lungs. For a second she panicked, her mind and body writhing in her father's grip. But then she steadied herself, and slowly, with a massive effort, she resisted the pressure, pushing against its deadly grip, until Oskan was forced to release her.

She drew on the Power of the Dark, and her confidence grew. She knew she was stronger than Oskan; all she had to do was fight with precision and skill. "It's so nice to see you again, Father," she spat, trying to ignore the truth of the statement. "Did you hope I'd died when you exiled me?"

Oskan looked at his daughter and carefully masked all emotion. "I don't really know what I hoped, Medea. Your actions forced me to make a decision; you were a threat to the Icemark and everyone in it. I tried to end that threat, and now I must try to end it again."

Angry and hurt, Medea replied with a lightning bolt of searing energy that lanced into Oskan's face. For a moment he staggered and she thought she had him, but then, drawing breath, he absorbed the energy and spat back a bolt of such power that it threw his daughter across the width of the Great Hall. She landed heavily on the skull-cobbled floor, but leaped to her feet and renewed her attack, sending blast after bolt of energy against her father, forcing him back across the floor until he fell to his knees, exhausted and injured.

Medea walked slowly toward him, smiling brightly to mask the knot of fear and shame in the pit of her stomach. "Oh dear, is the most powerful warlock in the Physical Realms wounded? My, my, what a shame. No point in leaving him to suffer."

A crackling sheet of searing light suddenly appeared above his head, and gently, almost tenderly, it draped itself across Oskan's kneeling form. Swiftly it molded itself to his shape, and pulsating waves of broiling heat began to melt the wall of the Bone Fortress behind him.

Medea watched, her face a rigid mask, as the sheet crackled with heat. But then the kneeling form of her father climbed to its feet and turned to face her as though unaffected by her powers. Desperately fighting down an instinctive need to run to him, she began to turn away, but some unseen force held her in place.

"Come, Medea, we both need to end this quickly."

She screamed as she watched the white-draped figure advancing toward her. Oskan slowly opened his arms and gathered her in a hug.

Her hair and clothing burst into flames as his arms enveloped her in a crushing embrace so that she was unable to break free. The stench of her roasting flesh and choking smoke billowed into the atmosphere until her screams were cut short by her convulsive coughs.

Then, with a supreme concentration of willpower, she broke free and sent a flying dagger of lightning to bury itself in Oskan's chest. He fell to the ground, writhing in agony, as she staggered away, her skin charred almost to the bone. But as she watched, Oskan's hands slowly drew aside the white-hot sheet of plasma and wrenched the dagger from his chest.

"Your Gift has grown enormously, Medea. Why couldn't you have used it to help those who needed it?"

Medea was exhausted; his power appalled her, and nothing she'd so far sent against him had had any effect. His skin was unblemished, and not even a hair seemed to be out of place as he walked calmly toward her.

"Keep away," she screeched. "You should be dead! I've done enough to kill you three times over already."

Oskan now took the knife of lightning that had been buried in his chest and weighed it contemplatively in his hand as he desperately tried to remind himself of why he had to destroy his daughter's powers. Sharley, Mekhmet, and Kirimin were all in terrible danger, and if Medea was left with her Gifts intact, who could possibly tell how many others would suffer?

With a sudden cry of rage and desperation he threw the knife so that it buried itself deep in Medea's eye, throwing her to the cold white floor. He fell to his knees, his face twisted in agony, as though he'd inflicted the wound on himself.

The point of the dagger was lodged deep in Medea's brain, but incredibly, she was still conscious. The pain was hideous, bright, brittle, and scintillatingly sharp as the energy of the lightning blade pulsated slowly.

Lifting her arms, she tried to draw the dagger from her eye, but she no longer had the strength. Outrage and betrayal burned deep within her. "How are you going to kill me?"

Oskan climbed to his feet. "I'm not going to kill you," he answered quietly. "I don't want to kill you. But I must destroy your powers."

He stooped over her, and, gathering energy from the evil that surrounded him, he began to feed it into the blade lodged so deep in Medea's brain. Soon cells and synapses began to boil and burn away, and she felt her Gift beginning to fade. She screamed in horror and fought back madly, but Oskan diverted all energy into his attack, even draining it away from his defenses and psychic shields as he struggled to destroy the powers of the daughter he knew he still loved.

Without warning a black and ragged shape hurled itself out of the shadows. Carrying a dagger of ice, it crashed into the Witchfather and buried the icy blade deep in his now undefended neck. With a roar of pain the warlock staggered to his feet and wrenched the dagger free.

Oskan's psychic guards and defenses were already down as he'd channeled all of his strength into destroying Medea's powers. But Orla's attack had distracted him further. Seeing her chance, Medea broke away in desperation and hit him full force with a plasma bolt that burned his flesh to the bone. "I have you now, Daddy dearest," she sneered. "Prepare to meet the precious Goddess you hold so dear!"

Drawing on the Power of the Dark, she gathered herself to deliver the final blow. Her body grew and expanded, and a maniacal grin split her face as she raised her hands above her head. But then something stopped her. She paused; this man, her father, was the only other living thing in all

Creation she'd ever loved. How could she destroy him?

Then a sudden shriek of pain distracted her. She spun around to watch as Orla's broken body flew through the air and landed at her feet.

"Cressida!"

"Well, well, if it isn't Medea, my long-lost little sister." The Crown Princess had appeared as if from nowhere.

"How did you get here?" Medea hissed.

"Dad brought me; how else?"

Medea's face contorted with rage, but then smoothed out to a sneer. "Well, he won't be taking you back again." She waved her hand contemptuously at the hideously burned figure that lay in a smoking heap on the floor.

Cressida gasped as she realized it was her father, but with the control of the experienced warrior, she turned back to face her enemy. "That will cost you more than you have to give, Medea," she said quietly.

But before she could move, her sister sent a blast of lightning roaring and crackling across the Bone Fortress's Great Hall and it struck her with a huge explosion. Medea let out a great shriek of laughter; she had no doubts or qualms about killing Cressida. She'd always hated her sister, just as she hated the rest of her family. But Medea's laughter abruptly stopped in mid-peal as she suddenly realized that Cressida was still standing, completely unscathed.

"NO!" she raged and sent bolt after bolt against her hated sister, but still Cressida stood, unaffected and smiling gently.

"Medea, let me introduce you to an old friend of mine," Cressida said as she strolled unhurriedly across the floor. "This is my favorite mace. I must have killed dozens with it in the last few wars. . . . Oh, and I've also caved in the heads of several Ice Demons with it just now."

"Why aren't you dead?" Medea raged, ignoring her sister's words entirely. "Why aren't you incinerated?"

Cressida smiled. "Oh, that; Dad tells me I'm immune to magic, so that means you can't do anything to me, apart from fight me physically, that is. I tell you what. . . . I'll take you on with one hand behind my back, *and* I'll let you choose weapons. . . ."

Medea gave a shriek and turned to run. But with the complete ruthlessness of the veteran she was, Cressida smashed her a crushing blow with the mace, breaking her shoulder, her collarbone, and several of her ribs. Like a rag doll in a high wind she was sent cartwheeling across the palace floor until she struck a huge ice table and lay still.

Now that the enemy was rendered senseless, Cressida remembered her father, and hurried over to the blackened remains that still smoked faintly on the icy floor of the palace. The stench of burned flesh was overpowering, and she stepped back in grief and horror, convinced she was looking at a corpse.

But then the blackened skull that had been a face turned to her, and she watched as the charred skeleton climbed to its feet. She was mesmerized, torn between revulsion and a deep sorrowing compassion for her hideously injured father. But as she watched through a distorting river of tears, the figure raised its hand. Medea was struggling to rise again.

Cressida drew her sword, but Oskan held her back and bowed his head as he opened himself once more to the Dark. Immediately his frame was filled to the brim with a snapping, crackling surge of power, and with a guttural cry he drove it at Medea.

It hit her like an avalanche, destroying her defenses and smashing her back against the walls of her palace. For a moment she was pinned to the ice, but then she slipped slowly to the floor and lay still.

"Forgive me, Medea," he whispered. Only he knew that he was asking her pardon for failing to guide her properly along the Paths of Light when she'd still been a little girl.

She wasn't dead, and he knew he'd only partially damaged her powers, but there was nothing more he could do. The laws of the Cosmos prevented him from killing her. Terrible consequences could arise from such an act, consequences he wasn't prepared to allow. Besides, he was too badly injured, and he only had sufficient reserves of strength left to rescue Sharley and his friends.

Cressida hurried forward to help him, but he waved her away. With a supreme effort he raised his hands above his head, gathered Cressida, her werewolves and housecarls, and then drove into the sky, bursting through the roof of the Bone Fortress like a shooting star. Scanning the Plain of Desolation, he quickly found what he wanted. Medea could no longer mask them.

The roar of the Witchfather's arrival above them made Sharley, Mekhmet, and Kirimin leap to their feet. But the silken hiss of scimitars being drawn and the warning snarls of Kirimin were suddenly stifled as Oskan gathered them together, horses and all, and wrenched them back to the Icemark.

They erupted into the Great Hall of the citadel just as dinner was being served. Tables were heaved aside, housecarls shouted, werewolves howled, dogs barked, and over it all Thirrin's voice rose in power and joy. "Put up your weapons! Put up your weapons! The Witchfather has brought them home!"

At last silence descended, and everyone gazed at the tangled heap of boys, horses, Snow Leopard, werewolves, housecarls, Crown Princess, and a gently smoking skeleton.

Thirrin was the first to shake herself free of the shock of their sudden appearance, and she stepped forward, gazing at the wreck and tangle before her. Her youngest son was home! Her little Sharley was safe and so were his friends.

She laughed aloud for joy, but then suddenly stopped as her eyes came to rest on the hideously charred skeleton. "Oskan!"

The blackened skull turned to look at her. "Thirrin, I can use the Dark! I can use the Dark!" it croaked.

16

Cressida sat in the chamber of the High Command busying herself with details, to distract herself from worrying about her father. When they'd first gotten back to the Icemark from the Magical Realms, Oskan had remained conscious just long enough to give directions about his care. But then he'd collapsed into a coma and been removed to the cave where his burned body had been magically regenerated in the last war against the Polypontus. Cressida's mind was eminently practical, and she knew full well that there was nothing she could do to help Oskan recover from his terrible injuries, so she'd decided to grill Andronicus about arrangements for the upcoming invasion of the Polypontus.

"So, your son will rendezvous with us just south of the Dancing Maidens," stated Cressida in brisk tones.

"Yes," Andronicus confirmed distractedly as he helped himself to another fruit pie. "I do hope your mother will allow me to take a few recipes along when we march south."

"General, concentrate!" came the snappy reply. "I'm trying to finalize details here."

"Yes, yes, quite," Andronicus agreed and tried to look suitably martial and efficient.

The other places around the huge table were empty. Grishmak, Tharaman, and the others had made good their escape as soon as Thirrin had closed the earlier meeting, but Andronicus just hadn't been fast enough and the Crown Princess had swept down on him before he could slip away.

"Now, am I right in saying that he's been leading a resistance movement against the northward advance of Erinor and her Hordes?"

"Yes, that's right," Andronicus confirmed, trying to sound efficient through a mouthful of pastry. "We agreed that I should lead a body of men into exile where they could recover, regroup, and re-equip, while he did all he could to slow down the enemy. With the help of the werewolf relay, communications between us have been swift, and it's thanks to him that we know so much of Erinor's movements."

Cressida nodded and made copious notes while Andronicus surveyed the sorry wreckage of the refreshment table. Grishmak, Olememnon, and Tharaman had left very little that was worth salvaging, but his Polypontian efficiency had so far unearthed two pies and a fruit tart. But now it really did look as though there was nothing left but crumbs, and a few jam tarts, with suspiciously large teeth marks, that had been sampled and then thrown aside.

With a sigh, Andronicus turned his full attention to the irritatingly exacting Crown Princess, who was speed-reading her notes. "Now, I take it he's fully aware of rendezvous times and places, and that he's familiar with his future role in the invading army?"

The general considered pointing out that all of these details had already been discussed ad nauseam, in the earlier meeting with the Queen, but quickly abandoned the idea. Cressida was the sort of young woman who took careful and painstaking delight in informing people that they had appalling faults, but could never accept criticism herself.

She'd told him only that morning that her mother had spent literally days going over plans that had already been studied and discussed and had then insisted on this detailed reexamination. The irony of the situation was completely lost on Cressida.

"General, are you listening to me?"

Andronicus jumped and sat up. "Er . . . yes, yes, of course."

"Then what did I just ask you?"

Feeling like a naughty schoolboy, he racked his brains. "Er . . . you wanted to know if Leonidas knew where we were meeting, and at what time."

"Leonidas? Is that your son's name? It doesn't sound Polypontian."

"No, it's Hellenic. His mother was a Hellene, and fortunately for him he takes after her rather than me," Andronicus replied, patting his enormous belly and smiling contentedly.

"*Was* a Hellene?"

"Yes, she died in childbirth. I never remarried. . . . Nobody could ever replace her; nobody could even come close. . . ." His voice trailed away sadly, and Cressida gazed at him, puzzled by the response she felt for someone she'd never known.

"Was she beautiful?"

"As a moonlit night, as a summer dawn. And Leonidas is a mirror of her."

"Good-looking, then."

Andronicus gave a bark of laughter. "Every young Polypontian lady who ever meets him begins a campaign to win him. But none ever has."

"Why not?"

"Well, he may have his mother's looks, but he has his old dad's inability with the opposite sex. Put him within sight of a young woman and he suddenly acquires feet that belong to somebody else and a tongue that's never even heard of language. He stutters and staggers and spends most of his time an interesting shade of red."

"And this man has command of an army?"

"Oh, that's different. There are very few women in the Polypontian forces, and the few female soldiers he's met from the Icemark he treats in exactly the same way as his men," Andronicus explained. "No. I think it's only when he meets women in a social context that he has difficulties."

"I see," said Cressida and valiantly resisted an almost overwhelming desire to ask more about Leonidas. "Now, back to details. How many soldiers does he have under his command?"

"Well, circumstances dictate that they fight in small autonomous units, using hit-and-run tactics, but as an approximation, I'd say he has over thirty thousand men altogether."

"Good, good," said Cressida, scribbling furiously. "And does he have any other names?"

"I'm sorry?" said the general, confused by the sudden change in the direction of the questions.

"Leonidas. Does he have any other names?"

"Er . . . yes, yes, of course. He's known as Leonidas Apollodorus Andronicus. When he was a boy, everyone called him Leo, and as his name suggests, he was brave as a little lion. But put him anywhere near a girl, even at that age, and he became as daft and as timid as a kitten."

"He should have had sisters. He wouldn't have been afraid of women then."

"Yes, he should. His mother always said she wanted a large family. But it wasn't to be," said Andronicus sadly.

"You ought to have married again," said Cressida in her practical mode. "It's not too late even now—Uncle Ollie . . . I mean Olememnon of the Hypolitan married the Basilea when he was positively ancient."

"As opposed to just old and decrepit like myself?"

Cressida smiled, acknowledging her faux pas. "I'll keep an eye out for someone; there are quite a few eligible ladies at court. Baroness Hildegard, for example. She has a small, comfortable castle near the Dancing Maidens, and her kitchens are famous throughout the Southern Riding. Ideal for a man of such culinary tastes as yours."

The general mustered his resources like the brilliant tactician he was and changed the subject smoothly. "I tell you what—shall we continue this over lunch? I'm supposed to be meeting Tharaman, Grishmak, and Olememnon in the Great Hall, and I'm sure there's still lots you need to finalize with them."

Cressida sighed. Men just didn't have the stamina needed for true organizational flair. "I suppose beer and wine will be involved."

"Well, we are talking about lunch here."

"Fine," she agreed, putting away her pens and notes. "I'd more or less gotten everything I wanted, anyway."

Medea was aware that her magic was damaged, but it would recover given time. Her eyeball, where the shard of lightning had pierced her skull, was healing only slowly, trickling thick mucus down her cheek like sticky tears. And her brain was desperately trying to find new pathways that would allow what Abilities she still had to be used. It was obvious she'd need to become "dormant" for a while and allow her body to repair itself properly. Ironically, when she was fully healed, she'd be stronger than she had been before Oskan had attacked her. In fact, her defeat in the battle with her father had been very useful; things had been put into a proper perspective. She'd been forced to face the fact that beneath the hatred and need for revenge, she still loved Oskan Witchfather. And now she was almost convinced that, knowing such a weakness existed in her psyche, she could eradicate it once and for all.

In the meantime, all she required was to be left alone and given the peace in which to recover from her injuries. She sighed and stretched, preparing her body for the long healing sleep that would add the final touches to her regeneration. When she was completely healed, one of her first tasks would be to thaw another soul from the tundra to act as a handmaid. Annoyingly Orla had managed to die in her clash with Cressida, her spirit ripped apart by the huge levels of magic that had seethed through the atmosphere.

A distant echo of footsteps interrupted her thoughts, and she waited quietly for her long-expected visitor to appear. Eventually the figure of her grandfather emerged from the shadows and she turned to watch as he drew nearer.

"Elegant," he said, in reference to the velvet eye patch that covered her injuries. "And do you have a patch for your damaged brain?"

"That's healing. I'll be stronger than ever in less than a month."

As her grandfather drew closer, Medea hurriedly stood and stepped to one side, and he sat in her great chair and turned his blank, crushing gaze on her. "True, you will be stronger. But will it be enough?"

"To defeat my father? Undoubtedly."

"You've always underestimated Oskan, Medea. Make sure you're not doing it again."

"No. This time I've got it right. You can't fight someone almost to the death without getting an accurate feel for their Abilities."

"Normally I'd agree with you, but the Witchfather is different. No one else has ever been able to call on the Power of the Dark as he did in his battle with you, and then resist being consumed by it. He should have been destroyed or become possessed by it." His lips drew back over his pointed teeth. "Consider yourself; you're completely submerged and saturated in the Darkness. You're part of its fabric, and every bit of you is made up of its hate and evil. But the Witchfather can use the evil power of the domain at will, and then walk away completely untouched by it."

"And that is his weakness," snapped Medea. "He uses it as a resource, whereas I *am* the Dark."

"No, *you* are one small part of it; the Dark would continue without your unimportant contribution, but you would die without its presence in your life."

"What do you mean? I existed before the Dark came into my life."

"Yes, but now it's consumed you. You need it like the creatures of the Physical Realms need oxygen or water. And that's *your* weakness."

"All who dwell in the Darkness are the same," she answered, unconcerned.

"Do you think so?" her grandfather asked quietly. "Haven't you realized yet that the greatest Adepts exist with it, whereas the weakest live on it, or even because of it."

"But I'm one of the greatest Adepts there's ever been!" Medea cried proudly. "I survived an all-out attack by Oskan Witchfather, and I almost killed him!"

"Yes, but he survived. My son is hampered by goodness, by emotions, and by his refusal to answer completely the call of the Dark, and yet still you couldn't defeat him." Cronus stood up, and a swirl of icy particles eddied around him like a cloak. "There's a fatal weakness in you, Medea. You can't see beyond your own arrogance and emotions. Even now your mind deals only with the small-scale and petty; why try to kill only your father when entire populations could be destroyed? The obvious still hasn't occurred to you, has it?"

His deep and dreadful eyes regarded her for a moment, and then he turned and walked away, the shadows coalescing and scuttling after him as they were drawn to his negative power.

Medea watched him go in puzzlement. "But what do you mean, Grandfather? What do you mean?"

Thirrin wasn't magical at all; she hadn't even the slightest latent tendency toward a Gift of any sort, but she *was* a creature of instinct, and some deep visceral feeling had drawn her to this vigil in the cellar above Oskan's cave. The torch she held flared and smoked fitfully, and she considered calling a housecarl or werewolf guard to bring another, but she eventually decided that she preferred that no one knew where she was.

She'd been waiting for over an hour so far, and though she wouldn't admit, even to herself, exactly what she was waiting for, she'd made sure that she had a complete set of Oskan's clothing with her, as well as a flask of brandy.

Eventually she found an old crate to sit on and occupied herself running over the marching order of the army that would set out in two days' time. She and Andronicus had agreed that for the sake of Polypontian morale his regiments should be at the head of the line. After all, in effect they were the remnants of several defeated armies that had been forced into exile, and if they were tagged onto the end of the marching line, this idea would be reinforced among the soldiers. No, for the Empire troops to be truly effective members of the invasion force, they had to believe themselves to be an integral part of it.

Thirrin smiled as she thought back over her meetings with the Polypontian general. At first they'd been frosty, formal affairs, but eventually Andronicus's natural exuberance and friendliness had broken down her reserves and she'd even begun to acknowledge to herself that she quite liked him. He really wasn't that bad, for a Polypontian.

A sudden noise from the depths of the spiral staircase caused her head to snap up, and she listened intently, head on one side and frowning in concentration. There it was again; a soft dragging sound, like bare feet on stone. Quickly she seized the lantern that sat beside her on the crate and lit the candle inside it. The panels were of red glass, and when she doused her torch, only a faint glimmer lit the area around the head of the stairs.

She held her breath and continued to listen. Nothing for almost a minute, and then the unmistakable sound of a cough echoed up from the black depths. She almost called out, but forced herself to stay quiet. If she startled him, he could lose his footing on the treads, which were worn and broken in several places.

The footsteps were coming regularly now, even if they were a little slow and hesitant, and she quietly stood and waited. The cough sounded again, and once she thought she heard a gasp, as though he'd just seen the light. For another five minutes she waited, in a quiet frenzy of anticipation, then suddenly he was there, stepping into the dim light and shielding his eyes from the glare.

"Oskan!" she whispered.

He turned toward her and lowered his hands, but his eyes still squinted in the glare. He was completely whole and regenerated, and as she gazed on his face, she realized that all the signs of aging had gone. His skin was unlined and his hair was jet-black again.

He looked at her blankly, as though trying to remember who she was, and when she stepped toward him, he stepped back. Forcing herself to remain calm, she held out the flask of brandy, and after a moment he took it and swallowed a long draft. The strength of the spirit took him by surprise, and he went into a long paroxysm of coughing and sputtering that forced him to his knees.

She rushed forward and put her arms around his shoulders, and he grasped her wrist in a grip of iron. His black eyes focused on her and suddenly he relaxed and smiled. "Hello, Thirrin. Bit cold in here."

She hurriedly fetched the clothes she'd brought with her and helped him to dress, while he took another, smaller drink from the flask of brandy. "How long have I been . . . away?"

"A week. You were burned black. Even your bones were charred."

"Yes. I remember."

"What happened?"

"I fought . . . the sorceress, and I suppose I won. . . . The kids! How are they?"

"Unharmed. They said you just suddenly appeared in the sky above them, and the next thing they knew they were in the Great Hall."

He nodded. "I broke her hold over them."

"Is Medea . . . is she dead?"

"No. Just injured. I can't kill her, Thirrin. There's a price to pay if an Adept kills another who's a family member. But I can say no more about that; the Goddess has imposed a sanction. So Medea's probably back to full strength again, just like me."

"But she tried to kill you."

"Yes. And she nearly succeeded. Clearly my magic may not always be enough to protect us."

Thirrin stopped and looked at her husband. It was one of those moments when she wished they were just an ordinary couple somewhere, perhaps farmers or bakers, or maybe merchants of some sort with no worries about wars or evil magic. She settled a thick cloak on his shoulders and then she kissed him. Just a small peck, but Oskan suddenly gathered her in a hug and returned the kiss with a passion that surprised her.

"Excuse me! I thought you'd just recovered from horrendous burns and a coma!"

"And so I have, but *everything's* restored and I've just realized the sheer wonderful joy of life!"

"Well, good," she said primly. "But you seem to have come back younger. How ever am I going to keep up?"

"Oh, you don't have to worry about that. There's not a speck of gray in all that glorious fire of hair, and not a line or wrinkle anywhere."

"I should hope not. Some of us have a country to rule."

"Well, just for tonight it can manage on its own. Come on, let's see what we can find to eat. I'm so hungry I could beat Tharaman in one of his pie-eating competitions!"

Thirrin sighed. "I'll have to see if there's anyone still in the kitchens; it is three o'clock in the morning, you know."

17

Sharley and Mekhmet were relaxing in their room. Neither of them had yet gotten used to the idea of easy access to food again, and they were just finishing off a huge plate of cheese-and-pickle sandwiches.

"You know, if we'd had a few pounds of this Southwold Stinker to give us strength on the Plain of Desolation, I'm sure we could've fought off any number of elephantas," said Sharley, nibbling appreciatively at a hunk of the cheese.

"Well, either that or we could have used it as a chemical weapon," said Mekhmet. "The smell's enough to drive off an army of demons. Still, it tastes good."

"Pickled onion?" Sharley inquired, handing over a jar.

The Crown Prince of the Desert People was just spooning two of the fiery pickles onto his plate when a knock came at the door. "Come in," he called, and then stared in amazement as Cressida appeared.

The Crown Princess never knocked on any door, and Mekhmet had often found himself holding a small washcloth in a very strategic position and having a conversation with Cressida while otherwise completely naked.

"Are you busy at all?" she asked quietly.

"No, sit down," said Sharley, waving at a chair.

She sat and smiled. "I just thought I'd drop in and see how things are going after all the time you spent on the Plain of Desolation."

"Fine. We must all be as tough as old boots," said Sharley, but then his face clouded as he remembered how they'd been rescued. "I'm just worried about Dad. . . . I mean, did you see the state he was in . . . ?" He fell silent and shuddered.

"Yes, horrible," Cressida replied, her face a mask of worry. "But I'm sure he'll be all right. He's been put into the cave where he was regenerated during the first war against Bellorum, and the witches caring for him expect him to make a complete recovery."

"I know," said Sharley. "It's just that it was such a shock seeing him like that. I mean, can he *really* come back from such horrible injuries?"

"Yes, he can," said Cressida with characteristic firmness. "By all accounts his injuries were at least as bad when he called down the lightning in the war against Bellorum, but he regenerated perfectly."

"But how can we be sure he'll make the same recovery this time?"

"We can't," she answered brusquely. "There's no such thing as certainty in this world, Sharley. You know that. All we can do is hope." But then her manner softened and she went on: "Look, Sharley, we're all soldiers here and we know that the end could come at any time. Dad knows it, too. All we can do is be ready for any eventuality and make sure there are no loose ends in our lives. So with that in mind, there's something else I want to say . . . something important."

She paused and shot a glance at Mekhmet, who immediately took the hint. "I . . . er . . . I think I'll just go and check on the horses," he said. "They seemed to be recovering nicely the last time I checked, but you can never be too careful. A good bran mash should help to build them up."

Cressida watched him leave and waited until the door had closed behind him before turning back to her brother. Then with the sudden determination of a warrior confronting her fears, she leaned forward and took his hand. "Look, I, er . . . I just wanted to say that I'm . . . *really* pleased you're safe, and that, er . . . you know, I'd miss you quite a lot if anything had gone wrong on the Plain of Desolation."

Sharley smiled; he was much more in touch with his emotions than his older sister was, and he knew what making such a statement must have cost her. "That's all right, sis. I'd have missed you, too. You might be a bit of a battle-ax at times, but we all know you mean well."

"Do you?" she asked plaintively. "I know I can be blunt, but that doesn't mean I feel the less for any of you, in fact, for *all* of you: Mom, Dad, Eodred, Howler, Maggie, Grishmak, Tharaman, Krisafitsa, Kirimin, Mekhmet . . ."

"All right! All right! I understand what you're saying," Sharley interrupted. "And we all know how you feel. You don't have to spell it out."

"Good. It's just that with another war approaching, and all *that* entails, I didn't want anyone thinking I didn't care."

"Nobody thinks that, sis," he replied, and standing, he kissed her.

"Fine!" she said, becoming brisk. "Well, I won't take up any more of your time. There are things to do."

"Stay and have a sandwich; the Southwold Stinker's really good."

"No, no, thank you. There are supplies to check and troops to drill. I must get on."

"Fine," said Sharley and smiled. "But you know where I am if you want to talk again."

"Yes, I do," she replied, and, standing abruptly, she crossed to the door, wrenched it open, and stormed off along the corridor, completely unaware that her capacities as a fully rounded human being had been expanded enormously.

Erinor rode at the head of her army. As far as the eye could see, rank upon rank of infantry, cavalry, chariot regiments, and Tri-Horns advanced toward their next objective. They were now on the boundaries of the Polypontian heartland and had spent the last week reducing six border fortresses to rubble. Admittedly they'd hardly been the latest design in military architecture, being over three hundred years old, but when the Polypontian government had realized that the homeland itself was in danger of attack for the first time in more than four centuries, they'd spent huge amounts repairing the crumbling walls and sending the few remaining cannon to help in the defense. But it had all been to no avail; Erinor had arrived and picked off each fortress one by one. None of them had been able to resist the ferocious onslaught of Shock Troops, elite regiments, and the Tri-Horns for longer than a day, and so in less than a week Erinor had turned her attention toward the heartland of the Polypontus and its glittering prize of the capital itself.

The city of Romula had stood for more than two thousand years and had never fallen into enemy hands. It was surrounded by four circuits of massive curtain walls and a complex system of ditches, and during its long existence it had been besieged only twice. Both times the enemy had been annihilated by the defending Polypontian soldiers, and soon it had become a byword for impregnability. Over the centuries many other enemies had marched on the city, but each time the sight of its huge walls was enough to make the attacking armies turn around and go home.

But this would not be the case with Erinor and her Hordes. She had sent out many spies, who had returned with detailed reports of the walls' decrepit state; the masonry was crumbling, and it was also pierced with dozens of gates in woefully indefensible places. In the four hundred years since Romula had last been attacked, the defenses had been neglected, and the money that would have been spent on their maintenance had been used to lay out pleasure gardens and to construct beautiful soaring buildings of marble. Worried military planners and engineers had pointed out the dangerous condition of the defenses to the Emperor and his Senate, but they'd simply replied that Romula's walls were the Imperial legions that had built an everlasting empire, and that its gates were the fighting spirits of her citizen militias.

But that had only been true before Scipio Bellorum and his ruinous wars with the Icemark. Since then the powerful Polypontian economy had collapsed, broken by the demands for more and more armaments to fight the countless rebellions that had erupted throughout the Empire after the general's defeat. And since then the Polypontus had lost many of her trade routes and access to raw materials as many of her former colonies had regained their freedom and turned against their old rulers. In fewer than three years the Empire had become bankrupt; there was no money to make or buy weaponry, or even to pay the soldiers of the legions. Almost all of the armament and munitions factories had closed; no new cannons or muskets had been made, and even the manufacture of gunpowder had ceased. There had been huge stores of the explosive, but these supplies were now dwindling, and firearms were no longer the chief weapons of the army.

The Empire was wounded and exhausted, and when Erinor and her newly unified Hordes had broken out of the land of Artemesion, destroying the Polypontian fortresses and walls that had kept them imprisoned, the Imperial legions were too weakened to stop her. She'd rampaged through the provinces and countries of the Empire, even destroying those who'd recently thrown off Imperial rule themselves. Some had offered to join with her in an alliance against the hated Polypontus, but she had rejected every overture of friendship and peace, sending the headless bodies of their ambassadors back to their governments and smashing their gifts to glittering shards. Erinor had no need for alliances. Why should she care? Her ambitions allowed for no equality among neighboring states; she was destroying the Polypontian Empire only to remake it, with herself as Empress.

And once that monumental task had been completed, she would then have the leisure to invade the Icemark and destroy those who dared to call themselves the Hypolitan and every one of their allies. Their so-called Basilea would die, along with Queen Thirrin, who was herself the daughter of the treacherous peoples who had fled the ancestral home of Artemesion centuries earlier, when the land was beset by enemies.

Erinor's corrupt and debased interpretation of the Goddess allowed for no compassion and brooked no thought of forgiveness. In her view the Goddess was vengeful and judgmental; she was stern and unloving. Those who broke her laws died, suffering slow and painful deaths, and Erinor had appointed herself as the Mother's weapon of retribution on earth. What greater proof of her right to fulfill this role was needed than the fact of her unending military genius and her victories against all who dared to take the field against her? Erinor was Basilea of her people, the true Hypolitan, and she was, in her opinion, undeniably the Mother's general. Let all who looked upon her tremble and fall to their knees in homage; and let those who carried the burden of guilt, be it centuries old, die before the justice of her striking hand.

But even though her power was undeniably great, Erinor was aware that her brilliance came directly from the Goddess, and she was determined that she would never forget this. Ever since she'd been a little girl she had offered sacrifice to the Mother, and she'd found that the greater her love for a possession, the more powerful it was as an offering. So it was that as an eight-year-old, she'd sacrificed her favorite puppy, cutting its throat herself, and pouring its blood over the altar. She believed that her prayers had been answered almost immediately when the tribal elders had chosen her, from among dozens of other girls, to be groomed as the old Basilea's successor.

Erinor smiled at the memory, and turned in her howdah to survey the great army that marched with such power and resolution behind her. She had achieved much, and now the greatest prize of all lay before her: the very heart of the Polypontian Empire, the city of Romula itself. Once it had fallen, she would undeniably be the successor to the power that had conquered almost all of the known world. But in her heart she knew that to achieve such a prize, a truly great sacrifice would need to be made. And what possession did she own that was greater than her pride, greater than her glorying joy in the victories she'd achieved? She had made her decision, and when the camp had been set for the night, she would call together her commanders and announce it to the world.

With this in mind she brought her Tri-Horn to a halt and waited quietly. Immediately orders were bellowed and the entire army stamped to a standstill. At a single nod of her head, her people then scurried to set up the camp, and she watched quietly as streets and walkways, parade grounds and smithies, kitchens and stables began to grow from the wide plain around her like a city of hide and of wood. Soon her attendants bowed low before her Tri-Horn and announced that the royal yurt was prepared. Digging her goad deep into the hide of her beast, she waited until it lowered itself to the

ground, and then she stepped lightly down and waited until
her usual complement of body servants had gathered in an
obsequious ring and escorted her to the huge hide-covered
tent.

She took supper alone that night; she had no time or inclination for small talk with Alexandros. Her every thought and
act was concentrated on, and dedicated to, her interpretation
of the Goddess. Even chewing and swallowing her food was
offered in homage to the Mother, as she nourished the body
that existed only to do her bidding; the body that was the
instrument of her will on earth.

But at last her hunger was satisfied, and, calling the
guards, she gave instructions for her generals and councillors
to be called. They arrived within minutes; nobody dawdled
when Basilea Erinor sent out a summons. They gathered in
a silent, watchful ring around her.

Alexandros, as consort, was the only man present, and he
knelt on the floor by her side, but the rest all squatted on
a semicircle of low divans that faced Erinor's high-backed
chair.

"The march on Romula begins tomorrow," she suddenly
barked without any preamble or delay.

A murmur rose up from the generals. Here it was at
last! Here was the moment when the power of the Empire
would be finally taken and placed in the hand of Erinor of
Artemesion. "May the Goddess smile on the task that lies
ahead," said Commander Ariadne, the army's second in
command.

"She does," said Erinor with quiet certainty. "And when
we've won, the new Artemesion Empire will have been
created."

Spontaneous applause broke out from the generals and
councillors, and Erinor smiled. "But there's something more
you should know." The yurt fell silent as all caught the

portentous note in the Basilea's tone. "The assault will be led by Commander Ariadne."

The shocked silence was the closest that any of the generals dared come to open dissent and disapproval. Then at last, the second in command herself drew fearful breath and asked: "But why, my Basilea? This will be the crowning glory of your whole campaign, perhaps even of your entire time here on earth."

Erinor regarded her in stony silence until Ariadne almost squirmed and writhed under the cold scrutiny. "And that's why my self-denial will be exactly the right act of sacrifice to the Goddess," she finally said.

Understanding nods were now exchanged between the generals. Here was a fitting reason for Erinor's absence from the assault. Every soldier in the army would approve of such a towering act of self-denial and would know that only their Basilea had the strength to make such a sacrifice to the Goddess. Their victory was now even more assured.

"May I request that the Basilea review the army before it embarks upon its historic invasion of the Polypontian heartland, and that she ask the Goddess to guide us in our war?" Ariadne asked quietly.

Erinor looked at her second in command, understanding her petition perfectly. This would be the first campaign in which she would be the sole tactician and strategist. Even though there would be many seasoned heads to consult, the ultimate and final decision would be hers, and the thought was overwhelming. "You needn't be afraid, Ariadne. The Goddess will guide you; the walls of Romula will crumble, and the defenders will lay down their arms."

Ariadne bowed her head in acknowledgment of the Goddess's bounty, but couldn't ignore the nagging fear that whispered failure in her mind's ear. Just then, almost as though confirming her dread, a distant mutter of thunder rolled over the sky, and the steady hiss of rain sounded beyond the walls of the yurt.

All of the commanders' heads turned to listen; rain could be the enemy of a marching army, especially if it turned the roads to mud and literally dampened the morale of the soldiers under drenching sheets that soaked uniforms to the skin and heralded illness.

Erinor sat back in her high-backed chair and offered a prayer to the Goddess, requesting perfect marching weather and the removal of any obstacles that might stop them from reaching the walls of Romula in less than a week. But the Basilea's corrupt and debased interpretation of the Mother caused the supplications to reach no divine ear and receive no such blessings.

The rains settled in for almost ten solid days, and they turned the Empire's once well-maintained roads into quag-mires; they soaked through the thickest and most waterproof layers covering the yurts and drenched every soldier to the skin. Foodstuffs, blankets, even boots rotted in the down-pour, and the normally brilliantly polished weapons became rusty no matter how often they were cleaned.

In such conditions the march on Romula was impossible, and the Hordes settled down to wait for better weather while their Basilea raged and roared through the camp, hanging anyone who caught her maddened eye and demanding a witch hunt to find out who it was who'd earned the anger of the Goddess, never believing that it might be herself.

Through all of this Cronus had quietly watched from his icy pinnacle in the Darkness. The fact that the attack on Romula had been delayed by the rains concerned him not at all. The Icemark and her allies were now committed to invading the Polypontus, and, once their armies had crossed the borders, his invasion of the Physical Realms would be uncontested. Surprise would be complete, and he would have established control over the entire country before anyone knew what was happening. So would begin the building of a new empire whose core and center would be the Darkness; so would begin the first move in a war that would ultimately challenge the Goddess herself for the right to rule Creation.

But one more piece needed to be put in place before the glorious jigsaw puzzle of his plans was truly complete. He would succeed, anyway, no matter what happened, but he felt he owed it to the overall elegant effect of his strategy to try to convince Oskan Witchfather to join with him and Medea in establishing the new order. Besides, it had to be admitted that everything would be so much *easier* if his son would join them.

What a truly magnificent triumvirate they would make, and how pleasing in its symmetry that three members of one diabolical family should rule the Physical and Spirit realms. He, Cronus, would of course be the senior partner within the ruling trinity, while Medea, who was still not aware of the true scale of his plans, would be a very junior contributor indeed. He had almost completed the molding of her thoughts and attitudes, but in one area she remained stubborn. No matter what Cronus did to alter her mind-set, she retained a love for her father.

But Oskan . . . Oskan had a potential whose range and power nobody really understood. With him on board, limits really wouldn't apply. But as yet, neither he nor Medea was aware that they were simply pawns in the game Cronus controlled. Oh, how he loved his ability to manipulate the worlds around him. Not only simple-minded barbarian queens, but even those of his own blood. Medea really had no idea that her grandfather had *orchestrated* her battles with her father as a means of testing both their abilities, and he'd found the results most informative.

All that remained to be done now was to convince Oskan to finally accept his true heritage within the Darkness. And Cronus was convinced that his son wouldn't be able to resist the call of true evil when he fully understood exactly what was being offered.

Sharley felt nervous. In fact, he was close to panicking as he waited with Mekhmet and Kirimin in the small room next to the comfortable family apartments that he'd known for years. He told himself he was being ridiculous; he was, after all, only waiting to see his father for the first time since he'd rescued them from the Magical Realms! But then the memory of the blackened skeleton that had erupted in the sky above them on the Plain of Desolation came back in vivid clarity and he shuddered. He now knew that his dad had fought Medea, and that she had lured them into the Magical Realms and kept them trapped. After his initial shock, he was hardly surprised. His sister had hated him since they were children, so this attempt to kill him was just one more in a long line of her attempts on his life.

His and his friends' survival was entirely due to his father, who despite his terrible injuries had managed to rescue them and bring them all home. But somehow Sharley couldn't get the image of that smoking skull out of his head, or the way its empty eye sockets had turned on them and seemed to glow, as though it could still see and was excited by its find!

Sharley knew that his dad had been magically regenerated in the cave beneath the citadel, but somehow he couldn't quite believe that his dreadful wounds could have been healed completely. Surely there'd be at least some scarring; surely he'd be disfigured in some way?

Mekhmet reached over and squeezed Sharley's hand, understanding how he felt perfectly. "No matter what he looks like, he's still your dad," he said. "And a brave man."

Sharley nodded. "I know, but how can I . . . how can I even touch him when . . ." His voice trailed away.

"Well, I won't flinch from him," said Kirimin. "The Witchfather's always been my favorite adult human. I remember when I was a little cub, meeting him for the first time. He understood perfectly that a smile would look like a snarl to a Snow Leopard, so instead he blinked slowly and purred, just like a cat. Of course as I grew older, I learned all about human facial expressions, but I've never forgotten that first meeting. He was . . . kind."

"You're talking about him as though he's dead!" said Mekhmet. "He's not; he's only injured, and we should all be adult enough by now to see through the disfigurement and look on the man beneath."

Suddenly the door to the sitting room opened, and all three leaped to their feet as though stung. They glared almost fearfully at the opening space, and breathed a sigh of relief when a neatly dressed chamberlain they all knew stepped out. "Ah, there you are! The Queen and Witchfather were wondering where you'd gotten to."

"We didn't like to just barge in unannounced," Sharley explained.

The chamberlain looked puzzled. "Why not? You always have before."

"Yes, but it's different now—"

"Are they there, Ranulph?" Thirrin's voice interrupted. "What are they dithering about?"

"I'm not sure, Ma'am," he answered. Then, turning back to the friends, he added, "Well, come on!"

They followed him into the living room in single file and stood in silence, as close to the door as they could. Thirrin was sitting next to the fireplace in her third-best dress, determined to be as normal as possible before the demands of the coming war had her wearing armor for weeks on end. She was talking to someone in a high-backed settle that was turned away from them.

"Well, come in!" she said when she saw them. Sharley had already been reunited with his mother earlier, and his ribs still felt bruised from the mighty hugs she'd given him. There was also something about motherly kisses that made your hair stand up in odd tufts, which no amount of brushing and wet combs would tame.

"They're here, Oskan," she said to the settle, and the wood creaked as a tall figure stood up. For a moment he paused as he poked the fire, and then he turned to face them.

They all gasped aloud. He was perfect! In fact, he looked younger, with no gray hair or wrinkles. "Well, it's about time," he said, smiling broadly. "It's not every day you get burned to a crisp rescuing people, so it's nice when they finally find a space in their busy lives to come and see you."

"Dad . . . Dad, you were burned black. You were a skeleton!"

"Yes, but I'm not now."

"But how?"

"I'm a healer and a warlock," he answered simply, as though that explained everything. Which of course, it did.

Kirimin leaped forward, almost knocking the Witchfather into the fire, and licked him vigorously, her thunderous purrs filling the room. "Kiri, this face is still quite new and tender; please leave some of it on my skull!"

She sat back and let out a crashing roar of joy that rattled the windows and had the werewolf and housecarl guards pouring through the doors, ready for battle.

"It's all right, it's all right!" Thirrin called as the soldiers stormed in. "It's only Princess Kirimin greeting the Witchfather."

Mekhmet joined in the pandemonium by calling aloud a prayer in his own language that proclaimed that there was no God but the One and mighty was his Messenger, and then he salaamed deeply and grinned hugely.

Only Sharley continued to stare at his father in silence. Then at last he said, "I thought you were as good as dead."

"So I was," said Oskan. "But the Goddess allowed me to be healed. Obviously I have other tasks to perform in my life before I'm called home to the Summer Lands."

"I see," said Sharley. Then, stepping forward, he took his father's hand and inspected the smooth, youthful skin before holding it briefly to his cheek. "Thanks for rescuing us, Dad," he said simply and smiled.

"That's all right, Charlemagne. I'd fight an entire Darkness of sorcerers for you, if I had to."

"Good. Greetings over," said Thirrin briskly into the silence that followed. "Now, while I have you all here, can you please do something about that imp you brought with you? He's causing chaos in the palace kitchens."

Almost on cue, a sudden rattle of wings sounded on the air and the object of discussion flew in. "Where have you been? I've been looking everywhere!"

Kirimin sighed wearily. "I'm sorry, but I don't think anyone can control him."

"Oh, I think I could," said Oskan darkly.

Pious gave a squeak of alarm. "Oh no! It's that warlock!"

"One moment, my little bundle of chaos," the Witchfather said commandingly as the imp prepared to flee. "I want to know exactly why you allowed yourself to be transported here when I rescued Charlemagne and Co."

"Well, actually I didn't 'allow' any such thing. It was purely accidental. One moment I was taking a well-earned siesta in one of the Prince's saddlebags, and the next thing I knew, I was in the Icemark with pandemonium erupting all around me!"

"I see," said Oskan quietly. "So you claim that you were a reluctant stowaway."

"Absolutely."

"All right. I'll accept your story for now. But I think it only fair to warn you that if I suspect, even for one moment, that you're acting as an . . . *agent* for a certain sorceress, or for anyone else, then you can expect to die slowly and horribly. Do I make myself clear?"

"As the finest crystal, oh powerful one," said Pious, managing to bow ingratiatingly as he hovered in midair.

Oskan then turned his full magical attention on the imp and held him in an unblinking stare that seemed to paralyze the small demon as he probed deep into his head. "Your brain and mind are as devious and as twisted as I would expect from one of your ilk; yet I detect no malice toward my son or his friends. In fact, I'm surprised to see a stirring of emotion deep in your dark little psyche. Could it be, creature of the night, that you even feel the first glimmerings of friendship for our children?"

"Witchfather, as a demon, I hardly know what I feel," Pious answered uncomfortably. "As you can no doubt appreciate, affinity and empathy have never been high on my list of priorities."

"Indeed," Oskan replied, and smiled. "Welcome to the world of humanity, my dear little imp, and be prepared for a ride of the most extreme emotional turmoil."

For a moment Pious gazed at the Witchfather, but then he was seized by a terrible panic attack as the full implication of what he'd been told hit him. With a squeak of pure terror he shot away, and the crash of breaking glass filled the room as the imp flew off through the window, allowing the cold, snow-scented wind to howl around the room.

"Do we have a glazier in the citadel?" Thirrin asked resignedly.

Medea woke slowly, her mind gradually expanding to fill the physical limitations of her body, but then extending beyond mere flesh and blood to explore the world around her. She'd been dormant for several days, allowing her body and powers to regenerate fully as she lay as still and quiet as the dead on the table of ice she'd conjured.

But if her body had been quiet while it repaired itself, her mind had been working feverishly as she sought a means of gaining revenge and destroying Oskan. Her grandfather had said that she was "missing the obvious" and that she only worked within the "small and petty." This had scarred her deeply. She was desperate to impress Cronus with her abilities, both psychic and intellectual. Her father had already rejected her when he'd exiled her to the Darkness, and the thought that Cronus thought her less than brilliant was more than she could bear. She'd spent hours thinking things through with meticulous care before she'd entered her healing sleep. But she'd reached no obvious conclusion.

She scanned the Darkness around her, observing and absorbing the terrifying beauty of its icy wastes. A full moon like a deformed skull glowered over the tundra of frozen souls, and a low howling moaned monotonously, almost as though a wind were blowing over the frigid wilderness. But the desolate sound had nothing to do with the movement of air; it was the "spirit of ghosts," a phenomenon quite unique to the Darkness, where the very *essence* of the many millions who'd died trying to enter the evil realm escaped from their captivity and wandered in torment over the wastes.

"So many lost souls," said Medea to herself. Shuddering at the thought of such desolate helplessness, she began to examine her body as it lay quietly on the ice table. The healing process was now complete, and her powers were completely restored. But she knew at last that the time had almost come to escape the limitations of puny physicality. If her form had been expressed in pure spirit, then her father would have been unable to destroy her magical Gifts. If a brain did not physically exist, it could hardly be damaged. Such freedom from the physical would be so liberating.

Her grandfather was the perfect example of "bodyless existence"; his form was conjured from the ectoplasm of light and shadow, and he built a body from whatever materials were at hand. This gave him a physical form that he could use whenever it suited him.

Medea knew that once she'd shed her body, her powers would manifest purely in spirit and so could never be damaged again. By the time her plan was put into action, she would need to have made this transition from physical being to spiritual, but somehow she wasn't quite ready to take this step. Her subconscious mind felt a need to hang on to the past that her real body represented. As much as she hated the memory of her old life in the Icemark, it was also there that she'd spent time with her father as he'd taught her how to use her fledgling talents as an Adept. It was there, and then, that Oskan had loved her.

But all of this was hidden deep in the shadows of her mind, and as she hung in the ether, she cleared her thoughts and finally descended through the Bone Fortress and entered her body. Its limitations were stifling and more than a little disgusting; it was rather like forcing her arms and legs into a tight rubber suit that'd been lubricated with someone else's cold and sticky mucus. Shuddering, she positioned her consciousness behind her eyes and between her ears, and then forced her eyelids up. She opened her mouth and drew the breath that was needed to keep the thing living, and she coughed to clear tubes and passages.

At last she stood up and stretched. The sense of disgust was beginning to fade as she grew used to her body again, and her thoughts quickly returned to her plans for inflicting death and mayhem on her family.

The Vampire Queen sat alone in her throne room. She often found the incessant chatter of the courtiers wearing; despite their immortality they seemed endlessly fascinated by the petty and ephemeral and would talk for hours about the weather, fashion, and the latest scandals. Better to suffer the loneliness of the cold throne room than endure the isolation to be found within the crowds of facile courtiers.

Time passed without acknowledgment from Her Vampiric Majesty; untouched by the needs of a living body, she could sit for days in the shadows of the palace. Only Lugosi, her loyal chamberlain, ensured that she remembered to feed the few needs of the corpse that contained her personality, and she would step out into the long night of a northern winter and fly in search of a victim. But when she came back to the Blood Palace, she would spend a few brief moments with her courtiers, before dismissing them and returning to the shadows and grief of her throne room.

Then, on one particular night of silence, as she reached across and laid her hand upon the arm of the king's empty throne, she became aware of a distant disturbance in the unending quiet of the room.

"Who's there?" she called into the shadows. Only a faint echo replied, and she stood gazing into the dark. "Show yourself, before my soldiers rip you apart and drink your blood!"

"I'm afraid they couldn't actually do that, Your Majesty," a voice replied. And then a slight figure emerged from the dark. It walked with the poise and elegance of a swordsman, which contrasted sharply with a pronounced limp.

"Prince Charlemagne!" she gasped in surprise. "But when did you arrive? I wasn't warned. . . ."

"I didn't arrive. I'm not actually here," he said with a charming smile. "My dad . . . I mean, the Witchfather is projecting my image and words using his powers."

"I see," she said quietly. "Then what is the purpose of your . . . visitation?"

Sharley smiled at her less than polite directness. "I have a message for you, Your Majesty, a very *personal* message."

For the first time in years her curiosity was aroused. "Personal?"

"Yes. You see, until recently I was trapped with two friends of mine in the Magical Realms. Fortunately Dad was able to rescue us, but before he could do so, we faced quite a few dangers. And when we were in the Circle of Ghosts, we were almost killed. In fact, I'm certain we would have been, had it not been for the intervention of a friendly spirit."

"*And?*" the queen snapped irritably. The adventures of young mortals interested her not at all.

"And . . . and the spirit was His Vampiric Majesty," Sharley replied quietly.

The queen sat in silence, her white skin seeming to glow in the dimness, like snow washed in moonlight. Then at last her voice whispered on the cold air, "But . . . but how can this be? His Vampiric Majesty was lost to oblivion when Bellorum destroyed him in the last war. Vampires have no ghosts! Vampires have no afterlife!"

Sharley shrugged. "The Vampire King has been granted a soul, and he exists still in the Spirit Realms."

"But how?"

"Because he learned compassion, and how to love, when he lived and worked with humans."

The queen's eyes glittered with rage. "And what human did he learn to love? Tell me her name, that I may tear out her heart!"

"He loved no human, Your Majesty. He loved only you."

Her Vampiric Majesty slowly bowed her head and felt a deep and overwhelming longing fill her to the utmost capacity. "He told you this?"

"Yes. He asked me to visit you and tell of his feelings for you. He also asked that you, too, should open your heart to emotion and compassion, so that you also could develop a soul and so join him when you finally lay down the burden of your physical existence."

Suddenly the queen's head snapped up, and she glared at Sharley. "Tell me, Prince Charlemagne, if my consort has developed a spirit and still exists, then why hasn't he ever appeared to me in this Land-of-the-Ghosts? Surely such a domain would be particularly conducive to spiritual manifestations!"

"To that I have no answers, Your Majesty," Sharley answered honestly. "I can only guess that some law or directive in the Spirit Realms prevents him from doing so. And, that being the case, I suspect that it may have something to do with you developing a spirit of your own. You must make your own choices and not be influenced by the sight and presence of your dead consort."

The queen fell silent again as she considered this. After a while she looked at Sharley again. "That could be so, I suppose. The Spirit Realms have their own arcane laws and rules that we can only guess at." With a sudden softening of her icy features, she asked, "How did he look? Is his spirit whole, or is it damaged by the hated Bellorum's weapons?"

"He looked strong and powerful, Ma'am. He looked confident and proud. He looked every inch a king."

Her Vampiric Majesty nodded in pleased satisfaction. *"Now* I believe you have seen my consort!" She raised her head and straightened her shoulders, glaring arrogantly over the empty throne room. "We were powerful indeed when we ruled this land together!" But then, slowly, her shoulders slumped, and she lowered her head to gaze at the floor. "But now I rule alone, denied the presence of my consort and with no certainty of ever meeting him again. How can I know that I will ever have a soul? How can I bear the thought of oblivion alone in the endless night, alone in non-existence?"

Sharley stepped forward. "Your Majesty, if the Vampire King developed his spirit as a result of his capacity to feel love, then I'd say you are already a treasury of souls! What else is grief but the emotion of love denied the presence of the loved one? Your feelings for His Vampiric Majesty have made you a spirit-bearer!"

"Do you truly believe so?"

"I do."

The Vampire Queen gazed at the young Prince, and tears trickled slowly down her cheeks.

"And remember," Sharley went on. "No matter how long the separation, reunited spirits will have eternity together."

"And you really believe this?"

"I do, Your Majesty, with all of my heart."

"Then I, too, must find a function for that long-defunct organ. His Vampiric Majesty waits for me in eternity, and I must prepare myself for everlasting life in spirit!"

18

The army of the Alliance continued to wind its way through the frozen countryside of the autumnal Icemark. No significant amounts of snow had fallen yet, but there'd been enough light flurries to give the land an interesting piebald look as patches of powder coated the rich black soil of the surrounding fields. The Great Forest was now out of sight, but it still made its presence felt in the low endless moaning of the wind through its now almost leafless branches. It was the familiar voice of autumn and winter, and would follow the army for a few more miles before distance finally silenced the voice of the massive stand of trees.

By this point the marching army had begun to warm up nicely, and many of the larger housecarls and all of the horses, Snow Leopards, and werewolves had begun to literally steam as the warm, moist air rising from their bodies condensed on the cold atmosphere.

"How lovely," said Thirrin ironically as she turned in her saddle and looked back over the lines of marching warriors. "We seem to have become a mobile sauna. It's a good thing no one's trying to track us; I should think even a noseless dog could follow our scent!"

"I'm sure we emit the wholesome aroma of resolution and martial fervor," said Oskan with a smirk. "Unless you're

Grishmak, in which case you probably just smell like cheesy feet."

"I do not smell like cheesy feet! More like cheesy *paws*, actually."

"Same smell, different anatomy."

"Acknowledged," said the Werewolf King and grinned.

"Well, I'm sure neither myself nor Tharaman smell particularly. And you and Oskan have the usual human fragrance," said Krisafitsa.

"I'm not sure I like the sound of that," Thirrin replied.

"Oh, I wasn't being offensive. It's just that all species have a distinctive odor. Humans smell of whatever they wash in, if they bother; werewolves smell of fur and . . . and . . ."

"Cheese?" suggested Oskan.

"Quite. And Vampires . . . well, I'm afraid they often smell of blood and death. Apart, that is, from His Vampiric Majesty, who seemed to regain his human perfume just before he was killed."

"That's because he developed a soul," said Oskan.

"Talking of Vampires, whether they smell or not, we could do with them here," said Grishmak.

"Agreed," said Thirrin. "But I just couldn't bring myself to disturb the queen's grief. Our relationship with The-Land-of-the-Ghosts has changed so much that the earlier tactics of threats and bullying just can't be used. You don't threaten friends, so I can't make the Vampires participate in this war any more than I can force the Holly and Oak kings to join us. We can only hope they'll decide to help later."

Oskan nodded in agreement. "There's a good chance that some of the Vampire warriors will take part in a private capacity. There was talk of it, I believe, and the queen hasn't forbidden it."

"Well, they'd better hurry up about it, then, hadn't they?" snarled Grishmak. "At this rate we'll be fighting Erinor herself before they turn up."

"At least we don't have to worry about a Sky Navy this time," said Thirrin with relief. "If we had wasp-fighters and bombers to deal with, we'd have no chance without the Vampires."

"That's true," said Oskan thoughtfully. "In fact, I think Erinor's reaction to the Sky Navy gives us an interesting insight as to the workings of her mind."

"What do you mean?"

"Well, we all heard the reports that the Hordes overran the bases of the Imperial flying fighters and destroyed them without even bothering to try and use them in their war. Obviously they just didn't recognize their potential; it's almost as though something didn't want them to understand the Sky Navy's value, especially if they knew the Vampires were no longer an integral part of our force and so we'd be easily wiped out by an aerial attack. . . ." His voice trailed away, but then he dismissed the idea as absurd. What possible reason could there be for prolonging a war? "This failure to recognize a weapon's worth," he went on, "is easier to understand if you realize that Erinor and her Hordes are simply tribal levies without either the sophistication or experience of a truly professional army."

"Well, these amateurs are doing pretty well against the Imperial legions, and let's face it, they're the second-best army the world's ever seen!" barked Grishmak.

"Who's the first?" asked Tharaman curiously.

"We are, of course!" said the Werewolf King with a huge grin. "Not even Bellorum himself could crush us, and he had two tries!"

"True, very true," said Thirrin warmly. "A fact that our soldiers should be reminded of."

"And just how do you intend to do that without alienating the Free Polypontian units?" Oskan asked.

"Ah yes. I see what you mean."

"Besides, that has nothing to do with my point about the Hordes. They're not even a proper army. They're a nation of tribes on the march!"

"What difference does that make?" said Grishmak. "The only real and important point is that they're winning battles. In fact, they're sweeping aside all opposition and seem unstoppable. Nicely debated points about their status and origins mean bitter little when you've got an arrow in your guts or when your army's been routed."

"I'm afraid he has a point," said Krisafitsa quietly. "I personally don't care if I understand Erinor's motives or not; all I want to do is stop her."

This seemed to end the discussion, and the comrades marched along in silence as the autumnal countryside of the Icemark slowly unfolded around them.

The Vampire Queen was surrounded by the usual throng of courtiers, sipping gently at crystal goblets of sherry, greeting one another with simpering bows, and chatting with great volume at huge speed about nothing. Her Vampiric Majesty allowed her eyes to pass languidly over the slowly circulating crowd of sycophants, unconsciously searching for something to distract her from the unending, crushing tedium of her undead existence.

Beside her stood the empty throne of the Vampire King, and each time she saw the shadows and the dust and the unending void that were its only occupants, she remembered anew the death of her consort. Prince Charlemagne and his message from the spirit of the Vampire King might have given her more hope than she'd known in years, but the fact remained that she ruled alone, sat on her throne alone, and expected to continue alone down the centuries until a violent end finally released her from her undead existence. And even then she couldn't be sure that her personality in the form of a soul would survive her physical destruction.

To her undying mind, time still had no relevance, and its passing brought no reduction of the pain and horror she'd felt when His Vampiric Majesty had died at the treacherous hands of Scipio Bellorum and his Imperial soldiers. Her grief would remain as searingly fresh as the moment she had heard her love's death cry high above the battlefields of Frostmarris. She bowed her head and watched as an icy teardrop fell to glisten like crystal on the black silk of her gown.

But then a sudden blast of freezing wind moved through the Great Hall of the Blood Palace, and she raised her head to look out over the marble floors, elegant statues, and monochrome furniture to where the hall's huge double doors were slowly opening. A great shout rose up into the air, and the simpering courtiers scuttled aside like black leaves to watch as a force of Vampire soldiers marched in. Their elegant black armor was dusted with snow, as a blizzard was raging in the living world beyond the walls of the palace, but the cold had no effect on the undead warriors, and they marched with unwavering resolution toward Her Vampiric Majesty's throne. She watched their approach, a tiny spark of interest lighting her eye.

The column of soldiers reached the foot of the dais, and their commander, Bramorius Stokecescu, saluted and then bowed. "The Vulture Squadron reports for Her Vampiric Majesty's inspection."

The Vampire Queen observed the warriors appreciatively for a moment or two; this squadron had been the personal guard of His Vampiric Majesty, and as such it commanded her interest and patronage. Then at last she said, "I believe,

Commander Stokecescu, that it had been agreed your squadron would use no official name or number."

The officer bowed again. "Yes, Ma'am, and beyond the walls of the Blood Palace it will indeed be nameless."

Her Vampiric Majesty nodded in satisfaction. Rising from her throne, she descended to the floor of the Blood Palace's Great Hall and glided among the armored soldiers. "They appear to be suitably martial, Commander," she finally said. "Do you leave immediately?"

"With Your Majesty's permission."

"And that you have. But remember, you and your warriors are private citizens who are simply volunteering to fight in a foreign war. I will sanction no official Vampiric force to take part in any campaign that's designed to save the hateful Polypontian Empire, that nation of regicides who murdered our king!"

The officer saluted but said nothing.

"Friend Thirrin may fight who and as she wishes, and I'm sure her reasoning is politically and militarily sound. But I can only rejoice that the Imperial legions have been smashed, and that the Empire itself teeters on the edge of oblivion. . . ." Her voice rose to a screech of hatred, but with some effort she regained control, and added, "But I have neither the right nor the inclination to stop any Vampiric citizen whose conscience compels them to help the Icemark and its Queen."

Stokecescu took the queen's hand and kissed it, clicking his heels smartly as he did so. Then, straightening, he barked an order and the squadron turned around and marched for the double doors. Her Vampiric Majesty followed, her hand lightly resting on the officer's arm.

Beyond the doors a blizzard blasted the darkness of the arctic night, but the queen's undead eyes could easily make out the rank upon rank of waiting soldiers filling the wide terrace that surrounded the palace and spilling out into the wild darkness beyond.

"I see your numbers have increased somewhat of late," said Her Vampiric Majesty, her quiet voice perfectly audible above the screech of the raging wind.

"Many have volunteered to join the most famous squadron of the Royal Vampire Army," Stokecescu explained.

"So it would seem," said the queen. "I would say that over half our warriors will be flying south, and all without a single threat from the Witchfather. Friend Thirrin will be very happy."

"Please don't think that any of us hold the memory of His Vampiric Majesty in anything other than the highest esteem," Stokecescu suddenly said. "We fight to defeat a new threat to our lands, not to help the Empire."

The queen patted his arm. "I know it, and doubt the motives of my people not at all. But understand, I cannot lead an army whose success will mean the saving of the Polypontian Empire. Such a royal sanction would dishonor the king who died as a result of Imperial treachery."

The officer dropped to one knee. "Then at least give the Vampire warriors your blessing, that we may return home safely to The-Land-of-the-Ghosts and our queen."

Throughout the darkness the soldiers sank to their knees and bowed their heads, moving Her Vampiric Majesty to tears. "Gladly I would give you my blessing," she answered, and her fangs glittered like ivory daggers as she smiled. "But blessings are made of life and spirit, and so not for the undead to give, even if they have hopes of developing an immortal soul. I can merely confer upon you my best and most fervent wishes, and hope that even a godless people can be favored by the gods."

"Ma'am, your words will be as a shield to your soldiers in their coming war," said Stokecescu, climbing to his feet.

"And now, we must assume our wings and fly to the aid of our allies."

The queen nodded and stood quietly while the army of Vampires beat black sword on black shield in salute to their monarch. Then, as the rhythmic beating rolled to a crescendo and died slowly away, they leaped as one into the air, transformed into giant bats, and wheeled away, screeching.

Her Vampiric Majesty watched and waved as their flying ranks were absorbed by the swirling snows of the storm. But then she stopped and held her head on one side as though listening. Her undead senses had detected a shift, the tiniest change of intention in the order of the worlds, and the implications were enormous.

Slowly her lips drew back over her fangs and she hissed threateningly. "It would seem, Commander Stokecescu, that yours will not be the only Vampire army seeing action in the coming weeks."

Then, turning, she strode back into the Blood Palace, calling for Lugosi, her faithful chamberlain, as she went.

19

"Then . . . then *you* caused the Polypontian Empire to invade the Icemark?"

Medea sat in silence as the enormity of what Cronus was saying sank in. She was appalled, she was thrilled, she was breathless with excited amazement.

"Of course."

"And so *you* have caused all the wars there've ever been?"

"Not *all* the wars there've ever been. Human beings have always had a capacity for violence. I just helped them along a little."

"And all the fighting and killing were just part of a master plan to distract the human race while you invaded and took over the Physical Realms."

"Exactly."

Medea nodded in silence again as she absorbed this incredible idea. But then her shrewd mind found an anomaly, and she shot Cronus a piercing glance. "So why are you telling me this now?"

"Because now I'm almost ready to carry out my final plans, and despite the weakness of your emotional mind, you are one of the most powerful Adepts that has ever been. An alliance with you would be useful to my cause."

Medea was flattered, but oddly she was also disappointed. If Cronus wanted her help, then he couldn't be as powerful as she'd liked to believe. In her imagination the Arc-Adept was the mightiest being in all of the Multiverse, before whom even the Goddess trembled, and yet here he was asking her help to invade the Physical Realms. Her disillusioned mind began to search for further flaws and immediately raised an obvious question.

"So, if you've been planning to invade the Physical Realms for so long, why haven't you done it yet?"

The temperature in the Great Hall of the Bone Fortress seemed to drop even lower, and the ice particles that flowed around Cronus's form swirled in agitation. "The Goddess has watched me closely for eons and opposed my plans, but my strength has now outgrown even her ability to stop me."

"That being the case," Medea said, "I must ask the question again: Why haven't you invaded the Physical Realms before?"

"Because there is another to consider."

"Who?"

Cronus paused as if to heighten the dramatic effect, then said, "Oskan Witchfather."

Medea gasped in amazement. Cronus's plans were being thwarted by her father! Once again her shrewd mind was forced to make an adjustment. Oskan was powerful enough to thwart the Arc-Adept's invasion plans! True, he was the most formidable Adept now living in the Physical Realms, and his power combined with that of the witches would be daunting opposition to any invasion. But once she and her grandfather had taken control of the Icemark and established their defenses, surely they'd be unassailable!

Unless . . . unless, of course, there was something else to consider. She could hardly believe it, but eventually she had to accept the obvious.

"You're afraid!" she said in appalled amazement. "You're afraid of my father!"

"Fear is an emotion I cannot feel, Granddaughter. But, my child, you have no idea of the extent of his powers. And neither, incidentally, has he."

"He's simply an Adept! *I'm* more powerful than he!"

"No, you're not, Granddaughter. If Oskan were to truly accept his position within the magical ecology of the Darkness, there'd be none who could even approach his Abilities. He'd be mighty . . . mightier . . . the mightiest! Terrible and unbearable would be his rule, and we would all be his groveling subjects!"

She gazed at him in horror. "Even . . . even *you?*"

"Even I," Cronus confirmed.

"But this can't be true!" she managed to croak at last.

"It can and is," said Cronus. "The only thing that has saved the whole of the Magical and Physical realms is the fact that Oskan refuses to accept what he secretly knows. He's chosen the path of goodness and truth, and he rejects the Dark. But in the extremity of our invasion of the Icemark, he might be forced to use every weapon and Ability he has."

He paused, and the dead, empty eyes turned to regard her. "This is why we must form an alliance with him; this is why we must convince him to join us, then all nations can unite and human feeling can be discarded forever."

Medea was appalled. In the long, bitter years she'd spent in the Darkness, the one comfort she'd had was the belief that her Gift was greater than her father's. Now Cronus was telling her that she was badly mistaken. The Witchfather had the capacity to be the greatest and most evil Adept of all time. . . . All he had to do was accept his true potential, and all Creation would be at risk!

For the briefest of moments she was almost prostrated by fear, disappointment, and even grief. But mixed in with all the negatives was the quiet note of admiration and love for her father. She did her best to quash these feelings and desperately began to search for a flaw in Cronus's revelation.

After a while, a small light of hope was ignited in her brain. Oskan would never embrace his true potential.

"No, Grandfather. It'll never happen. Oskan won't dare accept the Power of the Dark, especially if he knows it really could make him the greatest and most dangerous Adept ever."

"Why?" Cronus boomed.

"He loves my mother too much."

A silence fell. The Arc-Adept's flat black eyes looked at her blankly for a moment, then he spoke. "Are you saying that offspring of mine would put emotion before power? That he'd reject ruling both the Darkness *and* the Physical Realms because of love? Impossible! No one could resist the call of such limitless power. Once he'd established his rule, he'd even be in a position to attack the Goddess! Who could reject the chance to rule all Creation?"

Medea smiled, reveling in the power of the knowledge she held. "You obviously don't understand my father. If he accepts the Power of the Dark, he'll become immortal, right?"

"Of course."

"If he's immortal, he won't ever die?"

"Also undeniable."

"So, if he can't die, he'll never be able to enter the designated heavens, in whatever form they take. The very nature of the universe won't allow it!"

"Yes and yes again! Look, child, what are you trying to say?"

"It's simple. He won't be able to face eternity without my mother. He'd sooner die and be with her in whatever heaven they're eventually sent to!" Medea paused, allowing the enormity of what she was saying to percolate through. "Don't you see what this means? We *can* invade the Icemark; he'll never risk turning to the Dark in any war he fights against us, and there'll be no need to take him into an alliance! We can rule alone; just the two of us."

"To think that a son of mine could value mere *love* over all that the Dark can give him. I am truly amazed and ashamed."

"But you accept I'm right?" Medea asked breathlessly.

"Yes," he answered at last. "Yes! But even now, I still think that we need your father in our alliance. We must at least try to convince him to join us. With him we will certainly succeed, but without him the contest will be less certain, the final victory longer in coming."

"But what does time matter to an Immortal such as yourself?" she asked, desperate to exclude Oskan from their future empire. "Besides, I've already told you why he'll always refuse to accept the Dark; he'll never abandon my mother, and if he remains human, he'll be just one more Adept in a Cosmos that *we* rule and dominate."

Cronus returned to his seat, staring to the middle distance as he thought things through. "But his decision to value mere love higher than the ultimate prize of pure power sullies the line of Cronus the Great and poisons the purity of the Darkness. Our battle with him weakens our strength. And because of this, I insist that we at least make the attempt to draw him into our cause."

Medea almost wailed in desperation. "But you've said yourself that he's dangerous; how can we be certain that he won't discover our plans if we even meet with him?"

"Because my mind is protected by psychic shields of adamant; nothing could penetrate them, not even the Goddess herself. And nor will he be able to break through yours, with a little help from me." He paused again and Medea waited as patiently as she could while his white lips faintly mouthed the words running through his head. "Besides," he continued at last, "Oskan Witchfather is one of the very few creatures whose mind *I* haven't been able to fully penetrate. His defenses throw me out every time I try, but I know he's tempted by the Dark. He believes he can control it. And perhaps in direct conversation he will reveal more of himself than he realizes."

Medea opened her mouth to protest again, but then she was struck by the possibility that her grandfather simply *wanted* to meet his son, and that perhaps Cronus was more influenced by emotions than he knew. A sudden surge of jealousy flamed up within her. Once again she was being excluded; once again she was being placed second in her family's affections.

She began to sputter objections, but Cronus raised his hand. "Enough! I have decided; we shall meet with Oskan Witchfather, and then we shall test his mind in a competition of willpower. Be content with the fact that your words have shown me I am now able to invade the Physical Realms with or without Oskan's collaboration!"

20

Erinor sat in silence. Her yurt was in darkness, the only light source being the gray glow of dawn that glimmered through the entrance flap. The camp, too, was unusually silent, the normal sounds of waking and early-morning preparations muted and subdued. Even so, today was to be momentous. Today the final phase of the campaign against the Polypontian Empire would begin. The march on Romula itself was to commence, and a new empire would rise from the foundations. But despite this, there was an atmosphere of quiet and of waiting.

Erinor drew breath, but denied herself the sigh that waited locked in her lungs, and she exhaled quietly. A sigh might denote regret; a sigh could hint at emotional weakness.

At the sound of approaching feet, she turned her eyes to the entrance flap and waited. Ariadne, her second in command, entered and bowed.

"Your Majesty, all is prepared."

"Is the sacrifice waiting?"

"No, Ma'am. As agreed, the victim will be paraded through the camp before being dispatched."

Erinor almost gave orders to change the plan, but remained silent and nodded. She stood, already fully armed and armored, and strode out of the yurt. Her Tri-Horn was approaching, and she waited until it lumbered to a halt before her. It raised its huge head and bellowed, but even it seemed to be affected by the atmosphere, and it subsided into silence. The Basilea then climbed onto its raised foreleg, up via its bony ruff, and into the howdah high on its back.

From her vantage point Erinor could see far and wide over the camp, the tangle of yurts resolving themselves into a grid pattern of temporary streets, wide parade grounds, and training squares. Already representative regiments were drawn up in the central square: over ten thousand of the male Shock Troops and fifteen thousand of the elite female soldiers. The rest of the teeming Hordes that made up the army were drawn up beyond the boundaries of the yurt city, no square or parade ground being big enough to accommodate them all. Even so, they would know precisely when the sacrifice had been made, because the Tri-Horns would roar and a great beacon would be lit.

Erinor gave the word, and the mahout urged the giant beast forward. Soon they were pacing through the streets, and a phalanx of horse-mounted officers followed behind, led by Ariadne. The Basilea allowed the rhythmic swaying of the howdah to lull her mind into a nonthinking state as she approached the parade square. To think would be to regret. The sacrifice had to be made, and for it to be truly efficacious it must hurt the giver. . . . It must hurt the giver badly.

As the Tri-Horn entered the square, the waiting soldiers began to sing a hymn of praise to the Goddess and to Erinor, her representative on earth. Round and round rolled the song, its melody doleful and sad, as befitted a day of sacrifice. All accepted the belief that making a painless offering to the Goddess was worthless. It never seemed to occur to her worshippers that the Mother of All would be deeply saddened to think of her children hurting themselves, or denying themselves some much-needed commodity, just to make what they considered a fitting offering.

Erinor's giant mount advanced to the center of the square, where it halted, and a silence descended. Nearby stood a flock of goats, a herd of cows, and over fifty handpicked warhorses. All of the creatures were bedecked with garlands of flowers, and their coats had been brushed and cleaned until they gleamed.

The Basilea nodded and the sacrifice began. Soon the square was awash with blood as hundreds of jugulars were slit and the animals sank slowly to the ground as their lives ebbed away.

Erinor nodded again and the mahout dismounted, leaving her to place the huge chisel at the base of her Tri-Horn's skull where its spine entered its brain. Taking the hammer, she struck the chisel three times and the massive creature collapsed as suddenly as a felled tree.

But still the sacrifice was not complete. With perfect timing, Alexandros, the royal consort, entered the square. His escort of soldiers stamped to a halt, and he advanced alone to where Erinor was stepping from the wreckage of her dead Tri-Horn. He bowed low, then stood waiting.

His wife nodded in greeting, and then advanced to meet him. "Welcome, Alexandros. Are you made ready?"

"Your Majesty, I am."

"What is it you wish?"

"Nothing but a kiss," he said quietly.

"Gladly given," she answered, and for a moment the two embraced and kissed as though no one else were present. "Forgive me," she whispered in his ear.

"Of course," he whispered back. And then they stepped apart, and, drawing her sword, Erinor ran its glittering length through his heart.

A muttering rose up from the ranks of the Shock Troops as Alexandros, their commander, slipped slowly to his knees. And then, as Erinor gently laid him on the ground, a deathly silence fell. Tears coursed down her face. If sacrifice without pain was worthless, how great—how enormous—must be the worth of this offering to the Goddess?

The army seemed to gush out of the narrow entrance of the pass, like wine from an opened bottle. Thirrin hadn't been allowed time to sit and gaze upon the lands of the Polypontus, or to savor the moment in which she now led an invasion force into the Empire that had twice invaded her little land. The press of the following army was such that she'd been carried forward and down onto the wide grassy plain that flowed from the foothills of the Dancing Maidens and out toward a network of cascading mountain streams.

She frowned to herself; the relay of orders back along the ranks would need to be tightened. No way could they afford such a breakdown in communications when in battle.

"For goodness' sake, woman, lighten up!" snapped Grishmak, reading her mind perfectly. "Everyone got their orders, but they just couldn't resist the temptation to push forward and see the Polypontus. This is history in the making, you know, and understandably everyone wants a piece of it!"

"I know, Grishy. But we can't allow one moment of lapse when we're fighting Erinor. I'm just worried that if excitement can make the army ignore orders, then what about fear, and what about bloodlust? Just one slip against that woman, and she'll have us!"

"Well, there won't be any slips. The army knows that different rules apply in a battle situation. . . ." He trailed off as he watched Cressida gallop by, her face a mask of fury. "Someone's going to cop it! I wonder how many'll be on charge before we make camp this evening, and for that matter how many'll be flogged?"

Thirrin sighed. "I know, I know. Leave it with me. I was going to have a few strong words with the section commanders myself, but Cressida can never quite get things in proportion!"

"You'd better go and sort it out now, then, before the Crown Princess makes herself the most unpopular woman in the army."

Thirrin nodded and galloped after her daughter.

"Well, Grishy, we're here!" a booming voice called over the noise of the marching army. The Werewolf King waited quietly as Tharaman-Thar and Krisafitsa-Tharina trotted up. "The farthest south I've ever been, and probably about as far as I ever want to go, for that matter."

"The snow got here before you, though, just to make sure you got a good welcome."

"Call this snow? This isn't snow! It's just a sprinkling of powder to cool my tootsies," said the Thar contemptuously.

"Oh, I don't know," argued Grishmak. "It's drifted quite deeply in parts."

"Huh, not enough to come up to my—"

"That will do, Tharaman," said Krisafitsa primly. "We want no crudities, thank you."

"Don't we? Funny, I was only going to say it wasn't deep enough to come up to my knees."

"Were you?" asked the Tharina skeptically.

"We'll have to keep an eye on the supply wagons," Grishmak said, hoping to interrupt any bickering before it started.

"Why, are there problems?" asked Tharaman, almost panicking.

"Don't worry; the beer and wine are safe, and so's the food convoy. I'm just saying that the drivers might need a bit of help through the deeper drifts, that's all."

"Right, I'll send some of my strongest leopards to the supply commander. We can't be having any difficulties, now, can we?"

"I'm sure Thirrin's already thought of everything, Tharaman," said Krisafitsa. "There's no need to panic."

"Who's panicking? I'm just taking proper precautions, that's all."

"You're a fine commander, my dear—always concerned with the basics of planning," said Krisafitsa with amused irony.

"Well, yes, indeed. 'An army marches on its stomach,' as the old saying goes! Who *did* say that, anyway?"

"Some idiot," Grishmak observed acerbically. "A snake, perhaps?"

"Perhaps," Tharaman replied absently as he watched a wagon struggling through one of the snowdrifts. "Come on, let's give the driver a hand. There could be important supplies on board!"

"There are," said Krisafitsa. "Toilet paper, I believe."

"Bog roll?" asked Grishmak incredulously. "On campaign?"

"Do you mean the stuff humans wipe their . . . you know, after they've . . . ?" Tharaman said.

"Yes, that's right. Oskan insists on it. There are tools for digging proper latrines, too, complete with instruction manuals for the correct dimensions and depths."

"What on earth for?" the Thar asked.

"Hygiene, apparently. He says more soldiers have died of diseases caused by bad sanitation than were ever killed by the enemy."

"I suppose he's right," observed Grishmak. "There's nothing worse than bum trouble when you're on the march."

The army rumbled on under a cold and sparkling blue sky, and slowly, over the course of several hours, the landscape changed from the rocks, scree slopes, and tough grasses of the mountains to the gentler slopes and vegetation of the lower altitudes. And then, as the sun started to slowly dip toward the horizon, a halt was called and the process of setting up camp began.

Even though they'd left the mountains behind, they were still quite high up in the foothills, and when night fell, so did the temperatures. Several degrees of frost coated every surface in a thick crystalline crust of ice, and the cloudless night sky glittered with stars. All through the camp, fires crackled and roared in the freezing winds, and allied soldiers of all species gathered around their warmth, eating and drinking and sometimes singing or telling stories.

Thirrin's campaign tent felt very empty. Oskan was away in a different part of the camp with the witches and healers, and even though Cressida and General Andronicus sat with her, both were silent as they gazed into the middle distance and thought their own thoughts.

"Of course, with the support of an allied army behind them I'm sure the pike regiments will be more than a match for the Tri-Horns!" Andronicus suddenly said, as though they'd been discussing tactics.

"I'm sorry?" said Thirrin.

"Pike regiments, beat the Tri-Horns . . . you know, in battle."

"Oh yes. Perhaps . . . We'll have to see."

"I think the general's right," said Cressida, waking up from her own thoughts, and then making it clear to everyone exactly what she'd been thinking about by adding, "We should rendezvous with your son, Leonidas, tomorrow, shouldn't we?"

"All being well, yes. I've received no news from him, but that's not unexpected in a land at war. We don't have the advantage of the werewolf relay."

"You've no reason to think there're any problems, have you?"

"Well, no more than the usual ones for a cavalry commander on active service. But I'm sure if anything . . . bad had happened, I'd have been told somehow."

"Good," said Cressida with feeling.

Thirrin waited for her to ask the usual questions about troop size and disposition, but after a few minutes of silence, she was surprised to find that she was the one who finally did the asking. "How many soldiers will he have with him, General?"

"That rather depends on depletion, I'm afraid. But hopefully at least three thousand cavalry and perhaps a sizable number of infantry."

"A sizable number?"

"I'm sorry, I can't really be any more precise. If he's had to move fast through enemy territory, the foot soldiers will have been left behind."

"Yes, of course."

The general stretched and yawned. "Please forgive me, Ma'am. But it's been a long day, and we've an early start tomorrow, so if you don't mind, I'll say good night."

"Of course," said Thirrin and inclined her head as Andronicus saluted. She watched as he then saluted Cressida and left the tent. Thirrin marveled at how quickly she'd accepted his presence in the Allied High Command. If anyone had told her six months ago that a Polypontian general would be one of her most trusted officers, privy to all the secrets of the allied army, she'd have laughed. But here he was, an integral part of her planning, and an indispensable member of her inner circle, along with Tharaman, Grishmak, and Krisafitsa. She still had problems with Polypontians in general, but the particular of Andronicus and his Free Polypontian forces she'd accepted fully.

"I wonder exactly when we'll meet Leonidas and his cavalry," Cressida suddenly said, drawing Thirrin back to the moment.

"Who can say? Perhaps he won't be able to get through the enemy lines until later; or perhaps he won't even get through at all."

"Oh, don't say that!" said Cressida with surprising passion. "He *must* get through!"

Thirrin frowned. "Well, certainly his cavalry would be a useful addition to our numbers, and his experience of fighting Erinor can only be a bonus, but I wouldn't say it's imperative that he join us."

"Surely you can't be serious? Leonidas's presence would be invaluable, not only as mere weight of numbers, but also as a morale booster to the army generally."

"Perhaps, Cressida. But not everyone seems as eager as you to see him. Not even the Free Polypontians display the same levels of enthusiasm as you do. Hardly an hour goes by when you're not asking Andronicus for some tidbit of information about his son."

The Crown Princess blushed and snapped, "I don't know what you mean! Anyone would think that I . . . that I had a crush on him or something!"

"Yes, they would," Thirrin agreed. "Have you?"

"Oh, don't be ridiculous! I've never even laid eyes on him!"

"It's possible to fall in love with an ideal, you know," Thirrin answered gently. "What young woman hasn't created an image of a hero in her heart, fed it with fantasies of perfection, and become infatuated with the picture she's created?"

Cressida snorted. "Well, *I* haven't, for one!" But her fiercely burning complexion belied her scorn.

Thirrin sat back in her chair and sighed. A country at war was a terrible place to grow up emotionally; everything was so heightened, so pressured. There was no room or time to make the mistakes that everyone made. Cressida might almost be a fully grown adult, and have a huge experience of fighting and killing and even running a country, but when it came to matters of the heart, she was still an immature little girl. "Cressida, don't expect too much of Leonidas. It's not fair, either to yourself or to him! Heroes tend to be all too human when scrutinized."

Her daughter stood up, her face blazing and an angry retort waiting in her throat. But then she paused, drew a deep breath, and slowly sat down again. "Did you expect too much of Dad?" she finally asked shyly.

Thirrin snorted. "Your dad was different. I just hoped for the best and settled for what I could get."

"And what was that, in the end?"

Her mother grinned, realizing she was about to undermine her own argument. "A hero," she said.

Cressida nodded. "Yes, he is, isn't he? I think that might be part of the problem; when we're growing up, every little girl's daddy is a hero, and then when we get older, we find that he has problems and faults like everyone else. But little girls still love their daddies even when they realize they're just human; perhaps those faults even make little girls love them more. But you see, I don't have that advantage; my daddy really is a hero, and as for him being human, well . . . that really doesn't apply, does it? What man could possibly live up to the standard of Oskan Witchfather? Of course I create ideals in my head; it's the only hope I have of ever meeting a man worthy of him."

Thirrin reached across and took her hand. "Perhaps you should lower your sights a little."

"Perhaps. But until I'm forced to do so, I'll keep on waiting for my hero."

"Cressida, you're too hard on yourself, and the world."

"No, sometimes I think it's too hard on me."

Thirrin hugged her daughter and rocked her gently as though she were still a child. "Oh, my fierce warrior-princess, my vulnerable little girl. You might have to wait too long."

"Better that than be hasty and be disappointed later," Cressida replied. Disentangling herself from her mother's arms, she wiped her eyes and smiled. "I have to go to bed; we have an early start tomorrow."

Thirrin nodded and watched her go, imploring the Goddess to send her daughter a man who could live with, if not up to, her ideals.

The snow had frozen overnight, making the route treacherous underfoot. Oskan and the witches had been kept quite busy setting broken wrists and binding up strains and sprains, but in the main, the army marched on without undue incident. By midday they'd left the foothills behind and begun to march over a wide undulating plain of good farmland.

Thirrin sent werewolf scouts ahead, even though the few reports they'd had clearly indicated that Erinor and her Hordes were still well to the south. Try as she might, she couldn't help feeling deeply uneasy. She knew perfectly well why she felt like this; after all, she was invading the Polypontian Empire, a regime that was, at one time, the most powerful domain the world had ever seen.

General Andronicus rode at the head of the column beside Thirrin and Oskan, and the Imperial Eagle of Polypontus was the only banner that was on display. Thirrin wanted no misunderstandings with any Imperial legions there might be in the region. The general's own forces also headed the column of marching troops, and the entire army maintained a stony silence. At the present time the plan was to march on Romula and secure the safety of the Emperor, but circumstances could change at any moment, and they must be ready to react to whatever happened.

Tharaman and Krisafitsa also marched at the head of the column, as did Grishmak, Basilea Olympia, and her consort, Olememnon. Thirrin stole a glance at the Hypolitan leaders, but their faces revealed nothing. In a way, they had more to lose than anyone else in the coming war; Erinor had already declared the northern Hypolitan traitors and said that she intended to wipe them out without mercy. The threat sounded horrendous, but in reality it was little different from what Erinor and her Hordes did in every country they conquered. Their entire campaign so far had been an exercise in genocide and scorched earth. Whether you died because Erinor called you a traitor, or because you just happened to be in the way of her ambitions, made little difference when the knife cut your throat or the sword pierced your heart.

The rest of the day passed in a gradual but inexorable accumulation of distance from the mountains and the border, so that by the time they halted to make camp for the second night, they were already thirty miles inside Polypontian territory, having traveled at a speed that even Cressida accepted as exceptionally fast for a marching army. Thirrin watched as the usual controlled chaos ensued as tents were unloaded from wagons, and everyone got in everyone else's way as they were put up. Cressida, as usual, spent the next hour or so almost purple with rage as she tried to instill a sense of discipline into the assorted warriors and soldiers of the Alliance. But despite her rantings, the camp was habitable by the time the moon came up and the frost came down.

Thirrin was just settling into her and Oskan's campaign tent and wondering how to discuss the fact with Andronicus—and more important, with Cressida—that Leonidas still hadn't appeared when a huge clattering and screeching sent her running back out into the freezing night air. All over the camp human soldiers were scrambling for weapons, and werewolves and Snow Leopards were snarling and craning their heads skyward. She glared into the sky and then quickly beckoned a nearby bugler.

"Sound 'stand down,'" she ordered brusquely. "Now!"

The brittle, brassy notes echoed over the camp and were quickly taken up by other buglers, and gradually alarm and panic were replaced by a tense, wary curiosity as the entire army accepted the bugles' assurance that all was well, and they gazed into the skies.

"What do you think, Thirrin?" asked Tharaman as he strode over to stand at her side.

"Vampires. More than a thousand, I'd say, judging by the noise."

"Ha! Wonderful. Just what we need: an airborne division."

"Yes," agreed Thirrin and smiled.

Soon the huge forms of Vampire bats became visible as they descended into the dome of light created by the thousands of torches and fires that illuminated the camp. A great howling and roaring rose up from the Snow Leopards and Wolf-folk, as they greeted the arrival of their allies with relief, and the human soldiers beat swords and axes on shields.

A space opened up around Thirrin as housecarls forced back their comrades and cleared away wagons and stands of weaponry, creating a landing space for the Vampires. Then, at last, the squadrons swept in low and, transforming into their human forms, they stepped out of flight and into neat formations of black-armored, pale-skinned soldiers.

With perfect timing and faultless elegance, they saluted and then bowed as one body to the Queen. An officer stepped forward and bowed again. "Commander Bramorius Stokecescu reporting for duty, Your Majesty."

Thirrin smiled. "Welcome, Commander, and welcome to your squadrons. We're all very happy to see you."

"Her Vampiric Majesty extends her greetings to her sister monarch and ally, and wishes a swift victory to your campaign," Stokecescu continued smoothly. "She also assures you that your home territories and borders will remain secure under her personal unending vigilance and the guard of her remaining squadrons."

Thirrin's secret thoughts about it being easy to defend borders and territories that were not under threat were interrupted by the arrival of Oskan, who'd been supervising the witches and medical supplies in a distant part of the camp.

"The Vampire squadrons have arrived," the Queen explained to her consort, as though their presence had never been doubted.

"So I see," Oskan observed. "But without the official sanction of Her Vampiric Majesty's presence."

"Our queen has taken personal responsibility for the defense of the Icemark in your absence," Stokecescu explained warily.

"I see," the Witchfather said expressionlessly. Then, catching Thirrin's eye, he raised his shoulders in an almost imperceptible shrug and turned back to the Vampire commander. "We must indeed be grateful for the Vampire Queen's vigilance, but even more are we happy to welcome your squadrons to our war."

The atmosphere suddenly relaxed and the commander bowed low. "We're happy to fulfill our obligations to the Alliance. May our victory be swift."

"You can say that again!" Oskan replied, suddenly abandoning the formal language of diplomacy. "But somehow I think it ain't going to be easy."

21

Medea sat quietly in the private chamber she had conjured. She was about to become an integral part of one of the greatest events ever beheld by the Darkness and the Physical and Spiritual realms. Cronus was about to conquer the world, and after that . . . well, after that she now had no doubt that he intended to make war on the Goddess herself!

And so it was that Medea judged that the time had finally come to cast aside her physical body. Like all of the greatest Adepts, she would negate the deterioration of old age, and the finality of death, by simply ridding herself of her body. Then, in the same way that her grandfather created a physical form from his surroundings, she, too, would conjure a temporary body that would house her spirit whenever she needed it. As one of the most powerful Adepts the worlds had ever seen, she felt it incumbent upon her to assume the proper atmosphere and mystique of evil. And if this meant the death of her physical form, then so be it.

Besides, she'd subconsciously begun to accept that there was no way back into the past. She could never again be Medea, Princess of the Icemark; she could never again be the young girl who'd loved her father. A brief spasm of grief gripped her, but she thrust it aside and forced herself to concentrate on her plan.

For Medea, such a momentous occasion needed to be marked with a ceremony of "divestment." Layer by layer she would divest herself of her physical being until nothing remained. With this in mind, she sat quietly and willed her skin to split. With leisurely smoothness, the outer layers of flesh peeled open like the pod of a pea, revealing the muscles and tendons beneath, then with a damp slumping noise the flayed skin fell to the ground.

The muscles began to tear themselves from the bones beneath, swiftly followed by the intricate tracery of veins and arteries. Only her skeleton, central nervous system, eyes, and organs now remained. And these oozed from chest and abdominal cavities like strangely bloody fish, to pulsate on the white cobbles at her feet. Finally her eyes rolled away from their sockets, and her brain emerged from the bony triangle of her nasal cavity to drain away onto the floor, where it lay like a sticky gray puddle.

Medea's skeleton stood and surveyed the gatherings of offal that had been her physical life, and then one by one, the individual bones disarticulated and formed a neat pile next to the mounds of meat and slime.

Suddenly a raging fire burst into being and incinerated the remains until all that was left was a pile of gray ash, at which point a wind sprang up and blew the ash away. Medea's physical form was no more, and immediately the livid, evil essence of the sorceress began to create a new body, forming limbs and shape from the raw material that permeated the Darkness. Her hair was formed from cosmic dust, her eyes from photons, her flesh from radiation and electricity made tangible, and her brain from the dark matter that shaped and held together universes.

Soon she was complete, terrible, and awful in her beauty, awesome in her perfection, and terrifying in her evil. She looked almost the same as she had before she began her transformation, but all of her natural defects had been polished to an unnatural perfection. Her hair was lustrous, her skin flawless, her bone structure perfectly symmetrical and balanced. She could even sigh in satisfaction without her lungs as she did now, and then she laughed. She laughed in the knowledge and certainty of her power, and she laughed to think of the Icemark, just waiting to be destroyed.

The army waited in silence. The scouts had just reported seeing a large contingent of Polypontian cavalry on the road ahead, and a halt had been called. No order to ready weapons had been given, but the atmosphere was heavy with a nervous expectation that seemed to tingle through the air.

Cressida could hear the tiny creaks and groans of saddle leather as her horse breathed. In the nervous silence, the rustle and snap of the cold wind in the Empire's banner sounded as loud as the mainsail of a galleon in a storm.

Then, far off in the distance, an indistinct gathering of shadow and color slowly resolved itself into a large contingent of horses that cantered toward them. Andronicus snapped open his monoculum and peered without comment for a few seconds, before giving a bark of relieved laughter.

"Yes. It's Leonidas. And by the look of it, he has upward of two thousand cavalry with him."

Thirrin held out her hand wordlessly and, after receiving the monoculum, looked long and hard at the troopers heading toward them. "I see, yes. I presume the good-looking young man at their head is Commander Leonidas?"

"Yes, indeed. Luckily for him, he has his mother's Hellenic beauty."

Thirrin looked meaningfully at Oskan, who sat next to her on a droop-eared mule, before she silently handed the monoculum to Cressida. The Crown Princess showed masterly control and barely snatched at all, then she quickly trained the lens on the advancing cavalry, and just as quickly snapped the instrument shut and handed it back to Andronicus.

"I have an inspection to carry out," she said and started to turn her horse around.

"The Crown Princess will stay exactly where she is," Thirrin said, recognizing this sudden call of other duties as an acute case of nerves.

Cressida's horse sidled close to her mother's, and she leaned from the saddle to whisper, "I can't stay! He's . . . he's . . . and I'm . . . well, I'm a veteran of too much fighting and not enough taking care of my appearance."

Thirrin felt an almost unbearable upwelling of love for her daughter. She really had no idea how beautiful she was—not only beautiful but striking, with a pale, flawless complexion and profile, coupled with the family coloring of flame-red hair and green eyes.

"You will carry out your duties as the Crown Princess of the Icemark," Thirrin whispered, knowing that it would be useless to tell her daughter that any young man would fall over himself to spend even a minute in her company— unless, of course, he was a soldier under her command who'd done something wrong. "To gallop away now would be an insult to the commander!"

Cressida's eyes blazed with anger for a moment, but then she nodded curtly and guided her horse back to its position next to General Andronicus. By now the thunder of the approaching horses' hooves could clearly be heard, and a murmur ran through the gathered ranks of the army.

"They ride well," said Tharaman-Thar.

"And their horses are beautiful," Krisafitsa added.

"From the Imperial riding stables in Romula itself. The finest blood stock in the Empire," said Andronicus proudly.

"It shows, General. And may I add that your son, too, is a fine-looking young man."

"Thank you, Ma'am," he replied, bowing in his saddle. "His mother was as beautiful as moonlit snow."

"But do they fight as well as they look?" asked Grishmak brusquely.

"The fact that Romula still stands at all is almost entirely due to the Imperial cavalry and its tactics of harassment and containment."

"Hit and run, you mean?"

"Precisely."

"And what about a toe-to-toe slug-out?"

"The cavalry performed as well as poor supply and equipment allowed in the later battles with Erinor," Andronicus replied openly. "But Leonidas and his cavalry have now perfected the art of meeting their own needs."

"So they forage and plunder."

"I prefer the term 'living off the land.'"

"Leave the general alone, Grishmak," said Oskan, who'd been deep in silent thought as he watched the cavalry approach. "We'll be 'living off the land' ourselves as soon as our supplies have run out."

"True enough," the Werewolf King agreed. "I'm just trying to gauge the young man, that's all. And if I were you, Oskan Witchfather, I'd do exactly the same, especially if I had a daughter who suddenly seems to have gone off her feed."

"Oh, I've been gauging for quite some time now," said Oskan quietly.

Luckily for all concerned, Cressida had been too preoccupied with the approaching cavalry to hear the exchange, and her eyes narrowed as the horses reined to a halt and stood sidling and snorting only a few feet away. All of the troopers, and the horses themselves, looked hard-bitten and tough, with none of the usual glitter and finesse of the Imperial cavalry. They had the air of soldiers who'd been fighting for months, and who still had the energy and will to fight on for many more.

Leonidas, their commander, scanned the people before him, and his face broke into a radiant grin as he spotted his father. Quickly he dismounted, threw his reins to a companion, and strode forward. It looked like he was going to greet his father first, but then, seeming to collect himself, he slowed, stopped, and bowed low to all.

Andronicus dismounted and the two embraced with much backslapping and a rapid tumble of words in Polypontian. But then the general reverted to the language of the Icemark and, leading his son toward Thirrin's horse, he introduced him.

"Your Majesty, may I present my son, Leonidas Apollodorus Andronicus. Commander of cavalry, loyal son of the Empire, and, I'm proud to say, of myself."

Thirrin observed the young man through unconsciously narrowed eyes that assessed him coldly. "Commander Leonidas, I see you have a sizable force of cavalry with you. Have they recently seen action?" Even now, when the young man who'd reduced her daughter to an emotional wreck without even being seen stood before her, the needs of the war and of tactics came first.

"Yes, Your Majesty. Erinor and her Hordes have begun their advance into the Polypontian heartland, and we've been doing everything possible to disrupt their march."

"They've begun the attack?" asked Tharaman eagerly. "What're their numbers? How long before they reach Romula?"

Leonidas gazed in wonder for a few moments at the power and majesty of the Thar, the almost legendary talking Snow Leopard who'd figured so largely in the defeat of the Bellorum clan. Then, collecting himself, the young man bowed low and answered, "Great Thar, their numbers are impossible to count accurately; will it be sufficient for me to say that they outnumber this army of allies by many count- less thousands?"

Tharaman nodded. "It would, young man, and I suppose strict accuracy isn't really necessary; ever since I first began to fight in the wars of human beings, I've always been out- numbered. It seems to be the natural order of things. But what of Romula; how long before it's besieged?"

"I'd estimate a week. There are still several units of cav- alry resisting their advance, but they're unstoppable."

"Wouldn't they be better dismounted and defending the walls of the city?" asked Grishmak, stepping forward from among the horses.

Leonidas paused again as he was confronted by yet another walking legend. Who else could this huge and mon- strous creature be, other than King Grishmak Blood-drinker of the Wolf-folk? "Your Majesty, the walls of the capital city are indefensible, they're crumbling and breached in many places, and the defensive ditches have become mere hollows in the ground, choked as they are by centuries of debris. Not only that, but there are huge distances of walls and too few soldiers to man them. The military governor of the city has decided it will be easier to defend Romula by fighting for control of the streets."

"And the Emperor?" asked Thirrin succinctly.

"He is in the Imperial palace, along with all senior mem- bers of the Senate. Barricades have been thrown up around it, and the greatest concentration of troops are stationed to defend the precinct."

"I presume the squadrons of cavalry now harassing Erinor's advance will fall back to the city and join the defense?" Thirrin asked.

"Yes, Your Majesty."

"Then the race for Romula is on! How far to the city from here?"

"Ma'am, an army of this size will take at least eight days to reach its walls."

"Too long; the Hordes will have it by then. We'll do it in six!" She barked a tumble of orders to all around her, and immediately heralds scrambled to take the news of Leonidas's arrival and the development of the war to all sections and units. Within minutes the army rolled forward. All now knew the need for speed, and the massive host advanced over the land like an unstoppable flood.

Leonidas and his cavalry were assimilated into the whole with almost frightening ease, and he found himself trotting along between his father and Queen Thirrin.

"Have you and your men eaten, Commander?" a voice suddenly asked, and Leonidas turned in his saddle to see a tall, slightly built man riding on a mule. A strong sense of power and authority seemed to beat on the air around the figure, and he suddenly realized with a pang of fear that he was being addressed by Oskan Witchfather.

"We have, thank you, My Lord," he answered, confused and puzzled that such a powerful warlock should be bothered about whether he'd had breakfast that morning.

"I'm a healer, Commander Leonidas. It's my principal concern on this expedition to ensure the health of the army," the Witchfather said in irritable tones. It was almost as though he'd read Leonidas's mind and found his confusion annoying.

"Of—of course, My Lord," the young man stammered, still amazed that someone with supposedly huge magical powers should concern himself with such mundane matters.

"Tell me, Commander, are you more likely to achieve success with a healthy, well-fed army, or with a disease-ravished, malnourished rabble?"

The warlock was still reading his mind! He immediately blushed and blurted, "Well-fed . . . and-and . . . healthy, of-of-of course."

"I'm sure the commander understands your point, my dear," Thirrin said gently. "Allow him a little time to come to terms with his new allies. It's not every day that a Polypontian officer speaks with werewolves, Snow Leopards, and warlocks."

"Ah, of course. You'll have received the much-vaunted Polypontian education in rationality, science, and all things quantifiable, will you not, Commander Leonidas? So how do you find conversing with physical impossibilities and abominations of nature?" Oskan asked in acid tones.

"Er . . . very nice, thank you," he answered lamely.

"'Very nice'? Is that all? But you're consorting with the totally impossible, according to your scientific beliefs!"

"Yes . . . I mean no. . . . I mean, it's *very, very* nice."

"Did you hear that, Grishmak? It's very, very nice to talk to you," Oskan called to the Werewolf King, who'd been chatting with Krisafitsa a few paces back.

"Is that right? I'm glad to hear it; I'll allow you to buy me a pint tonight in celebration, boy."

"Certainly, sir, it'll be my pleasure!"

"Will it? Good, in which case you can buy me two!"

"Stop it, both of you!" a voice suddenly snapped, and Leonidas turned to see a beautiful young woman who was so like Queen Thirrin she couldn't fail to be Cressida the Crown Princess. "This commander has risked his life to join us and bring vital information, and I won't have him pilloried by two vicious old stoats that seem to think they're being funny!"

"Strange, I thought I was introducing him to the rough and tumble of the Icemark's courtly life," said Oskan with a wicked grin.

"Were you? I thought I was just lining up a few pints of beer," remarked Grishmak. "Could you see your way clear to a pork pie and some pickles as well, Commander?"

"Er . . . yes, certainly . . ."

"Enough!" Cressida cut in loudly. "Grishmak, I believe you were talking to the Tharina, so you can just go back and carry on with your conversation. And Dad, one of your supply wagons has broken an axle. You'd better see to it if you don't want to be left behind; there's no room for stragglers, you know."

Oskan bowed ironically and turned his mule around, happy in the knowledge that he'd given his daughter a comfortable means of introducing herself to a young man she obviously found fascinating. When it came to social niceties, she was hopeless, but give her a bullied stranger to rescue and her sense of outraged justice would give her the confidence she needed.

"I'm sorry about that," Cressida said to Leonidas. "They don't mean any real harm by it; they've just got a funny sense of humor."

"Oh, that's-that's-that's fine. . . ." the commander said, trying not to let his jaw drop as he remembered how she'd dismissed the huge Werewolf King as though he were a naughty schoolboy.

"Dad normally has more of a sense of decorum, but what with the strain of the war, and having to look after the entire army, I suppose he just forgot his manners."

Leonidas shot her an incredulous glance; was she really talking about the most powerful warlock that had ever walked the earth? "Don't-don't-don't, you know, don't worry about it. It's-it's fine."

They both looked at each other and suddenly realized that they'd just about used up all the good excuses for talking, and immediately blushed like twin sunsets. "Well, I suppose

I'd better inspect the troops or something," said Cressida, her toes curling in excruciating embarrassment. What a stupid thing to say! "Inspect the troops"? Of all the moronic excuses!

"Yes, fine . . ." Leonidas mumbled. And then as an afterthought he added, ". . . Your Royal Highness."

"Oh no, don't. I mean *you* don't have to. I'm only an ordinary woman like everyone else. . . . I mean, like every other woman . . . not like everyone else because not everyone's a woman . . . obviously. . . ." Oh, Goddess! This was getting worse!

"I know what you mean. . . ."

Thirrin, who'd discreetly dropped back with Andronicus to allow the two to talk, could see that a crisis point had been reached, and she urged her horse forward again. "I believe the commander saw action recently. Isn't that right, Leonidas?"

"Yes, at Bright Water River," he answered, confident now that he had a safe subject to talk about.

"How many of the Hordes were there?" Thirrin asked, determined to keep the conversation going until Cressida felt confident enough to rejoin it.

"Quite a sizable party. They were advance engineers, trying to build pontoon bridges for the rest of their army."

"How fascinating!" Krisafitsa trotted up, desperate to help the "poor young things" get to know each other. "Did they put up much of a fight?"

"Yes, Your Majesty," he answered, bowing in his saddle, as this was the first time he'd spoken to the Tharina. "They'd dug defenses, and we feinted a frontal attack while I sent out detachments to take them in both flanks."

"Classic pincer maneuver," said Cressida, her interest in the skirmish at last overwhelming her crippling shyness. "Did it work?"

"Yes, eventually. But they fought hard, and we lost a few troopers. Still, we killed more of them, drove off the survivors, and destroyed the groundwork they'd laid for the bridges."

Crown Princess and commander ground to a conversational halt again and Krisafitsa stepped resolutely into the breach. "How long have you been in the field, exactly?"

Leonidas opened his mouth to reply, then paused as though taken by surprise. "More than a year without a break, Ma'am," he finally said, and then began to brush at the buff coat and breastplate of his cavalry uniform. "I probably look like a complete mess. I can't remember the last time I spent more than a few hours in a town of any size; we usually bivouac in the countryside somewhere."

"You look wonderful," said Cressida distractedly, and then realizing she'd spoken aloud, she coughed and blushed such a deep and fiery red that Thirrin wondered if she could set light to paper just by touching it to her daughter's cheeks.

Krisafitsa rallied once more, and went on. "Well, we've brought along a few home comforts that I'm sure you'd enjoy; there are baths, for example. I know humans like to soak their bodies in hot water, oddly enough, and perhaps Cressida could keep you company." The sputters and coughs that followed this warned the Tharina that perhaps this wasn't acceptable behavior in human circles, at least not among young humans who'd only just met. "Ah, but there again, perhaps not. Maybe Cressida could meet you after your bath and you could . . . chat."

The Snow Leopard retreated, bloodied but unbowed, and allowed Andronicus to step in. "Leonidas won several decorations in the opening stages of the war, didn't you, my boy? Of course, we still had hopes at that point of containing the Hordes, but then supplies dried up and we began the long defeat that we've suffered up until now. Still, if we'd had enough ammunition and reinforcements, I'm sure Leonidas would have been at the forefront of a glorious victory!"

This only succeeded in making the commander look even more uncomfortable, but Cressida couldn't hide her admiration. "What decorations were they?"

"Two Exemplary Conduct medals, and an Imperial Cross—which, as we all know, is the highest order for bravery that the Empire can bestow," said Andronicus.

The breathless silence that this fell into somehow signaled the end of the conversation, and they all rode on quietly, with Cressida and Leonidas staring resolutely ahead, but side by side.

Andronicus was more than happy with the unexpected turn of events. After all, if his son and the Crown Princess were to strike up a relationship, the political advantages would be enormous. *Bless the young,* he thought to himself, *and bless the mighty hormone.* But then a less cynical part of his brain took over, and he fell to reminiscing about his long-dead wife and the wonderful effect she'd had on a young, slightly overweight officer so long ago.

The cold forever night of the Darkness stretched as far as Medea's psychic eye could see. The light of the moon reflected from the white tundra of frozen souls and touched rank upon rank of twisted, gigantic, and hideous monsters. The Ice Demons were a truly appalling sight, and under rigid mind control they made a formidable fighting force.

"An army of armies, Granddaughter," an unexpected voice suddenly said beside her.

Medea leaped sideways, but recovered quickly enough to answer Cronus with some semblance of control. "An army of *conquering* armies, Grandfather."

"Yes," he agreed. "More Ice Demon regiments are marching in from the outlying reaches of the Darkness, and within a week we will be ready for invasion."

"If the Physical Realms knew of the danger they're in, the entire structure and fabric of human society would collapse in terror," said Medea happily. "To think there are even cultures that believed the mighty Cronus was imprisoned in the Darkness, and that the Goddess could prevent him from entering the world of mortals! How stupidly naive!"

"Yes, indeed, Granddaughter," said Cronus with quiet menace. "But soon the people of the Icemark will find out exactly how wrong they were, when they die in their countless thousands. And after that the population of the entire world will be forced into changing its views. Millions will perish, and those that survive will envy them!"

Medea shuddered with evil anticipation. Soon she would be joint ruler over a new world order, and then let her family see if they could escape her wrath.

Sister's coming home, she thought happily to herself.

Erinor watched as the messenger thundered through the camp toward her. Dust rose from the horse's hooves in choking clouds; the rains had finally stopped, and the bitingly cold winds had helped to dry the clinging mud. Even this far south, she'd had to break the ice in her washing bowl that morning. Such domestic details would normally have been dealt with by Alexandros, but since she'd sacrificed her consort to the Goddess to secure final victory in the war, she'd had to cope with such inconveniences herself. Of course she could have replaced him with a body servant of some sort, but that would hardly have been in keeping with the spirit of the sacrifice. The point was, his loss had to hurt, and the difficulties of dealing with domestic issues served to remind her of that loss.

The messenger's horse was now close enough for her to see the rider's features clearly. No one she knew, she thought dismissively, and waited quietly. The horse slid to a stop in a flurry of flying stones and dust, and then the young woman flung herself from the saddle, dropped to one knee, and presented the small leather case that contained letters and battle plans from Ariadne, the commander of the Hordes in the field.

Erinor took the case without a word and returned to her yurt. This was another effect of the sacrifices she'd made to the Goddess in the hope of victory; she'd denied herself the glory of finally taking the city of Romula, and now she was reduced to waiting for the reports that Ariadne sent twice daily so that she could keep abreast of events! Sometimes it was almost more than she could bear, and twice she'd dressed herself in her armor and prepared to ride north and join her army. But at the last moment, common sense had prevailed, and she'd returned instead to the huge map that filled the floor of her yurt and moved the markers that represented the opposing forces instead. She had made the offering to the Goddess, and even to attempt to take it back would be the most terrible blasphemy.

With a frustrated sigh, Erinor broke the seal on the document case and took out the papers. Quickly she scanned the contents, and immediately began to move the markers on the map again. Ariadne's advanced party of engineers had met resistance at the Bright Water River and had been repelled. Obviously Erinor would need to send a covering force of Shock Troops and archers to secure a crossing and construct the requisite number of pontoon bridges.

Erinor shrugged. At this point in the war, the enemy's resistance was of little consequence; the best they could hope to do was to slow down the Hordes' advance, which, at best, meant her soldiers' arrival before the walls of Romula would be delayed by a day or two. Of course if the enemy had had enough numbers to truly contest the crossing of the

Bright Water River, the results could have been very different, and the campaign could have ground to a halt and even
foundered. It was only by the grace of the Goddess that the
Polypontians were scattered, broken, and badly supplied.
The beneficial effects of the sacrifices Erinor had made could
be seen in this alone.

The killing of the Basilea's consort was enough to win any
war, especially if that consort was Alexandros, and especially
if he'd been loved as deeply as Erinor had loved him. For a
brief moment she allowed the grief and sense of loss to sub-
merge her, but then she straightened her spine and refused
to accept the presence of the tears that slowly coursed down
her face. Alexandros had been expendable, like all males;
in fact, by being offered in sacrifice to the Goddess, he'd
reached the highest pinnacle of honor possible for any man,
and in this way his name would be remembered forever.

Telling herself that she was cheered and comforted by this
thought, Erinor continued to adjust the markers on her campaign map and tried to ignore the mournful howling of the
wind around the empty streets of the camp. As Basilea, she
was above any superstitious nonsense that might have heard
the voices of ghosts in the wind, but as a mortal woman, she
couldn't help turning to look over her shoulder when a powerful gust rose to a shriek and rattled the walls of her yurt.
For a moment she shuddered. It felt almost as though some
great power that had been guiding her actions, and clearing
her way of obstacles, was about to abandon her and leave
her to her fate. But then she frowned and shook her head, as
though to empty it of such superstitious nonsense.

22

The camp stretched along the road, creating a city of tents that was illuminated by thousands of cooking fires. Sentries patrolled the perimeter and guarded the horse lines and baggage train, but overall the huge settlement was amazingly quiet as most of the army of the Icemark and its allies rested after the long and arduous march.

Thirrin slept soundly in the narrow bed hidden in the shadows at the rear of her campaign tent, completely exhausted by the demands of the day. And Oskan sat nearby in a canvas-backed chair, his eyes closed and his mind open as he listened to the sounds of the night.

Strange psychic voices had been calling to the Witchfather since early that morning, echoing through the ether and falling directly into his mind, and it'd soon become clear that no one else could hear them, including his witches.

He stood and opened a portal into the Magical Realms. The voices continued to call, wordless mind-notes of summons and invitation that echoed through the sky and filled his psychic ear to the brim.

He knew the calls came from Cronus and Medea, and as a result all of his psychic shields and defenses were at their highest levels. He couldn't even begin to guess why they were calling him, and dangerously he'd allowed his curiosity to override his natural caution.

He rose up into the air and then zoomed in on the Darkness. In a matter of seconds he'd pinpointed the calling voices to Medea's Bone Fortress. Quickly he scanned all around for signs of traps and then hovered above the turreted roof of his daughter's home.

He could clearly see that all Ice Demons had been banished from the area; in fact, the livid white tundra of the Darkness seemed even more barren and lifeless than usual. All the signs were that Cronus and Medea genuinely wanted a summit, and considering that the Icemark was completely distracted by its upcoming war with Erinor, Oskan knew he couldn't afford to ignore their call.

He sent out a reply to announce his arrival, then slowly descended toward the fortress. As he sank through the many layers of the multitiered building, he became aware that Cronus and Medea were waiting for him in a completely new area of the structure, conjured from the ether just for their meeting.

He emerged in an enormously wide and long space with a hammer-beam roof, the supports and spars of which seemed to be made entirely of long, sweeping thigh bones. Oskan scanned the space, which was steeped in areas of light and deep shadow. He soon found Cronus and Medea waiting quietly in the middle of the wide floor, and he was immediately aware that his daughter had discarded her mortal body of flesh and had constructed a new shell for her spirit. But it was Cronus who held his attention.

He couldn't remember if he'd ever actually set eyes on his father before, apart from in an earlier vision sent by his Gift of the Sight. But if he had, it must have been when he was a very little boy, before the Arc-Adept had finally left his mother to bring him up alone.

Nevertheless, this . . . man undoubtedly *was* his father. He wasn't aware of ever having been in the same physical space as him before, even though he'd felt his towering presence many times in the ether. But to actually stand before him as he was now doing, and to look upon his face, was an overwhelming experience. Emotions chased one another around his mind as he stood in silence, but Oskan's expression betrayed nothing.

"Welcome, Oskan Witchfather," Cronus said in quiet and refined tones. "Or should I say, perhaps, 'Welcome, my son'?"

"Should you? I'm not sure. Biologically speaking, it can't be denied that you're my father," he replied. "But in every other way, you are nothing to me but an enemy."

"Oh, come now, can we not set aside our difficulties and talk to each other with at least a measure of civility?"

"Possibly," Oskan replied. "But that very much depends on the subject matter."

"Ah, I see you're a man of my own stamp. Not for you the niceties of formality; we're of that kind who need to get down to business immediately."

"Yes. So tell me, why have you called me here?"

"Because Medea and myself have a proposition to put to you," Cronus said, and for the first time since arriving, Oskan turned his full attention on his daughter.

"Ah, Medea. I see you've fully recovered from your injuries."

She strengthened the shields that hid her mind and all its workings, and smiled. "Yes, Father. No one can physically hurt me now."

"No," Oskan agreed. "But your spirit remains vulnerable."

She recoiled from the open threat but ignored the emotional pain that lanced through her. "It's well defended," she replied evenly.

"Perhaps a little less sparring and more business?" Cronus said. "That was your expressed preference, was it not?"

"Yes. So what is this proposition?"

"That you join with us."

"For what purpose?"

"For the joint purposes of eternal rule and limitless power," said Cronus, interested that Oskan hadn't rejected the idea out of hand.

"Oh, really? But isn't that the exclusive right of the Goddess?"

Cronus was pleased that they'd already managed to side-step the issue of the pending invasion of the Physical Realms. "Indeed, yes, for the present. But perhaps a new power, a new *alliance*, could challenge her position."

Oskan gazed in wonder on the . . . *thing* that was his father. Even now, after eons of exile, he still plotted and planned to attack the heavens again. "And you and Medea are that alliance?"

"Yes, but three is such a good number, don't you think?"

"And you, Medea, do you think this . . . venture possible?"

Her father's tone made it obvious what he thought of the plan, but she answered with enthusiasm. "Yes, completely. Easily! Between us, Grandfather and myself could sweep aside all divine opposition and establish a new order of such—"

"Then why do you need me?"

"*Need you? NEED YOU?*" Cronus's harsh voice cut through the icy atmosphere. "My dear boy, please don't think that this offer of an alliance is anything other than an act of mercy on our part. When we come to power, everything will be swept aside and destroyed; everything that weak-minded, small-scoped, petty being that dares to call herself Goddess ever created will be expunged! We will begin again, and this time the basis of the universe will be the purity of evil, rather than the faint-hearted simpering of love!"

Cronus's voice echoed around the wide hall, and his white face was contorted into a rictus of pure rage. But then he seemed to relax, and his voice became soft and reasonable again. "But you, my dear Oskan, you are *family*, and it is *because* you are family that I . . . *we* have decided to offer you the chance to join with us in a towering triumvirate of eternal power."

"Well, thank you very much, I'm sure," the Witchfather answered lightly. "But to be honest, I think you've underestimated the opposition. Something that you were guilty of before."

"I was guilty of nothing but a slight miscalculation!" Cronus snapped. Again Oskan watched him with undiluted fascination. How could such a supremely powerful entity be so blind? In any other circumstances that were much less dangerous and potentially catastrophic, such an inability to understand the true nature of Creation and its Creator might be almost endearing.

Then, incredibly, the Witchfather suddenly felt a spark of affection for the unspeakable abomination that stood before him, but he quickly reminded himself of all the pain and suffering that Cronus had inflicted on the world.

"A slight miscalculation, you say?" Oskan eventually went on. "Well, I'm afraid you're guilty of much the same again. Nothing would, or could, ever induce me to form an alliance with such depraved creatures as my beloved father and daughter! If you have nothing else to offer or add, we must consider this brief summit at an end!"

"Consider well before you reject me, Witchfather!" Cronus snarled, his black eyes sparking for a moment. "The offer will not be made again!"

"Good, then it will save me the effort of rejecting it again."

The Arc-Adept drew a cloak of shadow and ice around him, and his voice fell to a low threatening growl. "Had we agreed truce terms before we finalized the details of this meeting?"

Oskan smiled coldly. "No. But please, if you feel you can pierce my defenses, you're more than welcome to try."

Suddenly the entire room was obliterated as a blinding, searing explosion of plasma engulfed the Bone Fortress. Cronus and his granddaughter stood within their jointly con-jured shield of protection and waited for the smoke and falling debris to clear. The only sound was the wind gently moan-ing over the tundra, and Medea tried to look unconcerned as she scanned the slowly dissipating smoke for her father.

Then the last billows and wisps were blown away and Oskan emerged unscathed. "Well, how entertaining; you blew up your granddaughter's home, Cronus. I suppose one can expect little else from the psychic scum of the universe," he said quietly.

And then, with a wave of his hand, he conjured the entire Bone Fortress back into existence.

"Father!" Medea suddenly called, but then fell silent as he turned to her, and she regained control.

Oskan nodded decisively, as though she'd added some-thing more.

Cronus said nothing, his face impassive as he gazed at his son, and after a few more moments of silence Oskan rose up through the charred floors of the fortress. Anger burned within him, and he burst through the roof like a destroying comet.

He shouted loud and long, venting his frustration into the sky of the Darkness, his voice echoing over the wide frozen wastes of the tundra of souls. He had left much more behind him than a ludicrous offer of alliance in a doomed campaign against the Goddess—he'd finally left behind his daughter and the father he'd never had a chance to know. Somewhere in the deepest depths of his mind he'd somehow hoped to reach them, to reason with them, but now he was finally forced to accept they were beyond redemption.

Now would be the time to use the weapon of knowledge against them, but why should Cronus and his renegade daughter rob him of his life? There was still a chance of defeating them without the need to destroy himself, if only he could control the full Power of the Dark without being corrupted by it. For the sake of his family, he was determined to find a way.

Ariadne gazed over the land to the towering walls and defenses of Romula. Thousands of Polypontian cavalry units could be seen streaming back to the capital city, as their hopeless campaign to stop the Hordes' advance had finally collapsed. The Tri-Horn squadrons had crossed the Bright Water River two days before, pushing back the Polypontian defenders and holding a foothold on the northern bank while the engineers had then built the dozens of pontoon bridges needed to allow the massive army to cross.

After that it was simplicity itself. The Imperial cavalry had continued to harass the advance, but they were about as effective as a mosquito against a charging bull, and within forty-eight hours the supreme prize of Romula itself had appeared on the horizon. Ariadne knew that this was the defining moment of her career. No longer would she be a footnote to the military brilliance of the Basilea herself. No longer would she be just one more name among the lists of the High Command, who had simply facilitated the tactics and strategies of Erinor. She would be counted as a great commander in her own right: Ariadne Minotaurus, the Conqueror of Romula!

Taking a deep breath, she looked ahead to the walls and, raising her hand, gave the order to advance. There was no need to set up siege lines, pitch camp, or dig defenses. The city was weak and just waiting to fall. Her only interest lay in how long it would take it to finally die. To achieve true greatness and everlasting fame, she needed to be in control of the city within twenty-four hours.

With a rumbling roar her Tri-Horn stepped out across the plain, and the creature's strange rolling gait made her feel as though she were aboard a ship that was bearing down on a port city she intended to raid. "The prize is before us! Seize it! Destroy it! Wipe it from the land!" The huge deep-throated war-horns of the southern Hypolitan now boomed on the air, filling the world with their threat and their power.

But the city remained strangely quiet, with no sign of any defenders on the clifflike walls, and Ariadne suddenly felt the first pangs of doubt. Had she been a less experienced field commander, she might have been fooled into thinking that Romula had been evacuated and abandoned to its fate, but she knew better than to trust to such illusions; after all, the Polypontian cavalry units that had been resisting the Hordes' advance had been clearly seen retreating through the many gates. The military governor of this prize of prizes obviously intended to fight the Hordes in the streets. Ariadne frowned; such urban warfare could be devastatingly costly and time-consuming. Every district, every road, every house would be contested, sapping the strength and draining the numbers of even the mighty Hordes.

For a moment she almost halted the attack while she reconsidered her tactics, but her army had already begun its advance, rolling down on the city like the shades of the world's last night. Nothing could be done to recall them. The decision had been made; it was up to her now to ensure this war reached its obvious and glorious conclusion.

Thirrin and her army had been advancing in a state of high alert all day. Scouts had reported that they were a matter of a few miles from Romula and that the city was under attack. Smoke was pouring from the streets, and the Hordes were entering many breaches in the southern walls. But, most important, the fighting was still going on. Over a quarter of the city was ablaze, but the central and northern districts seemed to be intact, and—as far as could be ascertained—the palace precinct was untouched. Obviously the Emperor and his senators were still safe. But if they should fall into the enemy's hands, all was lost: city, freedom, and war. It was imperative that Thirrin and the allies reached them before Erinor and her Hordes.

The allied infantry advanced at a sustained jog, eating up the remaining miles to Romula, but it still took all of Thirrin's iron control and experience not to dash off at the head of her cavalry to save the city. It was essential that the army arrived as one disciplined unit and entered the battle like a blade burying itself in flesh. As usual, they were heavily outnumbered, and their only hope of success lay in surprise and rigid order.

"General Andronicus, take all the Polypontian units and place them at the head of the army," she ordered. "And make sure they display every Imperial flag and banner they have. We don't want to have to fight the defenders on our way into the city; we come as saviors, not conquerors."

The Polypontian general saluted and galloped off to issue orders, and Tharaman-Thar pulled in alongside Thirrin. "Refreshing change, really, marching on a city instead of defending one."

"Well, we are defending it, really, we're just doing it in a roundabout way," she replied. "But once we're through the gates, and the Polypontian defenders realize we're on their side, that's when the real fighting will begin. It'll be interesting testing our mettle against the Hordes. They claim to be undefeated and unbeatable, and that simply has to be challenged!"

"My dear, I do believe you're actually looking forward to this!" said the Thar in amazement. "Here we are about to confront an army that's known nothing but success and your only interest is to test yourself against it!"

"Not my only interest, Tharaman. Don't forget that they've declared our Hypolitan allies traitors, and stated that they intend to wipe them out. After which, no doubt, they'd turn their attention on the rest of the Icemark and anyone else who gets in their way. And on top of that, I think it's pretty clear that they intend to reestablish the Empire with themselves as a ruling elite. So all in all, I think it's in all our interests to stop and defeat the Hordes."

"Yes, yes, no doubt you're right. But this old warrior for one is wondering when he'll be able to fight his last battle."

Sharley, Mekhmet, and Kirimin stood with Cressida's cavalry unit and looked out over the walls of Romula. The snows of the mountains and foothills had been left behind, and the huge city stood on the fertile plain below them, magnificent in its size and unassailable in its legend.

Far off on the southern horizon a dark smudge of movement discolored the greenery of the plain, and a murmur rose up from the ranks. This was the first sight they'd had of the fabled Hordes, and though the distance between the two armies was huge, the flash and glitter of weaponry as the invaders continued to pour reinforcements into the southernmost sectors of the city reminded the allies that the enemy was vicious and undefeated.

Sharley could see his mother at the head of the army, giving final orders to Andronicus and Leonidas. Then at last the army rolled forward and down onto the plain. The next few minutes would be crucial. If the defenders of Romula believed they were a second invading force, they could find themselves fighting to get into the city before they'd even struck a blow against Erinor and her Hordes.

The flags and banners of the Empire snapped and rattled in the wind of their speed, while above, the squadrons of Vampires flew in tight formations that perfectly reflected the cavalry ranks below. As the huge, crumbling walls of Romula loomed closer, Andronicus gave the order for bugles to announce their approach. The bright, brittle glitter of notes scythed through the air, and soldiers could be seen scurrying around the walls as they watched their approach. But then an answering bugle call sounded, and with it came the distant sound of cheering.

After a minute or so, the gates they were approaching slowly opened and a contingent of horsemen rode out. With Thirrin's consent, Andronicus and Leonidas spurred ahead and they met the Polypontian cavalry midway from the walls.

As far as Sharley could see from his position among the ranks of Cressida's unit of cavalry, there was a great deal of backslapping and hand-shaking going on as they approached. Farther off, the gates of the city continued to swing open, allowing the allied army access. Kirimin trotted briskly between Sharley and Mekhmet, her huge jaws slightly open as she sampled the air for scents. Nobody said a word—Cressida demanded silence in the ranks during action—but that didn't stop the odors conveying their stories of fear, fire, and fighting in the streets of Romula.

To Kirimin's acute senses, smells were as articulate as words, and the men that Andronicus was still conversing with gave off a tangled skein of scents themselves, ranging from the extreme stress of warfare to relief that an army had come to their aid. One or two also seemed a little wary of the host of monsters that was approaching, but with the supreme pragmatism of the desperate, they were content to accept help from anyone—even the hideous Vampires that kept perfect pace with the land army below.

Andronicus now drew his sword, and, after bowing in his saddle to the approaching Thirrin, he raised it aloft and called the army on. The pace rose to a gallop. The noise of thundering hooves and jingling weaponry masked any conversation now, and Sharley leaned from his saddle to run his hand through Kirimin's fur.

"This is it, meat-breath," he called affectionately. "Give 'em fury, but take no risks!"

"You, too," she called back. Then, raising her head, she gave the coughing bark that was the war cry of the Snow Leopards. Immediately all of the huge cats took it up and Tharaman-Thar roared thunderously, the sound echoing back from the city walls like the boom of artillery.

Imp-Pious flew up into the air as the push to the city began, but after hovering for a few moments, he hurried to catch up with his friends. Then, as the defenses loomed nearer and nearer, seeming to rise out of the plain like dark cliffs, Pious landed on Kirimin's neck and burrowed deep into her fur.

Sharley caught Mekhmet's eye and winked. They'd ridden together into many battles far to the south and beyond the borders of the Desert Kingdom as the Polypontian Empire had broken apart. But now they were about to enter the very heart of the old Imperial power that had dominated millions of lives in dozens of countries. From here Bellorum had plotted and planned to enslave as much of the world as he could, and yet now they were riding to save it from its final downfall!

The army rattled through the eerily quiet streets and reached a wide square, where a hastily convened welcoming committee had gathered. Here a halt was called, and all of the top-ranking officers gathered around for a council of war. Thirrin impatiently acknowledged the speeches of welcome and then demanded information. Obviously, to fight the Hordes effectively, they would need to know exactly where they were and counter their advance. Soon Polypontian officers arrived from the fighting and gave details of positions, numbers, and dispositions. Sharley felt like screaming as time passed and the distant sounds of the fighting sent ghostly echoes over the square. But then at last plans were finalized and orders given.

The army was divided under the separate commands of Cressida and Krisafitsa, who would lead their human troopers, Snow Leopards, and housecarls through the streets of the city; Thirrin, Tharaman-Thar, and Grishmak would take the other half of the cavalry back through the gates along with most of the werewolf infantry and the Hypolitan. Eodred and Howler were also to stay in the city and lead their mixed regiment of werewolves and housecarls as an independent command that could react swiftly to whatever need should arise. A similar role had been assigned to the Vampires, but their remit extended beyond the walls, too, and with this in mind Commander Bramorius Stokecescu had subdivided his force, ceding command of one half to Squadron Leader Petros Cushingoss.

Sharley, Mekhmet, and Kirimin were to stay with Cressida, and the boys couldn't resist grinning when they saw Commander Leonidas riding with the Crown Princess. But now that both Princess and field commander had very definite military objectives to achieve, they were talking to each other easily, and General Andronicus hardly needed to fill any silences at all. Besides, all talk was of the coming struggle, and human, Snow Leopard, and werewolf allies busily finalized details as they hurriedly marched to the front. Stokecescu and his Vampires were initially being used as scouts and were busily pointing out the quickest route to the fighting.

The allies' battle plan was simplicity itself: Those in Romula were to support the Polypontian defenders and stop the Hordes' advance if possible, while Thirrin and the rest of the army would ride around the walls and take the enemy in the flank and rear as they waited to enter the city. Hopefully their losses and demoralization would be so great, they'd break and flee. General Andronicus had assured them all that it wasn't impossible, and that he'd almost done it himself with much smaller numbers. All they could do now was pray to the Goddess and hope that Erinor's phenomenal luck would finally run out.

All of the allied soldiers in the city knew it was imperative that the Hordes did not reach the palace precinct, where the Emperor was sheltering. If the palace should fall, the battle and the war were lost.

Sharley, Kirimin, and Mekhmet trotted through the labyrinth of city streets as part of Cressida's cavalry. The marching formation of the army was lost as the warriors crammed into the narrow roadways and dark alleys of the poorer quarters, but they still moved forward at a tremendous pace as the clamor of fighting drew closer. This was it; this was where the fighting finally began. Then at last, under the guidance of the Vampires and the Polypontian scouts, the allied army began to enter the wider streets and boulevards of the governmental enclave. Here, in the time of the Empire's greatest power, foreign embassies and commissions had stood, and the streets had been peopled with politicians, diplomats, and rich merchants. But now they were empty of everyone and everything, apart from smoke and the occasional glimpse of a feral dog or cat slinking away.

Sharley tightened his sword belt and patted Suleiman's neck as the horse blew and sidled at the acrid stench of burning. "Steady, steady. We'll be able to see them soon," he said, knowing the charger would settle down when the enemy came in sight and was no longer a hidden threat.

Mekhmet was muttering quietly to himself, offering up a prayer to his One God. Sharley had heard his friend pray many times before and knew he never asked for safety in battle or deliverance from death; instead Mekhmet asked for bravery and the ability to do honor to his ancestors.

Sharley offered his own prayer to the Goddess, and then another to Mekhmet's One God. After campaigning and living for so long with the Desert People, it seemed only polite, and he knew the Mother wouldn't mind.

Spiritual duties done, Sharley glanced over at Kirimin, who was trotting silently beside him. "All right, meat-breath?" he asked kindly.

"Not really, no," she answered. "Is it always so . . . *fraught* before battle?"

"Oh yes," he replied. "Everyone's always pooing themselves; don't believe all these stern martial expressions you can see around you; we're all terrified."

"Really?" she asked incredulously.

"Absolutely."

A sudden flurry of wind brought the sound of shouting and screaming with it, and they both fell silent as they stared ahead. "How many of us will die?" Kirimin asked.

"Well, that's direct and to the point," said Sharley with a pained smile. "But I couldn't possibly say. If it all goes well, perhaps only a few hundred; if it goes badly, maybe thousands. Maybe all of us."

Kiri nodded, unconsciously using human body language after living in their company for so long. "Thanks for being honest at least."

"No point in being anything else, really. We're about to fight a battle and no amount of pretty lies is going to make it any easier."

A Vampire swept in low, screeching as it came, and then did a slow barrel roll. The enemy was within sight. Immediately a muted rustle and murmur passed through the ranks of soldiers as equipment was checked and voices swore oaths or simply prayed. Then suddenly the road they were following ended, and the army emerged from the twisting skein of back streets and onto the hugely wide Eppian Way. Immediately horse and Snow Leopard, housecarl and were-wolf, fanned out and redressed their ranks, filling the wide boulevard from side to side.

Cressida barked orders and the cavalry surged forward at a swift trot. She stole a glance at Commander Leonidas, who rode beside her, and she found herself deeply approving his bearing. He rode straight-backed and with an elegant ease, as though he were in a show ring. Next to him, his father, General Andronicus, rode with all the style of a sack of coal; as the old general himself was always saying, his son took after his mother. But then the demands of Cressida's command claimed her full attention, and she stared along the boulevard. In the distance she could see a makeshift barrier being swept aside by a squadron of truly mountainous creatures, which she guessed must be the legendary Tri-Horns. The Polypontian defenders were retreating before their advance but were still maintaining good order, and others were running to join them in what looked like a futile attempt to resist the Tri-Horns.

Strangely, the massive animals didn't seem to be wearing the heavy quilted surcoats, chain mail, and plate armor that reports had stated they wore in every attack. Perhaps this was simply an oversight on the part of the Hordes' High Command, or perhaps it was an indication of their growing arrogance and showed that they believed no one could stop the Tri-Horns. Whatever the reason, the oversight could well have made the allies' job of fighting the monstrous creatures a little simpler. Cressida nodded silently and almost smiled, then, continuing with her assessment of the enemy, she looked beyond the phalanx of Tri-Horns to where she could clearly see the mass of the Hordes themselves. Their ranks seemed to visibly boil and seethe as the front ranks constantly flowed and contracted, tightened and expanded, as the individual soldiers continually changed their positions. At first sight there seemed to be little evidence of any sort of discipline or control, but Cressida knew that no army could have had such brilliant success against the mighty Polypontian Empire without some sort of order. She was certain that, given time, the framework of the enemy's command structure would become evident. But in the meantime her only concern was to stop their advance toward the palace complex and the Emperor.

She raised her hand and immediately dozens of bugles clamored on the air, sounding the charge of the Polypontian cavalry. This had the desired effect: The retreating defenders turned to see the allied army and immediately drew aside onto the steep steps and porticoes of the fine marble buildings that lined the boulevard.

Cressida now stood in her saddle and, drawing breath, gave the war cry of the Icemark. "The enemy is upon us! They kill our children; they burn our houses! *Blood! Blast! And Fire! Blood! Blast! And Fire!*"

Back crashed the reply from thousands of throats: human, werewolf, and Snow Leopard: *"Blood! Blast! And Fire!"*

Just behind his sister, in the ranks of the cavalry, Sharley leaned from his saddle and embraced Mekhmet. "The Goddess keep you safe," he said into his friend's ear.

"And the One keep you safe also," the Desert Prince replied, and then both boys saluted Kirimin, who trotted beside them. The Snow Leopard raised her head and roared mightily, and all of her people replied, their voices echoing from the surrounding buildings.

Ahead the Tri-Horn squadrons redressed their ranks as they saw the allied army, but their pace never slackened. Cressida now stood in her stirrups again, and her voice rose like a banner of ferocity above the cavalry. "The enemy is before us! Show no mercy! *SHOW NO MERCY!*"

The cavalry leaped forward, the human troopers singing the fierce battle paean and the Snow Leopards giving the coughing bark of their challenge.

The Tri-Horns bellowed and roared, their huge feet thudding into the ground like muffled rock falls as they advanced.

Above the allied army the Vampires flew in tight formations, screaming and howling as they raced to meet the enemy. Cressida raised her sword above her head and screamed out an order. Immediately the Snow Leopards galloped ahead, and forming behind their Princess they charged the Tri-Horns.

With a shattering roar, the cats leaped at the giant beasts, swarming up their legs and bodies to attack the mahouts and warriors in the howdahs. The Tri-Horns bellowed and roared as a raging battle began on their backs. Cressida now led the human cavalry to gallop neatly through the pounding treelike legs of the beasts and with a roar they fell upon the soldiers of the Hordes that followed behind.

* * *

Eodred and Howler led the infantry at a steady swinging trot that ate up the ground before them, and soon house-carl and werewolf were dodging the careering legs of the Tri-Horns as many now blundered directionless across the battlefield. The housecarls charged on in support of the cavalry and their battle against the soldiers of the Hordes, but Eodred and Howler led the Regiment of the Red Eye to scale the living mountains that were the Tri-Horns and joined the battle on the beasts' broad backs. Soon the axes of the mixed regiment of human and werewolf were felling the enemy soldiers as they swarmed over the beasts in support of their Snow Leopard comrades.

The Polypontian defenders now rejoined the battle, pouring down the marble steps of the fine governmental buildings and throwing themselves into the fighting with almost insane ferocity. Eodred stood atop the largest Tri-Horn that had turned back in an attempt to trample Cressida's cavalry, which was fighting to its rear. The Prince of the Icemark swung his ax around his head, roaring out the war cry of the Icemark, and brought it crashing down into the beast's neck at the point where spine met skull. For a moment the massive creature seemed to freeze, and then, with a bellow of agony, slowly crumpled to the ground like a mighty avalanche of flesh and bone and finally lay dead.

The one weak spot of the Tri-Horns had been discovered, and with a cry of triumph, housecarl and werewolf raised their axes and felled the creatures, like woodcutters in a forest of giant trees. A huge cheer rose up from the allied army as the once-unstoppable fell in ruin and a welter of blood.

Cressida, like all good field commanders, felt the mood of the battle swing in the allies' favor, and led her cavalry to bite deeper into the seething mass of the Hordes that swarmed before her. The battle-trained horses struck out with their hooves at the enemy, and sword, ax, mace, and spear rained down on them in a glittering frenzy that stopped them in their tracks.

The housecarls charged the Hordes with locked shields, the impact sending shock waves through the enemy like a boulder suddenly dropped into a wide body of water. For almost fifteen minutes the allies drove through the massed ranks of the invaders, while Vampire warriors dropped from the skies to rend them with tooth and sword, and Snow Leopards and the Regiment of the Red Eye also attacked as the last of the mighty Tri-Horns were felled.

The allies were like an avalanche falling from the highest mountain in the world, smashing and rending all before it. But their power and ferocity were falling into the massed ranks of the Hordes, who spread like a mighty ocean before them, an ocean that could swallow deserts and continents, an ocean that could drown empires and armies.

Within minutes everything had changed; Cressida sensed the battle swinging away from the allies again, and orders flashed among the ranks to tighten positions and change tactics from offense to defense. While the cavalry held the line, the rest of the allied army withdrew a short distance, and quickly the broad boulevard of the Eppian Way was bisected by a hastily reconstructed barrier of timber, over-turned wagons, and sacks filled with earth. Defending it was a living defensive wall that stood ten deep and bristled with steel, tooth, and claw.

But before the wall seethed a mass of warriors who'd never yet been stopped. To any lesser force, fighting an army that contained werewolves, Snow Leopards, and Vampires would have been a terrifying prospect, but the Hordes were supreme in their arrogance and confidence. They believed themselves to be the avenging instrument of the Goddess, and nothing could stop them. They had no idea that their interpretation of the Deity was corrupt and blasphemous; they had no idea that before them stood Cressida Aethelflaed Elemnestra Strong-in-the-Arm Lindenshield, known as Striking Eagle, Crown Princess of the Icemark, and one of the most formidable warriors in the northern world.

Cressida and the rest of the cavalry now dismounted and joined the defensive wall. Beside her stood Leonidas, and he smiled shyly as their shields overlapped. But then the Hordes let out a huge roar and all attention was concentrated on a unit of truly enormous Tri-Horns that slowly rolled into view.

Cressida's quick military mind immediately spotted that this time the huge animals were wearing full armor, with heavy surcoats and massively thick iron collars that protected the vulnerable junction of spine and skull. Could this really be a reaction to the loss of the other Tri-Horns to the axes of the Red Eye? There'd been no obvious evidence of messages being sent down the line, so perhaps it was mere coincidence. But even so, it had to be admitted that such details could easily be lost in the chaos of battle.

"They're not going to be so easy to stop," said Cressida as she watched the distant Tri-Horns' ponderous advance. "Their necks are protected."

"No," agreed Andronicus, who stood next to Leonidas. "But there are ways. With your permission, Ma'am . . . ?"

"Certainly, General," said Cressida and watched as Andronicus beckoned a Polypontian commander.

"Antonius, your men are skilled with the pike?"

"That's their normal role, sir. But we thought long spears wouldn't be much use in street fighting."

"Well, they have a use now. My pike regiments almost turned the Tri-Horns in the last battle I had with Erinor. Where are the spears kept?"

"In the palace armory, sir."

"How long to fetch them and be back here to defend the wall?"

"Twenty minutes, sir. Half an hour at most."

"Make it fifteen. Take your men and run—run as if the survival of the city depended on it, because it does, Commander, it does!"

"In the meantime, we hold the line, I presume," said Cressida quietly.

"Yes, Ma'am," Andronicus replied.

23

The army of Ice Demons had been called by Cronus from all corners of the Darkness, and was resplendent in a glittering display of banners and panoplies of arms and armor. Somehow the accoutrements of human war added to the hideous effect of their presence, and as they bellowed and raged in their disciplined ranks, the beat of their wings sent out an icy gale that blasted over the rolling wastes of the Darkness. Cronus and Medea reviewed their "conquering host" from a balcony high on the walls of the Bone Fortress and smiled in triumph. They'd accelerated their preparations for invasion, and now it was a reality!

Both Adepts manipulated the army of ferocious creatures by mind control. Each dominated the psyche of the leading Ice Demons, and as they forced them to follow whatever tactics they wished, the rest of the massive army followed. Once they were within sight of the enemy, the rest was simple; the demons had an inbred instinct to kill and maim, and they did it to perfection.

Medea's new body reflected the power and pride of the army and was as polished and formidable as a weapon. When next she faced her father, no amount of damage to this physical form could hinder or endanger her. She had become, in effect, virtually immortal; only the most powerful of Adepts could extinguish the spark of her life.

In the entire army only one other, in the form of Medea's grandfather, would be able to function efficiently without his outward form. Cronus looked magnificent in white armor, complete with a large white shield and a helmet that was plumed with white ostrich feathers. In his bone-white hands he also held a long staff that was covered in mystical symbols and had a globe of crystal at the top. This was his Staff of Power, and represented his right to rule the Physical Realms. Medea shuddered with a delicate combination of horror and revulsion at the very sight of his expressionless white face and flat black eyes. He truly looked the part of the preeminent, all-conquering sorcerer, and a sense of deranged power surrounded him.

He stepped forward, the crystal in his staff glittering like a malevolent eye, and glared at all before him. "Soldiers of the Darkness. The land of the Icemark is waiting now for our conquering power! The repellent Witchfather and his sorceresses have left their home undefended, and by the time he learns of his mistake the land will be ours, the first in the Physical Realms to fall to our will. Savor this moment of history; you stand on the threshold of a new empire that will encompass all of the Physical Realms, and once that is secured, there remains only the stars and the very heavens themselves! Let the gods gaze on our actions and tremble, and let them look to their defenses; we go to strike the first blow in a war that one day will march on paradise itself!"

A great railing, howling, hooting cheer greeted his words. Then, as the sound slowly died away, Cronus raised his staff above his head and the hideous constellations of dark stars seemed to draw together and then slowly to spin. Gradually their speed increased until a swirling nimbus of light surrounded a widening mouth of blackness. Cronus had created a tunnel between the Darkness and the Physical Realms that could accommodate an entire army! Medea felt dizzy with awe; nothing could withstand them in any of the worlds or plains of the Multiverse!

The tunnel between the worlds drew them in, and the army, thousands strong, entered the space that bridged the Physical Realms and the Darkness. For the briefest of moments, all went black, and then gradually Medea saw a gray, pulsating half-light settle over them. They were in the dead and silent space between realms. Noise fell flat and echoless as a voice in a small room packed with soft linen. The silence permeated everything, worming its way into the listening mind like dust invading the intricate workings of a delicate instrument.

Many of the Ice Demons began to snort and bellow in panic, their huge voices falling tiny and useless in that massive void of silence. But Medea and Cronus exerted a rigid control over their army, and they stood in restless ranks as the Arc-Adept probed at the interstices between the Magical and Physical realms.

At last a breach was made. Sound rushed in like air into a vacuum, and a night of brilliant stars and a blazing full moon erupted around them. They were in the Icemark. Medea drew air into the cavity of her chest, as though filling the lungs she no longer had, and savored the pine-spiced, earth-scented air. She was home, and she wouldn't leave the Icemark again until she was its undisputed queen!

Quickly she looked around her; the army stood on the Plain of Frostmarris, close to the Great Forest, and already twisted and hideous forms were beginning to emerge from the shadows of the trees. Medea had expected this; the witches and warlocks of the Dark Craft had been hiding in the secret depths of the forest for decades, waiting for the opportunity to strike back at the human power that had banished them from the land. She smiled; their psychic

Gifts would be a useful addition to the army. She prepared to make them welcome.

As usual Cronus had planned everything perfectly; now that they were limited by the physical restrictions of the world, the army would be far too large to be contained within the city of Frostmarris itself when it inevitably fell. But even so, elite advanced forces would soon be attacking the city and strategic points throughout the land, silencing the werewolf relay. Within seconds the Wolf-folk would be dead, and the routine calls of the relay would be magically mimicked so that no hint of trouble would reach Oskan Witchfather far to the south.

Medea turned to watch as Cronus raised his crystal-topped Staff of Power again and prepared to give the order to march on the capital. He stood, imperious and commanding, seeming to tower over the land, which, Medea thought, was already as good as his. But before he could speak, a single high-pitched screech sounded on the night air. Medea snatched her admiring gaze away and scanned the skies, searching for the source of the call, which sounded all too familiar.

Their invasion of the Physical Realms had been discovered. As she watched, strange squadronlike formations appeared as black shadows against the dark sky. The high-pitched screech sounded again, and after a pause many answered, filling the night.

Cronus immediately amended his orders. The Ice Demons took up defensive positions for an aerial attack: Shields were raised and locked, and spears bristled beyond the makeshift roof of wood and steel.

Medea scuttled to safety beneath the shields of the nearest unit of Demons and watched as the Vampire squadrons folded their wings and fell from the skies in a vicious rain.

This had *not* been expected. When they'd considered the Vampiric army at all, both she and Cronus had assumed that they'd remain neutral at the very worst. There was even some hope that they might have joined with them in the battle to capture the Icemark. After all, the Vampire King and Queen had only ever been the most reluctant of allies of the House of Lindenshield. And yet, here were undead soldiers defending Frostmarris! The Arc-Adept was guilty of a monumental miscalculation, to say the least!

Before she could analyze the situation further, Medea was distracted by the Vampire attack. Dozens of bat warriors crashed through the Ice Demons' raised shields, and, as the undead warriors transmuted into their human forms, vicious hand-to-hand fighting began. Medea blasted three Vampires where they stood, leaving nothing but smoking ash behind, but elsewhere the black serrated swords of the Vampiric army traded blow for blow with the clubs and axes of the Ice Demons.

The monsters from the Darkness were bigger and stronger than the Vampires, but the undead warriors were lightning-fast, and moved with an intelligent and deadly elegance that left the Demons confused.

The roar of battle alerted the garrison in Frostmarris, and now giant ballista bolts were fired from the walls of the city and began to scythe through the ranks of the demon army, skewering many where they stood and causing a panic that threatened to get out of control.

Medea glared around her in horror as the ranks of the army began to waver. In the confusion of the attack she'd become separated from Cronus, and she desperately searched for his white armor among the milling bodies that surrounded her. But he was nowhere to be seen. She suddenly felt completely isolated amid the chaos of a growing disaster. Already, on the outer edges of the massive host, some of the demons had begun to run, and as the ballista batteries properly calibrated the range, a constant and deadly hail of bolts began to power through the ranks, cutting down hundreds of the creatures.

She was close to panic herself when Cronus's voice smoothly moved into her consciousness. "Join with me, Granddaughter. Assert mind control over the demons. Force them to stand their ground."

Of course! With a flood of relief she melded her powers with those of Cronus, and together they reached out and secured a grip of iron over the collective psyche of the army. Immediately the ranks steadied and began to fight back furiously against the Vampire warriors. Forced on to the defensive, many of them quickly leaped into flight, from which they harried the army as it resumed its advance on Frostmarris.

High on the battlements of the city, the housecarls and werewolves of the garrison were running to their stations and taking up their positions. Exactly who was attacking wasn't clear, but they were ready to defend Frostmarris to the last. Many of them took heart in seeing the Vampire squadrons already engaging the enemy, but as they watched, the undead warriors suddenly rose away from the battle and seemed to hesitate.

Now that the Ice Demons were making headway again, Cronus took a moment to reassess the situation. He found a weak spot in the enemy line. If he could get to the Vampiric commander, all would be well.

Cronus's mind reached out and sliced through the resistance of her mind like a razor; he located the Vampire commander's consciousness and began to squeeze, shape, and mold her thoughts to his will.

The commander found herself thinking, *We can't win; we're outnumbered. Better to disengage and seek orders from the queen.* For a moment she was shocked by the thought and began to give orders to renew the attack, but Cronus tightened his grip, crushing all independent thought and resistance.

I can't risk losing my patrol in a futile action; Her Vampiric Majesty would be furious. I must withdraw and report back to the queen.

She could resist no longer; throwing back her head, she gave the call to retreat and regroup.

Immediately the squadrons disengaged, transforming into their bat forms and wheeling away from the battle; then, after one brief circuit of the Plain of Frostmarris, the Vampires powered away into the darkness.

Cronus and Medea relaxed; they were now free to concentrate on the city garrison. Melding their mind powers once again, they reached out and crushed the simple psyches of the defending force, until the entire garrison was almost incoherent with fear. Cronus and Medea inserted nightmare images into their minds; playing on their worst fears of the dark, of death, of disabling injuries, they filled each individual's mind with blind terror to the exclusion of all other thought.

But the werewolf commander realized that the enemy was playing with his soldiers' minds. With a supreme effort he regained some control, and, leaping onto the battlements, he rallied his housecarls and wolf warriors.

"To me! To me!" he bellowed, over the roaring of the Ice Demons. "We've nothing to fear. These nightmares are just ghosts and phantoms sent by the enemy. Confront them; face them, and they'll fade away!"

All around him, his soldiers rubbed their eyes and shook their heads as though waking from terrible dreams. "We control the walls, and nothing can get in while we defend them!"

the commander went on. "Look to your comrades and nothing can break us. We are they who defeated Bellorum; we are they who stood against empires and won!" He threw back his head and let out a bloodcurdling howl that echoed through the night sky. "Now take up your weapons and follow me!"

With a great cheer the entire garrison then surged forward as one, and followed their commander as he leaped to his death from the highest battlements in Frostmarris. In a great cascade of armor, weaponry, and living flesh, over a thousand warriors fell to the rocks far below, where their bodies were smashed apart and their blood ran in a crimson stream to soak deep into the soil of the Icemark.

Out on the Plain of Frostmarris, Cronus smiled gently to himself. It was so sad how misguided mortals could be. After an initial setback, everything had gone wonderfully well. It really was so refreshing when plans and preparations bore the required fruit. Reaching out to his granddaughter, he placed a thought in her mind.

"Medea, I do believe the battle for Frostmarris is over."

"Yes, Grandfather," she answered simply. "I do believe you're right."

The Ice Demon army now swarmed over the Plain of Frostmarris and into the city, securing their victory and establishing control. The victory from start to finish had taken much less than an hour, and their casualty rate was negligible and unimportant.

Medea smiled happily. The hated land of her birth was already subdued, and the home from which she'd been banished was now hers to rule. After negotiating the mound of dead housecarls and werewolves that littered the base of the walls, she met Cronus at the gates of the city. He took her hand and escorted her to the citadel.

"So begins the new order," he said confidently. "Take a look around you, Granddaughter. History starts again with us."

*   *   *

Beyond Romula's walls Thirrin sighed with relief. Riding her horse through the streets of the city had been one of the most stressful experiences she'd had in a very long time. The thought that Bellorum himself had been spawned somewhere within its precincts had been enough to make her flesh creep.

But now she was free, and trotting with her army over the fields that surrounded the city to confront the army of Erinor. She took off her helmet and shook her head empty of the thought of Bellorum and his hideous sons, the wind stroking her long red hair. The day was bright and sunny, with just the right nip of winter in the air to make the exercise of riding a pleasure. She smiled, and then had to sternly remind herself that she had a battle to fight.

Surprise was essential and still theirs. If the Hordes remained unaware of them until they had begun their charge, they had a small chance of breaking them—and at the moment, all of their attention would be concentrating on the allied army, which, under Cressida, would be slowing their advance toward the palace and the Emperor.

"When do we raise the pace, my dear?" asked Tharaman, eager to reach the target.

"Not yet; the horses must be as fresh as possible when we hit them. We could be fighting all day."

"Not if I have anything to do with it," said Grishmak as he loped along beside them. "If we hit them hard enough, they'll soon bugger off."

"It won't be as simple as that, I'm afraid," Thirrin replied. "Erinor's never lost a battle, and with that sort of record she must be as steady as a rock. We can't allow ourselves to hope that they'll break after the first charge."

"All right. But that doesn't mean we have to trot along as though we're on some sort of pleasurable day out!" said

Tharaman. "The longer we take to engage them, the longer Kirimin, Cressida, and the others have to fight against the entire weight of their army."

Thirrin nodded decisively and raised the pace to a canter that ate up the ground.

The Eppian Way ran with blood as the Shock Troops of the Hordes powered into Cressida's defensive line again and again. The allied army showed no sign of giving way, but each time the enemy was repelled, their numbers had dwindled a little more.

"Why don't the Tri-Horns come in?" Cressida demanded as she watched the mountainous creatures to the rear of the enemy's line.

Andronicus laughed. "I do believe our earlier successes have worried them. Perhaps Erinor won't commit them until she's certain of victory, and then they can be used to clear aside the barricades."

Cressida shook her head. "No, she knows the Tri-Horns were only vulnerable to our axes without protection. But they're armored now, unstoppable. Something's not right. I can feel it."

Leonidas expertly skewered an enemy soldier, then said, "You're right. The entire attack feels wrong. It's almost as though there's a different . . . *tone* of command."

Andronicus frowned as he considered this, standing with head bowed and hands resting on the hilt of his sword as the chaos of battle raged around him. "That's it," he said quietly, and looking up, he scanned the enemy lines before him. "That's it!" he shouted. "Leonidas! Your eyes are younger than mine; can you see Erinor anywhere? The Tri-Horns are the most likely position for the Basilea."

The young Polypontian commander scanned the Hordes with avid concentration, while his father sent an orderly scurrying to fetch his monoculum from his horse, which was tethered behind the lines.

"No, I can't see her!" Leonidas eventually announced.

"Well, what does that prove?" snapped Cressida as she beheaded a Shock Trooper scaling the barricade before her. "Perhaps she's organizing reinforcements or guarding the rear."

"Never! Erinor always commands from the front," said Andronicus. "There's something afoot, and I think . . ." At that point the orderly returned and placed the monoculum in his general's hand. "Ha, now we'll see," he said. Raising the viewing instrument, he scanned the ranks before him again. "I think the impossible . . . I think Erinor's not here!"

Leonidas snatched the monoculum from his father and glared at the Hordes. "You're right," he said incredulously. "She's not here!" Drawing breath, he suddenly bellowed, "She's not here! Erinor's not here! The Basilea's not commanding the Hordes!"

For a brief moment an unearthly silence settled on the Polypontian troops, who'd spent the long months of their defeat running before the power of the invincible Basilea. Then a disbelieving mutter and murmur ran through their ranks, until finally a great shout of joy and relief rose up. "Erinor's not here! Erinor's not here!"

A lull descended on the Hordes, and the assault on the barricades seemed to falter. But then a great bellow rose up as the Tri-Horns began to advance. Erinor might not be directing the battle, but Commander Ariadne was deeply experienced and could easily recognize a crisis. Now was the time to commit her greatest asset, the unstoppable armored Tri-Horns. Countless times she'd witnessed the Basilea snatch victory from a seemingly hopeless situation, and now she, Ariadne, would prove her abilities as a tactician and do exactly the same.

Standing in the howdah on the back of the leading Tri-Horn, she bellowed the order to attack. The heaving sea of bodies before her parted as the ranks of Shock Troops drew aside, and a corridor opened up that led directly to the flimsy barricade.

Ariadne screamed an order, and a flight of arrows rained down on the defending humans and Snow Leopards. But then a cheer rose up from the ragged collection of allies, and Ariadne watched as the long spears of pikemen came into view. Quickly the soldiers of the Polypontian phalanx took up positions all along the top of the barricade and lowered the massively long pikes, so that a bristling hedge of steel spearheads defended the line.

With a roar, the Shock Troops and elite women soldiers of the Hordes surged back into battle as they attempted to break down the barrier of steel, but the pikemen were defended by the swords and axes, teeth and claws, of their human, werewolf, and leopard comrades, and the line held.

No matter, no matter, thought Ariadne. *The armored Tri-Horns are unstoppable.* And she snapped out orders, urging on the mountainous creatures. Forward they surged, trampling through the rear lines of Shock Troops as they waited to engage the enemy, their bellows echoing from the buildings that lined the Eppian Way. Then, with a great rising crescendo of screaming and roaring, they crashed into the barricade.

Hundreds of the pikes splintered and snapped like dry twigs as the creatures smashed into the hedge of razor-sharp steel, but for every one that was rendered useless, two more of the long, deadly spears swung down into the engage position.

"Hold them! Hold them, soldiers of the Empire!" Andronicus roared above the din of battle. "Drive them back, warriors of the Alliance!" His sword flashed and glittered as it rained death down on the ranks of the Shock Troops that still swarmed up the barricade.

The Tri-Horns continued to move against the barricade like a horizontal landslide, but the pikes bristled before them, finding every gap and chink in their armor and driving deep into the creatures' hugely thick hides, their own strength and momentum adding power and effectiveness to the Polypontians' weaponry.

In the center of the defensive line Sharley, Mekhmet, and Kirimin fought side by side as they defended the pikemen from the soldiers of the Hordes, who were desperately trying to fell the hedge of steel. The lightning scimitars became a shining blur as the boys held the line and Kirimin let out the coughing bark of the Snow Leopard challenge while striking at the enemy with her huge claws.

But then suddenly the Snow Leopard Princess reared up onto her hind legs, and with a roar she leaped onto the head and neck of the huge beast before her and swarmed up onto its back, where she attacked the enemy soldiers in the howdah. Giving the battle cry of the Icemark, Sharley followed, as did Mekhmet, proclaiming that there was no god but the One, and mighty was his Messenger.

Along the line Cressida saw what was happening, and after issuing orders for the rest of the allied soldiers to hold their position in defense of the pike phalanx, she and Leonidas joined with Eodred and Howler's Regiment of the Red Eye and charged over the heads of the Tri-Horns, where battle was joined with the mahouts and the Hordes who fought in the howdahs. Overhead the Vampire squadrons folded their wings and dived into the attack, screeching as they swept down on the Hordes to rend them with fang and claw.

Ariadne screamed out orders that sent the Tri-Horns surging against the barricade, again and again, but incredibly the phalanx of pikes held, more and more of the huge spears swinging down to engage the beasts, which roared and bellowed as they tried to breach the line. Andronicus redressed the ranks continually as men fell, and replacements stepped forward over their dead and injured comrades to maintain the position. For a time arrows and spears rained down from the howdahs, killing hundreds of the Imperial soldiers, but with blood-freezing howls Eodred and Howler led their regiment against the archers and spear throwers, leaping from Tri-Horn to Tri-Horn like sailors fighting from ship to ship.

Out beyond the city walls, Thirrin led her force in a rising gallop. The massed ranks of the enemy were now in view, seething and writhing like smoke around the smashed southern gate of Romula. Surprise was complete; even those members of the Hordes who'd seen the army bearing down on them probably thought they were just another contingent of their own massive host. They weren't close enough yet for details to become clear, but they soon would be.

Olympia gazed ahead to the enemy host that was composed of her own race of people, and for a moment she bowed her head.

"They hate us, my love," said Ollie, who rode beside her. "They hate us and have sworn to destroy us. Let that knowledge give you strength to fight."

"I know it," the Basilea replied. "But that doesn't end my regrets."

"Nor mine. But the death of one allied soldier certainly would."

"Yes," Olympia whispered. Then, squaring her shoulders, she said in a louder, firmer voice, "Yes, it would."

"I think now would be an appropriate time to announce our presence," Tharaman said calmly to Thirrin, who galloped beside him.

"Yeah, let's put the fear of whatsit right up 'em!" Grishmak agreed.

Nodding, Thirrin drew her sword, stood in her stirrups, and gave the battle cry of the Icemark: "The enemy is upon us! They kill our children; they burn our houses! *BLOOD! BLAST! AND FIRE! BLOOD! BLAST! AND FIRE!*"

Back crashed the reply from thousands of throats, and with a roar they leaped forward in a charge that raised a cloud of dust like smoke from a raging fire.

At last the enemy realized their danger, and almost half of the Hordes waiting to enter the city had turned to face the new threat. Once again Thirrin gave the war cry of the Icemark, and again the entire army replied. Amazingly, the enemy surged forward to meet them, and the roar of onset rose over the city in a banner of sound that reached the ears of all who fought within its walls. Thirrin struck out at the warriors before her, fighting with an economy that conserved her energy. She knew the struggle would be long and any victory hard-won.

Tharaman and Krisafitsa led their Snow Leopards in a considered advance through the ranks that seethed before them. The Hordes showed no surprise that they were fighting beasts and monsters; they were unbeaten and invincible. The land itself could rise up against them and still they'd be convinced they'd win, blessed as they believed they were by the Goddess's favor.

Soon the momentum of the allies' charge was absorbed by the densely packed ranks of the enemy, and their advance ground to a halt. Now the strength and stamina of the fighters would be tested to the full as the toe-to-toe struggle began. The Hordes closed ranks and surged forward, trying to swamp the enemy, but the Snow Leopards stood like a ferocious dam that held their spate in check.

Thirrin scanned the lines before her; now they needed the immovable strength of the housecarls, who could stand all day while the enemy beat themselves to pieces on their shield-wall, but such infantry as they'd had stood now in the streets of the city holding the line against the Tri-Horns.

Grishmak immediately saw the problem, and once again led his warriors to break the strength of the enemy. Snarling out his commands, he suddenly leaped at the densely packed ranks of the Hordes and ran over their heads and shoulders, leading his werewolves to drop between their lines, prying apart the force's cohesion as they tore open their bodies like putrid leather and drank their blood.

The Werewolf King was joined by the Vampires as he led his people over the heads of the Hordes, levering apart the solid density of their army and leaving them to be hacked to pieces by the Snow Leopard and human cavalry that steadily advanced through the seemingly endless throng. The undead Vampiric warriors flew above the struggling masses in their bat forms, and then transformed to black-armored soldiers who dived into the ranks of the enemy, wielding their viciously serrated swords and biting out throats with their glittering fangs.

Slowly, painfully, bit by agonizing bit, the Hordes were being broken apart and annihilated. But Thirrin realized that the rate of advance was so slow, it would take more time than they had to wipe them out. The allies were losing soldiers, too, and such was the size of the enemy host, Thirrin knew that every human, werewolf, Snow Leopard, and Vampire of her army could be killed before they'd even confronted a quarter of their number.

She gasped for breath, exhausted by the effort to kill and kill again. Her charger's legs were red to the shoulder as he struck out with his hooves at the enemy before him and every one of her warriors of all species was barely recognizable beneath a brilliant crimson coating. This was the Hordes' greatest strength: They absorbed their enemies' power and then drained them of strength until they were ready to be overwhelmed.

But then, over the clamor of battle, a strange sound came from the city, a great bellowing and roaring, as though all the beasts that had ever lived had been packed within its walls and were now fighting to break free.

Quickly Thirrin looked toward the shattered southern gates and watched in amazement as a huge stampede of Tri-Horns suddenly burst into view. The massive beasts trampled all before them, cutting a huge bloody swath through the unfought ranks of the enemy, and a shudder passed through the Hordes, as though through the pelt of a giant animal.

The Tri-Horns raged on, unchecked, unstoppable. And as they came closer, Thirrin could see that some carried the remains of smashed howdahs that were populated by corpses, all rolling and lolling with the rocking gait of the animals.

Then slowly the cohesion of the Hordes began to falter. At first the units in the path of the stampeding Tri-Horns started to move away, rolling apart like a bank of fog before a blowing wind as the soldiers tried to escape the massive feet of the panicking and enraged creatures. Others then caught the movement, as section collided with section, and soon there was a general movement away from the gates of the city. At first there was no panic and no sense that a rout was beginning, but then a ragged tangle of fleeing soldiers burst from the city, Shock Troops and elite female regiments following the Tri-Horns as close as they dared. The Hordes were in retreat! Such a thing was unknown! Such a thing hadn't happened since the coming of Basilea Erinor! And so shocking was the sight that the regiments still waiting to enter Romula fell back before their running comrades.

Field marshals tried to regain control of the massive beast that was the Hordes, but still they rolled away from the gates, and then when the strange army of giant leopards and hairy monsters that was attacking their flank suddenly drew back and charged them again, a great howl rose up, and the plain surrounding the city was suddenly filled with fleeing soldiers as the Hordes laid down their invincibility and ran in defeat.

In the streets of Romula the Tri-Horns pushed forward, bellowing and roaring as they came in to attack the barricade, but the *feel* of the battle was changing. Cressida could sense the change; it tingled along her limbs and filled her belly with a fire that drove her on over the heaving backs of the giant beasts. And always beside her strode Leonidas, his whip-thin, elegant figure fighting with the speed and finesse of a dancer, his sword flashing and flickering as they attacked the soldiers in the howdahs, his face calm and peaceful as if he were strolling in a pleasant garden. To her right, Cressida could see Sharley and Mekhmet fighting beside Kirimin as they drove forward over the sea of backs, and to her left, Eodred and Howler led the Regiment of the Red Eye in a murderous advance.

But then she and Leonidas leaped onto the back of one of the largest of the Tri-Horns, and suddenly they were both aware that something was different. The howdah was the biggest they'd encountered, and around it stood a unit of enemy soldiers dressed in uniforms that were edged with purple. Immediately they realized they'd reached the Tri-Horn of the commander. Erinor herself might be absent from the battle, but whoever rode this beast must, by definition, be high ranking and vitally important to the war of the Hordes.

With cold calculation, Cressida and Leonidas waited until their following unit had caught up with them, and then with a roar they leaped to the attack. The action was sharp and bloody, sword and spear, shield and ax trading blow for blow as Cressida led them to sweep aside the enemy soldiers.

Now they were in the howdah itself, and suddenly before them stood the commander of the Hordes, tall and powerful and wielding a double-headed ax that felled all before her like wheat before a scythe. Cressida waited until the swing of the giant ax was at its widest reach, and then she leaped in, her sword striking forward and slicing open the commander's throat.

Ariadne fell in silence, relieved that she wouldn't have to face Erinor, and the remains of her bodyguard fled, wailing that the commander was dead.

Down on the barricades Andronicus was still directing the pike regiments' struggle with the Tri-Horns, the men holding their position unflinchingly and driving the razor-sharp steel of the giant spears through the beasts' armor and into their flesh. To the massive animals the stings of the pikes were like those of giant hornets: maddening, enraging, fearful. They bellowed and pushed forward, breaking hundreds of the spears, but more swung down into the engage position and continued to cut and sting.

Andronicus roared out orders as the stifling stench of the beasts billowed around him. Nearby, a pikeman fell with an arrow in his throat, but the general seized his giant spear and raised it to fill the gap in the hedge of steel while he continued to direct the defense.

"Hold them! Hold them, lads! They're weakening; they're giving ground!" He'd been shouting similar phrases for over an hour as he encouraged his men, but suddenly he realized it was true. The Tri-Horns were falling back!

As one the phalanx of pike surged forward, biting deep into the flesh of the giant animals that still stood before them. Then, with a sudden bellow of rage, a solitary beast turned, crippling its neighbor as its vicious horns scored deep wounds along its flank, and blundered away, crushing dozens of Shock Troops that were advancing in support.

Andronicus maintained an iron hold on the phalanx, not allowing them to break the line as they continued to push forward at the solid wall of Tri-Horns. But then, at last, more and more of the beasts began to turn away, dislodging the fighting howdahs as they smashed into one another in their haste to get away from the biting blades of the pikes.

"We have them! They're running! They're running!" Andronicus screamed in elation. Suddenly the entire line took up the call, and cheering spilled out over the battle-field.

The Tri-Horns were in full stampede, crushing the Hordes that had been marching in support of their attack. For a moment the Shock Troops and elite female regiments stood in awe as the monstrous animals rolled toward them, pounding and maiming thousands of their comrades. But then, with a roar of despair, they forgot their invincibility, they forgot that they were an army that was rendered invulnerable by the favor of the Goddess, and they turned and ran.

The Snow Leopards, werewolves, and human soldiers that had been fighting the enemy in the howdahs now leaped to safety, falling from the giant creatures' backs like droplets of cascading water. Overhead, the Vampires harried the retreat, diving down on the fleeing soldiers and screeching in triumph as they tore off their heads.

It was over, the battle was won, and Romula was saved. Now would begin the long chase, as the enemy was pursued and cut down in their thousands. The Eppian Way was suddenly almost shockingly silent as both defeated and victor ran from the city. Only Andronicus and his pikemen still held their position on the barricade, but after a few moments he quietly gave the order to ground pikes. The phalanx stood to attention for almost five minutes, and then, when he was finally certain the enemy had been routed, the Polypontian general told his men to stand down.

Wearily he removed his helmet, and, finding an old stool in the rubbish and flotsam that had been used to make the barricade, he sat down and waited for Thirrin to reenter the city.

24

O skan and the witches had been working for almost ten hours without a break. Many warriors of all species had been brought into the complex of tents he'd set up as an infirmary, and he and his healers had begun the long battle to save as many lives as they could.

His clothes were stiff with blood and other bodily fluids, and his boots were soaked as he paddled through the puddles of gore and slime that washed across the floor. He had calculated that they were losing five patients for every one they saved, and of those who survived almost half would be crippled in some way by their injuries. But he was enough of a realist to know that he could expect little better in the way of results, and at least some lives were saved from the horrors of the battle.

He suddenly noticed, with an almost detached interest, that the canvas of the tent he was working in was drenched with great sweeping swaths of blood, which made quite pleasing patterns against the brightness of the sunset outside. But then his patient groaned, and he returned to the task of trying to remove the arrowhead that was buried deep in his side.

Eventually, after long minutes of cutting, he managed to free the barbs and slide the thick piece of iron free of the wound. Now all he had to do was close the arteries before they emptied themselves of their precious contents. The young man had slipped into unconsciousness by this time, making Oskan's job of stitching and closing much easier.

He put in the last suture, and stood back while the orderlies removed the patient and brought in another. This was a young woman with a badly broken leg. The thick thigh bone was sticking through the flesh, and Oskan knew that forcing the jagged and glistening break back through the wound, and then lining it up with the other half so that it could mend, would be so hideously painful that the patient could quite easily die of shock.

Quickly he made a decision. Taking a key, he opened a small chest that stood against the canvas wall of his operating theater. This was where he kept his precious supplies of poppy. The rough morphine would take away the pain and shock, making survival more likely for the patient. But supplies were scarce and getting scarcer by the day, it seemed. As he decanted a measure of the liquid from a flask, he calculated how much they had left. Much less than was needed, that was sure—but as the main supply route came from the south, and probably began in Artemesion, the homeland of the Hordes themselves, they were very unlikely to get any more.

He helped the patient to drink, and watched in unfading wonder as her face relaxed and the screaming stopped. Just how did it work? If only he knew, then perhaps he could find some other source for its miraculous painkilling properties.

But he must move quickly before its effects wore off. With incredible speed, he and his assisting witch straightened the badly mangled leg, removed all bone splinters from the wound, and pushed the shattered ends of the break back through the chaos of torn muscles, tendons, and skin, until it met with the corresponding break deep inside the leg. They then twisted and rotated the limb until it looked as straight as they could judge it, after which they washed everything in old wine and garlic juice and proceeded to stitch the ragged wound, bandage it, and then set everything in a rigid splint. Perhaps the patient would never run again, Oskan thought to himself, but at least she'd walk, and as a cavalry trooper, she might even go to war again, and create more work for the healers to repair. Such was the role of the medic in a militaristic society.

Another wounded soldier was then brought in, and Oskan was so busy concentrating on the job in hand that at first he didn't notice the pricking sensation in the back of his neck that often warned him of some sort of psychic event. But eventually he was able to leave the patient to one of his witches, and he looked up and applied his Eye, trying to track down the source of the magical disturbance.

For almost five minutes he searched the ether, until gradually it dawned on him that perhaps he'd experienced a premonition or a warning. But whatever it had been or was going to be, the sense of foreboding had now gone, and though it left him feeling deeply uneasy, he didn't really have the time to search any longer. There were just too many wounded soldiers to treat, and maybe the feeling was just an anomaly of some sort: nothing important, just a small glitch in the ether.

The Vampires fell screaming and raging through the sky over Frostmarris. Below them the Ice Demons milled about in near panic as the attack began, but then suddenly they steadied and began to raise spears and shields to ward off the aerial assault. The Vampire Queen had been watching for this; the commander of the first attempt to defend the city had warned her of the enemy's use of mind control, and now she knew that Cronus and Medea were manipulating the simple but vicious creatures of their army.

She raised her head and screeched as the battlements of the citadel rushed up to meet them, and then, instantly transforming into her human form, she stepped out of flight onto the cold stone and drew her sword.

Leading the attack, she smashed into the ranks of the enemy before her, driving back the lumbering beasts by the pure ferocity of her charge, while all around her, the Vampire Army struck and parried with deadly elegance, killing dozens of the demons.

The queen waited in cynical patience, and smiled when the expected attempt to control the minds of her Vampires began. With a swaggering contempt, she raised the powerful psychic shields that protected herself and her army. Obviously the enemy must be completely naive if she believed it was possible to exist for more than twelve hundred years without learning a thing or two about protecting oneself against psychic power.

At the height of their combined abilities, the Vampire King and Queen had been the match of any witch or warlock; only Oskan Witchfather had been stronger, but then again, *he* was the exception to almost every magical rule. Even now that she was alone, Her Vampiric Majesty found that as long as she kept up the highest levels of concentration, her methods of magical protection were more than a match for Medea and the horrendous *thing* she'd brought with her.

But the Vampire Queen had to admit that though she wasn't shocked that the Witchfather's daughter had returned from exile in the Darkness, she *was* deeply disturbed by the depths of depravity to which Medea had managed to sink. It was all well and good being evil, as long as one remained within the limits and parameters of the Goddess-given universe, but Medea and the creature she'd brought with her obviously wanted to change *everything*. Truly, to some people nothing was sacred.

Now more and more Ice Demons began to swarm up onto the battlements, bellowing and roaring as they attacked, forcing Her Vampiric Majesty to concentrate on the immediate task in hand. It soon became clear that the position was indefensible, and as the queen screeched out an order, her army leaped into flight and powered away to attack the weak point of the outer walls, namely the main gatehouse of the city.

Within minutes they'd landed, driven out, or killed the demons, and established the foothold the Vampires needed. Sitting at ease in the main chamber of the barbican, Her Vampiric Majesty directed operations as her undead warriors attacked the rest of the city. Half of the squadrons dug in to protect their position, while the rest flew off to drop pots of flaming pitch into anything flammable they could find. Soon huge areas of Frostmarris were a raging inferno.

Once the fires were well established, the queen regrouped her warriors and led them on a devastating rampage through the city. Soon they were fighting from street to street, driving against the lumbering Ice Demons and scything through their defensive lines.

But then massive reinforcements arrived, bellowing and roaring as they ran up to help their comrades. The army of the Darkness now began to gain the upper hand, and once again the queen disengaged, leading her squadrons back into flight as she sought a new area of weakness to attack and destroy.

Medea and Cronus sat in the Great Hall of the citadel, their eyes closed and minds conjoined as they directed the defense of the city. The assault had been completely unexpected, but their powers were such that they'd soon recovered and mounted a counterattack that they were sure would ultimately destroy the Vampires.

The fact that Her Vampiric Majesty could resist their mind control had been something of a shock, it had to be admitted, but it was really only an inconvenience that would eventually be overcome. Once they'd destroyed the nuisance the Vampires represented, they could resume their program for the total domination of the Physical Realms.

But then the conjoined minds of the two Adepts registered puzzlement. Her Vampiric Majesty and her forces had disappeared. One moment the Ice Demons were gaining the upper hand in the barbican district of the city, and the next they'd withdrawn and vanished.

Suddenly the ceiling of the Great Hall exploded in a cascade of falling tiles, roof beams, and plaster as the Vampires smashed through the roof. The air was filled with shrieking and the clatter of giant leathery wings as the undead warriors rained chaos into the hall. Cronus and Medea leaped to their feet and ran to shelter among a tangle of huge oak tables that had been blasted aside by the queen's arrival.

"Are there no limits to this woman's impudence?" Cronus raged.

"Just blast her!" Medea replied and sent out a bolt of plasma that punched a hole through the wall of the Great Hall but left the Vampires unscathed.

"Waste of time and effort!" Cronus shouted. "She's shielded. So are her soldiers."

"What do we do, then?"

"Oh, there are many ways and means of dealing with those that have lesser Abilities. But first of all we call in the demons, of course!"

Quickly they sent out a mental summons, and within seconds hundreds of the gigantic soldiers of the Darkness powered into the hall, filling it with their size, noise, and choking stench. Now the battle for the citadel began in earnest; the ring of metal on metal filled the hall as sword traded blow with ax, and the hideous screeching of the Vampires mingled with the roaring and bellowing of the demons.

Soon the floors were awash with the black blood of the monsters of the Darkness and the decapitated bodies of the Vampiric warriors as the battle swung first one way and then the other.

Neither side could gain the upper hand, but then, during a natural lull in the fighting, a light and refined voice called into the relative quiet.

"Might I suggest a temporary truce?"

"You might," Cronus replied from his position behind the broken and blasted tables. "But to what purpose, other than to delay your inevitable destruction?"

"Oh, no particular reason," the Vampire Queen replied. "I just wanted to be certain I really am fighting the Arc-Adept of the Darkness."

"You are," Cronus said with pride. "And as a creature of evil and death, you owe your allegiance to me! Lay down your arms and swear fealty to your lord and master!"

"I don't think so!" Her Vampiric Majesty replied with contempt. "I show subservience only to those who are stronger than me, and I see no evidence of that as yet."

"Then your blindness is equaled only by your stupidity! Prepare to die, bat thing!"

"If I could just beg your indulgence for a moment longer," the undead queen's refined voice requested. "Could you please explain to me exactly what the staff is that you carry?"

Cronus proudly held the symbol of his power and authority aloft. "It is the scepter that denotes my control of the Physical Realms. All who defy me should look on it and tremble."

"Oh, I see! Do you know, I thought it was a giant toothpick, or perhaps something you shoved into other parts of your anatomy. I never realized it represented your supposed right to rule," said Her Vampiric Majesty lightly. "Do you really believe you'll ever be able to carry it with any degree of justification?"

Cronus screamed in rage, but once again the queen raised her elegantly armored hand.

"Just one moment. I know I'm being an awful bother, but I just wondered if it would be possible to talk to Medea."

"What do you want, you glorified leech?" the Adept asked, standing up from her position behind a fallen trestle.

"Oh, I want nothing from you. I feel only contempt for petulant teenage girls who are stupid enough to allow their tantrums to lead them into treachery. I was just curious to see you again." There was a pause as the Vampire Queen scrutinized her. "Yes. You've acquired a brand-new body and yet you still manage to look exactly what you are: a sullen, moody brat."

Medea sent out a blast of plasma that set fire to all the woodwork in the building. "I'm the second-most powerful Adept in the known universe. Take care I don't incinerate you where you stand!"

"But you can't, my dear. My defenses are far too strong. Oh, and incidentally, what on earth gave you the idea that you're the second-most powerful Adept in the universe?" The queen paused as though expecting an answer, but then went on: "Assuming you're misguided enough to think that *thing* with you is the most powerful, then that means you believe yourself more Gifted than your father. Well, let me leave you with this little thought: Whenever His Vampiric Majesty and myself conjoined and tried to raise defenses against Oskan, he tore them aside as though they were as insubstantial as wet tissue paper. Now, considering your little performance against my psychic shields today, what does that tell us about your powers when compared to your father's?"

Medea gave a scream of rage and sent out an explosion of fire, adding further to the flames that were slowly gaining a hold in the building.

"Though if one is to be totally honest about all of this," the queen continued conversationally, "there's one area of Magical Ability where you must excel to a level even greater than that of your father."

"Oh, do tell," Medea sneered. "I'm all agog for a blood-sucker's praise."

"Simple, really: mind-shielding. You've obviously managed to keep your intentions to invade the Icemark and Physical Realms completely secret. Something I find quite remarkable, especially as I know you've confronted the Witchfather and he must have probed your thoughts for information. All I can say is, well done. Your shielding must be exceptionally brilliant; we all know, don't we, that if Oskan had been aware of your intentions, he'd have been waiting for you and blasted your army to ash just as soon as you'd set foot on the Icemark's soil."

"For once your judgment is sound, leech-woman," Medea replied. "And by the time he finds out, we'll be so well established in his pathetic little kingdom, he'll have no chance of driving us out."

"Well, that's certainly debatable," Her Vampiric Majesty said calmly. "But rather a moot point really, because I intend to ensure that you and your army of loathsome demons never become 'established,' as you put it."

Both Adepts laughed contemptuously, and the Ice Demons rolled forward into battle once more as Cronus sent them against the Vampire squadron.

The roar of the resumed fighting mingled with that of the fire that was now leaping from furnishings and up into the rafters and beams of the roof. Ironically, the simple elemental power of the fire seemed to present more of a threat to the queen and her squadron than the combined Gifts of the two Adepts. But then Cronus drew on the elements and materials at hand, and a swirling vortex of power exploded into the hall as he fashioned a giant snake that coiled and snapped at the Vampires with long fangs like swords. Her Vampiric Majesty might have been able to shield herself and her warriors from the direct effects of magic, but she had no defenses against the physical fighting abilities of magically conjured creatures.

The huge snake swallowed two of the Vampires and crushed a third in its coils, which were constructed from granite and fire. Medea immediately seized on this chance to strike back at the arrogant queen, and conjured a giant ravening wolf that attacked the undead fighters and tore off their heads in its crushing jaws. The two Adepts now constructed more and more of the magical creatures, drawing on the very fabric of the city itself to make their bodies, until the Great Hall was filled with snakes and wolves, eagles and dragons, that fell on the Vampires in an ecstasy of killing.

The tide of battle had now turned, and though the undead squadron fought on with stubborn valor, eventually Her Vampiric Majesty gave the order to withdraw. The entire squadron then leaped into flight, and powered away through the hole they'd made in the roof when they'd first entered. But not before each and every one of the giant bats had emptied their bladders onto the enemy below to show just what they thought of them and their much-vaunted Abilities.

Thirrin led her warriors along the Eppian Way and into the city. Soon they were approaching the hard-fought position from which Cressida had led the defense of the streets, and all along the top of the makeshift barricade the mixed defenders cheered as their comrades approached. The long spears of the pike regiments stood like a winter thicket of trees, and the housecarls beat sword and ax on shield in salute.

Cressida, Andronicus, and Leonidas climbed down to stand before Thirrin's horse, where they drew their swords in salute. "Welcome to the liberated city of Romula, Your Majesty," said General Andronicus. "Its freedom is owed to your strategy and to your sword."

Thirrin nodded her acknowledgment, but then said, "The freedom of Romula is owed to the Alliance, General Andronicus. An Alliance that includes the fighting skills and bravery of many thousands of Polypontian soldiers."

A cheer rose up from the barricade at these words, and then, at a signal from Cressida, the soldiers climbed down from their position and drew aside the barrier. The combined army now advanced along the Eppian Way, where the survivors of the civilian population had slowly gathered from their hiding places as news of the unexpected victory had flowed through the city.

Rumors of the approach of the "Barbarian Queen" ran through the waiting crowds that lined the road, and her flaming red hair was greeted with as much awe as the spectacle of the giant Snow Leopards, werewolves, and Vampires. Beside her rode her daughter, and as both had removed their helmets, their hair seemed to lead the procession of the army like twin torches.

"I hear you and Leonidas led your troops with distinction," said Thirrin as the cheers washed over them. "Fighting side by side, I'm told."

Cressida blushed, as did Leonidas, who was riding beside her. "The flow of battle merely took us in the same direction. It's pure coincidence that we were at each other's side for the duration of the fighting."

"And what excuse do you have now?" asked Thirrin, unable to resist the temptation to tease.

"Perhaps I should . . . you know . . . go and lead my old command of . . . you know . . . cavalry," said Leonidas.

"You'll do no such thing, Commander," said Krisafitsa-Tharina, who'd been listening to every word. "Queen Thirrin is merely enjoying her own little joke. Aren't you, my dear?"

"Absolutely. I'm enjoying it immensely."

"Stay where you are, boy!" boomed Grishmak. "Things could start getting interesting later on, if you see what I mean!" and he winked hugely.

Tharaman caught Leonidas's cloak in his massive jaws as the commander almost fell from his horse, and then gently nudged him back into his saddle. "Steady on, Grishy! You know humans are a little less *earthy* than we are about these matters. And this pair is even more delicate than most."

"Eh? Oh, call a spade a spade, that's what I say. Come on, boy, what are you mucking about at? Get in there! Anyone can see she wants you!"

"Some of us prefer a little more romance in our wooing," said Krisafitsa loftily. "We don't all see relationships as mere wrestling matches."

"Don't we? Oh."

Cressida, who was almost writhing with mortified embarrassment, could take no more and suddenly exploded, "Who's wooing anybody around here? And what in all worlds does 'wooing' mean, anyway?"

"Right! Who's . . . you know . . . wooing anybody?" Leonidas agreed, and then immediately regretted it.

"Well, it looks like wooing to me," said Grishmak. "Not that I've ever had a woo myself. Sounds a bit too tame to me."

"I've had a woo," said Tharaman importantly. "Krisafitsa insists on it, don't you, my dear?"

"Have you?" asked Grishmak interestedly. "What's it like?"

"Bit tame, just as you thought," said Tharaman quietly out of the corner of his mouth.

"Is it? Not like the usual sort of . . . ?"

"That'll do, thank you," said Krisafitsa. "I do believe we're approaching the palace precinct and a little more decorum is required."

Thirrin unconsciously straightened her back and called a halt as the walls of the precinct came into view. Polypontian soldiers guarded the gates, their uniforms a pristine white that was emblazoned with the twin-headed Imperial Eagle. Here was the epicenter of the power that had sent two invasion forces against the Icemark; here sat the man who had controlled and manipulated the lives of literally millions of people when the Polypontian Empire was at the height of its powers. And now that the Empire was dying, millions more had been killed in the wars and rebellions that had followed the breaking of the Emperor's iron grip. Thirrin shuddered imperceptibly as she gazed in silence at the precinct; if Scipio Bellorum in all his cold, unthinking evil had been the servant, then what sort of depraved malevolence must reside in the master, in the Emperor himself?

The time had come to face him. She was a warrior-queen, and head of the Alliance that had not only defeated the Imperial legions twice but had also saved Romula itself from destruction. Let him come on his knees in all his evil arrogance and bow in gratitude and obeisance before her! She urged her horse forward, Cressida, Tharaman, Grishmak, and the rest of the royal party falling in behind.

As they approached the gates, the Imperial guard leveled their spears and demanded she announce herself and await permission to enter. But Thirrin's pace never faltered, and after a moment's hesitation the soldiers fell back before her. The gates swung open silently and a wide garden opened up before them. The beautiful pleasance of trees, lawns, and fountains swept down to a graceful and towering building of white marble. Rightly assuming that this was the palace, Thirrin rode slowly toward it, her head held high so that the sunlight made her hair a blazing halo of fire.

The soldiers of the Imperial guard ran before her, calling out in Polypontian that the Barbarian Queen was approaching, and soon the steps of the palace were thronged with what looked like hundreds of servants and officials, all straining to catch sight of the fearsome legend and her Alliance of monsters. Thirrin and her comrades rode on until they were a matter of a quarter mile from the lair of the Emperor himself, then they reined to a halt and waited until eventually a party of old men scrambled forward to greet her.

They bowed as they ran and smiled ingratiatingly, their long purple-and-white robes announcing their status as senators. "Welcome, welcome, Your Majesty!" they called as they ran up. "Please do us the honor of dismounting, and the Emperor will receive you in due course, in the Great Audience Chamber!"

Thirrin glared down at them, barely able to contain her fury. "The Emperor will 'receive' me nowhere! The Emperor will attend me here, and now, or my warriors will burn his audience chamber to the ground!"

Her voice cut clear and glittering through the air, like a razor through flesh, and a murmur ran through the officials who waited on the palace steps.

"Do not make the mistake of doubting my word, otherwise the ashes of the palace, and probably those of the Emperor himself, will serve as reminders of the weight of my meaning!"

Tharaman reared up, letting out a roar that smashed against the graceful marble gleaming brilliantly in the sunshine. The senators took one look at the Barbarian Queen's blazing eyes and scrambled away, calling out that they would inform the Emperor of her wishes.

In the silence that followed, Thirrin stared rigidly ahead, while Tharaman and Krisafitsa gave each other a wash and Grishmak leaned against Thirrin's horse, scratching absently. Cressida and Leonidas took the opportunity to sit side by side, ostensibly ignoring each other, but in reality basking in each other's presence as though in front of a warm fire on a cold day.

For fully fifteen minutes the royal party was kept waiting, and Thirrin was just considering riding her warhorse up the marble steps and into the palace itself when a sudden commotion at the top of a long, column-lined colonnade announced the arrival of a huge party of senators.

"What's up? Looks like business," said Grishmak. Pushing himself upright, he stretched until the sinews in his mighty arms and legs cracked.

"Well, I can see Imperial lackeys, but no Emperor so far," said Thirrin. "You've got the sharpest eyes here, Tharaman; what do you see?"

"Lots of old gents in those purple-and-white robe thingies. But no one else."

"Right. If this is just another senatorial delegation, the palace goes up in smoke!"

Grishmak nodded grimly and signaled to a cavalry trooper. "Fetch torches and tinder; I think we're going to have a bonfire."

As the soldier galloped off, the royal party waited in silence as the procession of elderly senators wound its way along the colonnade and down the flight of steps. They then set out across the wide sweep of lawn, all perfectly in step like a unit of geriatric infantry, and then at last came to a halt a few yards away from Thirrin's horse.

"You were warned that I would burn down—" Thirrin began angrily, but the most venerable of all the senators held up his hand commandingly.

"All hail his Imperial Majesty of the mighty Polypontian Empire. His lands stretch from the frozen wastes of the north to the burning deserts of the south, from the mountains and forests of the east to the mighty oceans of the west. His navies rule wave and tide, his sky-ships patrol the heavens, his legions' tread is thunder, and his will is life and death to all his subjects! All hail Titus Augustus Domitian Julianus, Divine and Imperial Majesty and Lord of all he surveys!"

A deathly hush fell upon the scene, and then the ranks of senators parted to reveal the Emperor himself.

A small boy in purple robes stood before them, and then an elderly servant took his hand and led the boy to stand before Thirrin's horse. The wide Imperial hat hid his features, but suddenly he took it off and scratched his head, making his hair stand in tufts.

"I said it would make me too hot, Silvanus. Here, you have it."

The servant fumbled to take the hat, visibly shaking before the red-haired monarch, but the boy smiled brightly and squinted up at the imposing figure before him. "Are you the Barbarian Queen? You've got a really fierce horse. What's his name?"

"Havoc," Thirrin replied quietly, her mind in turmoil. She wanted to hate the Emperor of the undeniably evil Polypontian Empire, but how could she hate a little boy? Could she really convince herself that he was a monster who was responsible for so many deaths?

"Can I sit on him?"

"You might find him a little rambunctious, I'm afraid."

"Oh, all right," the Emperor replied, his voice brimming with disappointment. "Will he let me pet him?"

Thirrin stared down at the boy, who looked incredibly small and vulnerable before the battle-trained hooves of her charger. She'd dreamed of just such a moment for so many long and bitter years that she was reluctant to let it go, and in her imagination she saw herself riding forward over the Emperor and crushing him to a bloody pulp. But in her fantasies he'd always been a man, tall and brutish with an evil, depraved expression, not a little boy with a pretty face.

"Will he let me pet him?" the boy asked again.

"I'm sure he will," Thirrin answered, desperately trying to retain the last dregs of her anger against everything he represented. She sighed, then, quickly dismounting, she held the charger's reins firmly and barked out a command. "Stand, Havoc!"

The huge horse snorted and laid back his ears, but stood like a rock while the boy reached up and stroked his muzzle. "He's all soft," said the boy in delight.

The warhorse whickered, then lowered his muzzle toward the child and snuffed at him. "Blow up his nose; it's the way horses make friends," said Thirrin quietly, still trying to maintain a proper coldness in her dealings with the head of an Empire she'd detested for years.

The boy blew, and giggled when the horse snuffled back at him. "Are we friends now?"

"For life," Thirrin answered.

The boy suddenly became serious. "Do you know, I lost my second front tooth this morning. Silvanus says that proves I'm growing up. Look!" and he grinned broadly so that Thirrin could see the gap where his two front teeth had been.

A memory engulfed her in devastating clarity, as she recalled a winter's morning long ago when Eodred and Cerdic had tumbled into her bed, squealing in delight because they'd both just lost their front teeth. They'd dropped the tiny pieces of ivory to nestle like pearls in her palm, and she'd solemnly told them that she'd give them to the tooth elf that very night and they'd each get a silver penny in return. Of course, Cerdic had argued that they should get two silver pennies each, as they were surrendering two teeth, and Thirrin had agreed to negotiate on their behalf.

For a moment she stepped back as the fullest impact of her emotions hit her, but, recovering herself, she looked down at the boy. "Where are your parents?"

"Oh, Mama died when I was born, and Papa killed himself not long afterward. Silvanus says he really died of a broken heart because he loved Mama so much. Do you love your husband?" The child's dark eyes held her in a frank and open gaze.

"Yes," she managed to mumble after a few moments. "Yes, very much."

"And do you love your children?"

"Yes."

"How many do you have?"

"I had five, but one . . . one has gone far away, and another was killed in the fighting between our peoples."

The child nodded. "Yes, the wars. I'm sorry they happened. Do you miss the ones you've lost?"

"I do, every day."

"I don't remember my parents, so I don't miss them. But I'd miss Silvanus if he was taken away. The senators told me that you could take him away if you wanted to, and that you'd burn my home. You won't, will you? I'd be very sad if you took Silvanus away from me; he's been my servant for always, and I like it when he tells me stories when I go to bed at night."

"I won't take him away, I promise."

"Do you promise on everything you love?"

"On everything I love."

The child smiled brilliantly. "You're a nice lady really, aren't you? But I think you're sad. I'd like to make you laugh and be happy. How can I do that?"

Thirrin looked down at the child and felt a hope stirring. "You could do that by promising our two lands and two peoples will be friends forever."

"Is that all? That's easy — yes, of course I will." The boy opened his arms wide and looked at her.

For a few seconds Thirrin hesitated, then suddenly she stooped and, seizing him in a hug, she swung the child off his feet. He giggled and then kissed her twice.

"The senators said you're called the Barbarian Queen, but that can't be your real name."

"No. It's Thirrin."

"I like that. I'm Titus."

"Hello, Titus."

"Hello, Thirrin," he said, and, giving her a smile of teeth and gaps, he kissed her on the cheek again.

A murmuring began on the steps of the palace, and grew and swelled until slowly it translated itself into applause. Titus smiled and waved, and cheering began to rise into the air, soon to be taken up by the royal party and all the palace guards, who'd been standing nervously nearby. It was going to be all right; everything was going to be all right. The Hordes had been defeated, and the little Emperor had won the heart of the Barbarian Queen.

Thirrin now placed the boy securely into Havoc's high war-saddle, and, keeping a tight hold of the reins, she led him toward the gate of the palace precinct. Sensing an impromptu victory parade, the commander of the palace guard ordered his men to fall in, and soon they were emerging into the streets, where the waiting population broke into spontaneous acclamation at the sight of the little Emperor riding the Barbarian Queen's warhorse.

For more than two hours they paraded through the streets, showing themselves to the people and giving a focus for the joy and relief they felt at the defeat of the Hordes and the saving of the city.

Her Vampiric Majesty had established her headquarters deep in the Great Forest, in the same complex of caves where Oskan Witchfather had lived as a boy. She'd even made her temporary throne room in the very cavern he'd used as his home and main shelter before he'd met and married the young woman who was destined to become the Queen of the Icemark. She almost smiled in a wicked enjoyment of the situation, but then became serious again as she thought through the battle she'd just been engaged in. Her squadrons had taken a severe beating, but even so, they'd fought with distinction and had destroyed many of the hideous Ice Demons that made up the bulk of the invading army. Of course, technically the Vampires had lost the battle, and the invaders had taken Frostmarris and established control over the plain. But they hadn't been expecting any form of resistance, and Her Vampiric Majesty just knew they were reeling with shock.

But now it was imperative that she got a message through to Oskan Witchfather and let him know what was happening. Only he could confront Medea, and the *creature* she had with her, with any degree of equality. The werewolf relay had been knocked out, so other means of sending word had been devised. But in the meantime, she could enjoy herself attacking the lumbering Ice Demons and doing her best to thwart their plans.

She sat back in her chair and stretched luxuriously. She hadn't felt so *alive* in years, if such a term could be applied to the undead. Thanks to the hideous Medea, she felt that she had a purpose and a reason to exist for the first time since the Vampire King had fallen. With Queen Thirrin absent from the kingdom and completely unaware of the invasion, it was Her Vampiric Majesty's job as ally to defend the land and people and, if possible, defeat the enemy.

The evacuation of noncombatants had been chaotic, she had to admit. But once the last child and screeching matron had been flown to safety in the Great Forest, the battle for Frostmarris had truly begun. Oh, and how *glorious* that had been! Medea and the truly horrendous thing she'd brought with her couldn't understand why their psychic weaponry had so little effect against the Vampires. Her Vampiric Majesty allowed herself a small laugh. Obviously the child, Medea, didn't know that the existence of the undead in the natural realms was maintained by pure magic. Well, now she did! They might not actually wield magic as a weapon, but their very presence in the world depended upon an incredibly powerful form of enchantment that made every Vampire more than familiar with psychic power.

And as for the Arc-Adept . . . well, the Vampire Queen had never known such depths of depravity and evil. To be expected, she supposed, but even so, there were limits to what even her own evil would consider doing. But he . . . he would attack the Goddess herself, if he could.

She smiled to herself. It was odd, but at one time she would have found such undiluted malevolence wonderfully admirable, whereas now she found it merely irritating and even boring. How times had changed since Thirrin had become Queen of the Icemark!

A polite cough interrupted Her Vampiric Majesty's thoughts and she turned to see Lugosi, her chamberlain, waiting quietly.

"Well?" she asked imperiously.

"Forgive me for disturbing you, Your Majesty, but the volunteers are waiting."

"Ah, yes. Send them in."

Lugosi bowed himself out of the Presence and after a few moments he returned with three Vampire warriors, who prostrated themselves before the throne that had been transported from The-Land-of-the-Ghosts.

"Oh, *please*, do get up," said the Vampire Queen, her voice suddenly tinged with an odd note that sounded almost like respect and sadness. "I hope you're all fully aware of what lies before you?"

One of the warriors stepped forward and bowed. "We are, Your Majesty."

"And yet you accept the mission, despite knowing the outcome?"

"We do, Ma'am."

Her Vampiric Majesty gazed at her subjects in puzzlement. "Why?" she asked simply.

The Vampire soldier looked at the floor. "Ma'am, I . . . we . . . we've all existed for many lives of humans. In my own case I myself have been one of the undead for almost a thousand years, and the burden has grown heavy, especially knowing that only violent destruction will bring release. But all of us are agreed that being destroyed in an attempt to save the city of Frostmarris and its people is a more . . . acceptable way to go."

"But how will that make your passing any easier?" the Vampire Queen asked, her voice almost wistful as she tried to understand. "You know that once you're beyond the protective power of the Vampire Army, you're almost guaranteed to be ripped apart by the psychic Abilities of the witch Medea and the one she calls her grandfather. You even know that in reality you'll be nothing more than a decoy to distract attention away from the party of werewolves who'll be the real messengers taking news of the invasion to Oskan Witchfather. So how can such a futile mission and your certain destruction be a comfort?"

The Vampire soldiers looked almost embarrassed, and there was much whispering and nodding before their spokesman finally said to the queen, "Ma'am . . . forgive us, but we've all heard about the visit of Prince Charlemagne and the message he brought you."

The Vampire Queen hung her head and remained silent for so long, the soldiers thought she hadn't heard, but then she finally looked at them. "What of it?"

"Ma'am, we know His Vampiric Majesty survives in spirit. We know that it's possible for even the undead to acquire a soul."

There it was again. Her people were positively *obsessed* with a desire to acquire souls. At times she was convinced Vampiric purity was being well and truly sullied, but somehow she found it difficult to be overly concerned about that.

"Ah, I see. And you think that your willing self-sacrifice for the people of Frostmarris will in some way endow you with spirits."

"Yes, Ma'am."

"And is this a general belief throughout the Vampiric host?"

"Yes, Ma'am."

The Vampire Queen almost laughed derisively at the naïveté of the warrior mind. Did they really think that hundreds of years of murder, destruction, and depravity could be expunged by one single act of goodness? Her eyes glinted and she opened her mouth to pour scorn on their stupidity, but something stopped her. Every single one of her soldiers could be destroyed in this war at any time, and who was she to deny them whatever comfort they could find as they faced the depraved monsters of Medea's army? Let them keep their belief; let them have their hopes. For herself, she believed that His Vampiric Majesty was an amazing exception to an otherwise unassailable law of the Multiverse: The physically mortal had immortal souls; the physically immortal had nothing.

She sat back in her throne and smiled at her soldiers. "I'm sure your act will be noted by . . . whatever Powers there may be."

The Vampires returned her smile and turned to embrace one another, as though the queen's acceptance of what they'd said somehow made it more valid.

The flight of Vampires fell from the sky, their wings torn to rags by the blast of psychic energy. Three of the party of six were already destroyed, their heads torn from their shoulders and their status as undead negated.

The remaining three fell uncontrollably. One crashed into a tree, his body impaled on the sharp stakes of broken branches, another disintegrated on impact with the ground, and the third landed in a fountaining shower of mud as he fell into the shallows of a small mountain lake. The collision smashed the winter ice and drove him deep into the silts that lined the bottom.

The psychic blast had hit the party of Vampires just as soon as they were beyond the collective protection of their army, and they died in the knowledge that they were nothing more than a distraction, a decoy that would allow the real messengers to slip through unnoticed.

The party of six werewolves moved with speedy silence across the land now, blending with the shadows of the night and making less noise than the gentle icy breeze that breathed across the route leading to the south and the border with the Polypontus. As they ran, the howling of the magically re-created werewolf relay sounded, sending the army of allies campaigning in the Empire its false message that all was well. The six creatures snarled with silent hatred as they heard the deceiving call but ran on unflaggingly; they couldn't send a vocal warning to Queen Thirrin and Oskan Witchfather themselves, not only because they'd attract the attention of the enemy, but also because the chain of relay stations that would be needed to send on their call had been destroyed. All they could do was keep running and hope to deliver their message in person. Medea, and the creature that shared command of her army, were probably still scanning the skies for more Vampire squadrons, and the Wolf-folk knew that they must be far away before the evil pair even thought of turning their attention to the ground.

The night wore on and the werewolves continued their flight south. They covered huge distances, taking secret routes over wold and dale, and even belowground, through cave systems that led them quickly beneath hills standing between themselves and the border. Desperation increased their speed dramatically, and as the winter dawn began to lighten the eastern sky, the mountain range known as the Dancing Maidens came into view, the snows on its rounded peaks blushing pink in the glorious sunrise.

With their target, and safety, in sight, the werewolves spurred themselves on to even greater speed, and soon they began to climb the foothills that led to the pass. But the creatures were wily, and suspecting that the Polypontian border would be watched, they veered off the path and headed for the mountain peaks. They'd take the least suspected route into the Empire, a route where blizzard and intense cold would kill any ordinary mortal. The evil witch Medea would never think of watching the heights.

Within two hours the Wolf-folk were nearing the tops of the mountains, and soon they'd be able to look down into the Polypontus itself. They whimpered with excitement and relief, and allowed themselves a rest for the first time on their mission. The eldest of their number, a gray-pelted female who'd commanded the citadel guard in Frostmarris before it was destroyed, stretched and smiled.

"I think we've made it. We're sa—" Suddenly her words were cut off as she disappeared beneath a crushing fall of wing and scale, talon and fang.

Ice Demons were falling from the sky, their huge wings beating on the air and sending up a blinding fog of powdery snow. Immediately the werewolves formed themselves into a fighting phalanx and charged the creatures that were tearing their comrade to pieces. The fight was ferocious and swift; blood cascaded over the pristine brilliance of the snows as the demons immediately ripped two of the five remaining Wolf-folk to gory rags of flesh.

The werewolves fell back, snarling defiance, as the monstrous creatures beat their huge wings and screamed. Command of the messengers now fell to Garstang Flesh-eater, and he quickly evaluated an almost hopeless situation.

"Right, youngster, slip down that way, through the boulders," he said to the smallest and nimblest of the werewolves. "Me and Scar-muzzle here will keep them busy while you escape down into the Polypontus. Don't argue, just go. The message must get through!"

Without another word the youngest of the party scrambled off and didn't turn to watch as his comrades attacked the Ice Demons again. He heard howling and snarling as the two werewolves fought with economy and intelligence, throwing huge boulders with a devastating accuracy that crippled one of the demons by breaking its wings. But not even the Wolf-folk could stand against the insane ferocity of the creatures of the Dark, and soon they fell in a welter of blood and smashed bone.

The youngster continued to tumble and scramble through the icy boulders toward the border of the Polypontus. All had gone quiet behind him, but he didn't dare stop to see what was happening. He could now see the Empire below him, the snowy foothills bathed in brilliant sunshine that was almost blindingly bright. He could even make out herds of grazing beasts of some sort, moving across the land as they looked for food. He was almost there! In less than half an hour he'd be safe! He ran on, suppressing an almost unbearable need to whimper with excitement.

He was so distracted that when the strange thud in his back came, he hardly noticed it. But at the same time two long and glittering talons seemed to grow from his chest, and he looked down at himself in puzzlement. It was only when the Ice Demon lifted him from the ground and he was carried high into the air that the agony enveloped him in a raging fire. But it soon ended when he was torn apart.

The demon dropped his corpse and flew back into the Icemark, but the werewolf's head bounced down the mountainside in a wild, careering journey that sent it soaring and rolling down the steep, snowy gradients, until it came to rest at last, a few feet inside the border of the Polypontus. For a moment, the young werewolf's eyes flickered open and the mouth worked, but then darkness descended and all movement stopped.

After another four hours of unbroken concentration Oskan finally stopped working. The wounded were still being brought in to lie in the ragged tatters of their own broken bodies, but the Witchfather knew he could do no more to help. There was every possibility he'd do more harm than good if he continued trying, so he ordered his watch of healers to stand down, and a second shift of witches and a few of the better doctors took over.

His attempts to wash away the blood and filth of the operating theater met, as usual, with only partial success. But he dressed in clean clothes and splashed himself with the cologne he kept in his personal traveling chest for just such emergencies. Smelling faintly of blood and strongly of roses, he then set out for the palace.

The field infirmary was pitched beyond the walls of Romula, and the palace precinct was deep inside the governmental district of the city, but despite this Oskan decided to walk. It might take him an hour or so, but he needed to blow away the stench and horror of the operating theater. As usual, no one seemed to recognize or even see him as he made his way over the battlefield—part of his mystery as a warlock that had its uses. He needed time to clear his mind and compose himself for the official victory feast in the palace.

By this time the moon was rising over the battlemented walls of the city, washing the hideous sight of so many broken corpses in the beauty of silver light. Oskan could also see looters systematically working their way through the dead, robbing them of anything of worth. Rings, coins, even boots and blood-soaked clothing would be taken by the poor of the city, who needed to seize every opportunity that came their way just to survive. To them, the battle was the biggest windfall they'd had in years, and thanks to the tragedy of such wholesale slaughter, many of their number could now hope to survive the Polypontian winter.

Oskan entered the broken southern gates of Romula and made his way quietly through the mounds of dead that marked the point where Cressida and the allies had defended the barricade blocking the Eppian Way. Nearby, starving dogs were fighting noisily over the corpses, and huge packs of them swarmed around the massive bodies of the fallen Tri-Horns.

Oskan stared resolutely ahead, his mind refreshing itself in one of the gentler circles of the Spirit Realms as he walked. But even so, his senses were alert in the physical world, too, and when one of the shadowy looters thought the slender, well-dressed figure would make better pickings than the dead, the man found himself hanging on a thread of nothing, his feet dangling a foot or so from the ground. He was then brought around to stare into the seemingly bottomless eyes of the Witchfather, who smiled with all the warmth of a glacier.

"Your dagger would look better in its sheath, friend," he said quietly. And when the looter was foolish enough to try to stab him, even the icy smile disappeared, and the man was drawn in deeper to the black eternal eyes.

"Shall I show you something, friend? Shall I show you what forever without hope looks like?"

The man hung limply, and then began to shudder as his mind filled with an unending despair and limitless fear. Only when he began to scream did the Witchfather release him, and he fell to the ground in a tangle of limbs and rags. For a moment, Oskan watched the man groveling in the blood and filth of the battlefield, and then slowly his eyes refocused, and human compassion and warmth briefly returned.

"Here, buy yourself some amnesia," he said and dropped a gold coin into the hand that was convulsively clutching and flexing in the air.

He turned and walked away, but now the aura of his power swirled around him like a threat of storms, and the dogs and looters scrambled away as he approached. He reached the gates of the palace precinct without further incident, but when the palace guard tried to question his right to enter, Oskan found his temper wasn't up to explanations, and the gates burst open. The soldiers fell back before the creature that advanced across the lawns of the precinct, a black shadow seeming to gather around it as it walked.

A large figure that had been drawn by some instinct to take a breather from the victory feast watched the encroaching shadow and then loped down the marble steps of the palace and across the lawns, until it stood just behind the retreating line of the palace guard.

Suddenly it threw back its head and howled. The soldiers stopped dead, as did the advancing figure. "Oskan Witchfather, have you forgotten your allies and friends; have you forgotten those who love you and those you love?" Grishmak called into the night.

The slender figure of the warlock stared at him without recognition, and the Werewolf King strode forward and seized his shoulders in his giant paws. "Come back to us. We still need you."

At last Oskan gasped and passed a hand over his eyes. "Grishmak, I . . . I'm sorry. It was the Dark. . . . My guard was down; it flooded in."

The giant werewolf nodded. "By the smell of the blood on you, you've just come from the infirmary; you must be exhausted, not to mention traumatized by the sights you've seen."

"Yes, but it wasn't that. I felt a . . . shift of some sort. As though power were flooding in from somewhere. It knocked me off guard." He frowned in confusion and puzzlement as his head cleared. "But it's gone now. No sign of anything unusual anywhere. It must have been some sort of . . . anomaly."

Grishmak scrutinized him for a moment, then nodded sharply once. "No harm done. Come on in to the feast. The food's amazing. The beer's crap, admittedly; these southerners have no idea about brewing. Perhaps we can call a few beer-masters down here to set up a brewery."

Oskan smiled, completely restored. "Directed by you and Tharaman, no doubt."

"Eh? No fear, it's too warm down here for me and the giant pussycat."

25

Basilea Erinor had been shaking with rage ever since the messenger had arrived with the news of the Hordes' first and only defeat since they'd broken out of their homeland of Artemesion over a year and a half ago. Even so, she had controlled her actions with an icy precision, and instead of racing off to meet the remains of her army, she had waited in the silent streets of the camp, knowing that they would soon return to face her. Of course, they could have deserted and run away to safety, but not one of the individual warriors in the vast military gathering that was the Hordes believed that there was anywhere in the entire world to hide from Erinor's wrath. Not even the highest mountain, nor the deepest forest; not the widest ocean, nor the most remote of valleys would conceal them from the unending power of the woman who was the Goddess's representative on earth.

Their defeat, they knew, was entirely due to the fact that she had not been in personal command of their attack upon the city of Romula. But the responsibility for their ignominy remained theirs and theirs alone; their faith in the Goddess had been somehow lacking, and knowing this, the Great Deity had punished them for the towering blasphemy of their doubt. And now they must return and face the righteous wrath of Basilea Erinor, who, as a living nemesis, would complete the punishment they must bear.

She glared now over the broken and ragged remains of the individual regiments that had failed to capture the capital city of the Polypontian Empire. But even now, in defeat, and after losing over a quarter of their number, the Hordes were so vast that no parade ground or square was big enough to hold them, and they'd been drawn up on the plain that surrounded the camp to silently await justice.

The regiments defined a space where the punishment would be meted out, and nervously eyed rows of gallows and scaffolding that waited neatly for their victims. Two separate sets of pits had also been dug, one set shallow and just large enough to accommodate individual soldiers, and the other set wide and deep, sending out great billowing waves of heat that shimmered in the cold winter air.

Erinor surveyed all from the height of her Tri-Horn, and her fury knew no limits. These were the soldiers, these were the warriors who'd not only been defeated in what should have been the crowning glory of their campaign against the Empire, but who, in their insolence, had also made as nothing her great and supreme sacrifice of Alexandros, her consort, the male she had condescended to love.

On the day that she'd made that most painful and bitter of all offerings to the Goddess, Erinor had known she'd finally secured the right to be the Empress of the regime that had conquered and ruled most of the known world. The horror and thrill of feeling the blade puncture her husband's heart had brought with it a certainty of her destiny, and yet her army had failed in its simple task to fulfill that destiny.

The temptation to kill in a frenzy of revenge and retribution had been enormous, but gradually the conflagration of her rage had been replaced with the ice-cold and vengeful calculation of anger. Whatever punishment she inflicted must hurt the individual warriors of her army without reducing their effectiveness as a fighting unit. It must cut them to the soul, yet leave them thirsty for revenge against those responsible. Not Erinor, not a vengeful Goddess, but the Polypontians and the Queen of the Icemark with her ragged Alliance of monsters. So as the defeated Hordes had staggered back to camp, she'd sent out spies and informants who could watch them and tell her what she needed to know.

She sat now before the gathered remains of her defeated army and prepared to inflict the punishment that would pay only the smallest retribution for their failure. Without the need for any notes or lists, Erinor gave the endless roll call of names to her executioners. Soon death squads were passing between the ranks of the army and dragging out the victims to stand in neatly arranged rows before their Basilea's Tri-Horn.

Field marshals, commanding officers, battalion leaders, senior and junior officers from all regiments were chosen to stand before her, each and every one personally selected for their popularity with the soldiers they commanded. But Erinor's wrath didn't end there; soon even the petty commanders of individual units were taken, and then the youngest and most vulnerable of each regiment, whose deaths would touch the hearts of even the most hard-bitten of the warriors.

For a moment the Basilea paused and wondered if enough had been selected. But then, with a supreme assertion of will, she decided to continue with the punishment that would strengthen the resolve of her army. She looked out over the vast gathering of warriors who waited in silent apprehension, and then she beckoned up her executioners and gave a further selection of names. Friends were then taken from friends who could only watch in hopeless horror as they were dragged away; lovers were parted from lovers who were left to stand in silent agony as they witnessed half their lives removed. Those who resisted and tried to fight for the lives of their friends were clubbed to the ground and then tied up, before being revived and made to stand and wait to watch the punishment.

All was almost ready, and Erinor gave the order. First the most senior officers were buried up to their necks in the specially prepared pits, after which the Basilea herself urged her Tri-Horn forward. A heavy pulsating silence now descended as all eyes turned to watch the figure standing as straight and rigid as a blade in the howdah. For fully five minutes she gazed out over the massed ranks, but then at last she drew breath to speak.

"Soldiers of the Hordes, these women have betrayed the trust of the Goddess! They have betrayed the trust of their Basilea! And they have betrayed the trust of every single individual warrior in our great and unstoppable army! Because of them our invincibility has been brought into question, and because of them you have suffered your first defeat since breaking out of the walls that once bound our homeland of Artemesion. Know then the wrath of the Goddess, and witness now the punishment that awaits all failure!"

And in full view of the army, she urged her Tri-Horn forward toward where the heads of the officers emerged from the earth like small and vulnerable pumpkins. With slow deliberation the huge creature approached the nearest officer, and, on Erinor's command, raised a mighty foot and brought it slowly down to break open the head like an egg.

A great sigh and gasp rose up from the ranks, but then silence returned as the Tri-Horn approached each officer in turn and crushed her head with the same deliberate precision.

"So die all traitors!" Erinor screamed. At a frenzied nod of her head, all the rest of the officers, from section commanders down to the most junior, were hanged from the scaffolding and gallows that stood waiting in neat rows. For several long minutes the figures kicked and convulsed as they swung by their necks, but gradually their struggles slowed and finally ceased altogether.

Only the friends, lovers, and youngsters taken from each regiment remained, and they were marched to the wide and deep pits, where fires had been lit earlier in the day. The flames had been fed with fuel throughout the morning, but then the fire had been allowed to slowly die down until a thick layer of red-hot coals glowed at the bottom of each pit that remained as hot as furnaces.

A murmur rose up from the army, and individual voices called out as friends and lovers were recognized. Erinor nodded, and the executioners took long poles and carefully raised the iron grids that covered each pit. Now over two hundred men and women were herded at spear-point toward the red-hot craters that exhaled great gouts of searing heat into the cold winter's air.

Those at the back of the huddle and press of humanity pushed forward to escape the circle of spears that jabbed at them, and their weight drove the mass toward the open pits. Soon the victims began to tumble into the red-hot depths, and a great screaming and wailing rose up as flesh was seared and hair and clothing caught fire. The terrible stench of burning skin and muscle drifted across the army that now stood in silence.

For more than half an hour the massed ranks of the Hordes stood to attention, listening as the cries slowly died down to a tortured moaning and then at last ceased altogether. Then once again Erinor stood in her howdah and glared out over her army.

"Know you, then, that ignoble death and unending shame is the price of defeat. The souls of those here executed will wander endlessly in the twilight world, forever tormented by their failure, forever tortured by remorse. And know you, too, that such will be the fate of those who allow the army of the Goddess to know again the bitterness of defeat. Now return to your fires and to your yurts, return to your regiments and units and talk on the events of this day. And then decide that never again will a soldier of the Hordes die in retreat, never again will a warrior of the Great Mother fall to a victorious enemy! Bind your wounds and salve your injured pride, then sharpen your swords and prepare to fight! The hated Queen of the Icemark still lives, and with her stand the treacherous Hypolitan who left our homeland so many generations ago. Not until their pride has been leveled in the dust will I deem you free of the shame of your defeat; not until this Alliance of monsters and broken empires has been reduced to blood and rotting flesh will I consider you worthy of my rule!"

In perfect silence the army now marched from the scene of carnage. Not one of the angry, embittered minds thought of mutiny; they had failed, and the Basilea had punished. Such was the order of life. Such was the decree of the Goddess.

Cressida waited quietly in her campaign tent and brushed her hair again until it shone. She could have requisitioned a comfortable room in the palace, just as her mother and the rest of the High Command could have done, but, like them, she preferred to remain in the camp the allied army had set up beyond the city walls. The thought of actually living in Romula itself set her teeth on edge, and though she knew it was a stupid prejudice, she couldn't rid herself of the idea that the capital city of the Polypontus was the center of all evil and depravity. Years of warfare and fear generated by the Polypontian Empire was ingrained in her soul, and though the Imperial legions were now allies, she couldn't easily set aside her feelings.

She peered now into the polished bronze of the mirror that she'd borrowed from one of the amazing bathrooms in the palace and was less than satisfied with her reflection. She'd tried to soften her usual military appearance and bearing by tying a pretty silk scarf around her mail-shirt and by letting down her hair, but she just looked like one of the male housecarls in a wig. She was glad Eodred and Howler couldn't see her, and with this thought she suddenly found herself scrambling out of her chain mail, until she stood in nothing but the long linen shirt every human soldier wore under her or his armor.

"You look about as feminine as Grishmak," she snapped at her reflection, but then she had an idea. She was almost certain she'd brought a dress with her, and quickly she hurried over to the large chests that lined the canvas walls of her tent. After ransacking three of them, she found what she wanted lying at the very bottom under several layers of mail gauntlets and spare surcoats.

She dragged it out and strode back to the mirror, where she held the dress against herself and surveyed the results. "Not too bad," she conceded. "A little crumpled, perhaps, but most of that'll fall out after I've worn it for a while."

She struggled into the yards of velvet and fine lamb's wool, and finally emerged through the neck hole red-faced and gasping, then had to struggle out of it again when she realized she'd left her shirt on. Rough linen didn't look good sticking out of a daringly plunging neckline.

Once she had the dress back on, she resisted looking in the mirror until she'd brushed her hair yet again and found the pretty tie-belt that went around the waist. Then, steeling herself, she took a deep breath and looked up. She almost gasped aloud as the reflection stared back at her. Who was that striking young woman in the mirror? She'd almost forgotten what she looked like in a dress, and in fact had only ever worn one once or twice, at her mother's insistence, for very special occasions like Yule. She didn't actually own a gown that had been especially made for her, but this wasn't a problem because she and Thirrin were exactly the same size, and she just wore those her mother had finished with. The one she was wearing now had been Thirrin's favorite for years, and though it was a little worn around the cuffs and hem, it was still perfectly serviceable, even if it did smell strongly of the herbs that kept the moths at bay.

Cressida turned to the side, and then peered over her shoulder as she surveyed the back. Yes, it definitely made her look like a young woman. But when she turned to view the front again, she began to lose her nerve as the plunging neckline met her gaze. She couldn't possibly be seen in public like that! She could just imagine what Grishmak would say!

Quickly she began the long process of struggling out of the gown, but the sudden sound of approaching feet made her drop the hem and hurriedly smooth the cloth back into position.

A werewolf and housecarl guard burst through the entrance. "Commander Leonidas to see you . . ." the wolf-man barked, then stopped in surprise as he saw the dress.

"'Commander Leonidas to see you, *Your Majesty*,'" Cressida corrected haughtily.

"Yeah, that, too," the werewolf agreed. "Shall I . . . erm, shall I let him in, then?"

"'Shall I let him in, then, *Ma'am*?'" she corrected again, finding it easier to hide behind her status as Crown Princess than acknowledge to anyone she was wearing a dress.

"Yeah, well, shall I . . . Ma'am?" the werewolf asked, surreptitiously nudging his housecarl comrade, who surrep-titiously nudged him back.

Swallowing hard, Cressida almost panicked and consid-ered telling the guard to send Leonidas away, but as usual she was almost desperate to see him and she nodded. "Send him in."

"Right, we will, then . . . Ma'am," the werewolf said, and the guards backed out, their eyes transfixed.

Leonidas appeared a few seconds later to find Cressida sitting in a high-backed chair she'd managed to position just in time. "Ah, Leonidas!" she squeaked, losing control of her voice completely. "Find a chair and sit down."

The commander stood staring at her stupidly as he realized she'd abandoned the safety of her usual military gear and was actually wearing a dress, of all things! "Oh . . . right, yes. A chair! Um, I don't think, you know, there is one." He felt almost angry; it had taken them days to reach a point where they were comfortable enough with each other to meet alone, as long as the conversation was strictly military, and now Cressida had gone and compromised everything by wearing women's clothing!

"I'm sure there's more than one chair in here, Commander," she said, her irritation at his incompetence allowing her to regain some composure.

Leonidas bumbled off on a quest for somewhere to sit, and Cressida rolled her eyes heavenward.

"There's nothing in here but a . . . oh! I'm awfully sorry, I seem to have inadvertently walked into your, you know, into your *bedroom!*" He reappeared rapidly, his face crimson. "Please accept my, you know, my *apologies.*"

"That's all right, Leonidas. I wasn't in it," said Cressida briskly, but the scenario she conjured up with the unthinking reply made them both blush painfully. "Oh, for the love of . . ." she went on, beginning to get angry with them both. "There's a stool over there in that alcove."

She watched him hurry off and stagger as he tripped over his own feet, and found herself wondering if this could really be the same man who moved with such grace and competence on the battlefield. She sighed, realizing, at last, that if their relationship was to go anywhere, then she would have to take firm control and guide it.

She squared her shoulders, feeling suddenly better. She'd given herself a task and an objective and felt immediately more able to cope. The trick would be to approach it as a military campaign, then she couldn't fail.

Leonidas made his way back carrying a heavy wooden stool and managed to knock over a box of campaigning maps, a wine jug, and the table it sat on, and finally a rack of spears that collapsed in such a spectacular crashing, thrashing, and clanging that the werewolf and housecarl guards came running in, thinking a skirmish was being fought. The commander was attempting to stand the rack back up by this point, and the guards stopped to watch with growing appreciation as he became more and more entangled in spear shafts and also sundry pieces of carpet he'd somehow managed to drag up from the floor. He looked like a man fighting a battle with a multicolored sheep, and the more entangled he got, the more obscene his language became. Fortunately it was all in Polypontian, so no one understood. But somehow the way it was said suggested he wasn't reciting moving and esoteric poetry.

"Well, don't stand there trying not to snicker, help him!" Cressida snapped at the guards, then immediately regretted it as the werewolf and housecarl dived into the melée with the sort of enthusiasm that made everything worse. In fact, if she hadn't known for a fact that all soldiers of every species treated her with the utmost respect and awe, Cressida might have believed that the guards were deliberately making matters worse. Soon more and more carpet became entangled in the spears, and at one point the werewolf seemed to be chewing the fringing off one particularly fine rug that was Cressida's favorite.

"Enough!" she suddenly bellowed at battle pitch, and the three figures in the middle of the chaos thunderously dropped the spears and carpet they were wrestling with. "Leave everything where it is; I'll find a chamberlain to clear it up later!" she said in tired tones. Then, reviving, she turned to the guards. "And you two! Get back to your posts! If I'd wanted clowns, I'd have sent for a circus!"

Leonidas tried to retrieve something of his dignity as he smoothed his tunic, but his mane of black curls now stood in tufts and had pieces of carpet fluff in it. Cressida took one look and fetched her brush.

"Sit still," she commanded and began to put his hair to rights. At first the commander sat rigid and tense under her ministrations, but slowly he began to relax, and even closed his eyes as she brushed and smoothed his hair. Later, neither of them was entirely sure how it happened, but as Cressida began to smooth his curls from his forehead, Leonidas opened his eyes, and somehow her lips were hovering the merest whisper from his. It would take only the slightest movement for them to brush together, and the intensity of it all was almost overwhelming.

"What are you doing, woman, trying to bite his face off?" Grishmak boomed as he erupted into the tent. Then he threw back his head and laughed.

Leonidas leaped from his stool as though he'd sat on a thistle and stumbled past the Werewolf King and out of the tent. Cressida whirled around in fury. "Grishmak! Don't you believe in knocking?"

"What, on canvas?" he inquired innocently.

She threw her brush in rage into the tangle of carpets and spears that still littered the middle of the tent, and Grishmak observed the mess interestedly.

"My, my, you two have been energetic, haven't you?" he said and gave her a huge wink. "That's the style, lass. Keep him busy and he won't stray far."

Outside the tent, the werewolf and housecarl guards winced as Cressida screamed an explosion of obscenities in both human and Wolf-folk speech.

Medea was almost content. She and Cronus had secured the vast majority of the Icemark after a lightning campaign that had raged through the land in a matter of days. Every major settlement was now under their control, all the roads were patrolled, and every fortress was garrisoned. Medea was now the virtual co-ruler of the land in which she was born. If only her family could see her now; if only Oskan knew of her incredible success and power! The Vampire Queen retained only a mere toehold in the Great Forest, and though the latest assaults against her positions had been repulsed with heavy losses, Medea was certain she'd soon be overcome. She was also certain that the "nuisance raids" that had slowed down preparations for the next stage of their campaign would also stop, just as soon as they could smoke out the Vampire nest hidden in the trees. In fact, her grandfather was trying to do just that as he led another assault against the Great Forest.

Medea rested her hands on the huge oaken arms of the throne that stood in the Great Hall of the citadel of Frostmarris and savored the coming victory. The citadel had already been destroyed once before by Her Vampiric Majesty's squadrons, but it'd been a simple magical matter to rebuild it. A situation that summed up the Vampire army nicely; they were a nuisance, a mere hindrance, and once they'd been destroyed, she and Cronus could continue with their plan to invade the Polypontus. And of course, as they were a force under the command of Adepts, there'd

be none of the tedious marching and drawn-out preparations that a mortal host would need to undergo. Once they
were ready, Cronus would simply transport them to their
destination via the Magical Realms in the blink of an aston-
ished eye.

She sighed happily. She already controlled the land of her
hated family, and soon she'd rule the world. How many
pathetic mortal tyrants had dreamed of such power, little
knowing they were doomed to failure? Only those with
Magical Abilities had any hopes of achieving such a goal,
and even among their august numbers, only Medea and
Cronus could ever succeed.

Her happiness was such that she decided to celebrate her
pending victories by feeding her magically created body
with wine and sweetmeats that it didn't actually need. But
before she could move, a hideous screeching sounded on the
air, echoing from the courtyard and filling the Great Hall
with its cacophony. Medea slapped her open palms down
onto the arms of the throne in amazed rage. The Vampires
were attacking again! They must have simply outflanked
her grandfather's attack on their lair and flown on to launch
their own assault on Frostmarris. The Vampire Queen was
outrageous in her arrogance! Without further delay Medea
hurried off to direct the defense of the city, collecting a
contingent of Dark Witches as she went, their tattered and
twisted forms gathering around her like the wind-torn rags
of storm clouds.

As she made her way down from the citadel of Frostmarris,
she could clearly see the formations of Vampire squadrons as they swept across the skies. Their numbers were
surprisingly large considering the losses they'd suffered in
the many battles and skirmishes they'd fought, but Medea
could only assume that this was the full complement of Her
Vampiric Majesty's remaining strength, and that somehow

she'd managed to completely avoid Cronus's attack on her stronghold.

No matter, the Vampires could just as easily be destroyed over Frostmarris as they could be over the Great Forest, and when Cronus realized that the enemy had literally flown the nest, he'd guess what was happening and return to the city immediately.

Medea found the Ice Demon garrison ready and waiting for orders on the walls, their scaly bodies and scarlet-feathered wings incongruously encased in armor and their ferocious tusked heads somehow made even more hideous by the polished metal and plumes of their helmets. She rapped out orders as she strode up, and immediately the hideous creatures leaped into flight. She then watched as wave after wave of them poured into the sky, their huge wings sending up a clamor of rapid beats as they powered toward the enemy.

The Vampires now let out screeches of challenge, and section by section they folded their bat wings and dived to meet the demons. The roar of onset echoed over the sky and through the streets of Frostmarris, and Medea watched as the giant bats smashed into the even bigger Ice Demons. It took two or even three Vampires to successfully challenge one of Medea's warriors, and she watched avidly as they tore at each other with fang and claw.

Soon the sky was dark with falling bodies, as fighters of both species fell in ruin to smash into the ground hundreds of feet below. Medea sent more and more of her demons into the battle so that soon they heavily outnumbered the enemy, but incredibly, they were losing! Her warriors were being torn limb from limb, and even those that safely reached the ground were then attacked by the Vampires as they transformed into their human shapes and fought against the demons using weapons of silver and pure iron. The talismanic metals ripped open the Ice Demons' bodies, spilling their black blood in great gouts and fountains that melted the winter snows.

The Vampires were slowly gaining mastery over the sky, and as Medea watched, entire squadrons peeled away to drop small barrels of blazing pitch onto the streets and empty houses below. Soon entire areas of the city were in flames, yet again, and Medea raged in frustration as her defending army seemed unable to stop them.

The time had come for her to intervene. Throwing wide her arms, she drew on the Power of the Dark and gathered all she needed from the materials that surrounded her. Atoms of stone and steel, ice and iron, were drawn into her body, adding to its bulk and strengthening the framework of skeleton and sinew in her magically created form. Soon she'd gathered enough material to expand and grow, and her face acquired a viciously hooked beak, as her feet became ripping talons and her arms powerful wings that stretched wide across the sky. Medea had assumed the form of a gigantic eagle, and with a high-pitched call of pure hatred she soared into the sky, snatching Vampires from the air and ripping them to bloody shreds as she flew. Entire squadrons fell to her rending beak and talons, and soon the streets of Frostmarris were littered with the broken remains of the undead.

High above the battle, observing all, Her Vampiric Majesty flew with her elite flight of bodyguards. She could clearly see that the tide of battle had turned in Medea's favor, as the evil Adept swept through the army of undead warriors and sent thousands to oblivion. Without hesitation the Vampire Queen folded her wings and dived at the eagle that was Medea. Her entire squadron followed in an avalanche of silent wing and fang, the wind of their speed roaring in their ears and cascading over their flesh like icy water as they dived, and as one they smashed into their enemy, driving her to the ground in a tangle of broken feathers.

The rending crash of impact broke Medea's wings and shattered her body, but she roared in defiance and struck at them with her razor beak. The Vampires wheeled away out of range, and then dived into the attack again, the queen screeching a challenge as she powered toward her enemy.

Medea hit the ground with a force that drove her body deep into its own impact crater. Still defiant, she sent out a lightning blast against the Vampire Queen, but the undead squadron flew on, shielded by Her Vampiric Majesty's protective magic. They stepped now out of flight and into their human forms as they simpered and swaggered before Medea's broken body.

"My dear child, I do believe you're injured," said Her Vampiric Majesty with mocking concern. "Does it hurt?"

The evil Adept now sloughed away her eagle form to stand before the Vampires in her usual body. "I am beyond pain, you stinking corpse!" she spat.

"I'm so glad. I'd hate to think we'd caused you any discomfort." The Vampire Queen smiled, revealing glittering fangs that seemed to glow against the deep blood red of her lips. "Oh, but I do believe we're too late in that respect. We seem to have destroyed your city. Such a shame; where will you direct your invasion from now?"

Medea involuntarily glanced at the fires that were sweeping unchecked throughout Frostmarris, but she quickly rallied and sneered, "Do you really think that mere physical damage can stop myself and Cronus? We'll have restored all of this within moments." Then, in a display of her towering talents, she stopped time itself. All around them warriors stood frozen in the acts of fighting, killing, and dying, and the flames of the blazing city arced against the sky in solid bursts of static brilliance, as though a sculptor had taken his chisels and carved light itself into abstract forms.

"Yes, but it's such a distraction having to redirect your Powers, don't you think?" Her Vampiric Majesty said dismissively. "Especially when you're trying to establish control over a country that just won't give up fighting."

Medea laughed with such confidence, she almost believed in her own invincibility. "Oh, I can assure you that my Powers will hardly notice the tiny effort any restoration will need."

Her Vampiric Majesty smiled condescendingly. "Has no one ever told you that overestimation of Abilities is the mark of the inexperienced and deluded?"

Medea raised her hand, releasing time from her psychic grip, and immediately flames flickered and writhed against the smoke-filled sky, and warriors continued their fighting with a frenzy. Then a sudden bellowing and roaring sounded on the air, and they all turned to watch as another huge army of Ice Demons materialized in the sky above them.

"I overestimate nothing, corpse-breath," Medea snapped in triumph. "Cronus himself has arrived. I suggest you make yourself scarce."

The Vampire Queen nodded to her squadron, and they immediately began to transform themselves into their bat forms. "Yes, the time has come to go. But I'll leave you with this small thought: If you and Cronus really are so infallible, why was it so easy for us to trick him into trying to attack us in the Great Forest while we destroyed Frostmarris? Intriguing, isn't it?"

The Vampires wheeled away, sending out screeches that gathered the rest of the undead army, and they streamed across the sky back to their stronghold among the trees.

Medea watched them go, a small frown creasing her brow.

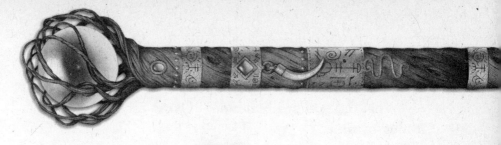

26

Thirrin closed the door to her room with a weary sigh. At last she could lock out the world and have a bit of peace and quiet.

"You can lock out *most* of the world, Thirrin Lindenshield, but I'm afraid I'll always find my way through," said a voice from the shadows.

She spun around, drawing her sword with lightning speed to level it between Oskan's eyes. "Oh, it's you!"

"Who else were you expecting in your bedchamber? Is there something I should know?"

"Judging by the way you keep reading my mind, you know everything about me, anyway."

"True," Oskan agreed with a grin.

Thirrin sheathed her sword and walked into the room. "Where were you today, anyway? I could have done with your input; those senators drone on for hours about nothing in particular; the gods alone know how they managed to create the biggest empire the world's ever known."

"I suspect that had a lot to do with Bellorum, and the fact that he never consulted the Senate about anything unless forced to."

"You're probably right," Thirrin agreed. "And so was Bellorum. Well, I won't make the same mistake again.

From now on all discussions will be restricted to the High Command and the best Polypontian officers."

"What did you finally decide?" Oskan asked, handing her a mug of wine.

"You mean you can't read what happened directly from my head?"

"Not always; in fact, rarely."

Thirrin nodded, relieved, but the fact that she'd had to ask at all was proof that her husband's powers had continued to change and grow throughout their married life. "Well, basically we've decided to go in pursuit of Erinor," she finally said, answering Oskan's earlier question. "There's no point sitting here in Romula and waiting for her to rebuild her forces. We have the advantage now, and we've got to keep it. It'll be something of a novelty for the Polypontian forces to go on the offensive again; they've been fighting a defensive war ever since Erinor first broke out of Artemesion."

"When do we march?"

"Tomorrow, if Cressida had her way!"

"Of course," said Oskan with a smile.

"And in three weeks if the senators had theirs."

"And in actuality?"

"In four days' time. Preparations began a while ago, anyway. It's just a matter of completing the process."

"Fine. Medical supplies are almost replenished. Romula has some superb pharmacies and some remarkably good doctors."

Thirrin paused in the act of peeling off layers of chain mail and unbuckling sword belts and daggers. "Doctors? That's the first time I've heard you say anything good about doctors!"

"Yes, well, the Imperial medics are different from the charlatans and quacks that plague the Icemark. I've taken the opportunity to study some of the medical treatises in the university libraries and they're astonishingly good. But, interestingly, most of them aren't Polypontian; they're Hellenic, and incredibly ancient."

Thirrin shrugged. "Unfortunately there's no time for studying now, my fine scholar. I've got a war to fight, and you've got to repair the damage inflicted on my warriors. You'll have to wait till after the fighting."

"And, talking of which, will we win?" Oskan asked quietly as he began to extinguish some of the candles and torches around the room.

Thirrin fell back onto the bed with a relieved sigh as the last of her armor fell with a clatter to the marble floor. "I don't know," she answered in matter-of-fact tones. "It was a hard-fought struggle last time, and Erinor wasn't even in command then. Who knows what the outcome will be when she's directing operations?"

"I see. And where is she now?"

"Four days' march south of here, and according to the Vampire scouts she's sending out messengers to Artemesion."

"For reinforcements?"

"Yes. The Vampires captured one of them and brought the papers back. It didn't take Grishmak long to get a prisoner to translate them."

"Can there be any warriors left in Artemesion? I thought the Hordes were an entire nation on the march!"

"So did I," Thirrin replied from the depths of her nightgown as she wrestled her way into it. "But it seems Erinor's expecting thousands to answer her call. That's why we must hit her as soon as possible, before they arrive." She climbed into the huge bed that occupied the center of the room, and snuggled down under the sumptuous covers of silk and fur from where she smiled at her husband. "Hurry up and get in. My feet are freezing!"

"I'm nothing but a glorified hot water bottle to you, am I?" Oskan answered as he extinguished the rest of the candles.

"Well, that's your main function, I suppose. But you do have other uses, too."

"So glad to hear it."

Thirrin became serious again as she thought through the difficulties facing her and the army. "At least we have no problems about leaving a garrison in Romula or organizing administration. The palace guard already carry out garrison duties, and the Senate's been the government for literally hundreds of years."

"But you're still not completely happy," said Oskan, climbing into bed.

"No. Things are too quiet."

"Quiet? Excuse me, but did the battle for Romula pass you by?"

"No, it didn't. But I'm beginning to wonder if perhaps other things have."

"Other things?"

Thirrin remained quiet for so long, Oskan began to wonder if she'd fallen asleep. But then she said, "Oskan, what's Medea doing?"

He'd been expecting a question like this for so long that he'd rehearsed the lie to perfection. "Nothing, at the moment. She's cooking up something, that's for sure, but she's obviously not ready to set things in motion yet."

"Are you sure about that?"

"As sure as anyone can be when talking of one of the most powerful Adepts in the Spirit Realms." He kept his voice as even and as steady as he could. He was determined not to distract his wife any more than was necessary from her upcoming battle with Erinor. Cronus's insane ambition to attack the Goddess was something that could be worried about if and when he ever decided to actually do it.

"Fine," Thirrin said, her voice tinged with relief as they left a topic she hated but felt she couldn't ignore. "But other things are bothering me."

"What now?" Oskan almost wailed. Would the woman never sleep?

"I'm worried about Titus. He's all right being looked after by Silvanus while he's still a little boy, but the Senate is acting as a sort of collective Regent for him at the moment, and I'm afraid there are some very ambitious men in that particular body."

"You think they'll exploit him?"

"Undoubtedly."

Oskan lay back with his hands behind his head. "Well, the solution's simple enough. Appoint a Regent, or Regents, you trust."

Thirrin turned over on her side and looked at the dark shadow of his profile. "Fine, but who?"

"Andronicus and Leonidas, because they're Polypontian, and Cressida, because she has the most developed sense of justice I know. Not only that, but it'll allow her a few years of stability while she and Leonidas get used to the idea of being married."

Thirrin sat up as though on springs. "What? Married? What do you know? What have you been shown?"

"Calm down, woman. Nothing's definite. I've seen shadows and possibilities, that's all. And none of it'll come about unless we defeat Erinor." He fell silent as he considered his words. "There's something else, too. . . . I'm not sure what. Some indefinable danger I can't pin down . . ."

But Thirrin was too excited about the possibility of Cressida's marriage to even notice his last sentence. "Cressida and Leonidas married!" She leaped out of bed and began to pace the room. "Perfect! Just perfect! An alliance with one of the most politically and militarily important houses of the Polypontus, and . . . and not only that, but she loves him!"

"There's still the small matter of winning the war," Oskan said, distracted from his worries by his wife's excitement. "Unless you defeat the Hordes, none of it will happen."

"Then we'll just have to win the war, won't we? With Andronicus, Leonidas, and Cressida as Regents, Titus will have a mother, father, and granddad in one fell swoop; what could be better? I've been worrying about that little boy ever since I first met him, but now I know exactly what to do!"

Oskan looked at her appreciatively. "The most powerful monarch in the northern hemisphere you may be; mighty warrior and brilliant tactician you undoubtedly are; but under it all, you're still a mother, aren't you? I knew as soon as I saw you with Titus that he'd brought out all of your maternal instincts. I fully expected to find that we'd adopted him at some point."

"We may still do yet," said Thirrin, suddenly feeling the cold and climbing back into bed. "Wouldn't you like a child around the place again?"

"Not particularly, no."

"Oh yes, you would! You're not fooling me, Mr. All-Powerful Warlock! I saw you playing horses with Titus yesterday. Have you any idea how cute you both looked as you galloped up and down the Senate chamber?"

"I was simply keeping the child entertained," Oskan replied with lofty dignity. "Ye gods, woman, you're freezing!"

Thirrin laughed and ignored his protests as she snuggled up to him. He was right, he did make a very good hot water bottle.

The purges were complete and the sacrifices made for the terrible blasphemy of defeat. Erinor had cleansed the Hordes of most of its high command and also of great swaths of deeply experienced field commanders, but the worth of a sacrifice was directly proportional to the pain and damage it caused to the giver. The structure of the army, already weakened by its unexpected defeat, was now severely handicapped, but even so, Erinor was preparing to attack, happy in the knowledge that the Goddess had been placated and final victory was assured.

Cronus, distracted by his own concerns after invading the Icemark, no longer manipulated the thoughts and tactics of the Basilea, and as a result many of her actions were damaging and dangerous for her own people. She was no longer important to his plans, having fulfilled her role as a decoy to draw away Oskan and his witches. But Erinor, blissfully unaware of the withdrawal of her powerful patron, continued with plans she believed infallible. She could easily have waited for the reinforcements to arrive from Artemesion, and then have commanded an army even greater than the one that had invaded the Polypontian Empire a year and a half ago. But that would have taken weeks, and the enemy would have had time to prepare an attack that would force the Hordes to fight a defensive war, something of which they had no experience.

No; now was the time to attack, not least because the hated Alliance of monsters and the dregs of broken empires wouldn't believe it possible, but also because the Hordes themselves would expect nothing less of their undefeated Basilea.

Erinor listened as the camp beyond the hide walls of her yurt seethed and hummed with purposeful activity. This was what her warriors had needed: the strength of certainty, the belief in destiny! No matter how depleted their numbers, the Hordes still heavily outnumbered the enemy, and the shock of seeing Erinor herself leading an attack within days of her warriors being repulsed from the streets of Romula would probably crush all morale and cohesion within the ranks of the Alliance. Indeed, if she moved quickly enough, she might even arrive at the city before the enemy had time to counterattack, and then the second siege of Romula would begin—and this time the capital would fall and the new Empire would be established.

The bellowing of Tri-Horns echoed around the yurt-city as the huge creatures were brought up the line, and Erinor stood as she prepared to don her armor. Not even the Hordes themselves were expecting to advance just yet; the most optimistic expected the new campaign to begin tomorrow or even the day after. How surprised they would be; how shocked the world would be to see the Basilea marching on her enemies when any other tactician would have taken time to consolidate and reinforce their depleted armies. Not so Erinor! Not so the living representative of the Goddess on earth! She would strike now! She would fly like an arrow from the bow and bury herself deep in the enemy's heart!

Summoning buglers, she gave the order to stand to, and soon the brassy call to arms was echoing over the camp. She smiled quietly while her soldier-servants dressed her in the steel of war, and when her sword was placed in her hand, she strode from her yurt and into the light of day. The cold streets of the camp were thronged with soldiers of the Hordes, and when they saw her, a great collective roar rose up as they clamored to be led to war, as they begged to die in the service of the Goddess, as they beseeched to be made again the unstoppable machine of death that would crush all who dared to stand against it.

Erinor mounted her waiting Tri-Horn. As she stood in the howdah that rose like a small fortress from its back, the Hordes fell silent waiting for the speech that would raise them to a frenzy of killing power. But their Basilea was silent. What need for words of passion and violence? What need for orations of frenzy and hate? Victory was already granted, they simply had to advance and take it.

With a huge bellow of power the Tri-Horn stepped forward, and the entire army fell in behind: regiment after endless regiment of Shock Troops, elite fighters, chariots, cavalry, and the mountainous squadrons of Tri-Horns. No power on earth could stop them, no alliance of human, beast, or monster could hold them back from their destiny. The Goddess herself was their patron, and all would fall before them; all would die beneath their trampling feet.

27

Medea and Cronus sat in the comfortable chamber that had once been Thirrin and Oskan's private quarters in the citadel of Frostmarris. The city had been magically restored after the Vampires had destroyed much of it with fire, but in fact the citadel and royal quarters had been largely untouched. It was almost as though the Vampires had deliberately avoided attacking it. Medea privately thought that a little "fiery cleansing" might have improved the old fortress, but at least it'd meant that she and Cronus had still had a base to use as their center of operations.

The weak winter sun was just beginning to set, filling the room with russet light and giving an illusion of warmth. But even though the huge fireplace was piled high with blazing logs, a deep rime of frost coated the stonework that was carved with the fighting bear of the House of Lindenshield.

Medea remembered the room well from her childhood, and she took a perverse pleasure in thinking that she'd taken possession of the place by force of arms.

"The Vampires are almost exhausted. Their resistance can't continue for much longer. And even if it does, we control all of the major settlements of the Icemark, along with the entire road network and all fortresses and strongholds." Cronus settled back into Oskan's chair. "All of which basically means Her Vampiric Majesty and her valiant squadrons have been reduced to a mere inconvenience. They cannot stop us completing our plans."

Medea couldn't help remembering in graphic detail how the Vampire squadrons had so easily sidestepped Cronus's attack on their forest stronghold only a few days earlier. And the subsequent destruction of Frostmarris was hardly the act of a force that could be considered "a mere inconvenience." Not only that, but what difference would control of the roads, and even the fortresses, make to an enemy that flew everywhere and was as mobile and flexible as the Vampires? Feeling suddenly disloyal to the Arc-Adept, she smiled optimistically and said, "So, now we can begin the next phase of the war?"

"Absolutely. We conquer what remains of the Polypontus, then we march south to the Venezzian and Hellenic territories, the Desert Kingdom, and Arifica," Cronus continued confidently. "The campaign shouldn't take much more than a year at most, after which we must look to the east and west. In fact, I expect to be ruler of the entirety of the Physical Realms within three years."

"*We* expect to be rulers of the Physical Realms within three years, surely," Medea corrected sharply.

"But of course," Cronus replied placatingly. "A trifling slip of the tongue, no more."

"But of course," she echoed, after a few moments' silence, and then continued. "We'll be ready then for the most important phase of our campaign."

"Indeed, yes!" Cronus hissed, and tiny particles of ice gathered in a dense mist around him. "The assault on the Goddess herself!"

Medea watched him with interest and marveled that he seemed completely unaware of the very emotions he supposedly didn't feel. Jealousy of the Goddess, rage at her rejection of him, and a deep-seated need for revenge were all displayed for anyone who dared to look as his guard slipped in the excitement of his plans.

And once, much farther down, in the shadows and murk of his deepest subconscious, Medea had detected something else, something she'd found so shocking and so frightening, she'd never dared look again. Cronus the Great, Cronus the Defiant, Cronus the Seat and Fount of All Evil, felt a need to be forgiven, to be accepted back into the realm of the gods!

"What need have we of Oskan Witchfather?" he suddenly shouted, waking Medea from her thoughts and fears. "Together we can defy all opposition. Not even the Goddess herself can stop us now!"

"Indeed not," she agreed and felt the familiar upwelling of emotions that she experienced whenever her father's name was mentioned.

The sudden shattering of the windows was somehow almost expected. Whenever Medea began to feel confident in their campaign, the Vampires always contrived to spoil it.

"I'm beginning to make something of a habit of this, aren't I?" said Her Vampiric Majesty as she stepped over the demolished window and wall. "I really must learn to announce my arrival with a little more subtlety."

Both Adepts began to send out calls for the Ice Demon guards, but the queen raised her hand so imperiously, they stopped. "Oh, please! Can't we simply have a little talk, without those awful lumbering creatures cluttering up the place? I promise a temporary truce, if we can just have a 'frank exchange of views,' as the diplomats put it."

"What do you want to say?" Cronus asked simply.

"Well, I thought I'd explain why you can't win this silly war, and then I'll listen while you state quite categorically why you can. It makes such a pleasant change from all the death and mayhem, don't you think?"

"I have no time to take part in your pathetic charades, woman," Cronus snapped.

"But you have all the time in the world to fight my squadrons, or at least I assume you do, because you certainly seem to expend most of your effort doing just that." Her Vampiric Majesty crossed to a large chair that stood next to the fireplace, and sat with every appearance of comfort and ease.

"Soon the skies will be cleared of your menace," Cronus growled, the nimbus of ice crystals that hung in the air around him eddying and swirling in the complex air currents that perfectly reflected his anger.

"When?"

"Today! I'll lead the demons against you just as soon as they're summoned."

The queen searched for a way of inflicting as much psychological damage as possible. Finding it, she smiled coldly. "You can no more destroy my army than you can control the emotions you supposedly do not have!"

"I feel nothing but contempt for you and your squadrons."

"Granted," she replied. "And alongside that contempt you also feel rage, hatred, . . . and *fear*."

An earsplitting crack exploded through the room as lightning struck the stonework behind Her Vampiric Majesty's head. "I have long forgotten the experience of fear. It's the weakest of the emotions, and I've expunged it from my psyche!"

"Do you really think so?" the queen asked conversationally, suddenly staring at Cronus intently as though she could see his very soul. "Hmm, perhaps you're right. Then amend fear to 'terror,' and add to it uncertainty, lack of ability, and *in-com-pe-tence*." She sounded every syllable of the last word with mocking relish.

Medea found herself marveling at Her Vampiric Majesty's

barefaced cheek, not to mention her incredible bravery. Here she was, sitting at her ease in the presence of the most powerful Adepts in all Creation, and throwing out insults as though they were nothing more than a pair of novice witches!

Cronus stood with slow menace, and his form seemed to fill the entire room as his shadow flowed across the floor like a black flood. "And exactly what do you believe is causing me to feel this supposed terror?"

The queen inspected her bloodred nails and smiled gently. "Well, where shall I begin? Let me see, now . . . first yourself, and your own actions. You're terrified that you've gone too far, taken on too much. Can you really get away with it? Haven't you tried once before and been punished? There really are *so* many uncertainties to plague you, aren't there? And then, of course, there's the Witchfather. You're *very* afraid of him, aren't you? What will happen when he finds out what you've done?" She suddenly looked up from her nails, and her piercing eyes glinted. "Because he will find out; you can't keep an invasion of this scale secret for long. And then . . . oh, and then you'll die. Both of you will die a truly *horrible* death."

Cronus began to laugh, gently at first, so that neither Medea nor the queen could hear it, but then the sound grew to slowly fill the entire room, with huge guffaws of mirth that echoed back from the high ceiling. "Oh, you stupid woman! Do you really think that I've spent eons and millennia planning this war without being absolutely certain that I could win it? Do you imagine that I could have spent the long, endless ages locked in the desolation of the Darkness and not have calculated and computed every possible setback and danger? Can you really believe that I haven't applied my towering intellect to ensuring that nothing could possibly prevent my victory?"

Her Vampiric Majesty politely stifled a yawn behind an elegantly armored hand, then she smiled, revealing her fangs. "Yes."

Cronus roared, sending out a blast of deadly cold that cracked the stonework of the surrounding walls and froze the fire on the hearth to glinting fragments like carved crystal. "Then tell me, oh wise corpse, where is the flaw in my invasion? Where is the danger?"

The queen stood and crossed to the window. "Here, looking at you. My undefeated squadrons still control the skies; my warriors continue to kill your Ice Demons and disrupt your preparations; my army still fights to defend the land of Thirrin Freer Strong-in-the-Arm Lindenshield. And until every one of my Vampires is destroyed, until you've obliterated me and all of my people, you will never be able to claim that you've conquered the Icemark!"

Cronus sent a blast of energy that demolished the window and the wall, but once the dust had settled, Her Vampiric Majesty had disappeared. Medea rushed to the gaping hole that had been torn into the wall and gazed up into the skies. The dying reds and bronzes of the sunset dimly illuminated the dense formations of Vampire squadrons that filled the skies.

"They're here again, Grandfather," she said quietly.

Alarms! Alarms! The streets of Romula rang with bells and brayed with bugles as the army was roused. Erinor was advancing! Erinor was striking back!

Thirrin and Cressida strode through the corridors of the palace as they hurried to the mustering point. They emerged into the once-tranquil Imperial park, which now seethed with the cavalry of the Icesheets, then descended the huge sweep of steps that led from the palace's imposing entrance.

"How far off is she?" Tharaman asked urgently as Thirrin swept across the lawns and mounted her warhorse, acknowledging as she did so the howls of Grinelda Blood-tooth and the rest of her Ukpik werewolf bodyguard.

"We've been lucky; she's still a day's march away. But if the Vampires hadn't sent out a routine patrol, she could have been on us while we were polishing our swords! It's only good fortune that the army's almost ready to march!"

"Erinor's certainly an unpredictable woman, it must be said," Krisafitsa commented as the cavalry began preparing to move off. "How many other commanders would mount an attack mere days after a crushing defeat?"

"Not many," Thirrin agreed. "But you can be certain she didn't expect us to be ready for her, either."

Receiving a nod from her mother, Cressida now stood in her stirrups and gave the order to march, and the line of cavalry trotted briskly from the park. Once out in the streets, they were joined by the rest of the army, human, Vampire, Snow Leopard, and werewolf welded into a single fighting unit by comradeship and the shared horror of battle.

The wide Eppian Way was lined with people, but this time the cheers were more muted than they'd been after the Hordes' attempt to take the city had been defeated. Now the nightmare of Erinor had been resurrected, and her name alone was enough to strike terror and despair into the stoutest heart. Even so, the sight of the Barbarian Queen and her army of monsters restored their morale slightly, as did the Polypontian contingents with their disciplined step, polished armor, and dense thickets of pikes.

Erinor advanced in silence. She was now almost eager to see the woman who'd defeated her Hordes, an army that had never been beaten, no matter who commanded them, since the day they were first created from the combined warrior-tribes of Artemesion. The intensity of her curiosity about Thirrin Freer Strong-in-the-Arm Lindenshield almost made her tremble, and in the pit of her stomach was an odd sensation that any lesser warrior would have recognized as the first stirrings of nervousness.

Behind her, the great sweeping sea of her army glittered and shimmered under a brilliant blue sky. But the weather had changed again: The day was icy cold, and the rumblings and bellowings of the Tri-Horns were accompanied by great clouds of steam as their breath condensed on the freezing air. There was also a sharp scent of snow on the wind, even though there wasn't a cloud in sight. But those with any knowledge of weather lore knew that there'd be a fall within a day or so.

Erinor nodded to herself as she thought of the coming clash. It was almost certain the numbers of casualties on both sides would be enormous, and there was something pleasing about the thought that the bodies would be preserved for weeks in the freezing temperatures. What better monument could there be to the Goddess than an ice sculpture of the dead, sacrificed in the battle to establish a new empire that would reflect the Mother's glory on earth?

A sudden alarm call distracted her thoughts, and she looked up to see a formation of giant bats swooping in from the north. A flight of arrows was immediately shot into the air, but the Vampires were well beyond range and continued to observe the Hordes at leisure before peeling away and flying back to the north.

This was the Vampires' fourth detailed observation of Erinor that day, although it was the first that the enemy had actually seen. Everything was prepared now, and, judging by their line of advance, the Hordes were still unaware exactly how close the allies were, so it didn't matter whether they were observed or not. Besides, the staff officers had needed to know if Erinor herself was definitely in command, and low-level flight was needed for positive identification.

Erinor watched as the giant bats disappeared from view; the Thirrin woman would soon know exactly where they were and how great their numbers. But the Basilea didn't see this as a disadvantage; knowing that they were heavily outnumbered was more likely to make the enemy break and flee. She calculated that first contact would be made with the foe either by that evening, or — at the latest — by first light the next day, so her surprise was enormous when she suddenly saw the outriders of the allied army.

Erinor adjusted her mind to the new sensation of military shock. Normally she could accurately predict the enemy's every move, but Thirrin was proving difficult. She had no way of knowing that her uncanny ability to guess the enemy's every action had been courtesy of Cronus himself. But now that she'd served his purpose, he'd abandoned her, and she would no longer receive the Arc-Adept's help.

Oblivious to all of this, she raised her hand, and immediately bugles rang throughout the huge army. The enemy was in sight; the enemy had arrived to offer itself for sacrifice.

As soon as the Vampires had reported back from their first high-flying reconnaissance earlier that morning, Thirrin had ordered the army to march in battle formation. This had meant that the infantry had to leave the fast transport wagons that had been commandeered from the Merchants Guild in Romula and take up the fighting positions Thirrin and Cressida had devised. The wagons had done their job admirably, and the army had been able to advance at almost three times the normal rate over the superb Imperial roads, which had the dual advantage of putting more distance between the pending battle and the vulnerable capital city, and also of taking Erinor by surprise.

The army now advanced in its fighting dispositions, with the cavalry and the mounted archers of the Hypolitan Sacred

Regiment riding on the left and right wings, and the infantry in the center in a huge bloc. The housecarls, werewolves, and Polypontian shield-bearers formed a circular core around which dense ranks of pikemen literally revolved, like a gigantic cog that was toothed with a deadly array of their immensely long spears, held at all angles from horizontal to vertical. In effect, the infantry had become a mobile fortress with walls of shields and deadly steel.

Thirrin and Cressida had been well aware of Erinor's huge advantage of numbers when they devised the plan and knew that the infantry would be the anchor of the entire battle. Hard-pressed cavalry would be able to fall back on the mobile fortress, and even if they were completely surrounded by the Hordes, its deadly walls of locked shields and bristling pikes should keep out even the most determined assault. Only the Tri-Horns could be a problem, and the Regiment of the Red Eye and Grishmak's werewolves had been assigned to deal with them.

Thirrin knew that her battle plan was far from subtle; basically it entailed allowing the enemy to batter itself to pieces on the rock of the infantry while the cavalry tried to inflict as much damage as possible in high-speed hit-and-run tactics. All of which was little better than Grishmak's usual idea of "hit 'em hard, and keep hitting 'em hard until they bugger off!" but fighting a force with such a huge numerical advantage left her little choice. Of course, she could have tried to defend Romula for a second time, but its walls were too sprawling and in such poor condition that they would have been impossible to defend. And fighting in the streets again was too risky; directing a battle required a clear view and good communications, but fighting from house to house and district to district meant nothing was ever clear. Victory on one street could be countered by defeat on another. Last time they'd had no option but to defend the city, as the enemy had already broken through the defenses when Thirrin and her allies arrived, but given a choice, she far preferred to fight in as wide a space as possible, where the field lay as open as a giant book beneath the sky.

On the right wing of the advancing allied army, Olympia, Basilea of the Hypolitan, sat at the head of the Sacred Regiment of mounted archers. Only an hour before, she'd taken leave of her consort, Olememnon, who commanded the Hypolitan infantry as part of the army's central bloc. As usual he'd been as bright and happy as an affable bear, convinced that Erinor and her Hordes were about to be crushed. But Olympia wasn't so sure. As the commander of the elite regiment of the Hypolitan, she was all too aware of what fanaticism could do. Even a badly trained soldier could be an unstoppable force once contaminated with the uncompromising insanity of the extremist, but Erinor's warriors were certainly not badly trained. They were disciplined, deeply experienced, and highly motivated, and add to that the unquenchable fire of their fanaticism, and they were virtually unstoppable. The fact that they were defeated last time was probably due only to their ferocity being somehow redirected from fighting strength into a raging panic that swept through the entire force and caused them to break ranks and flee. Olympia thought that it was somehow telling that this was the one and only time the Hordes had been defeated, and the likelihood of mass panic affecting them again, with Erinor in personal command, was almost nil.

Suddenly the Vampire scouts returned, sweeping through the skies like the rags of miniature storm clouds, barrel-rolling as they came. This was the signal that confirmed Erinor was in command, and Cressida nodded grimly to herself as she led her contingent of cavalry to support Olympia and the Sacred Regiment. This would be the decisive battle, she thought to herself; neither her mother nor the woman who'd led the Hordes to endless victories would retreat. By sundown the war would be won . . . and lost.

Cressida looked to her left and watched Leonidas's superb riding style with appreciation. Now that he was in the field and away from the dangers of socializing, he was as elegant and deadly as a hunting cat. Sensing her scrutiny, he turned and raised his sword in salute, and she nodded coldly in reply, both of them expertly ignoring the hot flushes that were turning their faces crimson. But then the needs of the coming battle claimed their undivided attention, and they looked ahead to where the horizon of the flat featureless plain began to shimmer, as though a lake or sea was sparkling under the cold winter sun.

A brassy fanfare of bugles warned that the enemy had been sighted, and the werewolves began to howl, the ferocious sound rising into the air and contrasting sharply with the elegance of the Polypontian soldiers, who advanced in silent discipline, their armor gleaming and bedecked with lace collars and cuffs.

But then the young boys and girls of the drum corps began to rattle out a stirring marching rhythm, and this was joined by the deep bass notes of gigantic kettle drums that were mounted on huge draft horses whose pristine armor shone in the sunshine.

Ahead in the distance the Hordes had now swarmed into view, glittering with weaponry and moving with the inexorable power of a lava flow. The gigantic Tri-Horns led the host in a wide wedge formation, culminating in the apex of a truly enormous beast that wore armor of scarlet and gold and carried a howdah on its back. In this rode a lone figure, glimmering like a distant flame. So rode Erinor at the head of her warriors.

She scanned the enemy dispositions as they approached, and molded her response to them by signaling with her spear. Immediately the chariots thundered away, cutting left in a wide arc that would bring them into contact with the Sacred Regiment, Cressida's cavalry of horse and Snow Leopard, as well as the hateful Vampires. The Shock Troops of male regiments also swept away, at a swinging trot that moved smoothly to the right, while the Tri-Horns and elite female regiments continued the frontal assault.

Erinor searched the ranks of the enemy, looking for the banners and insignia that would show her where Queen Thirrin would fight. She found her on the left wing, the position of honor since ancient times. Of course, where else? Erinor raised her spear and a squad of male soldiers shot away, carrying a broad wooden stretcher that contained several barrels covered in a thick tarpaulin. With them went a squad of female archers carrying short compound bows, whose sole job seemed to be to protect their male comrades.

The Tri-Horns now set up a huge bellowing as they scented the enemy, and the faint howling of the werewolves reached Erinor's ears as she advanced. Before her was the infantry bloc, bristling with revolving pikes and walled with shields.

"How novel," she said to herself, and smiled. She knew that it had been the pikes, under the command of General Andronicus, that had turned the Tri-Horns in the battle of Romula, and in fact she herself had almost suffered a setback when she and the general had clashed in an earlier battle, but now she was eager for a rerun of the contest, with herself in command of the beasts. She stood in the howdah, and as she screamed out orders, the Tri-Horns surged forward in a turn of speed and stormed down on the thin barrier of brittle wood and steel.

* * *

General Andronicus marched with the infantry bloc he commanded, and at a word the pikes stopped their revolving but continued their advance. He watched as the wedge of massive beasts bore down on his soldiers, and waited for the moment when he'd give the order to stand.

Intermingled with the long spears of the pikes were the heavy round shields of the housecarls, which provided the defensive walls of the formation. In the wide O of the center marched the werewolves, the mixed regiment of the Red Eye, commanded by Eodred and Howler, and the Hypolitan infantry under Olememnon. These were the anchor, the rock, and the foundations of Thirrin's army. If they broke, the battle and the war were lost.

The Tri-Horns were close enough for the barnyard smell of them to reach Andronicus's nose, and he bellowed out the order to stand. Immediately the infantry stamped to a halt, and they watched as the enormous creatures rolled forward, looking almost as though the earth had raised itself up like a sea, and a tsunami was bearing down on them.

Andronicus knew Erinor would try to roll over them without slackening her charge. The first contact was crucial; the opening seconds would either end it or see the beginning of a monumental struggle. Closer they came, their huge feet pounding like heavy hammers into the ground.

Andronicus gave the order, and the circle of the infantry bloc compacted itself into a thick crescent, like a quarter moon, the "horns" sweeping back in an arc to protect the flanks, the pikes lowering into the engage position as the sharp spike of each of the long spears' butts buried itself deep into the frozen earth.

"RED EYE AND WEREWOLVES, PREPARE TO ENGAGE!"

Howler and Eodred quickly embraced and then rattled out orders. Then, at a nod from Andronicus, the human and Wolf-folk warriors let out a huge roar and howl of challenge and charged, leaving the housecarls and pikes to maintain their stand.

The Tri-Horns bellowed as they saw the enemy sweeping down on them like a gray cloud, and then Wolf-folk and human warriors were swarming up the huge treelike legs of the beasts, howling and snarling as they climbed. Soon they were leaping over the broad swaying backs of the Tri-Horns, cutting down enemy soldiers, and hacking at the thick armor of the beasts themselves with huge double-headed axes.

But still the creatures advanced. Erinor raged and screeched hatred as she rained arrow after arrow down on the stand of pikemen and housecarls that stood before her like a defiant thicket of trees before a hurricane. Andronicus called out orders in a steady voice as the Tri-Horns suddenly seemed to increase speed and rolled down toward the thin defensive line. The soldiers braced themselves for impact.

Then, with a deafening roar of human and beast, the creatures drove into the line. Hundreds and hundreds of pikes shattered on impact, but more swung down to take their place, and the soldiers leaned with all their might against the impossible velocity and weight of the Tri-Horns. The housecarls braced themselves three to each pikeman, holding him in position as Andronicus rallied them again and again.

"HOLD THEM! HOLD THEM! THEY CAN'T BREAK THROUGH! THEY CAN'T BREAK THROUGH!"

Erinor roared out the order to advance and the mighty squadrons surged forward, pushing back the crescent of infantrymen as their werewolf and Red Eye comrades continued to fight a vicious hand-to-hand battle with the warriors in the howdahs.

Andronicus gave the signal, and the two horns of the crescent suddenly swung around to smash into the flanks of the Tri-Horns, the pikes driving into the armor of the beasts and finding chinks and gaps in the covering mail.

Olememnon now raised his ax and led his command to strike at the beasts. Like armored lumberjacks they hewed at the massively thick legs that pounded the ground all around them; the Hypolitan commander took both hands to his ax and drove it with a roar into the haunch of a bellowing monster. With a scream of pain and rage, the beast suddenly leaned visibly as the steel bit through muscle and sinew. Hamstrung, it fell thunderously to the ground, where it disappeared under a swarm of werewolves and Red Eye soldiers as they tore into its bulk.

Four more of the giants fell in a welter of blood and screaming rage, but the majority still heaved and pushed on, driven forward by the will and power of Erinor, who was the killing apex of the charge. Still the pikes held their courage, slipping and sliding before the strength of the huge animals, and driving back against them with all their might.

Andronicus, watching the struggle, suddenly smiled. Drawing breath, he bellowed an order: "THE PIKE REGIMENTS AND HOUSECARLS WILL ADVANCE!"

For a moment all seemed to fall still in the massive crescendo of killing and fighting, and then someone laughed. Others joined in as the tension suddenly broke and the soldiers of the Alliance gave way to hysteria. Advance? It was all they could do not to be swept aside and trampled!

Then, slowly, a lone housecarl began the familiar chant: "OUT! Out! Out! OUT! Out! Out! OUT! Out! Out!" It soon spread through the ranks of Icemark soldiers, but then the Polypontians took it up, too, spitting out the simple syllable with venom and force: "OUT! Out! Out! OUT! Out! Out! OUT! Out! Out!"

Now the impossible seemed to be happening. The line was beginning to hold, the seemingly unstoppable buckling and bending was slowing, and the Alliance soldiers began to heave back against the massive, inexorable weight of the Tri-Horns. Slowly, slowly, the line began to hold, and the towering beasts seemed to waver as the razor steel of the spearheads continued to drive at them, cutting through their heavy surcoats of leather and gouging deep into their thick hides. Their small, hating, stupid eyes saw the werewolves and human soldiers swarming over them, and the forest of pikes still waiting to swing down into the engage position, and suddenly they stopped, immovable as gigantic boulders.

Erinor sensed the impossible. The enemy infantry were gaining the advantage! All around her, werewolves and human warriors were attacking the howdahs and inflicting terrible losses, and five Tri-Horns had actually been brought down and killed! Never had she known such carnage inflicted on her forces. But her military brain was without equal, and, quickly assessing the situation, she knew the Tri-Horns would break if she didn't regain control by ordering a withdrawal.

For the first time in her glorious rise to power, Erinor finally made the decision and gave the order to retreat. Slowly, ponderously, the huge beasts turned around and withdrew. But even as they retreated, another Tri-Horn was felled and disappeared under a swirling mass of werewolf and Red Eye soldiers.

Erinor was incensed and mortified. Never in her entire military career had she been forced to withdraw from an engagement. This was a personal defeat at the hands of the hated Polypontians, and all around her on the battlefield the soldiers of the Hordes were watching. She knew she must act quickly or lose her iron control over her soldiers. Raising her hand, she gave the signal for the elite female regiments to support the Shock Troops that were struggling against Thirrin and the cavalry of the Icesheets. There must be no more withdrawals!

Her hopes now lay with the small band of soldiers carrying the wooden stretcher, packed with barrels, which she'd sent off toward the Barbarian Queen's position right at the beginning of the battle. If they were still alive, they must be very close to their target by now. Quickly she scanned the line of battle before her, but the heaving masses of struggling warriors revealed nothing. The band of soldiers might already be dead, or they might be still fighting their way through the throng toward the Queen. Erinor could only watch and hope.

All of the men who'd set out on the mission had been killed, but others had taken their places as they struggled to deliver their barrels to the target. The honor of Artemesion was at stake, and even in the midst of the fighting, they knew that the battle wasn't going well. Unless they reached the objective, the unthinkable could happen and the war be lost.

All around them werewolves, Snow Leopards, and human cavalry fought with a controlled ferocity that equaled that of the Hordes themselves. But the men's task of reaching the Queen was made simpler by the fact that she led her cavalry from the front, accompanied by her bodyguard of Ukpik werewolves and also by Tharaman-Thar of the Snow Leopards and his Tharina, Krisafitsa. All they needed to do was to find the place where the fighting was at its most ferocious, and there the target would be.

The sway and sweep of the battle bore the men and their burden along. Two more fell, and two others took their places. Their escort of female archers shot and shot again, bringing down as many who threatened their mission as they could. On they fought, and on, until at last, just ahead, a brilliant figure of light appeared, with hair of fire, riding a great horse that fought like a creature of nightmares, lashing out with hooves that were shod in gleaming iron, crushing heads and smashing limbs. The figure wielded a sword that struck and struck again like fire made steel, and her green eyes blazed with an intensity the men had only ever seen before in the face of Erinor herself.

The female archers cried out in triumph, and immediately surrounded the men and their burden while they set it down and prepared. The world fought and died around them as the men uncovered the barrels and lit torches; they were now ready.

Suddenly the Queen herself burst toward them, and with her came Snow Leopards and werewolves. The men raised their torches and, breaking open the lids of the barrels, drove them deep into the precious cargo of gunpowder that had been saved from the magazines of so many fallen fortresses.

The explosion swept across the field like a scythe of fire, felling all before it, friend and foe alike. The ear-bursting boom echoed into the sky, and the shock wave traveled on and on, killing, maiming, ending all hope, destroying victory, ending the war.

Now a deathly quiet fell, as the bloom of flame rolled itself up into the sky and disappeared in a shroud of black smoke. It was a quiet of such intensity that the gentle sigh of the wind over the grass of the plain could clearly be heard, and all surviving eyes turned to look to where the blood and tangled carnage stained the already death-polluted land. Who had fallen? Who was killed? How had the balance changed?

Only Erinor knew the answer, and, standing in her how-dah, she let out a shriek of triumph that echoed over the battlefield. Now her Tri-Horn turned and paced toward the epicenter of the destruction. There lay the body of the fallen Barbarian Queen, and Erinor would defile it where it lay among the fallen Ukpik bodyguard and the shattered corpses of Tharaman-Thar and his Tharina.

To the rear of the lines Oskan Witchfather stood at the entrance to the hospital tent and felt a glittering blade of fear drive itself deep into his heart. With a gasp he fell to his knees, and then looked up to watch as the rolling ball of flame rose into the sky.

"THIRRIN!!!"

28

Cronus filled the chamber in the citadel of Frostmarris with shadow and presence. Medea watched him silently, trying to gauge his mood before she spoke. Then, no longer able to keep quiet, she suddenly asked, "Can I assume that the Great Forest is secured now, and that we control the entirety of the Icemark?"

Cronus rose from his chair and went to stand next to the fireplace, the ice crystals that swirled around him like a cloak hissing and spitting as they came into contact with the flames. "Yes, Granddaughter," he finally replied and turned to face her fully. "We reached the cave complex where Her Vampiric Majesty had her headquarters, and the fighting was vicious. Even so, the Ice Demons managed to break through their lines and capture the place, but there was no sign of the Vampire Queen, nor of the majority of her surviving squadrons."

"Then who exactly were you fighting?"

"A few Vampires, but mainly tree-soldiers of the Holly and Oak kings. But there was a strange atmosphere about the undead warriors who stood against us." He paused as he marshaled his thoughts. "I can only describe them as a 'suicide squad'; they were ready to be destroyed; in fact, they seemed almost eager. And when they died, I detected the passing of a . . . *soul.*"

Medea snorted. "The undead don't have souls!"

"These did, unmistakably."

She puzzled over the anomaly for a few seconds, then shrugged, dismissing it as unimportant. "So where's the Vampire Queen?"

"Still at large . . . somewhere. We can expect an attack at any time and from any quarter."

"Oh, *wonderful!*" Medea spat bitterly. "At least when she was in the Great Forest, we knew where she was!"

"Calm yourself, Granddaughter, please," said Cronus as he crossed to his chair and sat down again. "Consider this. Her Vampiric Majesty has been reduced to the role of a terrorist. The pride of her squadrons has been broken, and she's no doubt skulking in some dank and hideous hideaway with neither comfort nor dignity."

"The Vampire Queen creates her own dignity. You could sit her in a cesspit and cover her in dung, and she'd still have more regality than an entire roomful of emperors!"

"Perhaps, but the fact remains that her power base is destroyed, and she can no longer fight with any degree of effectiveness—"

Almost on cue, a sudden explosion of roof tiles and plaster interrupted the confident flow of his words, and the room was filled with hideous shrieking as five gigantic bats smashed through the ceiling. All was chaos as flames belched from the fireplace, where small barrels of pitch had been thrown into the blaze, and Medea found herself flying through the air and finally landing with a jarring thud. The Vampires' attacks were becoming so common now, she half expected them every time she and her grandfather were sitting quietly in the citadel.

Cronus appeared out of the smoke and helped her to her feet. "A nuisance raid. We may have to expect this. I'll go and lead the defense."

Medea watched him leave, then quickly crossed to the window and looked out over the city, where formations of giant bats swooped down over the rooftops and then disappeared from view as they dropped down into the streets. Soon the sounds of fighting rose up into the air as the Vampires metamorphosed into their human forms and attacked the Ice Demon garrison.

If such attacks continued, they might have to review their tactics. Nothing must stop their plans! The new world order must be established. But she was beginning to worry about how easy it was going to be.

Far away on the plains to the south of Romula, the battle against Erinor and her Hordes raged on. Many had fallen when the Shock Troops had set off a crude bomb, but in the broken and bloody chaos around the point where the gunpowder had exploded, a mighty form stirred. A fierce and untamed consciousness fought its way back to the surface of its mind again and the fire of amber glowed on the world as Tharaman opened his eyes. He remembered! He remembered everything, with a terrible clarity.

Slowly he raised his head and turned to look at Krisafitsa, who lay in a broken heap nearby. With a huge effort he climbed to his feet and forced himself to walk to where she lay. He opened his mouth and drew in her scent, but everything was overlaid with the acrid stench of gunpowder, and he could smell no life. Gently he began to clean her face, which was blackened by flame and smoke, but then he gave up and lay down beside her. He would mourn his mate in the dignity of silence, and allow his own life to ebb away so that he might join her in the Fields of Everlasting Ice.

But then some deep instinct stirred, and he became aware of a movement. Slowly he raised his head and saw a truly enormous Tri-Horn bearing down on where they lay.

"Erinor," he said aloud. "No doubt coming to triumph over the fallen." And he laid his head wearily down again. But then a surge of defiance rose up within him, and he looked around quickly. There was nothing he could do for his mate now. But the Basilea of the Hordes would not defile the body of Thirrin, the greatest warrior the world had ever known! Only treachery and gunpowder had been able to kill her. But she was light enough to carry away, and Tharaman was determined that she should be buried in the manner of her people, sealed in a mound on the Plain of Frostmarris.

Quickly he climbed to his feet and found the pain of his injuries miraculously sloughing away as purpose filled him to the brim. He then turned to Krisafitsa, and after licking her face, and promising he would return to be with her, he walked to where Thirrin lay beside her dead horse.

He stopped then to marvel at how untouched by the explosion she seemed, and finding it impossible to believe she could be dead, he began to draw in her scent . . . but then a sudden bellow reminded him of Erinor's approach and he turned to face her. The Basilea's Tri-Horn advanced alone, and she stood in her howdah, her face eager as she searched for her enemy's body.

"Come no farther. You will not have the body of Thirrin Freer Strong-in-the-Arm Lindenshield. She will lie with her ancestors," said Tharaman steadily.

"Stand aside, animal; as victor I claim her body as the spoils of war."

"I am aware of no victory for your Hordes, Madam. Look around you; the battle continues."

"Defiance only. The Alliance knows their Queen is dead, and when I display her body, your pathetic little army will lay down its arms and die."

"Oh, I think not," Tharaman replied. "If I were you, I'd go now before rumor of our leader's death reaches all of our warriors; there'll be no escape for you then, only destruction and mayhem as they wreak their revenge."

Erinor smiled coldly. "Your war is lost; capitulate now to the invincible!"

"Willingly," the Thar of the Snow Leopards said. "Exactly where is this 'invincible' chap, or should I say 'chap-ess'?"

Erinor shook her head impatiently. "You have made your choice, so die!" She drove the sharpened steel goad into the hide of her giant Tri-Horn, and with a bellow the creature surged forward.

Tharaman reared up and roared mightily, his voice blasting high into the air. Then he leaped at the beast, fastening himself to its face, his claws digging deep into its thick hide and raking huge bloody trenches across its snout.

The Tri-Horn bellowed, and with a convulsive heave it threw off the Snow Leopard. Erinor laughed and urged her beast on, but the Thar then reared again, and his mighty paws struck at the beast, knocking its head to the left and the right. It staggered to a standstill, and Tharaman then locked his forepaws around its horns. Bracing himself against the earth, he twisted its head with all his might.

Erinor seized her bow and loosed arrow after arrow into the Snow Leopard's body, but he seemed unaware of their bite as he wrestled with the huge Tri-Horn.

For a moment Oskan almost blacked out, but then he swam to the surface of consciousness again. Thirrin dead! Then how could he live? Without her, how could he resist the terrible call of the Dark? Without her, he, too, must die, and follow her quickly into the Spirit Realms.

But no! No! There was no sign! She hadn't passed! She was still here in the Physical Realms. But injured, unconscious. Quickly Oskan sent his Eye questing over the field of battle to where she lay beside her mutilated horse. At first he hardly dared look, but then he saw she was unmarked. At the last moment, some instinct must have made her duck down behind her shield, and it had taken the full brunt of the blast, shattering on impact, but miraculously protecting her. Havoc, her horse, must have reared and turned, too, absorbing the explosion and saving his mistress. Not one hair of her head was singed, while all about lay in broken ruin. Oskan shouted aloud in triumph, but then his Eye became aware of a titanic struggle.

Tharaman-Thar and a truly gigantic Tri-Horn were locked in battle. The Thar was fighting to fell the beast by twisting its head and neck down to the ground, while the Tri-Horn was trying to lift the giant Snow Leopard and throw him aside. Oskan immediately knew the battle was being fought to save Thirrin. Only once had he been allowed to kill in the first war against Bellorum, and as a result he'd been burned to a blackened skeleton, and only the mercy of the Goddess had restored him.

Even so, to save Thirrin he would have risked all, but he knew he had other tasks to perform that went beyond considerations for himself or even Thirrin. He had to live; he had to remain healthy for the struggle that was yet to come. He watched as Tharaman was borne backward, his hugely clawed feet digging for traction in the grass-trampled ground, all of the muscles in his mighty back bunched and knotted as he fought to fell the beast. The Snow Leopard roared, and roared again, and miraculously the Tri-Horn was stopped in its tracks.

Then Oskan watched as a powerful-looking woman shot three arrows, in quick succession, deep into the Snow Leopard's back. His once-beautiful coat was already blackened and burned by the explosion, and now huge slicks of blood were spreading across the surface of his fur, like wine soaking into fine linen. Tharaman roared again, and with a convulsive explosion of strength he forced the creature's head around, and further around, to an impossible angle. His back feet scrabbled for purchase, and once again he heaved with all his might, until at last there came a cracking, tearing sound, like a tree trunk snapping in a hurricane, as the Tri-Horn's neck broke, severing bone, muscle, and spinal cord as cleanly as a blade.

The beast fell like a landslide, and Tharaman stood, head hanging low, his flanks heaving, and blood dripping from his pelt. Slowly he raised his head and roared into the sky, then he slowly sank to the ground and lay still.

Oskan breathed a deep sigh of relief, but then, as his Eye watched, a woman stepped from the wreckage of the Tri-Horn. She was obviously unhurt, and, though powerfully built, she walked with the light step of a dancer, or a deadly killer. In one hand she held a long cavalry saber, and in the other a spear, and with an air of single-minded deliberation, she headed for where Thirrin lay beside the body of her dead horse.

The Barbarian Queen had to be dead. No human being could have survived such an explosion! But even so, she, Erinor of the Artemesion Hordes, would make doubly sure the Queen could be counted among the fallen by burying her spear deep in her chest, and then she would proclaim the death of Thirrin Lindenshield to all the world, and finally assume her Goddess-given right as Empress of the new Artemesion Empire!

Oskan watched Erinor approach and gathered himself to strike. He had no choice; the woman he loved lay helpless before a mad-minded killer! If the world ended because of his actions, if he died a blackened corpse in an eternity of torment, then so be it! He wouldn't let his wife be killed when she had no chance of defending herself. He opened his mind, gathering the power to strike from the very air around him. But then something made him stop, a small inkling of an idea that entered his head from some unknown point, and instead he turned to Thirrin. If only he could wake her! Quickly he dived into her mind and found only darkness. Desperately he searched through the stilled functions of her brain, and then at last found the tiny spark that was the mighty Thirrin Freer Strong-in-the-Arm Lindenshield, and guided it back to its seat within the recesses of her mind.

"Wake up!" he called desperately. "Wake up, and defend yourself!"

A tiny flicker creased her eyelids, and her breathing deepened, but Erinor was getting closer, a small smile playing about her lips as she hefted her spear and prepared to strike.

"Wake up!" Oskan called again. "Or are you happy to be skewered where you lie, like some helpless fawn?"

Thirrin's eyes shot open. "I'm no helpless fawn! I'm a ravening lion!" She leaped to her feet, sword in hand.

Erinor stopped in her tracks, her eyes widening. This was the woman who'd inflicted the only defeat her Hordes had suffered; this was the woman who was a rival to her claim as the greatest general and warrior that the world had ever seen! For the briefest moment, the two stared at each other, then Erinor gave a wild and mighty war cry and struck a savage blow with her spear. Thirrin parried the blow, knocked up the striking saber, and then ran her sword through

Erinor's chest. For a moment the two women stood almost nose to nose.

"Nice to meet you, Basilea Erinor," Thirrin hissed through clenched teeth. "Pity you have to leave so soon!" Then, stepping back, she wrenched her sword free and struck Erinor's head from her shoulders.

Imp-Pious had flown far to the north of Romula. For some time now he'd been wrestling with a troubling sense of divided loyalty. Did he want to risk further emotional contamination and stay with his mortal friends, or should he cut his losses and return to his homeland where no one and nothing felt any bonds of friendship—or, worse still, love? A few weeks ago the decision would have been easy, but the longer he stayed in the company of mortals, the more difficult it became.

Finally that morning, he'd sneaked out of camp and flown off. He needed to think things through carefully. He had no idea where he was going, but the fact that he hadn't actually made the jump back to the Magical Realms could only mean that he wanted to stay. It was a thought that shocked and horrified him, but even so, he was almost certain now that he'd finally reached a decision.

"Do you intend flying far, Pious?" he said to himself. "I believe I'm right in saying that those are the foothills of the Dancing Maidens below us, and if I go much farther north, the rising topography will necessitate attaining a higher altitude to ensure safe passage over the peaks and arêtes."

He had to admit that his emotions had gotten completely out of hand ever since he had left the Plain of Desolation. But even if his arrival in the Physical Realms, and his relationship with the three mortals, had been completely accidental, he was beginning to wonder if his feelings for them had been destined to happen for some as yet undisclosed reason. As a creature of the Magical Realms, he was fully aware that there was no such thing as coincidence, and that "accidents," if they were studied carefully, often turned out to be very well planned.

But then his thoughts were suddenly interrupted, and he stopped and stared at a black and ragged something that seemed to be struggling to fly some way ahead. "Hello," he said to himself. "I wonder what that might be. Funny-looking bird. In fact, it looks more like a big bat to me. I say, it couldn't be a Vampire, could it?"

He continued to scrutinize the object as it dipped and wavered over the sky. "It's not flying very well, whatever it is. In fact, it appears to be injured in some way. I think it would only be charitable to lend it a hand." And he shot off toward the bat at high speed. In a matter of seconds he was flitting around the Vampire and inspecting its ragged wings.

"I say. Whatever did that to you must have been a big brute. Does it hurt?"

The giant bat seemed to suddenly become aware of his presence, and, screeching in terror, it folded its damaged wings and fell from the sky. The imp powered after it, and, flying below its tumbling form, he reached out and lifted it back aloft. "Have a care; you could've hit the ground!"

"Leave me alone!" the bat screamed. "I know nothing, and I won't give you any information!"

"Fair enough. But I don't actually want any information. Now, who are you, and where are you going?"

"I'll tell you nothing!"

"All right, all right! Calm down. You don't have to say a thing. Though I suppose you want to join Queen Thirrin and the Witchfather to help in their war. There're plenty of other Vampires there."

"What do you know about the Queen and the Witchfather? You're . . . you're an imp!"

"Do you know, ever since arriving in the Physical Realms, I've suffered nothing but insults and blind prejudice. I suppose you're making the assumption that I have ulterior motives?"

"Well, yes," said the giant bat. "You're a small demon, and as a species you're evil!"

"Fortunately not all of us adhere to that particular stereotype," said Pious wearily. "I'm fully aware that my words will carry no weight whatsoever, but I mean you no harm, and you can rely on me completely."

"Why should I believe you?"

"Quite simply, because I could have ripped you to shreds by now if I'd chosen to do so; you're in such a bad way, you wouldn't have had a chance of defending yourself."

"Yes, I suppose so. But you'll forgive me if I ask a few questions before I make any decisions about trusting you."

"Certainly," Pious agreed. "Now might I suggest you ask for information that no enemy of the allies would be likely to know?"

The bat thought for a few moments, then said, "What's the name of the Queen's youngest son?"

"Charlemagne," Pious replied. "Sharley, to his friends. Next!"

"All right, then; what's the name of his closest friend?"

"Mekhmet. He's Crown Prince of the Desert Kingdom and—"

"Does he have any nonhuman friends?"

"Lots. Werewolves—myself, I'm proud to say—even a few Vampires. But his best nonhuman friend is Princess Kirimin of the Icesheets. She's a Snow Leopard, and daughter to Tharaman-Thar and Krisafitsa-Tharina. Any more?"

"No, I suppose I'll just have to trust you," the Vampire replied. "Besides, I don't really have any choice; if I don't get help soon, I won't reach the Queen, anyway."

"In which case, the question of my intentions toward you becomes quite academic, does it not?" said Pious. "If I help you, you'll reach your intended destination; if I don't, you'll die."

"True," the Vampire replied. "As I said, I have no choice really."

"None whatsoever," Pious agreed. "Right. Off we go!"

"Where are we going?"

"To find Queen Thirrin, of course. Last I heard, she was heading south to do battle with Erinor. It'll be interesting to see what the outcome of that little confrontation may be."

For the rest of the day Pious helped the giant bat to stay airborne, augmenting its feeble wing-beats by flying beneath it and holding it up. Progress was slow, and as the sun descended to its setting, they were silhouetted against the livid red of the sky.

They journeyed on through the night, flying over the city of Romula that was lit up below them like a galaxy in the darkness of the surrounding plain. And then, with surprising speed, they came upon a second city of lights—but this time the houses were tents, and the walls were the watchful eyes and spears of sentries posted at strategic points all around the camp's perimeter.

"Looks like we've made it," said Pious to the Vampire. But there was no reply. The undead warrior was unconscious.

With much slapping of cheeks and some very colorful insults, the imp managed to revive the Vampire enough to make it realize where they were. "You'd better warn your kindred you're about to come in to land," said Pious.

The Vampire nodded. Raising its head, it gave the high-pitched warning call of its kind.

"Do it again. We want them to know it's urgent, and not just some routine patrol coming back."

This time the giant bat let out a great screaming bellow that echoed over the sky, then slumped into unconsciousness.

Pious struggled to keep the Vampire airborne as they clumsily circled down to the ground. "The landing won't be textbook, I'm afraid," he gasped to himself. "I'd better look for something soft to crash into!" He desperately scanned the camp below him and saw only scurrying soldiers and general panic. "We're coming in! Move! Look out! LOOK OUT!"

"All right! We've got him!" said a sudden voice as four Vampires appeared and took the weight, their huge wings beating into the air as they slowed the descent. "Down there—the Witchfather's waiting."

The night boomed and pulsed with the sound of laboring flight as the Vampires gently lowered their injured comrade. A tall and slender figure then hurried forward and bent over the prostrate form. "These are injuries from a psychic blast," Oskan said as he quickly examined the burns and rents over the bat's body. "But he must metamorphose to his human shape. I can only work on his base form, not a magically derived simulacrum. The treatment won't take otherwise."

The other Vampires gathered around and helped the injured bat regain his human form. "Fine," said Oskan. "Now I can work."

Cressida fought to put aside the atmosphere of war and fighting that clung to her like the smell of blood. She'd washed again and again, combed her hair, shocked the guards once more by putting on a dress, and still she felt like a machine created purely for killing. It didn't occur to her that anyone else might feel the same; she presumed the struggle to regain a sense of humanity after such wholesale slaughter was hers alone. After all, Leonidas seemed to come alive when on the battlefield; gone was his social incompetence, his mumbling and shambling, and in their stead was an assured and elegant warrior who moved with the lethal grace of a wildcat. Why would Leonidas want to be anything else other than a fighter? Certainly, as a potential lover he was hopeless; even Cressida, who was a complete novice herself when it came to the gentle arts of finding a mate, could see he was ridiculous!

She sat back in her chair and considered the problem, artfully avoiding admitting to herself that concentrating on Leonidas and his bumbling was an ideal way to forget the horrors of the recent battle. She tried to settle the huge amounts of cloth that made up her dress, and failed utterly. Why did women put up with wearing such monstrosities? But eventually her mind returned to the commander and his social incompetence.

She'd sent a guard to fetch him less than five minutes ago, and she calculated that she still had another few minutes to decide on her strategy before he arrived. She'd already come to the conclusion that there was little point in waiting for Leonidas to make any meaningful moves, and so all she needed to do was to advance upon him herself and break down his defenses. She found that viewing him as a heavily fortified city that she must capture concentrated her mind wonderfully, and provided her with a modus operandi she would otherwise have lacked.

The sound of approaching feet alerted her, and she sat up straight and quickly patted her hair. Within seconds the entrance to her campaign tent was flung open, and the were-wolf and housecarl guard marched in with Leonidas between them. It almost looked as though he were under arrest, and after taking one look at her in a dress, he then managed to look like a man on his way to the gallows.

"Commander Leonidas," the human soldier announced with a huge grin. Escorting the Polypontian officer to and from the Crown Princess was swiftly becoming one of the highlights of his duties. Only payday came anywhere near to it for sheer joy.

"We found him having a bath," the werewolf guard added. "But as you'd ordered his presence immediately, we helped him finish off and dry himself."

Cressida looked at Leonidas and shuddered when she saw the huge red marks, like rope burns, all over the exposed areas of his flesh. Obviously a werewolf's idea of toweling someone dry was a little rougher than the average human being was used to. She dreaded to think what the rest of his body looked like and then immediately blushed at the very thought.

"Thank you," she finally said in her haughtiest tones. "You may leave us."

The guards looked deeply disappointed, but contented themselves with nudging each other as they backed out of the royal presence. With a bit of luck they'd be able to hear their conversation as they guarded the tent. It was amazing how people forgot that a canvas wall wasn't very sound-proof.

Cressida decided to start her campaign immediately, and after observing the commander for a few seconds, she said, "You can sit down, you know."

She pointed to a chair that was already positioned at an angle to hers. After the chaos and fiasco of Leonidas's last attempt to find somewhere to sit, she was taking no risks. He dropped into it, wincing slightly as his buttocks made contact with the seat. Obviously the werewolf had been *very* attentive when helping him to dry.

"You've recovered from the battle, then?"

Leonidas was relieved to have a familiar subject to talk about and nodded. "I wasn't, er, you know . . . *injured* really, as you know . . . er . . . just a few scratches and, you know . . . lots of bruises."

"Yes," Cressida agreed. "In fact you seemed to have suffered more being helped out of your bath."

"I think the werewolf meant well, but he was a little . . . robust."

"As a *species*, they're a little robust."

"Yes."

A huge silence now started to stretch out between them, and Cressida began to despair. Only the everyday sounds of the camp broke into the billowing silence as she desperately tried to find something to say. At one point she thought she heard a stifled giggle coming from outside the tent, and then a gasp that was suspiciously like the noise someone makes when elbowed hard in the midriff. But then the silence returned, and Leonidas's face began to burn.

Cressida could have howled in desperate frustration. Just what was it about the pair of them? Why couldn't they talk like the two responsible, intelligent human beings they obviously were? Why did their meetings have to descend into painful farce? But then at last she began to get angry, her military resolve asserted itself, and she threw caution to the wind.

"Good goodness, Leonidas. Do I have to spell it out? Are you willing . . . would you like . . . do you want to . . . would you consider . . . ?"

"*YES!*" Leonidas blurted, and a small, hastily muffled cheer sounded from outside.

"You don't even know what I was going to say," Cressida said irritably. "I might have been about to ask you to drink poison!"

"Oh! Er . . . yes . . . I mean, *no*. . . . I'm sure you wouldn't, well, you know, ask such a thing of anybody. . . . You're too . . . *perfect!*"

This time there were unmistakably two loud guffaws from outside the tent, but Cressida ignored them. She felt her

entire body burn in a combination of acute embarrassment
and pure pleasure. He thought she was perfect! Nobody
had ever accused her of that before. She was considered by
everyone to be overbearing, bossy, rude, unreasonable, and
pedantic, but never perfect! Not even her mother thought
she was *perfect*!

"Then you . . . you will?" she asked at last.

"Of course! With . . . er, you know . . . *immediate* effect.
Abso . . . you know . . . absolutely!"

A great, glowing, rushing flood of happiness and relief
swept through Cressida from top to toe, and she leaped to
her feet and spontaneously clapped her hands for joy. Then
she stopped. "But you still don't know what I was going to
ask!" she said with suspicious pessimism. Perhaps he thought
she wanted him to exercise her warhorse or something.

"Yes, I do!" Leonidas answered. "Or at least I *think*
I . . . er, you know, I think I do."

"Well, say it, then. What do you think I want you to
do? Or more to the point, what do you think I want you to
be?"

Leonidas now began to doubt his interpretation of events
and turned crimson with the mortifying idea that he could
have gotten everything horribly wrong. "I think . . . well . . .
I *thought* . . . you know . . . that you wanted me . . . to,
you know . . . be your . . . well . . . I'm not sure how to
say . . ."

"Oh, for god's sake! She wants you to be her mate," a
rough werewolf voice provided from beyond the canvas wall
of the tent.

"Yeah!" a human voice agreed. "She wants you to be her
'bit of stuff'!"

"That's right! She wants you for her partner in the great
wrestling match of love!"

"Yeah! Her Pillow Partner!"

"Not only that, she wants you to be her—"

"All right, thank you! We get the idea!" Cressida called out angrily. Then, turning to Leonidas, she said, "Well?"

"Oh! Er . . . well, you know, *definitely . . . absolutely . . . certainly . . . yes . . . no question . . . without doubt . . . indubitably . . .*"

"All right, thank you! We get the idea!" a rough werewolf voice called from outside the tent.

Thirrin watched her husband as he drank the wine she'd given him. "Well, what did you learn from the Vampire?"

"Not good," he answered, sitting back wearily in the chair that stood in the middle of Thirrin's campaign tent. "We're invaded again."

"What?!" She leaped to her feet and was just about to call for a bugler when Oskan held up his hand.

"Hear me out first. There're things to explain, and a few more minutes'll make no difference one way or the other."

She looked at him, then nodded, trusting his judgment. "Go on."

"It's no ordinary invasion. Medea's come home, in the company of my father."

The words fell as stark and hard as pebbles into the silence of the tent. But at last Thirrin swallowed and said, "What else did the Vampire tell you? Do . . . does the enemy control all of the Icemark?"

Oskan shook himself, as though breaking free from unwelcome thoughts. "Um? Oh yes . . . virtually. But Her Vampiric Majesty has been fighting hard to slow them down. Successfully, too, by the looks of things. If she hadn't been there to contest Cronus's control, he'd have broken out by now and would probably have conquered most of the Northern Continent. We've got a lot to thank the Vampires for."

"So it would seem," said Thirrin thoughtfully. "But what do you advise we do now?"

"For the moment, nothing. I need to make an in-depth reconnaissance, after which we can make plans."

"Fine. When do you go?"

"Right now," he answered. "Expect me back at nightfall." And with that he took one step away and disappeared, leaving Thirrin to brood in the sudden silence.

29

Tharaman and Krisafitsa had been unconscious for more than three days, but Kirimin had at last agreed to leave their tent in the infirmary block and take a rest, now that her parents' conditions were showing no signs of worsening. Leaving strict instructions to be called the moment anything happened, good or bad, she gently nuzzled Tharaman's and Krisafitsa's cheeks, then walked quietly back to her quarters and the promise of a few hours' sleep. After she'd gone, the witch-healers quietly checked their patients' progress before extinguishing most of the candles and finally leaving to complete the rest of their rounds.

After they had gone, the darkness and silence pooled in the large tent, and then, in the gloom of the deepest shadows, a pair of red, bloodshot eyes slowly opened and narrowed as they assessed the situation. Both Snow Leopards were obviously still unconscious, and there was no sign of guards or attendants of any sort. The coast was well and truly clear.

With the stealth of an assassin, a huge shape then detached itself from the darkness and made its way silently to where the Snow Leopards lay. Having satisfied itself that it had found the Thar, it uncorked a large flask, poured a bloodred liquid into a wide bowl, and placed it before Tharaman's muzzle. For a moment nothing happened, and then the shadowy figure dipped a huge, wickedly sharp claw into the liquid and trickled it across the Snow Leopard's nose. Again, nothing. But then Tharaman's muzzle began to twitch and the lips to curl, and eventually a large red tongue snaked out and licked up the liquid that was slowly running toward his nostrils.

The huge dark shape hissed in excited satisfaction, quickly trickled more droplets of the red substance across the Thar's nose, and waited impatiently, all the time looking cautiously over its shoulder for any signs of the witches coming back. This time, the tongue slurped out immediately, and the dark figure moved the bowl closer, until eventually the tongue fell into the red liquid and began to lap. The dark shape capered about, silently raising its fists in glee and shaking them wildly. But then it froze and turned to look at the Thar, as the unmistakable sound of a clearing throat boomed into the room.

"Oh, I say! Yes! Do you know, if I'm not very much mistaken, that has the distinctive palette of a very fine Gallian vintage. Yes . . . yes, chalky soil, south-facing vineyard, plenty of sunshine to aid the production of natural sugars." The tongue quested forth again. " Oh yes! I'm getting strawberries, vanilla, and just a soupçon of licorice; and . . . and . . . yes, at the end, citrus, lemons; a very fine, refreshingly piquant finish! "

The huge head of the Snow Leopard now swung up from its pillow, and the glowing amber eyes opened to illuminate the room. "Hello, Grishmak," he said warmly. "Did you bring the wine? It's very good."

"Just a little something I keep for emergencies, like bringing Snow Leopards out of comas," said the werewolf. "Finish off the bowl; I've got plenty more."

"Nothing would give me greater pleasure, but . . . er, just see if Krisafitsa would like some, too," said Tharaman in worried tones.

Grishmak produced a second bowl and repeated his technique of trickling the liquid over the Tharina's muzzle. Soon her tongue was lapping at the wine, too, and she opened her eyes.

"Well, my dear, you're certainly in need of a thorough wash," she said as she scrutinized her mate. "It looks like no one's been near your fur for days."

"I suspect you may be right, my love," said Tharaman with a deep purr of pure pleasure. "Exactly how long has it been, Grishmak?"

"You've both been unconscious for three days," he said. "Everyone's been pooing themselves thinking you were going to die."

"Oh yes. I remember now," said Krisafitsa slowly. Then suddenly she leaped to her feet. "There was an explosion. . . . Thirrin!"

"Calm down, there's nothing to worry about. She's alive and well," said Grishmak. "She didn't even get a scratch. In fact, she was well enough to fight Erinor and kill her."

"So, the Basilea survived me killing her Tri-Horn, then?" asked Tharaman as the memory of his struggle with the huge beast came back.

"Not for long," said Grishmak. "She's dead and the war's over."

"And Kirimin and the boys?"

"Also safe and well. In fact, Kiri left only a few minutes ago; she's been here ever since you were brought into the infirmary. She'll be spitting mad she missed you waking up."

The Snow Leopards began to purr enormously, the booming sound of their pleasure filling the space of their hospital tent so that it vibrated like a struck bell.

"I've brought something else with me, too," said Grishmak conspiratorially, and after fishing around his pelt for a few moments, he produced an enormous frying pan and a massive steak that flapped over the sides. "This came from Erinor's Tri-Horn. I thought it'd make a light convalescent meal. Now has anyone got any firewood?"

"I don't think it'd be very safe lighting a fire in a tent, Grishy," said Krisafitsa. "What we need is one of those charcoal griddles the cooks use in the mess tent."

"Of course! I never thought of that. Hang on a minute, I'll go and see what I can find." The Werewolf King headed for the entrance, then stopped to hiss conspiratorially over his shoulder: "We won't tell anyone what we're doing. You know how these healers fuss; they'll only moan on about steak being too rich for someone who's just come out of a coma, and all that malarkey. See you in a bit!"

In the following silence the Snow Leopards contented themselves with giving each other a thorough wash, and in an amazingly short time most of the discoloration and blackening caused by the explosion had been cleaned away.

"That's better! I feel almost human now."

"I beg your pardon, my dear?" Tharaman asked in puzzled tones.

"Oh, sorry. It's an expression I've picked up from Thirrin. It just means I feel better and much more in control."

"Well, in that case, I feel almost human, too!"

Suddenly a small, horned head peeped around the flap of the tent. "Hallelujah! You're awake! You're alive! Wait till I tell Kiri!"

"No, wait, Pious dear," said Krisafitsa urgently. "Let her rest. I hear she's been with us ever since they brought us in from the battlefield, so she must be exhausted. We can have a happy reunion when she wakes up."

The imp shrugged his agreement and flew into the tent. "Fine. But look at you two! You must be as tough as a Tri-Horn's fundament to have survived that explosion!"

"It takes more than a few fireworks to extinguish a Snow Leopard's light," said Tharaman proudly. "Though if I remember correctly, it looked as if Grinelda and the Ukpik bodyguard took the full force of the blast."

"Yes, all dead. An enormous shame," said Imp-Pious as he fluttered down to sit on the Thar's bed. "Still, they'll get full military honors at their funeral, and a new Ukpik guard's already being formed, so the tradition won't die."

"I see," said Krisafitsa quietly. "And will there need to be any other funerals with full military honors?"

Pious looked at her, an expression of pure panic slowly gathering on his face. "Oh, dear me! You've been unconscious, haven't you, so you won't know! And now I'm going to have to tell you, and I have absolutely no experience of this sort of thing because no one dies in the Spirit Realms!"

"Never mind about comforting phrases and all that sort of thing, Pious dear. Just tell us the worst."

"All right. Well, you asked for it, so here goes . . . For a start, thousands! Erinor's Hordes were tough nuts, and they weren't easy to crack. But I suppose the biggest names, so to speak, are Olememnon and Olympia. They were both killed, along with all the Sacred Regiment. In fact, the Hypolitan suffered truly appalling losses; the Hordes seemed to specifically target them. But worse than all of that was the fact that everyone thought you two were among the fatalities! And, in fact, a lot of Snow Leopards were killed in the explosion, including Taradan." The imp went quiet, and then, in an attempt to fill the lengthening silence, he added, "As I said, tough nuts . . . and they were perilously hard to crack."

"Yes," Krisafitsa agreed quietly. "Do you know any figures at all? Exactly how many Snow Leopards fell?"

"I'm sorry, I don't know for certain, but I know the casualties were heavy."

"In all reality, my dear, I don't think it will be of any use to know such details, just yet," said Tharaman. "I think our first duty is to ensure we both make a rapid and complete recovery, so that we may continue in our duties as Thar and Tharina."

"Yes, of course," said Krisafitsa, but her ears remained flat. "I'm just a little tired at the moment. Do you mind awfully if I have a little sleep?"

"Not at all, dear heart. In fact, I may join you. Imp-Pious, be a good chap and see if you can find Grishmak, will you? And tell him that we're very grateful for his trouble, but we'd prefer to rest right now."

"Certainly. Just leave it to me. Do you think you'll feel a little perkier tomorrow?"

"I'm not entirely sure, but I suppose it's a possibility. A good old-fashioned drinking competition might have helped to set me up, but somehow, without Olememnon to compete against, the idea's lost something of its savor."

"Yes," Pious agreed sadly. "His capacity was truly formidable."

"Yes, it was. I hope someone remembers to mention that in his funeral address. A gentleman quaffer of the ale and true appreciator of the viticulturalist's art. Not to mention a thoroughly decent sort of chap and all-around good guy."

"Yes," Pious agreed again, then quietly flitted out of the tent as Tharaman slowly laid down his huge head and closed his eyes.

30

Thirrin paced the floor like a caged beast. The Icemark had been invaded again, and she daren't say a word to anyone until Oskan had returned from his reconnaissance. Without hard facts and figures to lay before the High Command, she'd only cause chaos and panic. All she could do was wait, and the suspense was almost unbearable.

She crossed to the entrance of her campaign tent and watched the doings of the camp with sightless eyes for a few moments, then turned back to begin her pacing again, and bumped into the Witchfather.

"Oskan, at last! What's happening? Is everything destroyed? Is there any resistance? Are the Vampires wiped out? Can we fight them effectively? How long before we can counterattack?"

Oskan crossed quietly to a chair and sat down. "Which question should I answer first?"

"The most important!"

"Then we can counterattack. And as for the rest of your inquiries: Yes, there's a very vigorous resistance, thanks to the Vampire Queen and her squadrons of warriors, who incidentally haven't been wiped out. But having said that, the enemy has control of every major city and large town, and they're almost ready to march on the Polypontus."

He calmly poured himself a flagon of beer and took a long drink before going on. "Unless we hit them immediately, our beloved daughter and her . . . grandfather will begin a process that can only end in world domination."

"Then we'll hit them now!" said Thirrin decisively, ignoring the pangs of regret and longing she felt at the mention of Medea.

"Well, yes. But there are problems."

"Which are?"

"To be effective we must attack within hours rather than days, and that will require transporting the entire army through the Plain of Desolation."

Thirrin sat down heavily. "Can it be done?"

"In theory, yes. I must admit I didn't know that it could, but Cronus proved it as a means of transporting entire armies when he took his host of Ice Demons into the Icemark. But that required only half the energy and effort that will be demanded of us. After all, he only took them from the Darkness to the Icemark, whereas we'll need to transport our fighters to the Plain of Desolation, and then from there back to the Physical Realms again. The effort would be enormous."

"But it can be done?" Thirrin repeated sharply.

Oskan slumped back in his chair as though exhausted. "I think so, yes. If I work in concert with every one of the witches, we should be able to generate enough psychic energy to pull it off. To understand the process properly, you have to see the Plain of Desolation as a sort of conduit, a pipeline through which we can travel."

The Queen leaped to her feet, her face alight with the promise of battle.

"But the problems don't end there, I'm afraid," Oskan went on. "When we arrive in the Icemark, we then have the small question of fighting the Ice Demons, and believe me, they're truly formidable. Even with talismanic weapons like silver arrowheads, and swords and spears of pure iron, they're still going to be a terrible opposition. There are literally thousands and thousands of them, and I'm afraid the advantages are all theirs. Not only will we be the invaders of our own land, trying to oust well-dug-in defenders, but they're enormously strong and afraid of nothing."

A small cough suddenly sounded. "Not quite *nothing*, Witchfather, and I do apologize for the double negative." Imp-Pious flew into the tent and hovered before Oskan. "Sorry to interrupt what appears to be a private, not to say confidential, conversation, but I was just passing by on my way to taking dinner to Sharley, Mekhmet, and Kirimin and I couldn't help overhearing your chat. You see, I might be able to give you a valuable insight into a failing in the formidable armor of the Ice Demons."

"You can?" asked Oskan skeptically.

"Yes. I think people too easily forget that imps and Ice Demons are distantly related, and that we smaller cousins are privy to many of their foibles. For example, the Ice Demon is mortally afraid of fire. You see, flames are diametrically opposed to their element of ice, which, after all, is simply frozen water."

"Of course!" said Oskan, becoming truly animated for the first time since he had begun his conversation with Thirrin. "Now we have a chance! With this information, you and the army can keep the enemy's fighting forces busy while I deal with . . . Medea and Cronus, the driving force behind the invasion."

"What will you have to do?" his wife asked quietly, as though she already knew the answer.

"Quite simple, really. I'll have to destroy them."

The entire allied army stood on the wide plain beyond the camp and waited in a deep unbroken silence. Human, Snow

Leopard, and werewolf were drawn up in their respective regiments and watched as Oskan and the full complement of White Witches stood before them, arms raised and eyes turned up to the whites.

"They look dreadfully spooky when they do that," Tharaman whispered to Krisafitsa.

"Hush, dear, they might hear you."

"No chance of that!" Grishmak boomed. "Once they go into that sort of trance, you could probably tear off their legs and they wouldn't notice."

"Well, that's not an experiment I'd care to carry out," the Tharina replied. "I just hope they can generate enough . . . whatever it is to transport us all to the Icemark."

"What I want to know is, why didn't they try this before? It'd have saved a hell of a lot of marching when we first invaded the Polypontus if they had," said Grishmak.

"Oh, that's easy," said Tharaman. "It wasn't until Oskan had been back and had a quick chat with Her Vampiric Majesty that he even realized it *could* be done. It was only because she'd witnessed the arrival of the Ice Demon army that Oskan was able to guess what had happened—and, more important, how it had been done!"

"Well, I'm still worried they won't be able to call up enough power to take us all through the void thingy. I mean, look at the size of those Tri-Horns that Cressida and Leonidas are commanding, and there are over five hundred of them!"

"I don't think actual weight is a consideration, my dear," said Tharaman knowledgeably.

"What is, then?"

"Well . . . well, I'm not really sure. Something . . . magical, I expect."

Krisafitsa shot him an annoyed look. "Thank you for that in-depth and informative insight."

"Now, now, no bickering before battle," said Grishmak. "What's up! I think something's happening."

They all looked up and watched the witches as the fabric of light and reality itself seemed to slowly tear apart, revealing a black void that grew wider and wider, until a huge yawning chasm had opened up before the army.

A great icy blast spewed out into the day, and many of the horses reared and danced nervously as their riders tried to calm them.

Over in the ranks of cavalry, Sharley whispered in his mount's ear and stroked his neck. "Steady, steady, Suleiman. Remember who we are. You'll see the enemy soon."

Mekhmet smiled at him nervously. "I wish I could be calmed as easily. I can't say I like the idea of going into that at all."

"Me, neither," agreed Kiri, flattening her ears. "Why can't we just get on with it?"

"Any minute now," said Sharley, his confidence in his father's Gifts helping to steady his nerves. "Don't forget Dad's in charge. He'll get us through."

Then suddenly, a strange blackness seemed to bleed across the day, consuming the army and filling every eye and every ear with a deep and endless nothing. Each individual warrior was alone in the eternal emptiness that was the space between the Physical Realms, the Darkness, and the Spirit Realms. They could hear and see no one and nothing; it was almost as if everything had ceased to exist apart from their own individual fear. Mekhmet tried to draw breath to cry out in terror, but nothing entered his lungs, and the unending silence and blackness filled his head to the brim. Was this it? Would this be where they ended their lives, suspended forever in an endless nothingness while they soundlessly screamed in unending fear?

But then, abruptly, light, sound, scent, and every other sensation returned in screaming clarity as the army emerged onto the Plain of Desolation. But they were only there for a matter of seconds, as Oskan and the witches once again opened a portal, and then they were all plunged once more into the nothingness between realms.

Mekhmet felt he would die of fright in the emptiness, but then the Physical Realms erupted into his senses again, and he found himself on the Plain of Frostmarris. Bugles clamored and orders were shouted as the allied host regained its composure and realized that there before them was an army of Ice Demons waiting to be transported themselves through the Spirit Realms and far to the south. Above them squadrons of Vampires were harrying them with murderous attacks that carved great swaths through the ranks of the Ice Demon army.

They had them! They'd taken the enemy by surprise. Drawing her sword, Thirrin stood in her stirrups and gave the war cry of the Icemark: "The enemy is among us! They've killed our children; they've taken our houses! BLOOD! BLAST! AND FIRE! BLOOD! BLAST! AND FIRE!"

From every throat the reply crashed out: "BLOOD! BLAST! AND FIRE!" And as one the allied army swept down on the demons, firing silver-tipped arrows and drawing weapons of pure iron.

Oskan stepped aside and watched the charge in silence, allowing himself one brief moment of peace before he began the hideous task that lay ahead. Confronting Medea and Cronus would be a mighty struggle, but whatever the cost, he must stop them, and he'd already come to the conclusion that there was only one way to do it. He hardly dared allow himself to think of the plan he'd been formulating ever since he'd learned of the invasion, and in fact, he now carefully packed away his strategy behind psychic shields of steel and adamant, so that his beloved father and daughter couldn't read his mind and take steps to thwart his plans.

The outcome of the confrontation remained completely unclear. There were so many variables to take into consideration—not least his uncertainty that he could actually bring himself to do what he knew he must. Could any father inflict such a thing on his daughter? He didn't know. All he could do was make a beginning and leave the outcome to the Goddess.

Oskan now watched as Thirrin and her army smashed into the lines of the Ice Demons, and he raised his hand in a gesture that was part blessing and part farewell. Then, at last, assuming the form of an avenging eagle, he swept up into the sky and raged down on the citadel of Frostmarris, where he knew he'd find Medea and Cronus. Within seconds he'd located them in the highest room of the highest tower, where they'd been watching the triumphal mustering of their army as they prepared to transport them to the invasion of the Polypontus.

He wasn't surprised to find them ready and waiting as he crashed through the roof and landed before them in his human form.

For a moment they stood immobile, but then they struck at him with a double blast of fire and psychic energy that demolished the room around them, so that they all stood exposed to the watching sky. Oskan struck back, sending Medea reeling away, but Cronus stood his ground and advanced, sending out great bolts of lightning and sheets of flame that engulfed his son.

With an almost contemptuous wave of his hand, Oskan drained the power away and sent a flight of solid steel bolts that pinned Medea's body to the charred floorboards and pierced both of his father's eyes. With howls of rage, they wrenched themselves free and sent a rain of fire in return, setting Oskan's clothes ablaze and burning his flesh so that it hung in great weeping ribbons that smoldered and spat like cooking meat. Shuddering with pain and concentration as he drew power from the atmosphere around, he quenched the flames and healed his ruined flesh, then hit back with a vicious rain of pure acid that hissed and smoked as it ate away the remaining stones of the wall.

"You cannot win," Medea suddenly shouted, her mind a turmoil of conflicting emotions as she was forced to fight her father again. "Our bodies are mere shells for our undying spirits. How can you kill the lifeless?"

"But I've told you before, I don't want to kill you, Medea," he answered quietly. "I just want to destroy your powers." And, raising his hand, he slowly balled his fingers into a fist. A psychic force seized Medea's very soul and squeezed it in a viselike pressure that dragged great howls and screeches of pure agony from her throat.

Her cries were unconsciously echoed by Oskan as he felt the true horror of inflicting such pain on his daughter. This was the child he'd raised and loved; this was the child whose psychic Gifts he'd helped to develop. And yet now he was forced to fight her.

"My most beloved son," said Cronus lightly. "You will stop this, and you will stop it now!"

A sensation of freezing cold enveloped Oskan as his father revealed all of the stored hatred and negativity that he had gathered during the long, endless eons of his existence.

Gasping in pain and horror, the Witchfather fell to his knees.

"I was worried for a moment," said Cronus to his fallen son. "What a terrible shock to find an army attacking our Ice Demons just when we were ready to invade the Polypontus. But you were never really a threat. And despite your disloyalty, I am still prepared to offer you life and power again, my son. Join with us; join with your daughter and father and become part of a triumvirate of unstoppable force that will sweep aside even the Goddess herself."

Oskan slowly raised his head, and with an effort focused his swimming eyes on the two evil Adepts who stood before him. "I will never turn to the Dark!" he spat.

"But why not?" asked Medea, desperate to find a means of reconciliation. "With your power, you could . . . you could convert its polarity; you could make it a force for good!"

Even through his pain the Witchfather smiled sadly. "You know full well that the Dark is evil in its purest form. Nothing could convert it; everything is corrupted by it!"

"Then consider this option," said Cronus, and suddenly an image began to form, obscuring the chaos and destruction that surrounded them. It showed a room in the citadel of Frostmarris. A fire in the hearth gave off a cozy glow, and Cressida sat on a high-backed chair with twin babies cradled in her arms. Beside her sat a proud-looking Leonidas, as Thirrin looked on, her face wreathed in smiles. "Just imagine, my son, all of this could be yours, even now. All you have to do is join with us and you will live to see it. The need for fighting and death will be over. With the Power of the Dark you can achieve immortality, and you can also confer immortality on whomever you wish. You and Thirrin could live and . . . love . . . forever!"

Oskan fell silent. Slowly he bowed his head to the scorched and pitted floor. For a moment he considered the possibility, desperately wishing it could be true. Then he looked up. "This happy little scenario you paint could never be; you know that the Dark corrupts everything it touches. And, while I have the strength to prevent it, the purity of my warrior-queen will never be sullied by such evil! Rather than that I'd choose to be racked over a pit of white-hot lava for eternity!"

"That, too, can be arranged, if you're foolish enough to reject us," said Cronus quietly.

*   *   *

Down on the Plain of Frostmarris, Thirrin led the cavalry of the Icesheets in a charge that ripped into the ranks of the Ice Demons. All around her human troopers struck with iron swords at the massive bodies of the monsters, tearing great holes in their scaly flesh. But the demons were enormously strong and fought back ferociously, tearing gaps in the ranks of the cavalry, ripping bodies apart and throwing them contemptuously aside.

But then, with hideous screeches of challenge, the Vampire Queen and her squadrons dived at the enemy, while Cressida and Leonidas led a charge of Tri-Horns that powered into the enemy's ranks, their huge three-horned heads throwing aside the demons like fallen leaves before a wind.

The enemy host was at last forced to realize that it was not going to be transported through the Spirit Realms. Something had obviously gone wrong, and the invasion of the Polypontus had been postponed. But now the Witches of the Dark Craft appeared, like the fetid rags of storm clouds, sending blast after blast ripping through the allies' ranks. The balance of power was tipped yet again. The witches' screeching laughter echoed in triumph over the battlefield, and only Tharaman's mighty roar of defiance challenged it.

Back in the citadel Cronus watched his army of Ice Demons and smiled. "The army's holding its own. The constant attacks of Her Vampiric Majesty have honed their fighting skills, which allows us to concentrate on your father."

Medea smiled in answer, a rictus of agony stretching her mouth.

"Do you know, Granddaughter, I do believe the time has come for you to finally throw off the restricting chains of the family."

"What do you mean?"

"I want you to kill your father."

The words fell like small leaden weights into her soul. How could she kill the man who'd first shown her how to use her Abilities? How could she destroy her own father? For a moment, blank despair invaded her mind and she stood, head bowed, in the chaos of the destroyed citadel. But then, with a supreme effort of will, she turned her full attention on Oskan, who still groveled under the terrible weight of Cronus's hatred.

"Even now, can you not agree to join with us? None of this has to happen; together we can stand against the corruption of the Dark and change it!"

The beseeching tones reached the Witchfather in the extremis of his fear and pain, and slowly he gathered his willpower so that he could raise his head. "Medea, you know I can't join you. No power can ever change the Dark. It will always be evil in its purest form."

Medea looked at him, her face expressionless. Then, slowly, she raised her arms and began to draw power from the air around her.

Oskan had to act now; he knew he had no choice. With the deepest sorrow, he turned to the Dark. Shielding the core of his soul, he felt the boundless force of hatred channeling through him.

His body began to swell until it reached the proportions of an Ice Demon, and he lashed out with a mighty roar that smashed his father and daughter to the ground.

Medea's body was a mere tangle of wreckage, but even now she fought back. Drawing on her powers as a Weather Witch, she called lightning and storm to blast Oskan where he stood. Winds howled, thunder crashed, and temperatures plummeted and then soared. The rending power of tornadoes and hurricanes raged against him. But Oskan hardly flinched, and a deep and hideous laughter that burst from a mouth that was wattled and tusked was his only reply.

More and more of the Dark flooded into his frame. Hatred and evil permeated his very soul, and he looked on the prostrate forms of his daughter and father with pure loathing. His mind quested forth, probing and examining his fallen enemies, looking for weaknesses in their defenses. His mind swept over the figure of Cronus as he struggled to regain his feet and fight back. Oskan could now pierce the adamantine shields that had protected the core of his father's mind in all their confrontations and meetings, and what he found made him shout aloud in shocked amazement.

Beneath the appalling corruption and evil of the Arc-Adept's mind, Oskan found something else, something at complete odds with his entire mind-set. Cronus the Mighty, Cronus the enemy of the Goddess, loved his son! Like a tiny unsullied spark of brilliance in the entire quagmire and filth of his mind, Cronus harbored a secret love. A love he'd felt for his only child since the day he was born.

Oskan reeled; this . . . being had human feelings! How could he destroy him now, even if Cronus was still prepared to defy his own emotions and kill the son he had loved for so long?

Cronus at last scrambled to his feet and gazed at the monster that rose before him. "He has opened himself to the Dark," he whispered in horror. Convinced they were about to die, he called to Medea. "Quickly, Granddaughter, join your mind with mine. We have seconds to crush him before he becomes accustomed to his new strength."

Medea had always hated looking into the evil abyss that was her grandfather's mind, but now their very survival depended on their ability to act in unison. Gladly she surrendered her individuality, and together they created a greater Adept than the worlds had ever known.

As their minds became one, a whirling void gathered and the very atmosphere froze, to fall as ice crystals before the depth of its evil. "Look on us! Look on us, my father-son!" boomed its voice. "Look on what we have become, and despair! Know your individual futility before my-our con-joined powers, and now prepare yourself to die!"

On the Plain of Frostmarris, the battle continued as the Witches of the Dark Craft advanced against their enemy. Still they danced like corpses on the gallows as they sent out bolt after bolt of plasma, and still the ranks of the infantry fell before the continuing blasts. But then, slowly, a light began to pulse and push against their advancing darkness, and at last the Witches of the Light began to fight back. On they advanced, and they, too, danced as they came, flowing like a smoothly incoming tide, sailing like swans in flight, rolling like the considered arches of Romanesque architec-ture, and as they pushed forward, they sent out blasts of white light that crushed the darkness and sent it scurrying to find refuge in the deep shadows of vaults, in the darkness of noisome pits, and in the lightless eye of the corpse.

Thirrin now felt the tide of battle turning. Raising her sword, she led her host to smash once again into the Ice Demons, who howled as they fell back before the power of the enemy. Now a small figure flew up from the ranks of the allies and, leading squadrons of Vampires, it swept down on the demons with barrels of burning pitch that were dropped in a flaming cascade to burst in a mighty conflagra-tion among the huge beasts.

Their roaring and bellowing unfurled like a banner of agony over the battlefield, and, as though in answer, the clamor of battle-horns erupted from the Great Forest, and forward rode the armies of the Holly and Oak kings to smash into the enemies of the Icemark. Now, too, the very fabric of the day ripped open, and with a great roaring and wailing a host burst from the Plain of Desolation and rode forth into the light of the world. Ghosts they were, and at their head flew a giant Vampire bat whose screeches found an answer in the calls of the warriors of Her Vampiric Majesty. A pause now fell upon the battle as all looked to the ghosts, wondering which side would feel the wrath of their power. And then, with a great screech, the giant bat led his army to power into the ranks of the Ice Demons, tearing them limb from scaly limb.

With a despairing roar, the Ice Demons fell back before the many-headed beast that was their enemy, and then at last their ranks broke apart, and they scattered over the field like storm clouds before a cleansing wind.

Oskan fell to his knees as agony billowed over him in waves, and he almost gave himself up to despair. But then a small part of his mind that was not besieged by desolation made a plan, and he smiled.

Quickly he opened a doorway in the fabric of reality, and a black hole appeared that led into a place of nothingness: a void that contained neither light nor dark, sound nor silence. This was the negation of everything, the perfect prison for Medea and Cronus.

With a supreme effort of will, Oskan began to drag the swirling vortex of his enemies' conjoined minds toward the black hole. But Medea-Cronus were too strong. They threw him off and pinned him to the ground.

Again the Witchfather was wracked by a terrible intensity of pain; he was literally being torn apart. But then, in the deepest parts of his brain, a small note of resignation and final acceptance sounded. Immediately everything fell silent, as though the world itself were holding its breath. An incongruous sense of peace settled over him amid all the destruction and filth. He looked up to see a gentle figure in long flowing robes standing before him, her face relaxed and smiling, and he immediately recognized the Messenger of the Goddess.

"You have chosen, Oskan Witchfather, beloved of the Goddess?"

"I have chosen," he answered simply.

The Dark now drained away from his soul, and a sense of light and peace flooded in. The Goddess was with him. He knew that the conjoined minds of Cronus-Medea were completely unaware of the Messenger, and of the Power of the Mother of All. Now he had the strength to fight back; now he had the chance to save the Icemark and the world, where Thirrin and Cressida, where Sharley and Eodred, might live and love, and find their true selves after achieving their appointed ends.

The Ice Demons had broken and were being destroyed even as Thirrin watched. But she knew that the main part of the struggle had nothing to do with weapons of iron and steel and was still being fought in the citadel of Frostmarris. Turning her horse, she galloped away toward the city and was soon charging through the empty and echoing streets. Before her the ruined tower still spat fire and lightning as the Adepts fought their war. Within minutes she was racing across the courtyard of the citadel, something driving her on to find the stairway and race up it toward where she could see and hear the titanic struggle going on.

She reached the top step just in time to see a hugely swollen creature lower its arms and stand waiting quietly for the jagged bolts of power that ripped their way into its chest. For a moment it stood, head thrown back as though exalting, but then more and more bolts burst huge holes in its body and it sank slowly to the ground as a single voice screeched in triumph.

Thirrin watched as the body rested back on its haunches and its head fell forward onto its chest. Yet more blasts pierced it through, and the wild yells of triumph rose to a crescendo. But there was another voice mingled with them, and it seemed to be screaming in despair.

It was then that the horribly injured body began to transform, losing its huge bulk and extreme ugliness to diminish to the shape of a tall and slender man dressed in black.

"No!" Thirrin screamed in pain and horror as she recognized Oskan.

"Oh yes! He's dying! We are victorious!"

Thirrin staggered into the destroyed room and ran to cradle her husband's head. "No!" she screamed again.

A following silence was then broken as a sneering voice observed, "I do believe I have the pleasure of Queen Thirrin's company!"

Thirrin looked up to see Medea and Cronus drawing apart as their minds regained their individuality. "You!" she hissed in devastated anger. "You've killed your own father."

Medea remained silent, but Cronus smiled coldly. "Well, technically he's not dead yet, but he very soon will be. You see this is one of the many disadvantages of retaining a physical body; if it's damaged badly enough, it dies, and not even the most powerful Adept can save it. Especially if enough magical power has had the opportunity to alter the most basic building blocks of its structure."

Thirrin stood and reached for her sword, but before she could draw it, Oskan stirred. "No. Please sit with me quietly and wait."

She scrambled back to her husband. "Oskan! You're still alive. Quickly, do something, save yourself. . . . Carry out some magic. . . . Stop dying!"

He opened his eyes and smiled sadly. "I'm afraid my ever-loving father's right. I'm too badly damaged. Nothing can save me now."

"Well, what about the cave beneath the citadel?" Thirrin asked desperately. "You've regenerated before. Surely you can be saved again?"

"The Goddess has allowed me to return from death twice," he said weakly. "That's quite unprecedented, you know. But now I've fulfilled the last of my life's tasks and I must return to her."

Cronus laughed. "How gloriously loyal you are to this impotent deity, my son! I find it amazing that you still talk of her with respect even though she did nothing to save you."

"The choice to die was my own," said Oskan quietly. "I could have opened myself to the Dark completely and had enough power to defeat you many times over. But if I had, I would have become supremely evil. I would have been the very essence of everything negative, and so would have lost my right to the Spirit Realms and the Summer Lands."

"And now you're dying," said Medea. "What have you achieved? The world will now fall to myself and Cronus, and all you have loved will languish in torment forever. And, please, don't think we'll ever let Mother or the family die; they'll be maintained in an existence of pure agony for all eternity."

"No . . . Medea, you're wrong. You see, you're dying, too. In fact, you'll be dead before me."

"I admire your bravado," said Cronus contemptuously.

Oskan frowned. "You really don't understand, do you? Your emotions have destroyed you as well."

"What sick madness are you spouting . . . ?"

"I really am truly sorry," he said. "But perhaps the compassionate Goddess may find the ability somewhere to forgive you and you'll be spared oblivion. I can't quite believe it myself, but, then again, I'm only a mere mortal, and fallible." He paused, then went on. "Ah, it's beginning."

"What is?" asked Medea in confusion.

"Your death."

Instinctively both Cronus and his granddaughter glanced down at themselves and gasped. Their psychically conjured bodies were dissolving from the feet up. "Oh, really, how annoying," said Cronus. "We've obviously used too much energy in the battle. Never mind, we'll soon be able to carry out repairs when we've rested."

"No. I'm afraid not," said Oskan. "You're beings of pure energy, and that energy is now being negated. You see, you have contravened one of the universal laws of magic that you were never allowed to know. The Evil Ones, who defied the Goddess and fell into the darkness, murder themselves if they murder those they love. This was the weapon of knowledge I was given to use against you. That is the Power of the Law; if it was a secret, then no Adept could take steps to avoid the consequences of breaking it. I suppose it was the Goddess's way of slowly reducing your numbers over the eons. She knew most evil Adepts are murderous—particularly toward their own families, for some reason—and if they die as a result of killing their own, then the world enjoys the benefit of getting rid of two evil ones at a time. And both of you *have* killed one you love—namely me—and now you're both paying the appointed cost: dissolution."

"NO!!!" Cronus screamed. "I am unsullied, pure in my evil!"

"I'm afraid you're not," said Oskan lightly. "You see, during our battle I've been allowed to learn that none of us has the power to create pure evil; there's always a spark of love. That's the way of the Goddess."

"Quickly, Granddaughter, join with me again; together we'll be strong enough to fight this off."

Once again the black swirling void appeared as the two Adepts pooled their powers in a magical conjunction, and for a time they seemed to burgeon and grow in power. But then, slowly, they began to fade. Hideous screeches and howls emerged from the void as they fought for existence, but eventually these, too, started to fade, until only the smallest whisper could be heard.

Then at last all fell silent, until one final pleading word whispered into the world: "Father!"

The sound froze to black ice crystals and fell with a discordant tinkle to the floor, where slowly it melted away.

Oskan sighed, but before he could say anything else, the sound of a booted foot on the spiral staircase drew his and Thirrin's attention, and they waited until Cressida burst into the remains of the room. She skidded to a halt when she saw her father and mother, and after one look at Oskan's face, silent tears began to course down her face.

Thirrin now fell to her knees before Oskan, and he opened his eyes. "On your feet, Thirrin of the Icemark! My Queen kneels to no one!"

"But I do to love," she replied.

Her husband smiled. "Oh, that's all right, then. We all kneel to love."

His eyes were then drawn to the far side of the room, and as they all watched, a small coalescence of light gradually evolved into a large, friendly looking gray cat. "Ah, Grimalkin," Oskan said warmly. "You've been sent for me. Then it's time to go."

Thirrin and Cressida both knew that witches and warlocks were guided home to the Summer Lands by the Goddess's cat, and they hugged each other for comfort.

"Daddy," Cressida whispered.

Oskan turned his eyes to look at his daughter. "Oh, my powerful young Queen. You will rule countries and dynasties, and though you will live with your sword forever in your hand, it will never be used to oppress or control. Only love and respect will draw the world to your feet, and you will be crowned before all as the Queen of Wisdom, as the Queen of Compassion."

He smiled, then turned to Thirrin. "And you, my flame-haired warrior. What years you have yet to live! You will become the grandmother of nations, and when the fire of your hair becomes the silver of moonlight, look for me, and I'll come to you then and we can walk in the meadows of the Summer Lands."

"But I'll be in Valhalla," she said, her voice breaking in fear that they would never meet again.

"Oh, my love. Have you still not learned that all deities are one under the benevolence of the Goddess, and that all heavens are flowers in her infinite garden?"

Grimalkin then meowed. "I must go now, but remember, nothing but the mere facts of time and death separate us. Soon we'll be together again." Oskan then stepped from his broken body and followed the cat as he walked toward a slowly opening portal in the fabric of the physical world. But before stepping through, he turned and smiled. "When your hair becomes the silver of moonlight."

Then he stepped into the portal, and Thirrin and Cressida watched as he walked toward the figure of a beautiful woman. She was dressed in a flowing robe that seemed to be made of all the flowers and trees and growing things of the world. And all around her were the living souls of her children, every living species there was, had been, and would ever be. And as they watched, she smiled at them, her beautiful face as dignified as the most stately queen and as merry as the happiest young maiden. And as Oskan reached her, she enfolded him in a loving embrace, and kissed him like the Mother she was.

31

So came the time of funerals and weddings. Oskan's broken body was cremated on a towering pyre that rose out
of the Plain of Frostmarris like a mountain of wood. Within
its huge conical structure were built several staircases, so
that the werewolves and housecarls who were constructing
it could climb to greater and greater heights as they piled
massive bundles of wood toward the sky. Then at last,
when it was complete, the broad platform at its very peak
was draped in purple and white, and the flag of the Icemark
was unfurled, showing a fighting white bear on a blue
background.

Then, winding down from the citadel of Frostmarris, came
the cortege led by Thirrin, on foot and fully armored but
for her helmet. And on her belt, her scabbard was empty
of all weapons, and neither did she carry a shield. Beside
her walked Cressida, Sharley, and Eodred, and behind came
Tharaman, Krisafitsa, and Grishmak. The people of the
Icemark lined the streets of Frostmarris and spilled out onto
the plain surrounding the city like a many-headed sea, all
intent on witnessing the passing of the Witchfather, and
they gasped aloud at the spectacle of the escorting warriors
carrying the bier on which lay Oskan's body. Werewolves
and housecarls, Hypolitan and Snow Leopards, Vampires

and Polypontians, and even soldiers of the Holly and Oak kings all helped to bear the body of the warlock who had saved the world from destruction.

Out onto the plain wound the long procession, and the only sound that arose from that huge company was the steady *tramp, tramp, tramp* of disciplined feet. Then, as they reached the pyre, selected warriors from each of the allied species carried the bier up the internal stairways to eventually emerge on the platform at the apex of the huge mound. Now the bier, with its precious cargo of coffin and body, was placed gently at the very center, and as the bearers withdrew, the huge Solstice Bell that hung above the South Gate of the city began to toll, its sonorous voice booming over the plain and echoing from the eaves of the Great Forest.

Then, when all had emerged from the stairways and withdrawn to a safe distance, Thirrin was handed a longbow, and she shot a flaming arrow in a high arc that landed deep within the oil-soaked wood of the pyre. Immediately flames leaped up, and on a signal from their officers, rank upon rank of Hypolitan archers sent a barrage of blazing arrows to land at all points within the pyre, and soon a huge conflagration roared into the sky, destroying the body that had housed the indestructible spirit of Oskan Witchfather.

For many hours the flames raged, turning the encroaching night to day. But then, at last, when the fires had died to white ash, Oskan's bones were taken and laid in the cave, deep in the Great Forest, where Thirrin had first met him so many years before. Then Tharaman-Thar and Krisafitsa-Tharina broke down the entrance until it was blocked forever with fallen rock, and a holly soldier and an oak soldier began the vigil that would continue until the last tree had fallen.

And so the people were scattered to their various homes. The Snow Leopards traveled back to the Icesheets; Cressida traveled south to the Polypontus, where she became the

Regent to the Emperor Titus along with Leonidas and Andronicus.

Thirrin sat on her lonely throne, comforted by Sharley, Mekhmet, and King Grishmak, whose people stayed forever in the Icemark, living side by side with their human friends. The Vampire Queen, too, returned to the Blood Palace, where she ruled the shadows in splendor, remembering the strange Vampire bat that had appeared in the battle leading the ghosts against the Ice Demons. She was almost certain she'd recognized his form, but dared not allow herself the comfort of the thought that His Vampiric Majesty still existed in the Spirit Realms.

But then one night, as the dark shadows of the empty throne room stood in textured crowds around her, she heard a step echo across the floor.

"Who's there?" she called. But no one answered and, standing, she stared into the dark. Being undead, the night held few fears for her, but she was curious, and she called again. "Who's there?"

This time she was answered by the regular beat of a footfall, and she waited until a tall, shadowy figure came into view. "Who are you?" she asked coldly.

"One who has loved you for eons, oh light of my death."

Her hand was drawn to her heart and she gazed into the darkness. "Step forward, that I may know you."

"But you know me already, my love."

She stepped lightly down from the throne and crossed the floor to stand before him. "Oh, my dearest heart! Then it is true—oblivion has no hold over you."

"And neither does it over you, my only one. I've been sent to fetch you, the only one of our kind to be released from the prison of existence without violence. Come, step toward me now, and leave behind that hateful rag that is your body."

The Vampire Queen took his hand and walked away from her physical form, and together they danced in the darkness as music swelled around them.

Then the Vampire King whispered gently in her ear, "Do you remember long ago, my love, in the last war with the Polypontus, you told me you'd had a dream in which we'd had children? I believe you said they were called Lucretia and Belasarius." Her Vampiric Majesty nodded, and the king continued: "I remember reminding you at the time that the undead cannot bear young, and that your dream, though beautiful, could never become a reality. Well, my dear, I'm now in a position to tell you that souls are amazingly complex things, far beyond anyone's ability to understand. They can take form from love, wishes, and dreams. But mainly from love . . ." He paused and smiled, then, turning, he held out his hand to the shadows and called, "You may join us now, my little ones."

Strange particles of light then began to accumulate before him, and slowly two small forms coalesced from the shadows as though woven from photons. The Vampire Queen gasped and watched avidly as a boy and a girl began to emerge from the surrounding dark. They appeared to be about ten years old, and their faces were a mingling of the best features of Their Vampiric Majesties.

The king smiled. "May I present the twins Belasarius and Lucretia, oh my light and love? They are the children of our minds and dreams, if not of our bodies, and they have been given life in the Spirit Realms."

The queen held her hands to her mouth and gazed in wonder on the small forms. The king smiled and called them forward. "Children . . . it is time to meet your mother."

And so dawned the day of Cressida's wedding. The Great Hall of the citadel was bedecked with greenery, and all of the peoples of the Alliance had gathered to watch the Crown Princess take the hand of Leonidas Apollodorus Andronicus, Commander of the Polypontian Army.

Tharaman-Thar and Krisafitsa-Tharina escorted Cressida to stand with her consort before the Priestess, and then Queen Thirrin and General Andronicus placed the rings upon their fingers, after which Cressida and Leonidas took their vows, pledging to guide the people of the Icemark to happiness and prosperity. A breathless silence then fell as the two newlyweds turned to face each other. Their faces blazed like twin suns, but after much hesitation, and after maneuvering their noses into the appropriate positions, they finally managed to kiss before the congregation of allies. And as the cheering raised itself to the rafters, all fell to the feasting with power and might.

Tharaman took his place at the High Table along with his Tharina and Grishmak, but despite their best efforts, something was missing from the atmosphere. "I think it has to be said, happy day or not, somehow no feast is complete without a drinking competition," said Grishmak sadly. "And no drinking competition is complete without Olememnon."

"True, very true," agreed Tharaman. "I've been known to vomit for more than four hours after a session with dear old Ollie. But for some reason I just can't get into the *spirit* of the thing without him."

"Well, I'm not entirely sure that I miss the vomiting," said Krisafitsa. "But I do know what you mean about a feast not being the same without him. Of course you could always ask the new Basilea's consort if he would care to compete against you. I know no one will ever replace Ollie, but he may help to fill the vacuum."

Tharaman and Grishmak stared along the table to where the tall and slender consort of the Hypolitan Basilea sat, and they both shook their heads. "Looks a bit of a lightweight to me," said Grishmak.

"Absolutely. No stamina, by the looks of him," said the Thar. "Still, perhaps we should give him a chance."

"Go on, then, you ask him."

"All right, I will," said Tharaman determinedly. Clearing his throat, he called along the table, "I say . . . it's Philippos, isn't it? Yes? Well, Grishmak and I were just wondering if you'd care to partake in a little drinking competition."

The young man turned a serious face to look at them, and narrowed his eyes. "Ale or wine?"

"Ale," said Grishmak.

"Right, you're on! Nothing less than a pint per unit, and the first one sick or unconscious is the loser!"

"Done!" said Tharaman. "And Maggie here can be the referee."

"I'm not entirely sure I'm in any fit condition," the old scholar giggled. "I'm already at the stage where I can see two Grishmaks."

"Oh, never mind. You don't mind officiating, Krisafitsa, old girl, do you? No? Good! Right, to battle."

Sharley, Mekhmet, and Kirimin were just attacking their third dessert apiece, and the boys were feeling a little queasy.

"Don't you want those?" asked Kirimin hopefully, nodding at the two huge bowls of steamed custard that the boys were prodding at with their spoons.

"No, I think we've had enough," said Mekhmet. Pushing the bowls toward the Snow Leopard, he tried not to watch as she quickly demolished the contents.

"Kiri, we'll be going back to the Desert Kingdom in a few weeks' time," said Sharley, watching a globule of custard slowly descending her whiskers until a huge tongue quested forth and licked it up. "And myself and Mekhmet were wondering if you'd like to come with us. If your mother will let you, of course."

The Snow Leopard Princess turned a cream-covered face excitedly toward him. "Really? Oh yes, please, I'd love to. And don't worry about the Mumbo, she'll let me go now. Snow Leopards mature much more quickly than humans."

"Who's the Mumbo?" asked Mekhmet.

"My mother."

"But she didn't even want to let you go to the Great Forest a few months ago," Mekhmet pointed out.

"Yes, but as I just said, Snow Leopards mature much more quickly than humans. A few months in our terms can be the equivalent of a few years in human terms. I'm quite grown-up now and completely independent."

"Great, that's settled, then," said Sharley decisively. "I thought we'd go via Venezzia and the Southern Continent, and then, once we've explored the desert for a while, we can go on to Lusuland. You'll just love Queen Ketshaka."

"Oh, wonderful!" said Kirimin excitedly. "I can't wait to get going. When do we start?"

"Like I said, not for a few weeks yet. But if we travel south through the Polypontus, we can reduce the sea journey by several weeks."

"That'll suit the horses better," said Mekhmet.

"That sounds marvelous!" said a familiar voice as Pious fluttered up from under the table. "Can I come, too?"

"I'm not sure," said Mekhmet cautiously. "The people of the Desert Kingdom are deeply devout; just one look at your wings and scales and they'll know exactly what you are, and try to kill you as an act of piety to the One."

"Well, couldn't you explain I'm a reformed character, not to mention a war hero?"

"We could try, I suppose," said Mekhmet, though he didn't sound very confident.

"I've got an idea," Sharley interrupted. "We could dress him in those little red jackets and pantaloons the monkeys wear whenever you see them around the fairs and bazaars in the Desert Kingdom. Then if anyone asks, we can say he's our pet, and that he's been ill and his fur's fallen out."

"What exactly are monkeys?" Pious inquired.

"Small hairy creatures that look a bit like tiny people wearing fur coats," Sharley explained. "They're not very bright, and they're also extremely ugly, but lots of people keep them in the Desert Kingdom."

"An absolutely superb disguise in any other circumstances, I'm sure. But not, I think, for me. I'm sure that somehow my natural brilliance will just shine out."

"Oh, I think we'll manage," said Sharley airily. "Is everyone in agreement then—Pious comes with us?"

"Well, he can come along as far as I'm concerned," said Kiri.

"Me, too, I suppose," Mekhmet agreed eventually, and the four friends began to make plans, to the exclusion of all others. The ever-present thought and memory of Oskan dimmed their excitement, but quite rightfully thinking the Witchfather wouldn't have wanted them to be sad on this day of all days, they continued to discuss their journey.

Only Cressida and Leonidas seemed as self-contained, talking quietly and helping each other to tidbits from their plates. "It'll be a little awkward constantly traveling between the Icemark and Romula, but I'll have a word with my mother and see if we can establish a household in one of the southern towns near the border," said Cressida as she sipped from her goblet of wine. "That way everyone can come to see us whenever I come home."

"That . . . er . . . that . . . er, seems a little unfair, don't you think?"

"Not at all. I *am* the Crown Princess, you know."

"Well, yes. But, er . . . you know, Grishmak's a king, Tharaman and Krisafitsa are Thar and . . . er . . . Tharina respectively, and your mother's the Queen of the Icemark. So if you're talking social precedent here, we're . . . er . . . you know, *we're* the ones that should be doing the visiting."

"Are you going to be as argumentative as this all of our married life?" Cressida asked sharply.

"Well . . . er . . . yes . . . probably."

"Good," she said. Leaning across, she kissed him on the nose. She couldn't remember ever being so happy; she was just sorry that her father couldn't have been with them all to share the day. It seemed so unfair that, after everything he'd been through, he couldn't have been allowed a little time to enjoy the peace he'd been instrumental in creating.

For a moment tears threatened to well up, but, fearing a bad omen for her big day, she determinedly pushed aside the sadness and filled Leonidas's goblet to the brim with wine.

"Come on, drink up. There's lots more to come!"

Of all the huge gathering of wedding guests, only Thirrin seemed a little quiet, her hand resting gently on the arm of the empty throne that stood beside hers. It had been months now since Oskan had died, and, despite what everybody kept telling her, the pain hadn't gotten any easier to bear. He'd been with her since before she'd become Queen of the Icemark, and had shared with her the terrible burdens of rule and warfare and general everyday life. He'd kept her sane, lent support, and, most important, made her laugh just when it was most needed. And now he was gone.

She still woke up every morning expecting to see his head on the pillow next to hers, and she still lay on the left side of the mattress, as though he'd climb in beside her at any moment and make some ridiculous remark about one of the visiting dignitaries who'd arrived that day. But that was never going to happen again, and she began every morning in the awful knowledge that he was gone.

With an effort she cleared her throat and sat up straight. She was determined not to brood; this was Cressida's day, and she'd smile and look happy if it killed her! And anyway, she wouldn't be allowed to remain pensive for too long; Emperor Titus was too busy bouncing up and down on the cushions that bolstered his chair and asking Thirrin to explain exactly what some of the ruder housecarl songs meant. Having a young child to look after again had helped to give her day a purpose and structure, and she smiled as he stared around at the Great Hall drinking it all in. He repeated his question about the songs.

"You're a little too young to understand," Thirrin answered, in a voice she hoped was firm enough to put off further questions.

"No, I'm not. Go on, I won't be embarrassed. Just translate a bit of it, then!"

"Later."

"That's just adult speech for 'never ever,'" he said disappointedly. But then he suddenly brightened up. "Never mind, I'll ask Eodred and Howler. They'll tell me."

"Not if I get to them first, they won't."

Titus sighed heavily. "All right, then, if I'm not allowed to know what the housecarls are singing about, can I ride your new warhorse tomorrow?"

Thirrin threw up her hands in despair. "Yes, all right, anything to stop you pestering! But I'll hold the reins."

"All right," he answered, then began to bounce on his cushions again. "What does it mean when the men housecarls and male werewolves make that movement with their arms and then wink?"

Thirrin slumped on her throne. She'd forgotten just how demanding a child could be. "It means that if little emperors don't stop asking questions, their tongues will wear out."

"Does it? Funny, I was almost sure it had something to do with ladies."

Suddenly the Queen of the Icemark giggled, quietly at first, but then slowly the sound grew and, once started, it could not be stopped but developed into full-blown laughter that echoed back from the rafters and filled the Great Hall with joy. As one, all of the guests turned to look at Thirrin in silence. This was the first time she'd laughed since the death of Oskan Witchfather, and, quite rightly taking it as the best of omens for Cressida's marriage, the healing of the land and all its peoples, the guests stood and cheered.

Eating and drinking now began again with renewed vigor, but at the back of the hall several witches sat watching events unfold and chatting quietly to one another. Tomorrow they'd finally be selecting a new leader to take over for the much-missed Witchfather. But for now they were happy just to watch him behind his family at the High Table, his face alight with smiles and his head crowned with a silver light.

"Well, he'd have to come for this, wouldn't he?" said Old Meg. "I'm sure the Goddess wouldn't have expected otherwise. Here, I think this calls for more beer than is strictly good for us. Come on, you lot, let's raise a tankard to Oskan Witchfather. The Goddess bless him."

ACKNOWLEDGMENTS

Thanks are definitely long overdue to Julian, Jane, and Peter for years of listening to me moan on the phone, and also for keeping my wonderfully cooperative computer in line and online.

I'd also like to thank Immers and all the editorial team for their patience and for politely ignoring my barbed comments scribbled in reply on the typescripts.

Also to Nigel, in thanks for long years of support.

And finally to the G and the G, TM, TG, and all the Ts.

LAST BATTLE OF THE ICEMARK